Ain't She Sweet

Not exactly . . .

"FUNNY AND SEXY... [IT] SPARKLES."
Memphis Commercial Appeal

"WONDERFUL... A GREAT READ."
Columbia State

"FAST-PACED... CHEEKY."
Publishers Weekly

"NO ONE WRITES FUNNIER ROMANCE THAN SUSAN ELIZABETH PHILLIPS."
Detroit Free Press

SUSAN ELIZABETH PHILLIPS

Ain't She Sweet?

AVON BOOKS

An Imprint of HarperCollinsPublishers

The chapter epigraphs from the works of Georgette Heyer are re-printed with the permission of Sir Richard Rougier and Harlequin Books. They are copyright Georgette Heyer 1926, 1932, 1940, and 1950.

AVON BOOKS
An Imprint of HarperCollins*Publishers*
10 East 53rd Street
New York, New York 10022-5299

Copyright © 2004 by Susan Elizabeth Phillips
Excerpt from *Match Me If You Can* copyright © 2005 by Susan Elizabeth Phillips
ISBN: 0-06-103208-5
www.avonromance.com

First Avon Books paperback printing: February 2005
First William Morrow hardcover printing: February 2004

Avon Trademark Reg. U.S. Pat. Off. and in Other Countries, Marca Registrada, Hecho en U.S.A.
HarperCollins® is a registered trademark of HarperCollins Publishers Inc.

Printed in the U.S.A.

10 9 8 7 6 5 4 3 2 1

To Jayne Ann Krentz

*A dear friend, a wonderful writer,
and the romance novel's most eloquent
and insightful advocate*

No reference to examples in books. Men have had every advantage of us in telling their own story. Education has been theirs in so much higher a degree. The pen has been in their hands. I will not allow books to prove anything.

JANE AUSTEN, PERSUASION

Ain't She Sweet?

"I am afraid," confessed Pen, *"that I am not very well-behaved. Aunt says that I had a lamentable upbringing."*

GEORGETTE HEYER, *The Corinthian*

Chapter 1

*T*he wild child of Parrish, Mississippi, had come back to the town she'd left behind forever. Sugar Beth Carey gazed from the rain-slicked windshield to the horrible dog who lay beside her on the passenger seat.

"I know what you're thinking, Gordon, so go ahead and say it. How the mighty have fallen, right?" She gave a bitter laugh. "Well, screw you. Just . . ." She blinked her eyes against a sting of tears. "Just . . . screw you."

Gordon lifted his head and sneered at her. He thought she was trash.

"Not me, pal." She turned up the heater on her ancient Volvo against the chill of the late February day. "Griffin and Diddie Carey ruled this town, and I was their princess. The girl most likely to set the world on fire."

She heard an imaginary howl of basset hound laughter.

Like the row of tin-roofed houses she'd just passed, Sugar Beth had grown a little shabby at the edges. The long blond hair that swirled to her shoulders didn't gleam as brightly as it once had, and the tiny gold hearts at her earlobes no longer skipped in a carefree dance. Her pouty lips had lost the urge to curl in flirtatious smiles, and her baby doll cheeks had given up their innocence three husbands ago.

Thick lashes still framed a pair of amazing clear blue eyes, but a delicate tracing of lines had begun to make tiny fishtails at the corners. Fifteen years earlier, she'd been the best-dressed girl in Parrish, but now one of her calf-high stiletto-heeled boots had a small hole in the sole, and her scarlet body-hugging knit dress with its demure turtleneck and not-so-demure hemline had come from a discount store instead of a pricey boutique.

Parrish had begun its life in the 1820s as a northeastern Mississippi cotton town and later escaped the torches of the occupying Union army, thanks to the wiles of its female population, who'd showered the boys in blue with such unrelenting charm and indefatigable Southern hospitality that none of them had the heart to strike the first match. Sugar Beth was a direct descendant of those women, but on days like this, she had a tough time remembering it.

She adjusted the windshield wipers as she approached Shorty Smith Road and gazed toward the two-story building, empty on this Sunday afternoon, that still sat at the end. Thanks to her father's economic blackmail, Parrish High School stood as one of the Deep South's few successful experiments with integrated public education. Once she'd ruled those hallways. She alone had decided who sat at the best table in the cafeteria, which boys were acceptable to date, and whether an imitation Gucci purse was okay if your daddy wasn't Griffin Carey, and you couldn't afford the real thing. Blond and divine, she'd reigned supreme.

She hadn't always been a benevolent dictator, but her power had seldom been challenged, not even by the teachers. One of them had tried, but Sugar Beth had made short work of that. As for Winnie Davis . . . What chance did a clumsy, insecure geek have against the power and might of Sugar Beth Carey?

As she gazed through the February drizzle at the high school, the old music began to drum in her head: INXS, Miami Sound Machine, Prince. In those days, when Elton John sang "Candle in the Wind," he'd only been singing of Marilyn.

High school. The last time she'd owned the world.

Gordon farted.

"God, I hate you, you miserable dog."

Gordon's scornful expression told her he didn't give a damn. These days, neither did she.

She checked the gas gauge. She was running on fumes, but she didn't want to waste money filling the tank until she had to. Looking on the bright side, who needed gas when she'd reached the end of the road?

She turned the corner and saw the empty lot marking the place where Ryan's house had once stood. Ryan Galantine had been Ken to her Barbie. The most popular boy; the most popular girl. *Luv U 4-Ever.* She'd broken his heart their freshman year at Ole Miss when she'd screwed around on him with Darren Tharp, the star athlete who'd become her first husband.

Sugar Beth remembered the way Winnie Davis used to look at Ryan when she didn't think anyone was watching. As if a clumsy outcast had a chance with a dazzler like Ryan Galantine. Sugar Beth's group of friends, the Seawillows, had wet their pants laughing at her behind her back. The memory depressed her even further.

As she drove toward the center of town, she saw that Parrish had capitalized on its newfound fame as the setting and leading character of the nonfiction bestseller *Last Whistlestop on the Nowhere Line.* The new Visitors Bureau had attracted a steady stream of tourists, and she could see the town had spruced itself up. The sidewalk in front of the Presbyterian church no longer buckled, and the ugly streetlights she'd grown up with had been replaced with charming turn-of-the-century lampposts. Along Tyler Street, the historic Antebellum, Victorian, and Greek Revival homes sported fresh coats of paint, and a jaunty copper weathervane graced the cupola of Miss Eulie Baker's Italianate monstrosity. Sugar Beth and Ryan had made out in the alley behind that house the night before they'd gone all the way.

She turned onto Broadway, the town's four-block main street. The courthouse clock was no longer frozen at ten past ten, and the fountain in the park had shed its grime. The bank, along with a half dozen other businesses, sported maroon and green striped awnings, and the Confederate flag was nowhere in sight. She made a left on Valley and headed toward the old, abandoned train depot a block away. Until the early 1980s, the Mississippi Central had come through here once a day. Unlike the other buildings in the downtown area, the depot needed major repairs and a good cleaning.

Just like her.

She could postpone it no longer, and she headed toward Mockingbird Lane and the house known as Frenchman's Bride.

Although Frenchman's Bride wasn't one of Parrish's historic homes, it was the town's grandest, with its soaring columns, sweeping verandas, and graceful bay windows. A beautiful amalgam of Southern plantation house and Queen Anne architecture, the house sat on a gentle rise well back from the street surrounded by magnolia, redbud, azalea, and a cluster of dogwood. It was here that Sugar Beth had grown up.

Like the historic homes on Tyler Street, this one, too, was well cared for. The shutters bore a fresh coat of shiny black paint, and the fanlight over the double front door sparkled from the soft glow of the chandelier inside. She'd cut herself off from news of the town years ago except for the bits and pieces her Aunt Tallulah had condescended to pass on, so she didn't know who'd bought the house. It was just as well. She already had enough people in her life to resent, with her own name at the top of the list.

Frenchman's Bride was one of only three houses on Mockingbird Lane. She'd already passed the first, a romantic two-story French Colonial. Unlike Frenchman's Bride, she knew who lived there. The third house, which had belonged to her Aunt Tallulah, was her destination.

Gordon stirred. The dog was evil, but her late husband Emmett had loved him, so Sugar Beth felt duty-bound to keep him until she could find a new owner. So far, she hadn't had any luck. It was hard to find a home for a basset with a major personality disorder.

The rain was coming down harder now, and if she hadn't known where she was going, she might have passed the overgrown drive that lay on the other side of the tall, privacy hedge that formed the eastern boundary of Frenchman's Bride. The gravel had washed away long ago, and the Volvo's worn shocks protested the bumpy approach.

The carriage house looked shabbier than she remembered, but its mossy, whitewashed brick, twin gables, and steeply pitched roof still gave it a certain storybook charm. Built at the same time as Frenchman's Bride, it had never held anything resembling a carriage, but her grandmother had considered the word *garage* common. Late in the 1950s, the place had been converted into a residence for Sugar Beth's Aunt Tallulah. She'd lived there for the rest of her life, and when she'd died, the carriage house had been part of her legacy to Sugar Beth, truly a mark of the desperate, since Aunt Tallulah had never approved of her.

"I know you don't mean to be vain and self-centered, Sugar Beth, bless your heart. I'm sure someday you'll grow out of it."

Tallulah believed she could insult her niece however she wanted as long as she blessed her heart while she was doing it.

Sugar Beth leaned across the seat and pushed open the door for Gordon. "Run away, will you?"

The dog disliked getting his paws wet, and the look he gave her indicated he expected to be carried inside.

"Yeah, that's gonna happen."

He bared his teeth at her.

She grabbed her purse, what was left of the cheapest bag of dog food she'd been able to find, and a six-pack of Coke. The stuff in the trunk could wait until the rain stopped. She emerged from the car, her short skirt hiking to the top of her thighs and her long, thoroughbred legs leading the way.

Gordon moved fast when he wanted to, and he shot ahead of her up the three steps onto the small porch. The green-and-gold wooden plaque Aunt Tallulah's handyman had hammered into the brick forty years earlier still held a place of honor next to the front door.

DURING THE SUMMER OF 1954,
THE GREAT AMERICAN ABSTRACT EXPRESSIONIST ARTIST
LINCOLN ASH PAINTED HERE.

And left Tallulah a valuable work of art that now belonged to her niece, Sugar Beth Carey Tharp Zagurski Hooper. A painting that Sugar Beth needed to find as quickly as possible.

She selected a key from the ones Tallulah's lawyer had sent her, unlocked the door, and stepped inside. Immediately, the smells of her aunt's world swept over her: Ben Gay, mildew, chicken salad, and disapproval. Gordon took one look, forgot that he didn't like getting his paws wet, and turned back outside. Sugar Beth set down her packages and looked around.

The living area was stuffed with a cozy horror of family pieces: dusty Sheraton-style chairs, tables with scarred claw and ball feet, a Queen Anne writing desk, and a bentwood hat rack festooned with cobwebs. The mahogany sideboard held a Seth Thomas mantel clock, along with a pair of ugly china pugs and a silver chest emblazoned with a tarnished plaque honoring Tallulah Carey for her many years of dedicated service to the Daughters of the Confederacy.

There was no organized decorating scheme. The room's threadbare Oriental rug competed with the faded floral chintz sofa. A coral and yellow flame stitch on an armchair peeked out from beneath an assortment of crocheted cushions. The ottoman was worn green leather, the curtains yellowed lace. Still, the colors and patterns, muted by age and wear, had achieved a tired sort of harmony.

Sugar Beth walked over to the sideboard and brushed away a cobweb to open the silver chest. Inside were twelve place settings of Gorham's Chantilly sterling. Every other month for as long as Sugar Beth could remember, Tallulah had used the iced tea spoons for her Wednesday morning canasta group. Sugar Beth wondered how much twelve place settings of Chantilly sterling could bring on the open market.

Not nearly enough. She needed the painting.

She had to pee, and she was hungry, but she couldn't wait any longer to see the studio. The rain hadn't let up, so she grabbed a funky old beige sweater Tallulah had left by the door, draped it around her shoulders, and ducked back outside. Rainwater seeped through the hole in her boot as she followed the paving stones that led around the house to the garage. The old-fashioned wooden doors sagged on their hinges. She used one of the padlock keys she'd been given and dragged them open.

The place looked exactly as Sugar Beth remembered. When the carriage house had been converted into a spinster's home, Tallulah had refused to let the carpenters destroy this part of the old garage where Lincoln Ash had once set up his studio. Instead, she'd contented herself with a smaller living room and narrow kitchen, and left this as a shrine. The rough wooden shelves still held crusty cans of the paint Ash had dripped and flung from his brushes fifty years earlier to create the works that had become his masterpieces. Since the garage's single pair of windows admitted only a minimum of light, he'd worked with the garage doors open, laying his canvases out on the floor. Years ago, her aunt had covered the paint-splattered tarp with thick sheets of protective plastic, now so opaque from grime, dead bugs, and dust that the colors beneath were barely visible. A paint-speckled ladder, also draped in plastic, sat at one end near a workbench laid out with a toolbox, a collection of Ash's ancient brushes, knives, spatulas, all scattered about as though he'd stopped work to have a cigarette. Sugar Beth hadn't expected her cantankerous aunt to leave the painting propped by the door waiting for her, but still, it would have been nice. She suppressed a sigh. First thing in the morning, she'd start her search for real.

Gordon followed her back inside the house. As she flicked on a floor lamp with a fringed shade, the despair that had been nibbling at her for weeks took a bigger bite. Fifteen years ago she'd left Parrish in perfect arrogance, a foolish, vindictive girl who couldn't conceive of a universe that didn't revolve around her. But the universe had gotten the last laugh.

She wandered over to the window and drew back the dusty curtain. Above the row of hedges, she saw the chimneys of Frenchman's Bride. The name had come from the original homestead. Her grandmother had planned the house, her grandfather had built it, her father had modernized it, and Diddie had lavished it with love. *Someday Frenchman's Bride will be yours, Sugar Baby.*

In the old days, she would have given in to tears at life's unfairness. Now, she dropped the curtain and turned away to feed her disagreeable dog.

Colin Byrne stood at the window of the second-floor master bedroom of Frenchman's Bride. His appearance conveyed the brooding elegance of a man from another time period, the English Regency perhaps, or any era in which quizzing glasses, snuffboxes, and drawing rooms figured prominently. He had deep-set jade-colored eyes and a long, narrow face broken by sharp cheekbones with comma-shaped hollows beneath. The tails of those commas curled toward a thin, unsmiling mouth. He had the face of a dandy, vaguely effete, or it would have been were it not for his nose, which was huge—long and bony, aristocratic, and vastly ugly, yet perfectly at home on his face.

He wore a purple velvet smoking jacket as casually as another man would have worn a sweatshirt. A pair of black silk drawstring pajama bottoms completed his outfit, along with slippers that had scarlet Chinese symbols across the toes. His clothing had been perfectly tailored to fit his exceptionally tall, wide-shouldered body, but his big workman's hands—broad across the palm and thick fingered—served notice that everything about Colin Byrne might not be exactly as it seemed.

As he stood at the window watching the lights go on in the carriage house, the line of his already stern mouth grew even harder. So . . . The rumors were true. Sugar Beth Carey had returned.

Fifteen years had passed since he'd last seen her. He'd been little more than a boy then. Twenty-two, full of himself, an exotic foreign bird who'd landed in a small Southern town to write his first novel and—ah, yes—teach school in his spare time. There was something satisfying about letting a grudge ferment for so long. Like a great French wine, it grew in complexity, developing subtleties and nuances that a speedier resolution wouldn't have allowed.

The corner of his mouth lifted in anticipation. Fifteen years ago he'd been powerless against her. Now he wasn't.

He'd arrived in Parrish from England to teach at the local high school, although he'd had no passion for the profession and even less talent for it. But Parrish, like other small Mississippi towns, had desperately needed teachers. With a view toward exposing their youth to a larger world, a committee of the state's leading citizens had contacted universities in the U.K., offering jobs complete with work visas to exceptional graduates.

Colin, who'd long been fascinated with the writers of the

American South, had jumped at the chance. What better place to write his own great novel than in the fertile literary landscape of Mississippi, home of Faulkner, Eudora Welty, Tennessee Williams, Richard Wright? He'd dashed off an eloquent essay that vastly exaggerated his interest in teaching, gathered up glowing references from several of his professors, and attached the first twenty pages of the novel he'd barely started, figuring—rightly so, as it turned out—that a state with such an impressive literary heritage would favor a writer. A month later he'd received word that he'd been accepted, and not long after that, he was on his way to Mississippi.

He'd fallen in love with the bloody place the first day—its hospitality and traditions, its small-town charm. Not so, however, with his teaching position, which had gone from being difficult to becoming impossible, thanks to Sugar Beth Carey.

Colin had no specific plan in place for his revenge. No Machiavellian scheme he'd spent a decade mulling over—he would never have given her that much power over him. Which didn't mean he intended to set aside his long-held grudge. Instead, he'd bide his time and see where his writer's imagination would take him.

The telephone rang, and he left the window to pick it up, answering in the clipped British accent that his years in the American South hadn't softened. "Byrne here."

"Colin, it's Winnie. I tried to get you earlier today."

He'd been working on the third chapter of his new book. "Sorry, love. I haven't gotten around to checking my voice mail. Anything important?" He carried the phone back to the window and gazed out. Another light had gone on in the carriage house, this time on the second floor.

"We're all together for potluck. The guys are watching Daytona highlights right now, and no one's seen you in forever. Why don't you come over? We miss you, Mr. Byrne."

Winnie enjoyed teasing him with reminders of their early relationship as teacher and student. She and her husband were his closest friends in Parrish, and for a moment he was tempted. But the Seawillows and their significant others would be with her. Generally the women amused him, but tonight he wasn't in the mood for their chatter. "I need to work a bit longer. Invite me next time, will you?"

"Of course."

He gazed across the lawn, wishing he weren't the one who had to break the news. "Winnie . . . The lights are on in the carriage house."

Several beats of silence stretched between them before she replied in a voice that was soft, almost toneless. "She's back."

"It seems that way."

Winnie wasn't an insecure teenager any longer, and an edge of steel undercut her soft Southern vowels. "Well, then. Let the games begin."

Winnie returned to her kitchen in time to see Leeann Perkins flip her cell phone closed, her eyes dancing with excitement. "Y'all aren't going to believe this."

Winnie suspected she'd believe it.

The four other women in the kitchen stopped what they were doing. Leeann's voice had a tendency to squeak when she was excited, making her sound like a Southern Minnie Mouse. "That was Renee. Remember how she's related to Larry Carter, who's been working at the Quik Mart since he got out of rehab? You'll never guess who stepped up to the register a couple of hours ago."

As Leeann paused for dramatic effect, Winnie picked up a knife and forced herself to concentrate on cutting Heidi Pettibone's Coca-Cola cake. Her hand barely trembled.

Leeann shoved her cell in her purse without taking her eyes off them. "Sugar Beth's back!"

The slotted spoon Merylinn Jasper had been rinsing off dropped in the sink. "I don't believe it."

"We knew she was coming back." Heidi's forehead puckered in indignation. "But, still, how could she have the nerve?"

"Sugar Beth always had plenty of nerve," Leeann reminded them.

"This is going to cause all kinds of trouble." Amy Graham fingered the gold cross at her neck. In high school, she'd been the biggest Christian in the senior class and president of the Bible Club. She still had a tendency to proselytize, but she was so decent the rest of them overlooked it. Now she set her hand on Winnie's arm. "Are you all right?"

"I'm fine."

Leeann was immediately contrite. "I shouldn't have blurted it out like that. I'm being insensitive again, aren't I?"

"Always," Amy said. "But we love you anyway."

"And so does Jesus," Merylinn interjected, before Amy could get around to it.

Heidi tugged on one of the tiny silver teddy bear earrings she was wearing with her red and blue teddy bear sweater. She collected bears, and sometimes she got a little carried away. "How long do you think she'll stay?"

Leeann slipped her hand inside her dipping neckline to tug at her bra strap. Of all the Seawillows, she had the best breasts, and she liked to show them off. "Not for long, I'll bet. God, we were such little bitches."

Silence fell over the kitchen. Amy broke it by saying what all of them were thinking. "Winnie wasn't."

Because Winnie hadn't been one of them. She alone hadn't been a Seawillow. Ironic, since she was now their leader.

Sugar Beth had come up with the idea for the Seawillows when she was eleven. She'd chosen the name from a dream she'd had, although none of them could remember what it was about. The Seawillows would be a private club, she'd announced, the funnest club ever, for the most popular girls in school, all chosen by her, of course. For the most part, she'd done a good job, and more than twenty years later, the Seawillows were still the funnest club in town.

At its peak, there'd been twelve members, but some had moved away, and Dreama Shephard had died. Now, only the four women standing with Winnie in the kitchen were left. They'd become her dearest friends.

Heidi's husband, Phil, poked his head in the kitchen. He handed over the empty Crock-Pot that held the Rotel dip the men insisted on having at every gathering, a spicy tomato and Velveeta concoction for dunking their Tostitos. "Clint's making us watch golf. When are we eating?"

"Soon. And you'll never guess what we just heard." Heidi's teddy bear earrings bobbled. "Sugar Beth's back."

"No kidding. When?"

"This afternoon. Leeann just got the news."

Phil stared at them for a moment, then shook his head and disappeared to pass the word to the other men.

The women set to work, and for a few minutes silence reigned as each fell victim to her own thoughts. Winnie's were bitter. When they were growing up, Sugar Beth Carey had possessed everything Winnie wanted: beauty, popularity, self-confidence, and Ryan Galantine. Winnie, on the other hand, had only one thing Sugar Beth wanted. Still, it was a big thing, and in the end, it had been all that mattered.

Amy pulled a ham from one oven, along with a dish of her mother's famous Drambuie yams. From the other oven, Leeann removed garlic cheese grits and a spinach-artichoke casserole. Winnie's roomy kitchen, with its warm cherry cabinets and vast center island, made her house the most convenient place to gather for their potlucks. Tonight they'd parked the kids with Amy's niece. Winnie had asked her own daughter to baby-sit, but she'd turned difficult lately and refused.

As born and bred Southerners, the Seawillows dressed up for one another, which meant they spent the first part of every get-together discussing what they were wearing. This was the heritage passed on to them by mothers who'd donned ny-lons and high heels to walk to the mailbox. But Winnie wasn't a Seawillow, and despite her mother's nagging, it had taken her longer than the rest to figure out how to pull herself together.

Leeann licked a dab of cheese grits from her index finger. "I wonder if Colin knows."

"Did you get hold of him, Winnie?" Amy asked. "We got so distracted by the news, nobody asked."

Winnie nodded. "Yes, but he's working."

"He's always working." Merylinn reached for a paper towel. "You'd think he was a Yankee."

"Remember how scared we used to be of him in high school," Leeann said.

"Except for Sugar Beth," Amy pointed out. "And Winnie, of course, because she was teacher's pet." They grinned at her.

"God, I wanted him," Heidi said. "He might have been weird, but he sure was hot. Not as hot as he is now, though."

This was a familiar topic. Five years had passed since Colin had come back to Parrish, and they'd only just gotten used to having a man who'd once been the teacher they most feared as part of their adult peer group.

"We all wanted him. Except for Winnie."

"I wanted him a little," Winnie said, to redeem herself. But it wasn't really true. She might have sighed over Colin's brooding romantic aloofness, but she'd never really fantasized about him like the other girls. For her, it had always been Ryan. Ryan Galantine, the boy who'd loved Sugar Beth Carey with all his heart.

"What did I do with the oven mitts?"

Winnie handed them over. "Colin knows she's back. He saw lights at the carriage house."

"I wonder what he'll do?"

Amy stuck a serving fork on the ham platter. "Well, I for one don't intend to speak to her."

"If you get the chance, you know you will," Leeann retorted. "We all will because we're dying of curiosity. I wonder how she looks."

Blond and perfect, Winnie thought. She fought the urge to run to the mirror so she could remind herself that she was no longer lumpy, awkward Winnie Davis. Although her cheeks would never lose their roundness, and she couldn't do anything about the small stature she'd inherited from her father, she was slim and toned by five grueling sessions a week at Workouts. Like the other women's, her makeup was skillfully applied and her jewelry tasteful, although more expensive than theirs. Her dark hair shone in a short, fashionable bob, the work of the best stylist in Memphis. Tonight she wore a beaded T, a pair of periwinkle pants, and matching slides. Everything she owned was fashionable, so different from her high school days when she'd plodded down the hallway in baggy clothes, terrified someone would speak to her.

Colin, who'd been such a misfit himself, had understood. He'd been kind to her from the beginning, kinder than he'd been to her classmates, who were frequently the target of his sharp, cynical tongue. Still, the girls had daydreamed about him. Heidi, with her passion for historical romances, was the one who'd come up with his nickname.

"He reminds me of this tortured young English duke who wears a big black cape that snaps in the wind, and every time there's a thunderstorm, he paces the ramparts of his castle because he's still mourning the death of his beautiful young bride."

Colin had become the Duke, although not to his face. He wasn't the kind of teacher who inspired that sort of familiarity.

The men began to wander in, drawn by the smell of food and a desire to hear their wives' reactions to the news of Sugar Beth's return.

Merylinn flapped her arms at them. "Y'all are in the way."

The men ignored her, just as they always did when it was time to eat, and the women began their familiar dance around them, carrying the food from the kitchen to the late-eighteenth-century sideboard that occupied one wall of Winnie's graceful formal dining room.

"Does Colin know Sugar Beth's back?" Merylinn's husband, Deke, asked.

"He's the one who told Winnie." Merylinn shoved a salad bowl in his hands.

"And you sweet thangs complain because nothing ever happens in Parrish." Amy's husband, Clint, had grown up in Meridian, but he knew the old stories so well they sometimes forgot he wasn't one of them.

Brad Simmons, who sold home appliances, chuckled. He was Leeann's date for the evening. Leeann didn't really like him, but since her divorce, she'd been working her way through every eligible bachelor in Parrish, along with a few who weren't eligible, but none of them talked about that because Leeann had it hard. With two kids, one of them handicapped, and an ex-husband who was always behind on child support, she deserved whatever diversion she could find.

Winnie's husband was the last to appear. He was the tallest of the men, lean and fine featured, with wheat-colored hair, caramel eyes, and one of those perfectly symmetrical male faces that had, on several occasions, prompted Merylinn to tell him he needed to fulfill his God-given mission and sign up to be a regular sperm donor. The Seawillows were too polite to stop what they were doing and cross-examine him the way they wanted to, but they watched from the corners of their eyes as he picked up the corkscrew and began to open the wine Winnie had set out.

Winnie felt the old ache in her chest. They'd been married a little over thirteen years. They had a beautiful child, a lovely house, a life that was almost perfect. *Almost* . . . because no matter how hard Winnie tried, she would always be second best in Ryan Galantine's heart.

After two days living on Coke and stale Krispy Kremes, Sugar Beth couldn't put off buying groceries any longer. She waited until dinnertime Tuesday evening, hoping the Big Star would have emptied out by then, and drove into town.

Luck was with her, and she was able to pick up what she needed without having to speak with anyone except Peg Drucker at the register, who got so rattled she double-scanned the grape jelly, and Cubby Bowmar, who caught up with her while Peg was bagging and revealed a gaping hole where his right canine tooth had once been.

"Hey, Sugar Beth, you are even mo' gorgeous than I remember, doll baby." His eyes trailed from her breasts to the crotch of her low-rise pegged pants. "I got my own business now. Bowmar's Carpet Clean. Doin' real good, too. What's say me and you go toss back a few beers at Dudley's and catch up on old times?"

"Sorry, Cubby, but I swore off gorgeous men the day I decided to become a nun."

"Dang, Sugar Beth, you ain't even Catholic."

"Now that sure is gonna surprise my good friend the pope."

"You ain't Catholic, Sugar Beth. You're just bein' stuck up like always."

"You're still a smart 'un, Cubby. Tell your mama hi for me."

As she walked out of the Big Star, she refused to look at the poster that had stopped her dead on the way in:

The Winnie & Ryan Galantine Concert Series
Sunday, March 7, 2:00 P.M.
Second Baptist Church
Donation of $5.00 benefits local charities

The night felt as if it were closing in on her, so she headed toward the lake, only to realize she couldn't afford the gas. She made a U-turn on Spring Road, not far from the entrance to the Carey Window Factory, the business her grandfather had founded, except it was called CWF now. She found it hard to imagine Winnie and Ryan hosting a concert series. They'd been married for more than a dozen years now. The thought shouldn't be painful, since Sugar Beth was the one who'd dumped him. With her typical bad judgment, she'd taken one look at Darren Tharp and forgotten all about *Luv U 4-Ever.* Now, Winnie was the driving force behind the town's revitalization, and she sat on the boards of most of its civic organizations.

Cubby Bowmar's carpet cleaning van passed her going the other direction. In high school, Cubby and his cronies used to show up on the front lawn at Frenchman's Bride in the middle of the night, howling at the moon and calling out her name.

"Sugar . . . Sugar . . . Sugar . . ."

Her father generally slept through it, but Diddie climbed out of bed and sat by Sugar Beth's window, smoking her Tareytons and watching them. "You're going to be a woman for the ages, Sugar Baby," she'd whisper. "A woman for the ages."

"Sugar . . . Sugar . . . Sugar . . ."

The woman for the ages turned her battered Volvo into Mockingbird Lane and glanced at the French Colonial that had once been the home of the town's most successful dentist but now belonged to Ryan and Winnie. The past two days couldn't have been more dismal. Sugar Beth had cleaned up the carriage house so it was habitable, but she hadn't uncovered a trace of the Lincoln Ash painting, and tomorrow she faced the unpleasant task of searching that wreck of a depot for it. Why couldn't Tallulah have bequeathed her blue chip stocks instead of a shabby carriage house and a train stop that should have been torn down years ago?

She came to the end of Mockingbird Lane, then braked as the Volvo's headlights picked out something that hadn't been there when she'd left—a heavy chain stretching across her bumpy gravel driveway. She'd barely been gone two hours. Someone had worked fast.

She got out of the car to investigate. The quick-set cement had done its job, and a couple of hard kicks didn't budge either of the posts holding the chain. Apparently the new owners of Frenchman's Bride didn't understand her driveway wasn't part of their property.

Her spirits sank lower, and she tried to convince herself to wait until morning to confront them, but she'd learned the hard way not to postpone trouble, so she headed for the long walk that led to the entrance of the house where she'd grown up. Even blindfolded, she would have recognized the familiar pattern of the bricks beneath her feet, the point where the walk dipped, the spot where it curved to avoid the roots of an oak that had come down in a storm when she'd been sixteen. She approached the front veranda with its four graceful columns. If she ran her finger around the base of the closest one, she'd come to the place where she'd gouged her initials with the key to Diddie's El Dorado.

Lights shone from inside the house. Sugar Beth tried to tell herself the uneasiness in her stomach came from lack of a decent meal, but she knew better. Before she'd gone into town, she'd tried to boost her confidence with a tight candy pink T-shirt showing a few inches of belly, a pair of low-riding, straight-legged jeans that hugged her long-stemmed legs, and black stilettos that took her nearly to six feet. She'd topped the outfit with a copycat black motorcycle jacket and the pea-size fake diamond studs she'd bought to replace the ones she'd hocked. But the outfit wasn't doing a thing to boost her morale now, and as she crossed the porch of her old home, her heels tapped out a dismal reminder of what she'd lost. *Sugar Beth Carey . . . doesn't live here . . . anymore.*

She set her shoulders, lifted her chin, and punched the bell, but instead of the familiar seven-note chime, she heard a jarring, two-tone gong. What right did anyone have to replace the chimes at Frenchman's Bride?

The door opened. A man stood there. Tall. Imperious. It had been fifteen years, but she knew who he was even before he spoke.

"Hello, Sugar Beth."

"Shaking, eh?" said that hateful voice. "I shan't beat you if you behave yourself."

GEORGETTE HEYER, *Devil's Cub*

Chapter 2

$\mathcal{S}$he swallowed hard and spoke around a croak. "Mr. Byrne?"

His thin, unsmiling lips barely moved. "That's right. It's Mr. Byrne."

She tried to catch her breath. Tallulah hadn't told her he was the one who'd bought Frenchman's Bride, but she'd only passed on the news she'd wanted Sugar Beth to hear. The years fell away. Twenty-two. That's how old he'd been when she'd destroyed his career, barely more than a kid.

He'd looked so odd in those days with his Ichabod Crane body—too tall, too thin, his hair too long, nose too big, everything about him too eccentric for a small Southern town—appearance, accent, attitude. Naturally, the girls had been dazzled. He'd always dressed in black, most of it threadbare, with silk scarves looping his neck, some fringed, one a muted paisley, another so long it came to his hips. He'd used phrases like *bloody awful* and *don't muck about,* and, just once, *feeling a bit dicky, are we?*

The first week of school they'd spotted him using a tortoiseshell cigarette holder. When he'd overheard some of the boys whispering that he looked like a queer, he'd gazed down his long nose at them and said he regarded that as a compliment, since so many of the world's great men had been homosexual. "Alas," he'd told them, "I've been sentenced to a life of mundane heterosexuality. I can only hope a few of you will be more fortunate."

That had brought 'em out for the old parent-teacher conference.

But the young schoolteacher she remembered was a pale harbinger of the imposing man who stood before her. Byrne was still odd, but in a far more unsettling way. His ungainly body had become hard-muscled and athletic. Although he was lean, he was no longer skinny, and he'd finally grown into his face, even that honker of a nose, while the cheekbones that had once looked gaunt now seemed patrician.

Sugar Beth knew the smell of money, and it clung to him like smoke. When she'd last seen him, his hair had fallen to his shoulders. Now it was just as thick, but cut in a movie star's short, dramatic rumple. Whether an expensive salon product or good health had produced its dark sheen was hard to tell, but one thing was certain. He hadn't gotten a haircut like that in Parrish, Mississippi.

He wore a ribbed turtleneck with Armani written all over it and black wool trousers that had a thin gold pinstripe. Not only had Ichabod Crane grown up, but he'd also gone to grooming school, then bought out the place and turned it into an international franchise.

She hardly ever had to look up at any man, especially not when she was wearing dominatrix heels, but she was looking up now. Into the same haughty jade eyes she remembered. All her old resentment came rushing back. "Nobody told me you were here."

"Indeed? How amusing." He hadn't lost his British accent, although she knew accents could be manipulated. Her own, for example, could go North or South, depending on circumstances. "Do come in." He stepped back and invited her into her own home.

She wanted to give him the finger and tell him to go to hell. But running was another of life's luxuries she could no longer afford, right along with throwing hissy fits and maxing out her credit cards. The contempt that tightened the corners of his thin lips told her he understood exactly how much his invitation stung. Knowing he expected her to stomp off gave her the determination to set her shoulders and step over the threshold . . . into Frenchman's Bride.

He'd ruined it. She saw that right away. Another beautiful Southern home ravished by a foreign marauder.

The rounded shape of the entrance hall and its sweeping curl of staircase remained the same, but he'd destroyed Diddie's romantic pastels by painting the curved walls a dark espresso brown and the old oak moldings chalk white. A jarring abstract hung in place of the painting that had once dominated the space, which had been a life-size portrait of herself at age five, exquisitely dressed in white lace and pink ribbons as she curled at her beautiful mother's fashionably shod feet. Diddie had insisted the artist add a white toy poodle to the painting, even though they didn't have a poodle, or any dog, despite Sugar Beth's pleas. But her mother said she wouldn't have anything in the house that licked its private parts, or licked anybody else's for that matter.

White marble inset with bands of taupe had replaced the worn hardwood floors. The antique chests were gone, along with a gilded Marie Antoinette mirror and a pair of gold brocade chairs. Now, a gleaming black baby grand piano dominated the space. A baby grand in the entrance hall of Frenchman's Bride . . . Sugar Beth's grandmother with her avant-garde tastes might have enjoyed the oddity, but Diddie was surely doing belly flips in her grave.

"My, my . . ." Sugar Beth's accent headed deeper south, the way it did when she'd been put at a disadvantage. "And haven't you just put your own stamp on things?"

"I do what amuses me." He regarded her with the arrogance of a nobleman forced to speak to the scullery maid, but she deserved his hostility, and no matter how much he still raised her hackles, it was time to face the music. Long past time.

"I wrote you a letter of apology," she said.

"Did you now?" He couldn't have looked more disinterested.

"It came back. Return to sender."

"You don't say."

He intended to keep her cooling her heels in the entrance hall. She didn't deserve any better, but she wouldn't grovel, so she struck a compromise between what she owed him and what she owed herself. "Too little, too late, I realize that. But what the hell? Repentance is repentance."

"I wouldn't know. I don't have much to repent."

"Then pay attention to one who's been there and done that. Sometimes, Mr. Byrne, a simple 'I'm sorry' is the best a person can do."

"And sometimes the best isn't good enough, is it?"

He didn't intend to offer his forgiveness, no surprise there. At the same time, her apology hadn't exactly sounded heartfelt, and since he deserved heartfelt, her integrity demanded that she do better. But not here, not standing in the foyer like a servant.

"Would you mind if I look around?" She didn't wait for permission but swept past him into the living room.

"By all means." His drawl dripped with sarcasm.

The taupe walls matched the marble inlays in the floor, while the deep-seated leather chairs and streamlined sofa repeated the dark brown of the foyer. A symmetrically arranged group of four sepia photographs of marble busts hung over the fireplace, which wasn't the fireplace she remembered. The old oak mantel with its assorted scorch marks from the times Diddie had forgotten to open the flue had been replaced by a massive neoclassic mantel with a heavy cornice and carved pediment reminiscent of a Greek temple. In another home, she would have loved the bold juxtaposition of classic and modern, but not at Frenchman's Bride.

She turned to see him framed in the doorway, his posture reflecting the perfect arrogance of a man accustomed to being in control. He was only four years older than she, which would make him thirty-seven. When he'd been her teacher, those four years had formed an unbridgeable chasm, but now they were nothing. She remembered how romantic the Seawillows used to think he was, but Sugar Beth had refused to have a crush on someone who so stubbornly resisted her flirtatious overtures.

She needed to get to that apology again, and this time she had to do it right, but the derision in his inspection of her, combined with the desecration of her home, got in the way. "Maybe I did you a favor. A teacher's salary could never have bought all this. Congratulations on your book, by the way."

"You've read *Whistle-stop*?"

The skeptical arch of that elegant eyebrow got her hackles up. "Gosh, I tried to. But there were all those big words."

"That's right. You never liked to tax your brain with anything more challenging than a fashion magazine, did you?"

"Hey, if somebody doesn't read them, there'll be a whole shitload of women walking around in plaid polyester, and then think how sorry everybody'll be." She widened her eyes. "Oops . . . Now you're goin' to give me a detention for vulgarity."

Time hadn't done a thing to improve his sense of humor. "Detentions never worked with you, did they, Sugar Beth? Your mother wouldn't permit them."

"Diddie sure did have opinions about what was right and wrong for me." She tilted her head just enough so her hair fell away from her fake diamond studs. "Did you know she refused to let me compete for Miss Mississippi? She said I was sure to win, and she wouldn't allow any daughter of hers within spitting distance of that tacky Atlantic City. We had a big fuss about it, but you know how Diddie was, once she made up her mind about something."

"Oh, yes, I remember."

Of course he did. Diddie was the one who'd gotten him fired. Which made it time to drop the bull and take another stab at those long overdue amends.

"I am sorry. Really. What I did was inexcusable." Meeting his eyes was a lot tougher than she wanted it to be, but this time she didn't falter. "I told her I'd lied, but the damage was done by then, and you'd already left town."

"Odd. I don't recall Mummy trying to track me down. It's strange an intelligent woman never figured out how to ring me up and say that all was forgiven, that I hadn't—how did she put it that day?—betrayed my position of authority by compromising her innocent daughter's virtue?"

The way he lingered over those last three words told her he knew exactly what she and Ryan Galantine had been doing in the backseat of her red Camaro. "No, she didn't. And I didn't have the guts to tell my father the truth."

Griffin had found out, though, when he'd dug through her mother's papers a few months after she died, and discovered the letter of confession Sugar Beth had written. "You've got to admit, Daddy did all right by you. He practically took out an ad in the paper telling everybody I lied."

"Nearly a year had passed by then, hadn't it? A bit late. I'd already been forced back to England."

She started to point out that he'd managed to return to the States—his book jacket said he was now an American citizen—but she'd only sound as though she was trying to defend herself. He uncoiled from the doorway and wandered over to a wall unit that held a wet bar. A wet bar in Diddie Carey's living room . . .

"Would you like a drink?" It wasn't the invitation of a good host but the softly spoken gambit in a cat-and-mouse game.

"I don't drink anymore."

"Reformed?"

"Hell, no. I just don't drink." She was on a roll, peggin' the old laugh-meter. She was killing herself here.

He poured out a few inches of what looked like a very expensive single malt scotch. She'd forgotten how large his hands were. She used to tell everybody who'd listen that he was the biggest sissy in town, but even then, those meat-hook hands had made her look like a liar. They still didn't seem to belong to someone who'd recited sonnets from memory and occasionally tied back his hair with a piece of black velvet ribbon.

One night a bunch of them had left school late and spotted him on the intramural field with a soccer ball. Soccer hadn't caught on in Parrish, and they'd never seen anything like it. He'd bounced the ball from one knee to another, off a calf, a thigh, keeping it in the air until they lost count. Then he'd begun dribbling it down the field, running at full speed, the ball right between his feet. After that, the boys' opinions of him had changed, and it wasn't long before they'd invited him to join them at the basketball hoop.

"Three husbands, Sugar Beth?" He curled those working-man's fingers around a cut-glass tumbler. "Even for you, that seems a bit extreme."

"One thing never changes about Parrish. Gossip's still this town's favorite pastime." Cool air brushed her belly as she slipped her hands into the pockets of her black leather jacket and pushed it back. Her cropped candy pink T-shirt had the word BEAST written in glitter script over her breasts. It was a little flashy, but it had been marked down to $5.99, and she could make just about anything look trendy. "I'd appreciate it if you'd get that chain off my driveway."

"Would you now?" He sank into one of the leather chairs without inviting her to do the same. "You have a wretched track record with husbands."

"You think?"

"Word travels," he drawled. "I believe I heard that husband number one was someone you met in college."

"Darren Tharp, all-American shortstop. He played for the Braves for a while." She executed a nifty tomahawk chop.

"Impressive." He took a sip from his drink, the tumbler nearly swallowed by his palm, and regarded her over the rim of the glass. "I also heard he left you for another woman. Pity."

"Her name was Samantha. Unlike me, she managed to graduate from college, but it wasn't her degree that attracted Darren. Turns out, she had a natural-born gift for fellatio."

The tumbler came to a stop halfway to his lips.

She gave him her best Southern belle smile, the one that went from here to there without coming anyplace close to sincerity. With a few adjustments—and if Diddie hadn't possessed such a hang-up about Atlantic City—that smile could have put something more impressive than a homecoming crown on her head. "I guess brains can only get a girl so far."

Byrne had no intention of letting her sidetrack him. "Apparently you took off to Hollywood with your settlement money."

"I earned every dollar of it."

"But you weren't flooded with movie offers."

"And aren't you just the sweetest thang, taking such an interest in me."

"Surely I heard this wrong. Your second husband was some kind of Hell's Angel?"

"That would have been more exciting, but I'm afraid Cy was just a stuntman for the movies. Extremely talented— right up to the day he killed himself trying to jump his bike from the Santa Monica pier onto the deck of a luxury yacht. It was a film about the evils of drug smuggling, so I tell myself he died for a good cause, not that I wasn't smoking the occasional joint myself back then."

"And more than a few in high school, as I recall."

"A mistake, Your Honor. I thought they were just funny-smelling cigarettes."

He didn't smile, but she hadn't expected it from that granite-jawed face.

She'd left Cy a few months before that fatal stunt. No girl on earth had a bigger talent for marrying cheating losers than she did. Emmett had been the exception, but then, he'd been seventy on their wedding day, and age begot wisdom.

"After that, people seemed to lose track of you for a while," he said.

"I worked in the restaurant business. *Very* exclusive."

She'd started off as a hostess at a decent L.A. restaurant but had gotten fired for mouthing off to a customer. Next she'd worked as a cocktail waitress. When she'd lost that job, she'd served up lasagna at a cheap Italian restaurant, then gone on to an even cheaper burger joint. She'd bottomed out the day she'd found herself studying a help-wanted ad for an escort service. More than anything else, that had made her realize it was long past time for her to grow up and take responsibility for her life.

"Then you snagged Emmett Hooper."

"And you didn't even need the Parrish grapevine to hear about that." Her smile hid every drop of pain.

"The newspapers were quite informative. And entertaining. A twenty-eight-year-old waitress becomes the trophy wife of a filthy rich seventy-year-old retired Texas oilman."

An oilman whose investments had gone belly-up even before he'd gotten sick. Emmett had been her dearest friend, her lover, and the person who'd helped her finish the job of growing up.

Byrne tipped his drink toward her, looking like a bored, but very masculine, Gucci model. "My condolences on your loss."

The lump in her throat made it hard to come up with a smart-ass response, but she managed. "I appreciate your sympathy, but when you marry someone that old, you kind of know what's coming."

She welcomed the contempt in those jade eyes. Contempt trumped pity any damn day. She watched him cross his legs, the movement an unsettling combination of feline grace and male strength. "We used to call you the Duke behind your back," she said. "Did you know that?"

"Of course."

"We all thought you were a pansy."

"Did you now?"

"And stuck-up."

"I was. Still am, for that matter. I take pride in it."

She wondered if he was married. If not, the single women of Parrish must be lining up at the door with coconut cakes and casseroles. She moved toward the fireplace and tried to look assertive. "I'm sure it's just entertaining the knickers off you to block my driveway, but the fun's gone on long enough."

"As it happens, I'm still enjoying myself."

He didn't look as though he knew how to enjoy anything, except maybe conquering India. As she gazed at his immaculately tailored clothes, she wondered who'd done the dirty work of setting the posts in concrete on such short notice. "Don't you think it might be embarrassing when I call the police?"

"Not at all. It's my land."

"And I thought you were such an authority on Parrish. My father deeded the carriage house to my aunt in the 1950s."

"The house, yes. But not the driveway. That's still part of Frenchman's Bride."

She snapped upright. "That's not true."

"I have an exceptionally fine lawyer, and he pays attention to things like property boundaries." He rose from the chair. "You're more than welcome to look at the survey yourself. I'll send over a copy."

Could her father have been that stupid? Of course he could have. Griffin Carey had been meticulous when it came to matters involving his window factory but notoriously lax regarding home and family. How careful could a man be who kept his wife and his mistress in the same town?

"What do you want, Mr. Byrne? Obviously not my apology, so you might as well spell it out."

"Why, retribution, of course. What did you think I wanted?"

His softly spoken words sent a shiver down her spine. She resisted a longing glance toward the glass of scotch he'd just set down, but she hadn't had a drink in nearly five years, and she wasn't starting up again tonight. "Well, now, isn't this going to be all kinds of entertaining. Exactly where do you expect me to park?"

"I couldn't care less. Maybe one of your old friends will help you out."

This was the perfect moment to throw a temper tantrum, but she'd forgotten how. Instead, she sauntered toward him, putting a little sway in her hips even though her bones felt a hundred years old. "See now, here's where you're not thinking straight. I've already lost three husbands and one set of parents, so if you want real retribution, you'll have to dig deeper than a measly driveway."

"Playing the pity card, are we?"

That's exactly what it had sounded like, and she wanted to bite her tongue. Instead, she flipped up the collar of her jacket and headed for the door. "Fuck you, Mr. Byrne. And fuck your pity."

She'd barely taken three steps before she caught a whiff of expensive cologne. Her heart bumped against her ribs as he caught her arm and spun her around.

"How about this for retribution, then?"

The cold, hard expression on his face reminded her of Darren Tharp's right before he'd smacked her to kingdom come, but Colin Byrne had another kind of violence in mind. Before she could react, his dark head swooped, and he covered her mouth in a brutal, punishing kiss.

Kisses . . . So many of them. Her adoring mother's cheek-smooches. Aunt Tallulah's pursed dry-lipped ones. Those sex-drenched teenage kisses with Ryan. Darren had been a main-event man and a lousy kisser. Then there'd been Cy's sloppy drunken kisses and her own gin-soaked ones in response. After that, the kisses of a string of men she barely remembered, except that all of them had tasted like despair. Salvation had arrived in the form of Emmett's kisses, ones of kindness, need, fear, and, at the end, resignation.

The last kiss she'd received had come from his daughter, Delilah, who'd thrown her arms around Sugar Beth's neck and left a wet track on her cheek. *I love you more than anybody in the whole world, my Sugar Beth.*

All those kisses, and she couldn't remember a single one that had felt like this. Cold. Calculated. Designed to humiliate.

Byrne took his time administering justice. He cradled her jaw, not hurting, but forcing her mouth open just enough so he could attack with his tongue. She didn't respond, didn't fight him.

He didn't care.

She wasn't surprised when his hand went to her breast. She even expected it.

Another clinical exploration, as if no real person lived under her skin, merely flesh and bone without a soul.

He held her breast in one of his big hands and rubbed the slope with his thumb. As he brushed her nipple, a pang of longing pierced her. Not desire—she was too empty for that, and this was about revenge, not sex. Instead, she experienced a bone-deep longing for simple kindness, an ironic wish for someone who'd doled it out so sparingly herself.

She'd learned a lot about street fighting during her marriage to a stuntman, and she thought about biting him or bringing her knee up, but that wouldn't be fair. He deserved his retribution.

He finally drew back, and the scent of the scotch he'd been drinking fell softly across her cheek. "You said I stuck my tongue in your mouth and felt your breast." His jade eyes cut through her. "Isn't that the lie you told your mother, Sugar Beth? Isn't that how you chopped me up and sent me packing?"

"Exactly that way," she said quietly.

He ran his thumb over her bottom lip. Coming from another man, it would have been a gesture of tenderness, but this was the mark of a conqueror. She owed him contrition, but all she had left these days was a little dignity, and she'd die before she let a single tear fall.

He lowered his arm. "Not a lie now."

She reached deep down into the reservoir of strength that had almost, but not quite, run dry and somehow managed to dig up what she needed to lift her hand and touch his cheek. "All this time I've hated feeling like a liar. Thanks, Mr. Byrne. You've cleansed my soul."

Colin felt her palm cool against his skin and realized she was getting the last word. The knowledge stunned him. This should have been his victory. Both of them knew it. Yet she was trying to snatch it away.

He gazed at the mouth he'd just crushed. She hadn't tasted anything like he'd expected—not that he'd expected anything, since he hadn't planned his attack. Still, he'd subconsciously braced himself for the slyness, the pettiness, the monstrous ego that had defined her. *Who's the fairest in the land? Me! Me! Me!* Instead, he'd discovered something else—something gritty, determined, and insolent. At least the last was familiar.

She dropped her hand and pointed her index finger at him, a pistol straight through his self-respect. Just before she pulled the trigger, she flashed a wisdom-of-the-courtesans smile. "See you around, Mr. Byrne."

Bang. And she was gone.

He stood there without moving. The scent of her—spice, sex, obstinacy—lingered in the air even after the front door shut. That ugly kiss should have put an end to it. Instead, it had started things up all over again.

At eighteen, she was the most beautiful creature anyone in Parrish had ever seen. Watching her saunter up the sidewalk to the front doors of Parrish High was watching sexual artistry in motion: those endless legs, the sway of her hips, bounce of her breasts, dazzle of her long blond hair.

The boys stumbled over themselves watching her while the music from their boom boxes played the sound track to her life. Billy Ocean pleading with her to get out of his dreams and into his car. Bon Jovi taking one look, then living on a prayer. Cutting Crew more than eager just to die in her arms tonight. Guns n' Roses, Poison, Whitesnake—all the great hair bands—somehow she'd brought them to their knees and made them beg for the crumbs of her affection.

Sugar Beth was still beautiful. Those man-killer light blue eyes and perfectly symmetrical features would follow her to the grave, and that cloud of blond hair should be fanned out on a satin pillow in a *Playboy* spread. But the dewy freshness had disappeared. She'd looked older than thirty-three and tougher. She was thinner, too. He'd seen the tendons in the long sweep of her neck, and her wrists looked almost frail. But that dangerous sexuality hadn't changed. At eighteen, it had been new and indiscriminate. Now it was well honed and much more lethal. The bloom might be off the rose, but the thorns had grown poison tips.

He retrieved his drink and settled in his chair, more depressed by their encounter than he wanted to be. As he gazed around at the luxurious house that his money had bought him, he remembered the sneers of his Irish bricklayer father when Colin had been forced to return to England after he'd been fired from his teaching job.

"Comin' home in disgrace, are you, then? So much for you and your mum's fancy ways, boyo. Now you'll be doin' honest work like the rest of us."

For that alone, Colin would never forgive Sugar Beth Carey.

He lifted his glass, but even the taste of ten-year-old scotch couldn't erase the single-minded defiance he'd seen in Sugar Beth's eyes. Despite that assault he'd delivered in the disguise of a kiss, she still believed she had the upper hand. He set his glass aside and contemplated exactly how he would disabuse her of that notion.

*"Have I done wrong? So many prim persons
stared as though they could not believe their
eyes!"*

GEORGETTE HEYER, *The Grand Sophy*

Chapter 3

*S*ugar Beth finished the potato chips that made up her
breakfast and gazed across the kitchen at Gordon, who
lurked in the door, looking hostile. "Get over it, will you? It's
not my fault Emmett loved me more than you."

He experimented with his psychotic Christopher Walken
expression, but bassets were at a disadvantage when it came
to projecting menace. "Pathetic."

He looked offended.

"All right, punk." She rose from the table, crossed the living room, and opened the front door. As he trotted past, he
tried to bump her, but she knew his tricks and she sidestepped, then followed him out into another chilly, drizzly
February morning. Since this was Mississippi, it could be
eighty by next week. She prayed she'd be long gone by then.

As Gordon began to sniff around, she gazed over at
Frenchman's Bride. She'd been trying not to think about last
night's encounter with Colin Byrne. At least she hadn't
crumbled until she'd reached the carriage house. Old guilt

clung to her like cobwebs. She should have tried harder to make amends, but apparently, she hadn't grown up as much as she wanted to think.

Why, of all people, did he have to be the one who bought Frenchman's Bride? If he'd ever spoken to the press about moving back to Parrish, she'd missed it. But then he seemed to shun publicity, and there hadn't been that many interviews. Even his jacket photo was distant and grainy, or she'd have been better prepared for the dangerous man she'd encountered.

She made her way toward the boxwood hedge that separated their properties and pushed aside the bottom branches. "Right through here, devil dog."

For once, he didn't give her trouble.

"Make Mommy proud," she called out.

He took a few moments sniffing around, then found a satisfactory spot in the middle of the lawn to do his business.

"Nice doggie."

Despite what she'd told Byrne, she'd read *Last Whistle-stop on the Nowhere Line* right along with the rest of the country. How could she have ignored the story of people she'd heard about all her life? The black and white families, rich and poor, who'd populated Parrish during the 1940s and 1950s, had included her own grandparents, Tallulah, Leeann's great-uncle, and, of course, Lincoln Ash.

The public's appetite for atmospheric Southern nonfiction had been whetted by John Berendt's runaway bestseller, *Midnight in the Garden of Good and Evil*. But while *Midnight* had dealt with murder and scandal among the wealthy aristocracy of old Savannah, *Last Whistle-stop* had mined gold from small-town life. Colin Byrne's story of a Mississippi town recovering from a segregationist legacy had been filled with the eccentric characters and domestic dramas readers loved, along with a strong dose of Southern folklore. Other books had tried to do the same thing, but

Byrne's fondness for the town, combined with his wry observations as an outsider, had put *Last Whistle-stop* in a league of its own.

She realized Gordon was trotting toward the house, not one bit intimidated by its grandeur. "Come back here."

Of course he ignored her.

"I mean it, Gordon. I have to go into town, and if you don't come here right now, I'm leaving without you."

She couldn't be sure, but she thought he blew her a raspberry.

"You know you'll try to nip me if I come after you." He never went so far as to actually hurt her, but he liked to keep her on her toes.

She watched him trot up the steps to the veranda. "Fine. Do me a favor, and don't bother to come home." Contrary to the habits of the rest of his breed, Gordon refused to roam. He liked torturing her too much to hit the open road. She stomped back toward the carriage house. What did it say about a person when even her dog hated her?

She grabbed her purse, stuck an old straw cowboy hat on her head, and set out to search the depot for the painting. But as she tramped down the drive to her car, she found a ticket for unlawful overnight parking tucked under her windshield wiper. Terrific. She shoved it beneath the visor and headed for town.

Purlie's Auto Shop was still doing business, but an office supply store sat in the space once occupied by Spring Fancy Millinery. Diddie had taken her there every year to buy an Easter bonnet, right up until sixth grade, when Sugar Beth had rebelled.

Diddie's nostrils fluttered like butterfly wings when she was displeased. *"You ungrateful child. Exactly how is our Dear Lord supposed to know it's Resurrection Day if He sees you sittin' there in church bareheaded like some heathen? Answer me that, Miss Sugar Baby?"*

Sugar Beth had fluttered her nostrils right back. *"Do you really think Jesus Christ is goin' to stay in his grave just because I'm not wearin' a hat?"*

Diddie had laughed and gone to find her cigarettes.

A longing for her loving, imperfect mother welled up inside her so strong that it hurt, but her feelings toward her father were all bitter. *"He's not my real father, is he, Diddie? Somebody else got you pregnant, and then Daddy married you."*

"Sugar Beth Carey, you hush your mouth. Just because your father is a reprobate doesn't mean I am, too. Now I don't ever want to hear you say anything like that again."

The fact that Sugar Beth's silver-blue eyes perfectly mirrored her father's made it impossible to hold on for long to the fantasy of Diddie having a secret lover.

She supposed her parents' marriage had been inevitable, but they couldn't have been more ill-suited. Diddie was the extravagantly beautiful, fun-loving daughter of a local storekeeper. Griffin was the heir to the Carey Window Factory. Short, homely, and intellectually brilliant, Griffin was smitten by Parrish's reigning belle, while Diddie was secretly contemptuous of the boy she considered an "ugly little toad." At the same time, she coveted everything a union with him would bring her.

Griffin must have known that Diddie was incapable of giving him the adoration he craved, but he'd married her anyway, then punished her for not loving him by openly living with another woman. Diddie retaliated by appearing not to care. Eventually, Griffin raised the stakes by turning his back on the person Diddie most loved . . . their daughter.

Despite their mutual hatred, they never considered divorce. Griffin was the town's economic leader, Diddie its social and political one. Each refused to give up what the other offered, and the marriage ground on, dragging a confused little girl in its destructive wake.

Sugar Beth passed a McDonald's, spruced up since her high school days, and a travel agency sporting one of the downtown area's new maroon and green awnings. She turned on Valley. The one-block street, which was anchored at the end by the abandoned railroad depot, had escaped the town's revitalization efforts, and she parked her car on a crumbling patch of blacktop. As she gazed at the dilapidated redbrick building, she saw the place where Colin Byrne had stood for his fuzzy author photo.

Shingles had blown off the depot's roof, and ancient graffiti covered the splintered plywood boarding up the windows. Cans and broken bottles littered the weeds by the tracks. Why had Tallulah thought it was so important to preserve this old ruin? But her aunt had been obsessed with local history, the same as Sugar Beth's father, and apparently she hadn't seen the wisdom of bulldozing the place.

As Sugar Beth got out of the car, she thought of the letter lying crumpled in the bottom of her purse:

Dear Sugar Beth,

I'm leaving you the carriage house, the depot, and, of course, the painting because you're my only living relative and, regardless of your behavior, blood is thicker than water. The depot is a disgrace, but, by the time I purchased it, I lacked the energy and the funds for repairs. The fact that it was allowed to deteriorate so badly does not speak well of this town. I'm certain you'd like to sell it, but I doubt you'll have any luck finding a buyer. Even the Parrish Community Advancement Association lacks proper respect for history.

The carriage house is a registered national landmark. Keep Lincoln's studio as it is. Otherwise, every-

thing goes to the University. As for the painting . . .
You'll either find it or you won't.

Cordially,
Tallulah Shelborne Carey

P.S. No matter what your mother told you, Lincoln
Ash loved me.

Tallulah's insistence that she was the great love of Lincoln Ash's life had driven Diddie wild. Tallulah said Ash had promised to come back to Parrish for her as soon as his one-man show in Manhattan was over, but he'd been hit by a bus the day before it closed. Diddie told everyone the painting was a figment of Tallulah's imagination, but Griffin said it wasn't. *"Tallulah has that painting, all right. I've seen it."* But when Diddie pressed him for details, he'd just laughed.

Tallulah refused to display the painting, saying it was all she had left of him, and she wasn't going to share it with curiosity seekers or those pompous art critics Ash had despised during his lifetime. They'd only analyze the life right out of it. *"The world can gawk all it wants after I'm dead,"* she'd said. *"For now, I'm keeping what I have to myself."*

Sugar Beth worked the key in the lock. The door was warped, so she had to use her shoulder to push it open. As she stepped inside, something flew at her head. She shrieked and ducked. When her heartbeat returned to normal, she pushed her cowboy hat more firmly down and went the rest of the way inside.

She could see just enough to make her cringe. A putrid crust of bird crap and dirt covered the scarred old benches of what had once been the depot's small waiting room. Rusty streaks ran down one of the walls, a fetid puddle sat in the middle of the hardwood floor, and pieces of broken furniture lay scattered around like old bones. Beneath the ticket window, a pile of filthy blankets, old newspapers, and empty tin cans indicated that someone had once squatted here. Her dust allergies kicked up, and she started sneezing. When she recovered, she pulled out the flashlight she'd brought along and began to look for the painting.

In addition to the waiting area, the depot had storage rooms, closets, an office behind the ticket window, and public rest rooms that were unspeakably foul repositories of exposed pipes, stained and broken porcelain, and ominous piles of filth. For the next two hours, she unearthed splintered furniture, crates, battered file cabinets, mice droppings, and a dead bird that made her shudder. What she didn't find was any sign of the painting.

Filthy, sneezing, and grossed out, she finally sank down on a bench. If Tallulah hadn't hidden the painting in either the carriage house or the depot, where had she put it? Starting tomorrow, she'd have to begin searching out the surviving members of Tallulah's canasta club. They'd feel duty-bound to cluck their tongues over her, but they'd been her aunt's closest friends, and they were most likely to know her secrets. Just as dispiriting was the knowledge that she was down to her last fifty dollars. If she intended to keep eating, she had to find a job.

"Charming place you have here."

She sneezed, then turned to see Colin Byrne standing in the open doorway. He looked as though he might have come in from a stroll across the moors: boots, dark brown slacks, tweed jacket, fashionably rumpled hair. But the cold assessment in his eyes reminded her more of a frontier hunter than a civilized Brit. "If you're here to assault me again," she said, "you'd better have your jockstrap fastened up extra tight because I won't be so polite next time."

"My body only has a limited tolerance for venom." He slipped one stem of his designer sunglasses into the open collar of his shirt and took a few steps inside. "Interesting that

Tallulah left you the depot, although not surprising, I suppose, considering her feelings about family."

"I'll give you a great deal if you want to buy it."

"No, thank you."

"It made you a fortune. You could show a little gratitude."

"*Last Whistle-stop* was about the town. The depot was a metaphor."

"I thought metaphor was a weight-loss drink? Do you always dress like a stiff?"

"As frequently as possible, yes."

"You look stupid."

"You, of course, being the ultimate fashion arbiter." He cast a disparaging eye toward her filthy jeans and dirty sweatshirt.

She slipped off her cowboy hat and wiped a cobweb from her cheek. "You were a terrible teacher."

"Abysmal." He nudged aside a piece of cable with the toe of his boot.

"Teachers are supposed to build their students' self-confidence. You called us toads."

"Only to your faces. Behind your backs, it was a bit worse, I'm afraid."

He *had* been a terrible teacher, sarcastic, critical, and impatient. But every once in a while, he'd been glorious, too. She remembered the way he used to read to them, words cascading like dusky music from his tongue. Sometimes the classroom would get so quiet it felt like nighttime, and she'd pretend they were all sitting in the dark together around a campfire someplace. He had a way of inspiring the least likely students, so that the dumbest kids found themselves reading books, the athletes were writing poetry, and shyer students began to speak up, if only to protect themselves from one of his scathing put-downs. She belatedly remembered that he was also the teacher who'd finally shown her how to write a paragraph that made sense.

As she stuck her hat back on, he gazed with distaste at the pool of stagnant water on the floor. "Is it true you didn't go to your own father's funeral? That seems ignominious, even for you."

"He was dead. I'm figuring he didn't notice." She pushed herself up off the bench. "I saw you had your book photo taken in front of my property. I want royalties. A few thousand should do it."

"Sue me."

She pushed aside a section of pipe. "Exactly what are you doing here?"

"Gloating, of course. What did you think?"

She wanted to snatch up one of the broken chair legs and hit him with it, but he would undoubtedly have hit her back, and she forced herself to be practical instead. "How well did you know my aunt?"

"As well as I wanted to." He wandered over to investigate the ticket window, not at all put off by the grime. "As a history buff, she was an invaluable source, but narrow-minded. I didn't like her all that much."

"I'm sure she lost sleep over that."

He ran a finger along one of the iron bars, gazed at the dirt he'd picked up, and pulled a snowy white handkerchief from his pocket to wipe it off. "Most people don't believe the painting exists."

She didn't bother asking how he knew she was looking for it. By now, everyone in town was familiar with the terms of Tallulah's will. "It exists."

"I think so, too. But how do you know?"

"None of your g.d. business." She pointed toward a stack of crates. "There's a dead bird behind there. Make yourself useful and get it out of here."

He peered around the crates but made no move to do anything with the corpus un-delicti. "Your aunt was barmy."

"It runs in the family. And don't expect me to be ashamed.

Yankees lock away loony relatives, but down here, we prop 'em up on parade floats and march 'em through the middle of town. Are you married?"

"I used to be. I'm a widower."

If she hadn't become a better person, she'd have asked if he'd killed his wife with his keen sense of humor. At the same time, she was curious. What kind of woman would have bound herself to such a critical, impossible man? Then she remembered all the high school girls sighing over him even after he'd stung them with one of his scathing rebukes. Women and difficult men. She was thankful she'd finally broken the habit.

He abandoned his investigation of the ticket window. "Tell me about boycotting your father's funeral."

"Why do you care?"

"I'm a writer. I'm fascinated by the inner workings of the narcissistic mind."

"I swan, all these big words are makin' my lil ol' head spin."

"You were so intelligent." He inspected one of the joists. "You had a fine brain, but you refused to use it for anything worthwhile."

"There you go again, knocking the fashion magazines."

"Skipping the funeral took gall, even for you."

"I had a hair appointment that day."

He waited, but she had no intention of telling him about that horrible year.

It had started out so well. She'd been the most popular freshman girl at Ole Miss, so caught up in the whirl of campus life she'd forgotten all about the Seawillows, ignoring their phone calls and standing them up when they drove over for a visit. Then one January morning Griffin had called to tell her that Diddie had died in the middle of the night from a cerebral hemorrhage. Sugar Beth had been inconsolable. She'd thought nothing worse could ever happen to her until, six weeks later, when Griffin announced that he was marrying his longtime mistress. He expected Sugar Beth to be in the front row of the church for the wedding. She'd screamed that she hated him, that she'd never set foot in Parrish again, and even though he'd threatened to disinherit her, she'd kept her word.

She'd spent his wedding day in bed with Darren Tharp, trying to numb her grief with bad sex. Not long after, when Griffin was disposing of Diddie's things, he'd found Sugar Beth's guilty confession. Within days, everyone had known what she'd done to Colin Byrne, and the people who'd merely disliked her before now hated her. The Seawillows, already hurt by the way she'd abandoned them, had never spoken to her again.

She'd had no chance to reconcile with her father. Right before her final exams, barely three months after his marriage, he'd suffered a fatal heart attack. Only then did she learn that he'd made good on his threat to disinherit her. In the space of five months, she'd lost her mother, her father, her best friends, and Frenchman's Bride. She'd been too young to understand how many losses were yet to come.

"Is it true that you got married three days after they buried Griffin?" Byrne asked, with no particular display of interest in her answer.

"In my defense, I cried buckets through the ceremony."

"Touching."

She pulled the key from her pocket. "It's been hilarious talking to you, but I need to lock up and get on with my day."

"Manicure and massage?"

"Later. I have to find a job first."

One bold, dark eyebrow angled upward. "A job? I'm incredulous."

"I get bored if I have too much time on my hands."

"The papers said Emmett Hooper died bankrupt, but I was certain you'd manage to come away with something."

She thought of Gordon. "Oh, I did."

He gazed around at the awful interior of the depot, then

infuriated her by lifting one corner of his mouth in what she realized was a knife-thin smile. "You really are broke, aren't you?"

"Only until I find the painting."

"*If* you find the painting."

"I will. You can count on it." As she brushed past him and headed for the door, she had to force herself not to run. "Sorry you couldn't stay longer."

He took his time following her outside, the smile still hanging around the edges of that uncompromising mouth. "Let me make certain I've got this right. You're actually going to have to work to support yourself?"

"I'm very good at it." She twisted the lock with more force than necessary.

"Planning to wait tables again?"

"It's honest work." She headed for the car, trying not to look as if she were making a jailbreak. Just as she got there, he spoke from the steps of the depot.

"If you can't find a job, come and see me. I might have something."

"Oh, yeah, I'm going to do that, all right." She jerked open the door, then spun back to confront him. "Unless you want our range war to get really ugly, you'd better have that chain off my driveway by nightfall."

And didn't that just entertain the heck out of him. "A threat, Sugar Beth?"

"You heard me." She threw herself into the car and peeled off. As she glanced in her rearview mirror, she saw him leaning against the side of his shiny new Lexus, elegant, aloof, amused. Coldhearted bastard.

She stopped at the drugstore to buy a newspaper and met up with Cubby Bowmar at the register. He pocketed the change from a bottle of Gatorade. "Did you see my new van outside, Sugar Beth?"

"Afraid I missed it."

"Carpet cleaning business is real good right now. Real good."

He licked his lips and pressed her to join him again for a drink. She barely escaped with what was left of her virtue. Back in her car, she unfolded the paper over the steering wheel and checked the help-wanted ads. She wouldn't have to work for long, she reminded herself, just until she found the painting. Then she was heading back to Houston.

Nobody needed a waitress, which was just as well, because the idea of serving hamburgers to all the people she'd once lorded it over turned her stomach. She circled three possibilities: a bakery, an insurance agency, and an antique shop, then headed home for a quick shower. A copy of the survey leaned against her front door. She flipped it open and saw that Colin had been right. The driveway belonged to Frenchman's Bride.

Depressed, she showered, swiped on some mascara and lipstick, twisted her hair up, and slipped into the most conservative outfit she owned, an ancient Chanel skirt and a white T. She added a raspberry pink cardigan, pulled on nylons and a pair of boots, and set off. Since the insurance agency offered the best money, she decided to start there. Unfortunately, she found Laurie Ferguson sitting behind the hiring desk.

Sugar Beth had liked Laurie in school, and she couldn't remember having done anything particularly despicable to her, but it didn't take long to figure out Laurie had different memories.

"Why, Sugar Beth Carey, I heard you were back in town, but I never expected to see you here." Her heavy hair was bright red now instead of brown, and her earrings were too big for her small, sharp features. She tapped an acrylic fingernail painted with a tiny American flag on the top of her desk. "You're looking for a job. Imagine that." She took a drag from her cigarette without inviting Sugar Beth to sit.

"You have to understand. We can only hire someone who's really serious about having a career."

In Sugar Beth's mind, a general clerical job wasn't exactly a career, but she smiled. "I wouldn't expect anything less."

"And we need someone permanent. Are you planning to stay in Parrish?"

Sugar Beth had known this was coming, and despite the aversion she'd developed for playing fast and loose with the truth, she was forced to hedge. "You might have heard I have a house here now."

"So you're staying?"

The gleam of malice in Laurie's eyes made Sugar Beth suspect her question had more to do with Laurie's desire to feed the local gossip mill than to offer Sugar Beth a job. On the other hand, the idea of bossing around Griffin and Diddie's daughter might hold just enough appeal for Laurie to come through with an offer, and the nearly empty bag of dog food sitting in the carriage house kitchen motivated Sugar Beth to respond politely. "I can't promise to stay here until I'm dead and buried, but I plan to be around for a while." For how long was anyone's guess.

"I see." Laurie shuffled a few papers, then gave Sugar Beth a smug smile. "You don't mind taking our proficiency test, do you? I need to make sure you have the minimal skills we require in math and English."

Sugar Beth could no longer hold her tongue. "I don't mind at all. I'm especially good in math. But then, you must remember from all the times you copied my algebra homework."

Thirty seconds later, Sugar Beth was on the sidewalk.

The Crème de la Crème Bakery had been Glendora's Café when Sugar Beth was growing up. Unfortunately, the new owner needed someone who could do maintenance work as well as bake, and when she handed Sugar Beth a monkey wrench to demonstrate her skills, the gig was pretty much up. Everything rested on the antique shop.

The charming window display at Yesterday's Treasures included a child's rocking horse, an old trunk filled with quilts, and a spool-legged chair with a hand-painted pitcher and washbowl. Sugar Beth's spirits lifted. What a wonderful place to work. Maybe the owner was new to Parrish, like the woman at the bakery, and wouldn't know Sugar Beth's reputation.

The old-fashioned bell above the door tinkled, and the soft strains of Bach's cello suites enveloped her. She inhaled a spicy potpourri along with the pleasantly musty scent of the past. Antique tables gleamed with English china and Irish crystal. The open drawers of a cherry highboy displayed exquisite old linens. An unusual rosewood desk showcased an array of watch fobs, necklaces, and brooches. Everything in the shop was top quality, perfectly arranged, and beautifully tended.

A woman's voice called out from the back. "I'll be right with you."

"Take your time."

Sugar Beth was admiring a cheery tableau of Victorian hatboxes, silk violets, and handmade reed baskets filled with speckled brown eggs as a woman stepped from the dim depths at the back of the store. Her dark hair fell in a sophisticated cut that ended just above her jawline. She was neatly dressed in pale gray slacks and a matching sweater with a simple strand of exquisitely matched pearls at her neck.

An icy finger crept along Sugar Beth's spine. Something about those pearls . . .

The woman smiled. "Hello. How can I—"

And then she stopped. Right where she was, underneath a French chandelier, one foot placed awkwardly in front of the other, the smile frozen on her face.

Sugar Beth would have recognized those eyes anywhere. They were the same shade of crystalline blue that looked back at her from the mirror every morning. Her father's eyes.

And the eyes of his other daughter.

"If I had a daughter like you, I would be ashamed to own her!" said Mr. Goldhanger, with real feeling.

GEORGETTE HEYER, *The Grand Sophy*

Chapter 4

Old bitterness curdled in Sugar Beth's stomach. Intelligent men kept their legitimate children separated from their illegitimate ones, but not Griffin Carey. He'd plunked them both in the same town barely three miles apart and, in his utter selfishness, refused to acknowledge how difficult it would be for Sugar Beth and Winnie to go to school together.

He'd gotten two women pregnant within a year—first Diddie, then Sabrina Davis. Diddie kept her head high, expecting him to outgrow his infatuation with a woman she regarded as a mealymouthed nobody. When he hadn't, she'd chosen to be philosophical. *A great woman learns to rise above, Sugar Beth. Let him have his piece of trash. I have Frenchman's Bride.*

Whenever Sugar Beth raged over being forced to go to school with Winnie, Diddie turned uncharacteristically harsh. *Nothing's worse than other people's pity. You keep your back straight and remember that someday everything he owns will be yours.*

But Diddie had been wrong. In the end, he'd changed his will and left everything to Sabrina and Winnie Davis.

The stylish woman standing before her bore little resemblance to the introverted outcast who used to trip over her feet if anyone spoke to her. The old sense of powerlessness crept through Sugar Beth. As a child, she hadn't been able to control the behavior of any of the adults in her life, so she'd exerted her power in the only way she knew how—over her father's illegitimate daughter.

Winnie stood motionless near an old pie chest. "What are you doing here?"

She could never say she'd come looking for a job. "I—I saw the shop. I didn't know it was yours."

Winnie regained her composure more quickly. "Are you interested in anything special?"

Where had her poise come from? The Winnie Davis Sugar Beth remembered had turned red when anyone spoke to her.

"N-no. I'm just looking." Sugar Beth heard the stammer in her voice and knew by the flicker of satisfaction in Winnie's eyes that she'd heard it, too.

"I just got a new shipment in from Atlanta. There are some wonderful old perfume bottles." She curled her fingers over the strand of perfectly matched pearls at her neck. Sugar Beth stared at the pearls. They looked so—

"I love perfume bottles, don't you?"

All the blood rushed from her head. Winnie was wearing Diddie's pearls . . .

"Whenever I see an old perfume bottle, I always wonder about the woman who owned it." Her fingers caressed the necklace, the gesture deliberate. Cruel.

Sugar Beth couldn't do this. She couldn't stand here and look at Diddie's pearls around Winnie Davis's neck.

She turned toward the door, but she moved too quickly and bumped against one of the tables the same way Winnie used to bump against desks at school. A brass candlestick wobbled, then fell and rolled to the edge. She didn't stop to pick it up.

*Dinner's gonna be nasty tonight, and not just because
we're having steak, which I ree-fuse to eat due to
global warming, et cetera, but because of Her. Why
can't she be more like Chelsea's mom instead of having
such a stick up her butt all the time? I'm not anything
like her, no matter what Nana Sabrina says. And I'm
not a rich bitch, either.*

I hate Kelli Willman.

"Gigi, dinner's ready."

As her mother called from the bottom of the stairs, Gigi
reluctantly closed the spiral notebook that held the secret diary she'd been keeping since last year in seventh grade. She
pushed it under her pillow and swung her legs in their baggy
corduroys over the side of her bed. She hated her bedroom,
which was decorated in this gay Laura Ashley crap her
mother *luvvved.* Gigi wanted to paint the room either black or
purple and trade in all the prehistoric antique furniture for
some of the awesome stuff she'd seen at Pier One. Since
Win-i-fred wouldn't let her do that, Gigi'd stuck up rock
posters everywhere, the nastier the better.

Setting the table was her job, but when she got to the
kitchen, she saw that her mother had already done it. "Did
you wash your hands?"

"No, *madre,* I dragged them through the dirt on my way
downstairs."

Her mother's lips got tight. "Toss the salad, will you?"

Chelsea's mom wore low-riders, but Gigi's mom still had
on the boring gray slacks and sweater she'd worn to work.
She wanted Gigi to keep on dressing like last year in seventh
grade, in all kinds of crap from the Bloomingdale's cata-
logue. Her mother didn't understand what it was like to have
everybody call you Miss Rich Bitch behind your back. But
Gigi had fixed that. Starting last September she wouldn't

wear anything that didn't come from the Salvation Army Thrift Shop. It drove Win-i-fred nuts. Gigi'd also stopped acting like such a geek at school. And she'd found cool new friends like Chelsea.

"Mrs. Kimble called about your history test. You got a C."

"C's okay. I'm not as smart as *you* used to be."

Her mom sighed because she knew it wasn't true, and for a minute, she looked so sad Gigi wanted to tell her she was sorry for being such a brat, and that she'd start working up to her potential again, but she couldn't say it. Her mom didn't understand anything.

Gigi hated being thirteen.

Win-i-fred set the last salad plate on the table. They were using the tea leaf ironstone china tonight, probably because her dad was home for dinner for a change. Their oak pedestal table wasn't nearly as cool as this awesome French farm table Win-i-fred had sold right out from under them, even though Gigi'd loved it and they didn't need the money. Gigi wished she'd close the store, or at least hire more people to help out so they could eat something decent for dinner once in a while instead of frozen crap. Her mom said if it bothered Gigi so much, she should cook a few meals herself, *completely* missing the point.

The teak bowl held one of those salads-in-a-bag with nothing except lettuce and some dried-up carrot turds. In the old days, even with all her board meetings, her mom used to make salads with good stuff like fresh tomatoes and Swiss cheese and orzo, which looked like fat grains of rice but was really pasta. She'd even fix croutons from scratch, with lots of garlic, which Gigi adored, even if it made her breath stink.

"I want orzo in it," Gigi complained.

"I didn't have time." Her mom went to the back door and stuck her head out. "Ryan, are the steaks done?"

"On the way."

Her dad grilled on the patio all year-round. He didn't like grilling too much, but her mom said meat tasted better that way, and he felt guilty because half the time he didn't make it home for dinner. He was chief operating officer of CWF, which was a big responsibility. Her Nana Sabrina owned the window factory, but the board of directors ran it, and her dad had worked his way to the top like everybody else, except Gigi heard her mom tell Nana that he worked harder than ten people because he still felt like he had to prove himself. Nana lived in this really cool mansion on Scenic Drive in Pass Christian, down on the Gulf, which her dad said was almost far enough away.

Their finances were complicated. Some stuff like the window factory was Nana's, but Frenchman's Bride used to be her mom's. Her mom wouldn't live there, though, and it was closed up till Colin bought it. Gigi loved Colin, even when he got all sarcastic because she hadn't read crap like *War and Peace.* Two years ago he'd volunteered to coach the high school boys' soccer team, and last year they'd gone all the way to State.

Gigi dropped the salad bowl on the table. "I'm not eating steak. I told you that."

"Gigi, I've had a long day. Don't be difficult."

"Here we go." Her dad came through the door carrying the steaks on one of the tea leaf ironstone platters, which, even if Gigi liked tea leaf ironstone, which she didn't, she wouldn't have let herself get attached to because her mom would sell it right out from under them, too. Her mom was a history nut, which was why she liked the antique store so much.

Her dad winked at her as he set the platter on the brass trivet. He was thirty-three and Win-i-fred was thirty-two. Most of her friends' parents were a lot older, but Gigi'd been born while her parents were in college. *Premature,* like, ha-ha, anybody would believe that.

The smell of the steak made her mouth water, so she forced herself to think about all the cow burps that were screwing up the ozone layer and causing global warming. Two weeks ago when she'd decided to become a vegetarian, she'd tried to explain it at lunch, but Chels told her to stop talking like a geek. But that weird Gwen Lu had overheard and wanted to strike up this big intellectual conversation about it. As if Gigi's reputation could stand being seen talking to Gwen Lu.

"Wine tonight or not?" her dad asked.

"Definitely." Her mom took some disgusting frozen french fries from the oven and dumped them in a bowl.

Her dad pulled a bottle from the wine rack.

In seventh grade, when Gigi had still been friends with Kelli and everybody, Kelli had said Gigi's dad looked like Brad Pitt, which was a total lie. For one thing, Brad Pitt was short and old, and his eyes were squished too close together. Also, could anybody honestly imagine her dad going around with his hair messed up all the time and looking like he never shaved? It grossed her out when some of the girls said they thought her dad was hot.

Gigi mainly looked like him, her mouth and the shape of her face. But her hair was dark brown instead of blond, and she didn't have his goldy-colored eyes. Hers were like her mom's, light blue and sort of creepy. She wished they were goldy brown like his. No matter what Nana Sabrina said, Gigi was a lot more like her dad than her mom.

She wished he didn't work so much. Then her mom might not have opened the store. They sure didn't need the money. Her mom said with Gigi in school and Ryan working such long hours, there wasn't enough for her to do, even with all her committees. In Gigi's opinion, she could stay home and make some decent salads.

He carried the wineglasses to the table, and they all sat down. Her mom said grace, then her dad passed the steak platter. "So, Gi, how's it goin' at school?"

"Boring."

Her parents exchanged a look that made Gigi wish she'd kept her big fat mouth shut. They thought one of the reasons her grades were going down was because she wasn't getting enough intellectual stimulation from her classes, which was true, but that didn't have anything to do with her grades. Lately she'd started to get scared they might send her away to some boarding school for the gifted like Colby Sneed's parents had done, and Colby hadn't been half as smart as her.

"Mainly because of the kids, though," she said quickly. "Classes this week were very stimulating, and my teachers are excellent."

Her mom lifted an eyebrow, and her father shook his head. One thing about her parents . . . they weren't stupid.

He salted his french fries. "Funny that with all that stimulation, you couldn't do better than a C on your history test."

Gigi knew she was walking a delicate line. Being the class brain—except for that dorky Gwen Lu—and being the richest girl in town, too, had made everybody hate her, but if she let her grades drop too far, she might find herself in boarding school, and then she'd have to kill herself. "I had a stomachache. I'm sure I'll do better next time."

He got that worried look in his eyes she'd been seeing a lot lately. "Why don't you come to the factory with me on Saturday morning? I won't be there long, and you can mess around with the computers."

She rolled her eyes. When she was a kid, she'd loved to go to work with him, but now she thought it was boring. "No, thank you. Me and Chelsea are going over to Shannon's house."

"Chelsea and I," her mother said.

"Are *you* going to Shannon's, too?"

"That's enough, Gi," her father snapped. "Stop being a smart-ass."

She scowled, but she didn't have the nerve to talk back to him like she did her mom because it made him crazy, and she'd only just gotten her telephone privileges back.

Her mom didn't say much for the rest of the dinner, which was unusual, because usually when her dad showed up to eat, she tried extra hard to be entertaining, being all chirpy and offering stimulating topics of conversation and everything.

Tonight, though, she didn't even seem to be paying attention, and Gigi wondered if it had anything to do with the fact that She Who Must Not Be Named had come back to town.

It made her mad that they still hadn't said anything. Gigi'd had to hear the news from Chelsea, who heard it from her mom. Gigi's parents acted like she was still a child, but everybody knew that Nana Sabrina hadn't married Mom's dad, Griffin Carey, until Mom was a senior in high school, and he'd had this other family, and, like, who cared? Although Gigi had to admit she was very, very curious.

The phone rang, and she made a dash for it because she knew it'd be Chelsea. "Can I be excused?"

She waited for her mom to say *no* like she always did, but she didn't, so Gigi grabbed the phone and raced upstairs. Everything was too weird tonight.

Winnie watched Gigi disappear and wondered what had happened to the little girl who used to love just being with her. This time last year, Gigi had rushed in from school, so eager to share the news of the day that she'd stuttered over her words.

Ryan gazed toward the door. "I wish you didn't let her hang around with Chelsea so much. That kid looks like an ad for kiddie porn."

Winnie balled her fist in her lap, but she kept her voice calm. "Exactly how do you expect me to stop her?"

He sighed. "Sorry. Frustration. I keep thinkin' she's going to snap out of it, and we'll have our daughter back."

She and Ryan hardly ever spoke harshly to each other. They disagreed, but in more than thirteen years of marriage, they'd never done more than exchange a few chilly silences. She didn't know how couples like Merylinn and Deke could stand it. During one of their fights, Deke had punched a hole in the garage wall, and they'd actually told people about it.

"I couldn't punch *her*," Deke had said, and Merylinn had laughed.

Winnie didn't think she could tolerate that kind of strain.

Ryan leaned back in his chair. "She looks like a street kid in those clothes."

Something else that was her fault. Today Gigi'd worn that awful shirt she'd insisted on getting at the Salvation Army Thrift Shop. Winnie should have known Gigi's pricey wardrobe would eventually make her a target and backed off, but she'd wanted her daughter to feel good about herself, and she'd waited too long.

Winnie tossed her napkin on the table. "You'll have to talk to her about it this time. She hates me enough as it is."

How had it come to this? Winnie wondered. She'd been so determined to be the kind of mother to Gigi that she'd wanted so badly for herself when she was growing up. Sabrina had done her best, Winnie supposed, but her mother's economic survival had depended on Griffin Carey's goodwill, and Sabrina had devoted all her energy to his comfort, leaving nothing for an emotionally needy daughter. Sabrina had hated Diddie Carey with a passion, and knowing that Diddie had given birth to the dazzling Sugar Beth, while Sabrina had born such an unimpressive child, galled her. Even the fact that Griffin doted on Winnie hadn't eased her anxiety. Sabrina understood her lover's fundamentally ruthless nature and kept waiting for him to transfer his affections to his legitimate daughter. But he never had, and Winnie missed him to this day.

"Gigi doesn't hate you," Ryan said. "She's just being a teenager."

"It's more than that. I'd like to smack those girls for turning against her last summer. It was simple jealousy."

"Gigi played into their hands. She'll work through it."

Despite his words, Winnie knew he was as worried as she. She rose and began carrying the dishes to the sink. "I only have ice cream for dessert."

"Maybe later." Ryan wasn't particular about food. Half the

time he didn't remember to eat, which was why he stayed so lean, while she had to watch every bite.

She needed to tell him about Sugar Beth coming into the shop. Otherwise, she'd be giving it too much importance. But as she tried to frame the words, the wineglass she'd been rinsing slipped in her fingers and broke in the sink.

"You okay?" He rose and came toward her. She wanted him to wrap his arms around her, but he studied the mess instead.

"I'm fine. Why don't you make coffee while I clean this up?"

As she tossed the bigger pieces of glass in the trash, she wondered why she didn't feel more satisfaction about today. The years had taken their toll on Sugar Beth, and for the first time in their lives, Winnie had come out ahead.

She'd begun to bloom her senior year in high school after Sugar Beth and Ryan had left for college. She'd stopped overeating and found the courage to have her hair cut. Inside, she might have been the same awkward teenager, but outside she began to move with a new assurance that only grew more pronounced after Griffin and Sabrina's marriage. Suddenly, she was the rich girl who lived at Frenchman's Bride.

Winnie's fingers crept to the pearls on her throat. The stricken expression on Sugar Beth's face had been the culmination of every revenge fantasy she'd ever entertained. She should have enjoyed it more.

The past wove its way through the sound of the furnace clicking on and the smell of the coffee beans Ryan was grinding. She was sixteen again, taking a shortcut through the gym when she'd tripped and her algebra notebook had fallen open at Sugar Beth's feet.

"Give it back!" Winnie's voice, high and shrill, had bounced off the gym rafters. But Sugar Beth had only stepped higher on the bleachers, the algebra notebook open in her hands. Tall and willowy, blond and beautiful, Sugar Beth had been evil all the way to the bottom of her heart.

"Listen up, y'all. Winnie's been doin' a lot more than solving problems in advanced algebra."

The Seawillows abandoned their chatter. Winnie's heart was pounding so fast she was afraid it would burst. "Sugar Beth, I'm warning you . . ."

But Sugar Beth just smiled and took another step up into the bleachers. Winnie started after her, but her sneaker caught on the seat. She winced as she stumbled. "Give it to me."

Sugar Beth smirked. "I don't know why you're getting so uptight. It's just girls."

Amy touched the gold cross at her neck. "Maybe you shouldn't read it if Winnie doesn't want you to."

Sugar Beth ignored her. "Y'all aren't going to believe this."

Winnie blinked furiously against her tears. Just once she'd like to be able to defend herself, but Sugar Beth was too powerful. "That's private. Give it back right now."

"Oh, don't be so immature." The gold hoops at Sugar Beth's ears flashed as she flipped her perfect mane of hair. Then she began to read. *"He looked at my naked nipples."*

The girls laughed, even Amy, although she touched her cross again. Sweat soaked through the underarms of Winnie's blouse. She'd started writing her fantasies a few months earlier in a special notebook that she kept hidden in the back of her closet, but today in study hall she'd gotten careless. "Stop it, Sugar Beth."

"No, don't stop!" Leeann blasted her bangs with the Aqua Net she kept in her purse, but her eyes stayed glued to Sugar Beth.

Sugar Beth propped one of her metallic flats on the bleacher in front of her. *"Next, he slipped his broad, strong hand into my tiny lace panties."* The way Sugar Beth emphasized the word *tiny* served as a not so subtle reminder that Winnie's panties weren't all that small. *"I moved my legs farther apart."*

Winnie could never come back to Parrish High.

"He slid his other hand up the inside of my leg . . ." Sugar

Beth's blue eyes widened in fake shock. "Why, Winnie Davis, this is pornography."

"I like it." Leeann popped a bubble.

Sugar Beth turned the page. " *'I love you, Winnie, with all my abiding passion.'* " She paused, and her eyes raced down over the words, looking for more ammunition to destroy Winnie. It didn't take her long to find it.

"Ohmigod, y'all listen to this. *'I spread my legs even farther as his strong fingers started to tiddle me. I gasped out his name . . .'* "

Winnie's ears rang, and the gym began to spin. She made a soft, helpless sound.

" *'Oh, my darling, darling—'* Ryan!"

Winnie's blood froze.

"Hey, Sugar Beth. What're you guys doin'?"

Ryan Galantine was coming toward them from the back of the gym, with Deke Jasper and Bobby Jarrow, the three of them in their letter jackets because there was a game that night. Winnie only saw Ryan—tall, blond, and golden, the object of all her fantasies. Horrified, she watched him climb the bleachers.

"Hey, Sugar, I thought you had a meeting."

"I'm gettin' there. I've been reading something Winnie wrote. It's really good."

"Yeah?" He kissed her, ignoring the school's policy on P.D.A., then looked down at Winnie and gave her the leftover crumbs of his smile. "I want to hear, too."

Winnie would have to run away from Parrish forever, but as she stepped back, her foot slipped on the bleachers and she fell in an awkward tangle, her hips wedged between the rows of seats.

"Stop it," Amy said, but like the others, she was a little afraid of Sugar Beth, and she didn't speak with much authority.

"No, keep reading. I want to hear more." Leeann popped another bubble.

Sugar Beth's eyes flicked over Winnie, then returned to the notebook page. "Should I go back to the naked nipples or the tiny panties?"

Ryan laughed and draped a proprietary arm around Sugar Beth's shoulders. "Hey, this sounds good."

Sugar Beth looked down at Winnie, her voice syrupy with bad intention. "Or maybe I should start where she calls out her lover's name?"

Winnie was going to throw up.

"Yes, why don't I start there. *'Oh, my darling . . . '*"

"That's quite enough, Sugar Beth." They all whirled around at the sound of a clipped British accent. Winnie struggled to her feet and watched as Mr. Byrne, her favorite teacher, walked toward the bleachers. He was wearing a gray-and-white-striped vest today over his old black turtleneck, and he had his long hair tied back in a low ponytail.

Even though he was the youngest teacher in the school, almost everybody was afraid of him because he could be so sarcastic. But the kids respected him, too. He didn't show movies in class, and he expected everybody to work hard. Winnie adored him. He was never sarcastic with her, and he even gave her some of his own books to read because he said she needed to broaden her horizons.

Sugar Beth didn't look worried or nervous like the other kids would have. Instead, she stared him right in the eye. "Hey, Mr. Byrne. We're just goofin' off. Isn't that right, Winnie?"

Winnie couldn't make her lips move. She couldn't do anything.

"Both of you come with me."

"I have a meeting right now, Mr. Byrne," Sugar Beth said, all sweet and polite. "Homecoming court. Are you going to be in your room in about an hour?" She sounded exactly like Diddie, who was famous for scheduling the school board meetings around her favorite TV shows.

None of the other teachers ever stood up to Sugar Beth because they didn't want to get on Diddie's bad side, but Mr. Byrne still hadn't figured out how important Diddie was. "I don't really care what you have planned."

Sugar Beth shrugged and passed the notebook to Ryan.

"I'll take that," Mr. Byrne said.

Winnie's heart stuck in her throat as Ryan handed it back. First Winnie had been humiliated in front of her classmates, and now even Mr. Byrne would know what a pervert she was. As for Ryan . . . She could never look at him again.

Sugar Beth skipped down the bleachers with the notebook. Winnie couldn't swallow as she watched it pass from her hand to his.

The buff-colored walls closed in on her as they made their way from the gym to Mr. Byrne's classroom. Sugar Beth chattered away, not seeming to care that he wasn't answering back. Winnie trailed behind, her feet dragging.

When they reached the door of his classroom, Mr. Byrne stopped. Winnie stared down at the ugly brown tile floor. He was wearing the old black loafers he always kept polished.

"I believe this is yours, Winnie."

She looked up at him through her misery and saw the familiar haughtiness in his eyes, along with a kindness no one except her ever seemed to notice. He held out her notebook.

She couldn't believe he was returning it, and her hand shook as she took it. "T-thank you."

Sugar Beth gave a light little laugh. "Mr. Byrne, you should read what Winnie wrote first. Everybody knows how smart she is, but I'll bet you didn't know that she's so creative."

"I'll see you in class tomorrow, Winnie," he said without looking at Sugar Beth. "And I'll expect you to have something scintillating to offer about that dreary Hester Prynne."

She gave a jerky nod and pulled the notebook to her chest. Just before she turned away, she caught a glimpse of Sugar Beth's face. Her eyes glittered with the old familiar hatred. Winnie knew exactly why it was there. Why it would never go away. Even though Sugar Beth had everything Winnie didn't—beauty, popularity, self-confidence, and Ryan Galantine—Winnie had the one thing Sugar Beth most desperately wanted.

Their father loved her the best.

Winnie tossed the last of the broken wine goblet in the trash. Her mind skittered toward the other memory from that year, the one that was infinitely more painful than having her sexual fantasies exposed, but even after all this time, she couldn't think about it. Instead, she gazed at Ryan, all grown up now. He'd turned the cuffs on his light blue dress shirt. She loved his wrists, the way his bones were formed, the strength in them.

She'd been his rebound girlfriend, there to console him the summer after Sugar Beth had dumped him and married Darren Tharp. Although Winnie might not have transformed herself into a swan while he was away at school, she was no longer an ugly duckling, either, and he'd noticed.

Sex had been her plan, not his, and he'd almost seemed puzzled when he found himself in bed with her one afternoon while his parents were at work. When she'd realized she was pregnant, she'd been terrified to tell him, but he'd put on his game face and married her. He'd even said he loved her, and she'd pretended to believe him. But she'd known then, just as she knew now, that his love for her was only a pale imitation of what he'd felt for Sugar Beth. To this day, he'd never once looked at Winnie the same way.

She pulled two pottery coffee mugs from the cupboard and set them on the counter. "Do you remember . . . when Sugar Beth found my notebook in the gym and tried to read it to everybody?"

Ryan stuck his head in the refrigerator. "Is there any more half-and-half?"

"Behind the orange juice. I'd . . . written a sexual fantasy about the two of us."

"Yeah?" He straightened, the carton of half-and-half in his hand, and smiled at her. "What kind of sexual fantasy?"

"Didn't she tell you about it?"

"Hell, I don't know." His smile vanished. "That was years ago. You're way too hung up on what happened in high school." He closed the refrigerator door just hard enough to rattle the eighteenth-century tea box sitting on top. "I don't understand why it still bothers you so much. You ended up with everything. Frenchman's Bride, a few million in your trust. Even the plant's going to be yours someday. Why would you waste your time thinkin' about what happened in high school?"

"I don't."

It was a lie. Her entire adult life had been shaped by those difficult years: her intellect, her painstaking attention to her appearance, even her social conscience.

The coffeemaker gave its final burp, and Ryan pulled out the carafe. As he filled the mugs, she knew she couldn't put it off any longer. "Sugar Beth came into the store today."

Only a wife would have noticed the tiny pulse that jumped at the corner of his jaw. He filled the mugs, then replaced the carafe and rested his hips against the edge of the counter. "What did she want?"

"Just looking around, I guess. I don't think she knew it was my shop."

He liked half-and-half in his coffee, but he took a sip without opening the carton. "Parrish is a small town. You were bound to run into her sooner or later."

Winnie began rinsing the dinner plates. "Her sweater was cheap. She looked tired." She might as well have hung out a sign advertising her own insecurities. "But she's still beautiful. As thin as ever."

He shrugged as if he'd lost interest, but he was still drinking his coffee black. She wanted to change the subject, but she couldn't think of a single thing to say. Maybe he felt the same way because he set down his mug and let his eyes drift over her. "So tell me about that sexual fantasy."

She turned off the faucet and forced a smile. "I was only

sixteen, so it was pretty tame. But I could be persuaded to make up something better after Gigi's asleep."

He crossed his arms, and the corner of his beautiful mouth curled. "Yeah?"

She loved his smile, but she was tired, jangled, and what she really wanted to do was take a warm bath, then curl up with a book. Instead, she closed the distance between them and slipped her hand between his legs. "Definitely."

He nuzzled her breast. "Right now I wish we didn't have a teenager in the house."

She withdrew her hand and forced her voice to a sultry pitch. "Don't let me forget where I was, y'hear?"

"Oh, I won't. Believe me, I won't." He gave her a quick kiss. "In the meantime, I'd better go remind Her Highness that kitchen cleanup is her job."

"Thanks."

After he disappeared, she wrapped up the leftover piece of steak and stuck it in the refrigerator before Gigi could throw it out. Then she picked up her mug and carried it into the den. She had some paperwork to do for the Community Advancement Association and phone calls she needed to make about the concert, but she wandered over to the window instead.

She was only thirty-two, too young to have lost her libido. She should discuss it with her doctor, but Paul and Ryan had played football in high school.

"How long has lack of desire been a problem, Winnie?"

"A while."

"Could you be more specific?"

She could lie and say a year. That didn't sound as bad as three years or maybe four. Five at the outside.

"And have you discussed it with Ryan?"

How could a woman tell the man she loved that she'd been faking it? Ryan would not only be hurt, he'd also be mystified. He was a considerate lover, but they'd started out all wrong. Winnie hadn't wanted to come in second best to Sugar Beth, so she'd done everything before she was ready.

Even though he'd been the more experienced partner, she'd set herself up as the sexual aggressor, and somehow they'd never broken that pattern. She was always available, always responsive. She never pleaded a headache, never made him work for it. She was the pursuer, Ryan the pursued. And as much as she loved him, she resented him for that, too.

Not very much. Not all the time. Just every once in a while.

"Obstinate, eh? I'll tame you," Vidal said, and got up.

GEORGETTE HEYER, *Devil's Cub*

Chapter 5

*S*ugar Beth switched the grocery bags she was carrying from one hand to the other, but they were equally heavy, so the change didn't do much good. As she headed down Jefferson Street toward Mockingbird Lane, she tried to relax her shoulders. The few staples she'd bought, along with a box of doggie treats and another six-pack of Coke, had seemed a lot lighter in the store.

Ignoring her parking tickets hadn't made them go away, and that morning she'd been forced to pull out her arsenal of charm-weapons against the beefy young tow-truck driver who'd been assigned to haul away her Volvo. Afterward, she'd taken the precaution of moving her car to the Arby's lot half a mile away. It would have been a nice walk if she hadn't already made it twice today and if she weren't hauling groceries. Conjuring up a few gruesome revenge scenarios against Colin Byrne helped distract her for a while, except she'd already been there and done that, which pretty much spoiled the fun.

Her luck hadn't improved in the week since her disastrous

visit to Winnie's antique store. She couldn't find either a job or the painting, and she had nothing left in her wallet but moths. At least she'd succeeded in tracking down the surviving members of Tallulah's canasta club, but only Sissy Tooms said she'd actually seen the painting. Unfortunately, she'd also told Sugar Beth that she was on her way to Vegas to have dinner with Frank Sinatra.

Her cell rang in her purse. As she set down her grocery bags by the curb, she wondered how long it would be before they cut off her service.

"It's me!" a soft voice chirped as Sugar Beth answered.

She smiled. "Hey, baby."

"Me!" Delilah repeated, as if Sugar Beth wouldn't recognize the voice of Emmett's only child.

"How's my best girl doing?"

"Good! We painted yesterday. And Meesie said I could call you today."

Sugar Beth had forgotten it was Wednesday, the day she and Delilah usually talked. "How's your cold? Any better?"

"I'm taking cough syrup at night. It's helping. And I painted a picture for you."

Sugar Beth turned her shoulders to the sharp edge of the wind and hooked her boot heel over the curb. Yesterday had been warm, but the chill had settled in again today, and her fake leather motorcycle jacket wasn't up to the job. "What's it look like?"

Delilah went on to describe a painting she'd done of the ocean, then talked about the new angelfish in the aquarium. When it was finally time for her to go, Delilah said what she always did.

"I love you, my Sugar Beth. And you love me, too, don't you?"

Sugar Beth's eyes stung. No matter what she had to do, she was going to protect this sweet, fragile creature. "I love you bushels and heaps."

"I thought so."

Sugar Beth smiled at her certainty.

As she slipped her cell back into her purse, the old anger at Emmett came back. How could he have been so careless about protecting Delilah's future?

"*I made financial provisions,*" he'd said when they'd talked about it. "*But when things started to go south, I had to borrow. I'll never forgive myself.*"

Sugar Beth remembered her first visit with Delilah at Brookdale, the exclusive private institution where she'd lived most of her adult life. They'd fallen in love with each other on sight. Delilah's own mother had died a few years before Sugar Beth had met Emmett, and Delilah had desperately missed her. Much to Sugar Beth's surprise, Delilah had transferred her affections to her new stepmother. Delilah was sweet, funny, and so very vulnerable—a fifty-one-year-old woman with an eleven-year-old's mind. They both liked girly stuff—clothes and makeup, *Friends* reruns, Pixie Stix. Sugar Beth had read her most of the Judy Blume books, *The Witch of Blackbird Pond,* as well as Mary-Kate and Ashley's adventures. They gossiped about Leonardo DiCaprio, whom Delilah adored, played Clue, and held hands when they went for walks.

If it weren't for Delilah, Sugar Beth wouldn't have been forced to come back to Parrish, but the money for Delilah's care had run out. Now Sugar Beth couldn't keep her stepdaughter at Brookdale unless she found the Ash painting. Still, she wouldn't feel sorry for herself. Unconditional love was a precious gift, and Sugar Beth knew a blessing when she met one.

As she retrieved her grocery sacks, a familiar cognac-colored Lexus sedan pulled up and stopped next to her. The driver's side window slid down to reveal the imperious face of the Duke of Doom himself, sneer and all. "You look like a bag lady."

She assumed he was referring to her grocery sacks instead

of her jeans and motorcycle jacket. "Thanks, I hope you're having a nice day, too."

He regarded her through his invisible quizzing glass. "Would you like a ride?"

"You let peasants in your carriage?"

"If I'm feeling benevolent."

"My lucky day."

He made her wait while he took his time flicking the locks. She opened the back door and set the sacks behind the passenger seat. Then, since pride did count for something, she climbed in with them and closed the door. "Carry on."

He draped an arm over the seat and gazed down his long nose at her.

She gave him a haughty look. "I really don't have all day."

"Perhaps you should walk after all."

"Bad for the neighborhood. Having a bag lady around."

She was pleased to note that he stepped on the accelerator just a little harder than necessary, and his tone was withering. "You'll let me know, won't you, if there's anything else I can do to make you comfortable?"

She gazed at the back of those wide shoulders. "You could take that silly little chain off my driveway."

"But I find it so amusing." He turned onto Mockingbird Lane. "I saw a tow truck by your car this morning. I'm dreadfully sorry about that."

"Oh, don't be. The sweetest boy was driving it, so reasonable, not to mention attractive."

"So you managed to dissuade him from taking it away, did you?"

"Now, now. Southern ladies don't French-kiss and tell."

She waited for him to say she was no lady, but obvious jabs were beneath him, and he engaged in more subtle warfare. "How's the job search progressing?"

She managed a breezy flick of her hand. "Career decisions are stressful, so I'm taking my time. You can drop me off right here."

He ignored her and pulled into the drive that led to French-man's Bride, which took care of his tip. "A lot to choose from, is there?"

"Tons."

"So I've heard. The town is abuzz."

"I'll bet."

He parked near the house and turned off the ignition. "The rumor is that even Louis Higgins refused to hire you at the Quik Mart, and he seems to hire anyone who speaks even a modicum of English."

"Unfortunately, I was the driving force behind a rather nasty rumor about his little sister in ninth grade. He didn't seem to care that it was true."

"The chickens keep coming home to roost, don't they?"

"Clucking all the way." She opened the door and began to unload. He came around the hood of the car just then, and she nearly dropped her Coke because he was wearing an honest-to-God black suede duster. And, with his short, rumpled hair, looking way too good in it.

"Let me carry your sacks to the carriage house," he said. "It's the least I can do."

She was too stunned by the sight of the duster to answer. In Mississippi yet.

"I'd hoped closing off the driveway wouldn't be such an inconvenience. Alas, I was wrong."

"Not to worry," she said as she recovered. "With the added exercise, I've been able to dismiss my personal trainer."

Gordon had apparently been hiding out on the veranda be-cause he came trotting across the yard. Byrne astonished her by looking pleased. He shifted the sacks so he had one arm free and leaned down to scratch behind his ears. "So you haven't run off."

"Nice dog," she drawled.

"He showed up a few days ago. He's a stray."

"That could mean rabies. I'd call the pound if I were you."

"He doesn't have rabies." Byrne looked even more irritated than normal. "And you know exactly what the pound would do to him."

"*Gas* him." She glared down at Gordon, who could spot a sucker a mile away. Instead of snarling at her as he usually did, he played to his new audience by dropping his head, letting his big ears flop on the ground, and giving a little whimper, the perfect portrait of a pathetic pooch.

"That's remarkably unfeeling, even coming from you," Byrne said stiffly.

"Yeah, well, it's a dog-eat-dog world." Gordon trotted toward the veranda, more than a little pleased with himself. She noticed an extra waddle in his gait. "You haven't been feeding him, have you? He looks fat."

"And what business is it of yours if I have?"

She sighed.

They reached the carriage house. When she turned the knob, he got all critical again. "Why isn't this door locked?"

"It's Parrish. There's not much point."

"We have crime here, just as any other place does. Keep this door locked from now on."

"Like that's going to stop you. All you'd have to do is give it one good kick, and—"

"Not from me, you ninny!"

"I hate to be the one to break the bad news, but if they find my body, you're the one with the biggest grudge."

"It's impossible to hold a rational conversation with you." He gazed at the living room with distaste, despite the fact that she'd cleaned the whole place from top to bottom. "Did your aunt ever discard anything?"

"Not much. If you see something you like, be sure and make me an offer."

"I wouldn't hold my breath." He headed toward her kitchen, duster flapping behind him.

She shrugged off her own jacket, dropped her purse on a chair, and followed him. "I'll bet you'd take out your wallet for the Ash painting."

"I'm afraid that would stretch even my finances." He set the sacks on the counter, his big body filling up the small space.

She pulled out a package of E.L. Fudge cookies. "You talked to Tallulah. You believe the painting exists, right?"

"I believe it existed."

"I hope that's some kind of fancy Brit talk for, 'Yes, indeedy, Sugar Beth.' "

He leaned against the ancient refrigerator and crossed his ankles. "I think it's quite possible your aunt destroyed it."

"No way. It was her most prized possession. Why would she?"

"She refused to share the painting during her lifetime. Why would she want to share it after her death? And not to put too fine a point on it, why would she share it with a niece she considered a bit of a tart?"

"Because she believed in family, that's why."

He picked up the box of doggie treats she'd just dropped. "What's this?"

"I'm poor. They're nutritious." She snatched them away and tried not to brush against him as she put the Coke in the refrigerator.

"Bugger. That dog showed up the same time you did. He's yours, isn't he?"

"Believe me, I'm not proud of it." She set the Coke on the top shelf.

"You told me to call the pound."

She was pleased to hear a note of outrage in his voice. "We're all entitled to our fantasies."

"If you dislike the dog so much, why do you have him?"

She knelt down to put the doggie treats under the sink. "Because Gordon was Emmett's, and nobody else will take him. I tried to give him away, but he has a personality disorder."

"Rubbish. He's a splendid dog."

"He's just sucking up."

Apparently he decided she'd had enough fun because he began wandering around the kitchen, inspecting the glass-fronted cabinets and the old appliances. The china knob on the bread box came off in his hand. He smiled as he examined it. "It's unfortunate that you're having such a hard time finding work."

"Now don't you go worrying that arrogant big head about it." Her knit top rode up as she stretched to put a bag of chips on the top shelf. She knew he noticed because it took him a few beats too long to pick up the thread of the conversation.

"I almost feel sorry for you," he said. "You have a dog you don't like, no one will give you a job, and you're broke."

"On the other hand, I still have my charm."

He propped a shoulder against the wall and tossed the china knob from one hand to the other. "I believe I mentioned that I might have a job for you. Are you desperate enough yet?"

She nearly choked on her spit. "I figured you were funnin' me."

"I'm fairly certain I've never *funned* anyone."

"My mistake. Does the job involve letting you feel me up again?"

"Would you like it to?" The way his eyelids fell to half-mast told her she wasn't the only critter around who knew something about playing games.

"I'd worry so much about frostbite." Curiosity overcame her need to dish out the crap. "What did you have in mind?"

He inspected the bread box, then took his time screwing the knob on while she held her breath. When he was finally satisfied, he turned back to her, his eyes shrewd. "I need a housekeeper."

"A *housekeeper*?"

"Someone who keeps house."

"I know what the word means. Why are you offering the job to me?"

"Because it's more temptation than I can resist. The cherished daughter of Frenchman's Bride forced to sweep its floors and serve on bended knee the man she tried to destroy. The Brothers Grimm as interpreted by Colin Byrne. Delicious, yes?"

"The minute I find Tallulah's butcher knife, you're dead." She jerked open the nearest drawer.

He took his time moving out of stabbing range into the living room. "On the practical side . . . maintaining Frenchman's Bride is nearly a full-time job, and it's cutting too deeply into my writing. This would be six days a week, from seven in the morning until after dinner. Long hours and, it goes without saying, each one as difficult as I can possibly make it."

"Where the *hell* is that knife?"

"You'll answer the phone, take care of grocery shopping and simple meal preparation, although I suppose that will be beyond you. The household bills have to be organized, the mail sorted, laundry done. I want an efficiently run household with absolutely no effort on my part. Do you think you could manage that?"

He made no effort to hide his smug contempt, and she told herself she wasn't this desperate yet. Except she was.

He named a salary that lifted her spirits, and she shot into the living room. "I'll take it! You mean for a day, right?"

From across the room, Colin watched Sugar Beth's entire face light up and knew he should feel like a cad. He didn't, of course. He hadn't felt better since the day she'd arrived. "Don't be foolish." He gazed down his nose at her. "That's for the entire week."

She looked as though she was choking, and he didn't try to hide his smile. The idea of offering her a job had come to him that day at the depot. He'd had time to think about it since then, but until he'd seen her standing on the curb in those tight jeans, cell phone pressed to her ear, looking like a very expensive hooker, he'd rejected the idea as far more trouble than she was worth. Then the wind had caught her blond hair and sent it streaming behind her head like an advertising banner. She looked so untouched by the harm she'd caused, and right then he'd changed his mind.

He didn't plan to destroy her, but he bloody well intended to see some flesh wounds, or, at the very least, a few honest tears of regret. Even a forgiving person would have to agree that he deserved more than he'd gotten so far. Putting that chain across her driveway had been like going after an elephant with a peashooter. This, on the other hand, should do the job right.

She tightened her grip on the chair, still dazed by the insulting salary he'd offered her. "No human being could possibly be that cheap."

He regarded her imperiously. "Don't forget you'll be eating my food, doubtless using my telephone. Then there's the miscellaneous pilfering one expects from the help." Her blue eyes snapped like pompoms. "Just to prove I'm not unreasonable, I'll take the chain off the driveway." He paused as inspiration struck. "And, naturally, I'll provide the uniform allowance."

"Uniform!"

Oh, yes. Having her slink around his house in tight pants and seductive tops would be too much of a distraction. Just watching her put away groceries had tested his self-restraint: the stretch of those long legs, the four inches of rib cage that had shown when she'd reached for the top shelf. This was the downside of being male. His body didn't recognize poison, even when his mind knew it was there.

"You'll be a housekeeper," he said. "Of course you'll need a uniform."

"In the twenty-first century?"

"We'll discuss the details on your first day."

She clenched her small, straight teeth. "All right, you son of a bitch. But you're buying the dog food."

"My pleasure. I'll expect you tomorrow at seven." He began to leave, but he still wasn't quite satisfied. He needed to make absolutely certain she understood exactly how things would be, and he searched his mind until he found one last nail to hammer in her coffin.

"Let yourself in the back door, will you?"

Colin Byrne's housekeeper! Sugar Beth stomped around the carriage house until Gordon got so aggravated he clamped his jaws around her ankle and refused to let go until he was sure she knew he meant business. She bent down to examine the skin, but he was too wily. "One of these days, fatso, you're going to leave marks, and then you're out of here."

He lifted his leg and licked himself.

She stalked upstairs hoping a good long soak would calm her down. The bathroom had a claw-footed tub and a single window with a yellowed shade. She dropped her clothes on the old-fashioned black-and-white honeycomb tiles, clipped her hair on top of her head, and tossed some ancient lily of the valley bath salts in the water. As she settled in, she tried to look on the positive side.

She'd already combed every inch of the depot, the carriage house, and the studio, and she only had one place left to look. Frenchman's Bride. There was nowhere else for Tallulah to have hidden the painting. But why hadn't she removed it before Byrne had moved in? Unless she'd been too ill by then.

Lincoln Ash had arrived in Parrish during the spring of 1954. Until then, he'd been living in a cold-water flat in Manhattan and hanging out with the equally impoverished Jackson Pollock at the Cedar Bar in Greenwich Village. The established art community had sneered at the work of "the dribblers," as they tagged them, but the public had begun to take notice, including Sugar Beth's grandmother, who considered herself a patron of the avant-garde. She'd agreed to provide him with room and board for three months, a studio where he could work, and a small stipend. In return, she'd have bragging rights as the first woman in northern Mississippi with her own artist in residence. Griffin had been sixteen at the time, and he loved telling people that he'd learned to smoke cigars and drink good whiskey from Lincoln Ash.

The water had nearly reached the rim of the tub, and Sugar Beth turned off the faucet with her foot. She thought of Frenchman's Bride with its deep closets and odd-shaped cubbyholes. More enticing, the secret cupboard in its attic . . . Her grandfather had ordered it built "in case those fools in Washington ever decide to bring back Prohibition." Did Byrne know about that cupboard? Tallulah certainly had.

She wouldn't consider his theory that Tallulah had destroyed the painting, but as she sank deeper into the tub, an equally alarming thought hit her. Byrne had bought the house. Did that include its contents? What if he owned the painting now? She knew nothing about property rights, and she couldn't afford to hire a lawyer. If she found the painting, she'd simply have to get it out of the house without tipping him off, which wasn't an enticing proposition. But she'd risk that and a lot more because selling the Ash painting would finally give her the money she needed to keep Delilah at Brookdale. As for supporting herself, she'd go back to Houston and wait tables until she could get a real estate license.

She didn't fall asleep until well after midnight, and then a nightmare awakened her. She lay there for a moment, skin damp, heart thumping, the dream still with her. Usually she found Gordon's snores irritating, but now the raspy sounds coming from the bottom of the bed were a comforting reminder that she wasn't entirely alone in the world.

She'd dreamed about Winnie again. Not the sophisticated woman she'd seen in the antique store last week, but the insecure girl who'd hidden behind her hair and stolen what Sugar Beth wanted the most.

Daddy, you were a real jerk, you know that?

She could never recall exactly how she'd come by the knowledge of her father's other family—bits and pieces absorbed here and there, snippets of conversations, glimpses of her father in places he shouldn't have been. Eventually she'd come to understand some of the subtler dynamics of his relationships with the two women in his life. Diddie was Griffin's mercurial unobtainable Scarlett O'Hara, Sabrina his nurturing, loving Melanie Wilkes; but her earliest memories were merely of her father walking away.

"Watch me do a cartwheel, Daddy."

"Not now, Sugar Beth. I'm busy."

"You're coming to my dance recital, aren't you?"

"I don't have time. I have to work so I can pay for those shoes you're scuffing in the dirt."

She'd approach him with a book to read, only to have him stand up before she could crawl in his lap. He'd walk off to make a phone call just as she brought him a painting she'd done to please him. She suspected flirting came so easily to her because of the arsenal of little-girl tricks she'd used to get her father's attention. None of them worked.

She'd been in third grade when she'd discovered she wasn't her father's only daughter, and it had all happened because of his disapproval over her schoolwork.

"You got a C in arithmetic? You have the brain of a flea, Sugar Beth. One more thing you inherited from your mother."

He didn't understand how torturous school was for her. All that sitting when she wanted to giggle and dance, to jump rope with Leeann and play Barbies with Heidi. To decorate cupcakes with Amy and lip-synch Bee Gee songs with Merylinn. One day after he'd made her cry with another lecture about how stupid she was, she came to the conclusion that her bad grades were the reason he didn't love her.

For six whole weeks she'd tried her hardest to change that. She sat still in class and finished every bit of her boring, boring homework. She listened to the teacher instead of talking, stopped drawing happy faces all over her workbooks, and, in the end, she'd gotten straight A's.

By the time she brought her report card home that April afternoon, she was nearly sick with excitement. Diddie fussed over her, but it wasn't Diddie's approval she craved, and as she waited for her father to come home, she imagined how he'd smile at her when he saw what she'd done, how he'd swing her up in his arms and laugh.

"What a smart daughter I have. I'm so proud of you, my Sugar Baby. Give your daddy a big kiss."

She was too excited to eat dinner. Instead, she sat on the veranda and waited for his car. When it grew dark, and he still hadn't appeared, Diddie told her it didn't matter and made her go to bed.

But it did matter. On Saturday morning when she awakened to discover he'd already left the house, she grabbed her precious report card—that magic passport to her father's love—and sneaked out of the house. She could still see herself flying across the yard to her pink banana-seat bicycle and tossing her report card in the basket. She jumped on her bike and took off down Mockingbird Lane, sneakers pumping, her lucky horseshoe barrettes warm against her scalp, her heart singing.

Finally, my daddy's going to love me!

She no longer remembered how she'd known where to find the house he sometimes stayed in with the other lady, or why she'd thought he'd be there that morning, but she remembered the tidiness of the brick bungalow, the way it sat back from the street with the curtains drawn over the front windows. She'd left her bike in the driveway behind his car, taken her report card from the basket, and raced for the front steps.

The faint sound of his voice coming from the back of the house stopped her. She turned toward the stockade fence that surrounded the tree-shaded yard and approached the partially opened gate, the report card clenched in her sweaty hands, a giddy smile taking over her face.

As she peeked through the gate, she saw him sitting in a

big lawn chair in the middle of a flagstone patio. His yellow shirt was open at the collar, revealing the shiny tuft of dark hair there that she was never, ever allowed to pull. Her smile faded, and a creepy feeling came over her, like she had big spiders crawling up her legs, because he wasn't alone. A second grader named Winnie Davis lay curled in his lap, her head against his shoulder, legs dangling, looking like she sat that way every day. He was reading a book to her, using funny voices, just like Diddie did when she read to Sugar Beth.

Spiders were crawling all over her now, even in her stomach, and she felt like she was going to throw up. Winnie laughed at one of his silly voices, and he kissed the top of her head. Without being asked.

The magic report card slipped from her fingers. She must have made some sort of sound because his head shot up and he saw her. He set Winnie aside and leaped to his feet. His heavy black eyebrows collided as he glowered at Sugar Beth. "What are you doing here?"

The words stuck in her throat. She couldn't explain about the magic report card, about how proud he was supposed to be.

He stalked toward her, a short-legged, barrel-chested banty rooster of a man. "What do you think you're doing? Go home right now." He stepped on the report card, lying unseen on the ground. "You aren't ever to come here, do you understand me?" He grabbed her arm and dragged her back toward the driveway.

Winnie followed, stopping just outside the fence. Sugar Beth started to cry. "W-why was she sitting in your lap?"

"Because she's a good girl, that's why. Because she doesn't go places where she's not invited. Now get on your bike and go home."

"Daddy?" Winnie said from the fence.

"It's all right, punkin'."

Sugar Beth's stomach hurt so much she couldn't bear it, and she gazed up at him through an ocean of tears. "Why's she calling you that?"

He didn't bother looking at her as he pulled her farther away from the house. "Don't you worry about it."

Sobbing, she turned back toward Winnie. "He's—he's not your daddy! Don't call him that!"

A swift, silencing shake. "That's enough, Sugar Beth."

"Tell her not to call you that ever again!"

"Settle down right now, or you'll get a spanking."

She'd pulled away from him then and hurled her small body down the drive, running past her pink banana-seat bicycle, out onto the sidewalk, sneakers thudding, her little girl's heart exploding in her chest.

He didn't come after her.

The years passed. Sometimes Sugar Beth caught glimpses of Griffin in town with Winnie, doing all the things he never had time to do with her. Bit by bit, she began to understand how he could favor one daughter over the other. Winnie was quiet. She got good grades and loved history the same way he did. Winnie didn't throw temper tantrums because he wouldn't take her to Dairy Queen, or get dragged to the front door by the chief of police for underage drinking. And Winnie had certainly never given him heart failure her senior year because she'd skipped her period and thought she was pregnant with Ryan's baby. No, perfect Winnie had waited until after Griffin died to do that. Most important of all, Winnie wasn't Diddie's daughter.

Sugar Beth hadn't been able to punish Griffin for not loving her, so she'd punished Winnie instead.

Gordon stirred at the foot of the bed. Sugar Beth rolled to her side and tried to will herself back to sleep before the memories took her any farther down that dark path, but her mind refused to cooperate.

Senior year. The after-school poetry showcase Mr. Byrne had required his classes to attend . . .

At the end of the performance, the stage had fallen into darkness, and two figures smeared with yellow fluorescent paint stepped into a dim puddle of black light. Stuart Sherman and Winnie Davis. Sugar Beth no longer remembered anything about the poem they'd dramatized. She only remembered that something made her turn toward the back of the auditorium, and there she saw Griffin standing under the exit sign. The father who'd been too busy last October to spend five minutes waiting on the courthouse steps so he could watch her ride through town on the back of Jimmie Caldwell's vintage Mustang convertible with the homecoming crown on her head hadn't been too busy to come see his other daughter recite poetry. She knew what she was going to do.

She lingered after the showcase with Ryan and some of his friends in the parking lot until enough time had passed, then she announced that she needed to get the eyelash curler she'd left in her gym locker. The sound of the shower greeted her as she'd made her way inside the almost empty locker room. Winnie, with her yellow fluorescent face and neck, her painted arms and feet, was the only girl in the showcase who'd needed to clean up before she could go home. Sugar Beth worked quickly, and as she left the locker room, she envisioned the yellow paint washing down the drain and taking her father's illegitimate daughter right along with it.

"Guess what," she'd announced to the boys as she returned to the parking lot. "The girls' locker room's empty. Y'all've been threatening since sophomore year to go in there. This'll be your last chance before we graduate."

It hadn't taken any persuading to get them to follow her: Deke Jasper, Bobby Jarrow, Woody Newhouse, and Ryan, of course, the most important person in her plan. Woody and Deke started scrambling for paper so they could slip notes through the vents in their girlfriends' gym lockers. They were making too much noise, and she shushed them. "Some of the teachers might still be around."

It happened just as she'd imagined it. Winnie stood naked by the lockers as they came in, hair plastered to her head, water still glistening on her skin, a bewildered expression on her face as she looked for the clothes and towel she'd left on the bench. But they were gone, hidden in Sugar Beth's locker. Even the stack of towels that normally sat in the corner had disappeared, stuffed behind the equipment bin.

The boys froze. All the blood drained from Winnie's face.

"Holy shit," Woody whispered.

Winnie could have laughed and run back into the shower room—the whole thing would have been over. But she didn't. Instead, she stood there, paralyzed by the poisoned arrow she hadn't seen coming.

She wasn't long-boned like Sugar Beth. She had short arms and legs. Her hips and thighs were a little plump for her narrow shoulders. Not fat, just fleshy enough to make her ever so slightly bottom heavy. A dab of white caught Sugar Beth's attention, and something unpleasant quivered in the bottom of her stomach. A string poked through the damp patch of pubic hair between Winnie's thighs. She was having her period.

Winnie's eyes went to Ryan. Only Ryan. All the boys saw the string, but Ryan was the only one who mattered. This was exactly what Sugar Beth had anticipated, but now she felt sick, as if she were the one standing there, naked and humiliated.

Winnie let out a low, keening wail and stood in front of them, arms at her sides, the white cotton string poking through her pubic hair.

The door of the shower room burst open, and Mr. Byrne came in. "What's going on in—"

He uttered a low curse as he saw Winnie. His hands flew to the buttons of his old black shirt. Within seconds, he'd peeled it off and wrapped it around her.

He shot the rest of them a furious look. "Get out of here! Wait for me in the hall."

The expression in those green eyes chilled Sugar Beth. He knew this was no accident, and he also knew who was responsible.

She fled from the locker room, from the building, feeling

as naked as Winnie. Her stomach cramped, just as if she were the one having her period.

Ryan called out from behind her, "Don't run, Sugar Beth! You're only going to make it worse."

She ignored him and raced for her car, but she couldn't find her keys. She sank to her knees, pulled open her purse with both hands, and dug inside, plowing through wadded tissues, makeup, pens, and a field trip permission slip she'd forgotten to turn in. A tampon that had come unwrapped lay in the bottom of her purse. She bit her lip.

Out of the corner of her eye, she saw Mr. Byrne coming toward her. He was bare-chested, his dark hair long and loose. "Get back in here now."

Ryan's eyes were pleading. "Come on, Sugar Beth. Do what he says."

She fumbled with her purse. Tried to think what she should do. She'd lie and say she hadn't known Winnie was in there. Their principal was a friend of Diddie's. How much trouble could she get into?

Slowly her heartbeat returned to normal. There was no reason to be so upset. She grabbed her purse, shoved the contents back inside, and stood up. "What's the big deal? The whole thing was an accident, Mr. Byrne. We didn't know she was there."

"You knew, all right."

God, she hated him. The first day of school she'd thought he was cute—weird, but so sophisticated that he even made Ryan seem immature. But when she'd gone up to him after class to flirt a little, he'd been a jerk, completely unfriendly.

Deke, Bobby, and Woody were waiting inside the gym door. Ryan wouldn't narc on her, and Deke and Bobby were tough, but Woody was afraid of his dad, so she shot him a hard look that told him he'd better keep his big fat mouth shut or she'd do something ten times worse than anything his dad could dream up.

"Would anyone care to explain?" Byrne had a skinny

chest, and he looked stupid standing there without his shirt, but he didn't seem self-conscious about it.

Sugar Beth told herself she hadn't done anything that terrible. Winnie should have just run back into the shower room. God, she was such a dweeb. She should have laughed it off. That's what Sugar Beth would have done.

She wondered if Winnie would tell Griffin. In Sugar Beth's entire life, Griffin had never once mentioned his other daughter's name to her.

"We didn't know she was in there," Deke said. "We thought the room was empty."

Byrne had this little zit on the side of his chin. Sugar Beth focused on it because it made her feel better knowing he still got zits. "Is that right?" he said.

"Yes, sir." They nodded.

Byrne's gaze went from one face to the next, looking for the weak link and finding it when he came to Woody. "All of you?"

Woody gulped. His eyes went to Sugar Beth. "Uh-huh."

"Then what happened to her clothes?"

Nobody had an answer for that.

"Sugar Beth, come with me. The rest of you can go."

The boys scrambled away, all except Ryan, who stayed by her side.

"You, too, Galantine."

"If it's all the same to you, sir, I'll stay here with Sugar Beth."

"It's not all the same. I wish to speak with her alone."

Ryan got this stubborn look on his face that said he intended to stay right where he was. But he had a scholarship to worry about, and Sugar Beth was afraid Byrne might try to screw it up. Besides, she didn't want Byrne thinking she needed her boyfriend to protect her. "Go on," she said.

The locker room door opened just then and Winnie came out. She was wearing her gym clothes and carrying Byrne's shirt. Her hair hung in a wet tangle, the ends dripping on her gym shirt with its bulldog mascot. She didn't look at Sugar Beth but at Ryan, and her expression was so full of anguish that Sugar Beth wanted to shake her. Didn't she have any pride?

"We didn't mean anything," Ryan said softly.

Winnie ducked her head and walked away toward the front of the building. She was still carrying Byrne's shirt, as if she'd forgotten she had it in her hand.

Ryan gazed at Sugar Beth, his troubled expression filling her with shame. She didn't want him here, didn't want him to see any more. She rose on her toes and gave him a light kiss. "Call me when you get home from work."

He didn't look happy about it, but he finally turned away and headed for the parking lot.

Byrne opened the locker room door. "In here."

She realized she was a little afraid of him, and she hated him even more for that.

"Open your locker," he said as soon as they were inside.

Shit. She hadn't thought far enough ahead. "My locker?"

He waited.

She tried a counterattack. "You shouldn't be in here, you know. It's the *girls'* locker room."

"Open the bloody thing, or I'll get the janitor to cut off the lock."

She thought about choosing another locker, Amy's or Leeann's, but he'd figure that out pretty fast.

Screw it. If he wanted to make a big deal out of this, that was his problem. She walked around two banks of lockers until she came to her own and twirled the combination. Her fingers were clumsy, and it took her three attempts to get it right. Finally, it clicked, but she didn't open it.

His bare arm brushed her shoulder as he reached past her. He pulled open the small metal door.

Winnie's clothes lay in a crumpled pile on top.

He didn't say anything for a long time. He simply gazed at

her, and she got this awful feeling that he could see right through her skin.

"Is this the kind of human being you want to be?"

She felt small and ugly. She bit off the urge to tell him how her father loved Winnie and not her, how she'd tried to be pretty enough, sweet enough, special enough, to make him notice her, but nothing had worked.

"Please inform your mother that I'll stop by to see her this evening."

Relief swept through Sugar Beth. Diddie would chop him into little pieces. She wanted to laugh in his face, but she couldn't find a laugh anyplace inside her.

By the time he arrived at Frenchman's Bride that night, Sugar Beth had done her work, not accusing him of attacking her—it would be another few weeks before she thought of that—just complaining about him to Diddie. How he put her down in class, embarrassed her in front of her friends. How his attitude had upset her so much that she'd done something really stupid. Something involving Winnie Davis.

Diddie wasn't predisposed to feel sympathetic toward her husband's illegitimate child, and as she met Colin Byrne, steely politeness undercut her gossamer blond beauty. "I don't see the need to make such a fuss about a silly prank. I'm sure Sugar Beth meant no harm."

Since Byrne wasn't Southern, he didn't understand how much power a softly spoken woman could wield, and unlike so many other people, he wasn't rattled by Diddie. "She did mean harm, though. She's been systematically persecuting Winnie Davis all year."

His bluntness set Diddie's teeth on edge, not to mention the fact that he had long hair, something she'd disapproved of from the beginning. "You're an educator. I expect you to understand that the roots of this difficult situation lie not with Sugar Beth but with my husband's lamentable *bohemian* lifestyle. My daughter is every bit as much a victim as . . . that *girl*."

"What happened today was cruel."

"Cruel?" Icicles dripped from the magnolia petals. "The lateness of the hour must have fatigued you, Mr. Byrne. I can think of no other reason a teacher would say something so unprofessional about one of the finest young women to ever attend Parrish High."

"Perhaps it's a cultural barrier, Mrs. Carey, but in England fine young women don't subject others to humiliation."

"I'll see you out."

In the end, Sugar Beth received nothing more than a mild reprimand from the principal, a man who owed his position to her mother's influence. Winnie, in the meantime, let her hair grow longer and ducked to stay behind it.

Gordon raised his head from the bottom of the bed. Sugar Beth got up and went into the bathroom for a glass of water. Winnie had done well for herself. The best part of Sugar Beth—the part that believed in cheering on anyone who fought the odds and came out a winner—tried to feel good for her. But the old ghosts loomed too large, and she couldn't manage it. One more item to add to the long list of things she still needed to do penance for.

She headed back to the bedroom, hoping for sleep. Tomorrow stood a chance of being one of the most miserable days of her life, and she needed to be ready.

*"No doubt you thought I was sadly lacking in
manners. You may sit down. At my feet."*

GEORGETTE HEYER, *These Old Shades*

Chapter 6

*S*ugar Beth didn't like the butterfly rumpus going on in her
stomach as she crossed the damp lawn toward Frenchman's
Bride. Unfortunately, she was already an hour late. After her
uncomfortable trip down memory lane last night, she'd slept
so badly that she'd turned off her alarm without thinking.
Byrne wouldn't be happy. Tough. Neither was she.

Gordon stopped to sniff a patch of grass, and a mockingbird called out. She had no intention of slinking in the back
door, regardless of what he'd said, and she climbed the front
steps, but when she got to the top, she saw a note stuck to the
knocker. *Door locked. Come in the back.*

Bastard. The latch didn't budge, and she turned her wrath
on her nearest target. "Now what do you think about your
choice of friends, huh? I hope you're proud of yourself."

Gordon gave her a snotty look, but he stayed with her as
she stomped down the stairs, not out of loyalty, but because
she hadn't yet fed him. She followed the flagstone path
around the side of the house, then came to a dead stop.

A sleek new addition, invisible from either the street or the carriage house, rose from the space that had once held the unused patio. The addition encompassed a spacious screened-in porch and a sunroom with long, high windows. One more desecration.

She entered through the porch into what had once been the cozy kitchen where Ellie Myers, Diddie's cook and house-keeper, had reigned supreme. But nothing was the same. Walls had been knocked out, ceilings raised, skylights added, all of it coming together in a state-of-the-art kitchen. She took in the bird's-eye maple cabinets and stainless steel appliances. A thick, tempered glass eating counter hung suspended over a section of the natural slate countertop. One end curved in a sculptured peninsula that separated it from the sunroom, which was decorated with an Asian flair—light walls and lacquered, oxblood furniture, along with some European pieces. An Adams sofa covered in burnished gold upholstery with brass nail-head trim sat near a decorative Victorian wooden birdcage. A few lacquered bamboo jars and earthenware ceramic pieces held a lush display of house-plants. The muted pagoda print on the chair and ottoman blended with a neighboring chinoiserie chest, which held a pile of books and an abandoned laptop computer.

The house of her childhood was gone, and it took her a moment to work up the energy to slip off her jacket. As she did, she noticed a neatly typed list propped on the slate countertop. She stopped at the first item:

Breakfast in my office: fresh orange juice, blueberry pancakes, sausage, grilled tomatoes, more coffee.

No way did Byrne eat like this every morning, not with that lean body. She knew a test when she saw one, and she gazed down at Gordon. "He thinks I'm not up to the challenge."

Gordon's expression indicated he had his doubts, too.

She set to work. It took a while to find the dog food, which she poured into an exquisite Waterford bowl and set on the floor near the porch doors. "Only the best for you, right, champ?"

His mouth was already full, so he didn't reply.

She was gazing in disgust at the old-fashioned glass juicer when she heard footsteps. She didn't like the way her stomach plunged. She was accustomed to making men nervous, not the other way around.

Byrne entered the kitchen through a newly constructed archway. As his eyes skimmed over her, she gave herself high marks for her choice of work clothes. Housekeepers were supposed to wear black, weren't they? And didn't she just live to please?

Her stretchy black lace crisscross blouse had a plunging V neck, and her ancient black slacks still had enough life in them to hug her hips. He eyed the small turquoise butterfly that dangled from a silver chain in her cleavage. She wished she had a really spectacular rack to shove under his nose. Still, with the right bra anything was possible, and judging from the length of time it took him to move his eyes back to her face, she was doing just fine. *Uniform, my ass.*

In contrast to her semihooker's attire, he wore dark slacks, a long-sleeved burgundy silk shirt, and an elegant pair of suspenders. What kind of man dressed like that to work at home? As he looked down his imperious nose at her, she knew for sure he'd been trapped in the wrong century.

"Fresh from your morning trot in Hyde Park, m'lord?" She managed a slight curtsy, although it lost some of its effectiveness, since she was behind the counter, and he couldn't see her knees bend.

He regarded her cuttingly. "Would it be possible to have my breakfast now, or is that too much of an inconvenience?"

"Almost done."

He took in the nearly empty countertop. "I can see that."

"I'm learning the kitchen."

"You're an hour late."

"What do you mean? I got here before eight."

"You were supposed to be here at seven."

"I'm positive you said eight. Didn't he, Gordon?"

Gordon was too busy giving him love to back up her story.

She pulled an orange from a bowl on the counter. "Is it true your parents were members of the British royal family?"

"One step from the throne." Byrne noted the Waterford dog dish as he made his way into the sunroom, but didn't comment.

"Liar. You grew up poor."

"Then why did you ask?"

"So I could irritate you by pointing out the differences in our backgrounds. Yours, humble and squalid. Mine, pampered and privileged. And if you want fresh juice every morning, I'm going to need an automatic juicer."

"Tough it out."

"Easy for you to say. You're not the one with blisters on her palms."

He headed back toward the archway, the book he'd retrieved in his hand, the light from the tall windows sending a sluice of mahogany through his already dramatic hair. "I'll expect breakfast in my office in twenty minutes." He disappeared into the hall.

"Good luck," she muttered.

"I'll pretend I didn't hear that."

She shot around the end of the counter and stuck her head through the archway. "You're enjoying yourself, aren't you?"

His chuckle drifted back to her, low and diabolical. "The Cinderella story in reverse. I only wish there were ashes in the fireplace so I could order you to sweep them out. Come along, Gordon."

She watched in disgust as her turncoat dog slipped after him into the office.

Half an hour later, she'd assembled a semidecent breakfast of two poached eggs on toast, a bowl of old-fashioned oatmeal topped with a mountain of brown sugar, and an admittedly tiny glass of fresh juice. Unfortunately, she was already pushing open the old library door when it occurred to her that she should spit in it.

Like the rest of the house, the library bore no resemblance to the dark, walnut-paneled room she remembered. White plantation shutters, open to the lawn on the west side of the house, let in the light. The hodgepodge of antiques she'd grown up with had been replaced by sleekly styled glass and granite furniture. Gordon lay on the abstract rug not far from Byrne's feet, along with paper wads that had missed the wastebasket. She set the tray on the end of the desk. Byrne turned away from his computer screen and studied his breakfast through a pair of Richard Gere rimless glasses. "I assumed you could read."

She was getting more than a little tired of his inferences that she was stupid. "There weren't any cookbooks in the kitchen, and I don't seem to have a pancake recipe memorized."

"Cookbooks are on the top shelf of the pantry." He studied the oatmeal. "I detest porridge, and where are my grilled tomatoes?"

He pronounced it *toe-mah-toes,* which sounded pretentious as hell, even coming from a Brit.

"I know you're technically an American citizen, but if you keep talkin' like that, you're goin' to get your sorry ass kicked right out of Mississippi. And what kind of person wants to eat *toe-mah-toes* for breakfast? Hell, I can barely get one of those suckers down for dinner." She pointed to the bowl. "And *that,* my friend, is good ol' fashioned Quaker Oats. Nobody over the age of three says *porridge.*"

"Are you done?"

"I think so." She grabbed the oatmeal bowl, along with his spoon, and carried it to the couch, where she perched on the arm and dug into the brown sugar. "It's better with raisins, but I couldn't find any. Or blueberries, for that matter, so those pancakes were problematic from the beginning." She rolled the oatmeal on her tongue, savoring its warm, comforting glue. It had been forever since she'd had anything decent to eat, but she never seemed to get around to cooking for herself.

He pulled off the Richard Geres. "Go grocery shopping. That's what you're here for, isn't it? And did I invite you to sit down?"

She dragged the spoon upside down from her mouth. "We need to discuss my paycheck."

"We already discussed it."

"I want a raise." She gestured toward the poached eggs. "Eat before they get cold. The point is, you get what you pay for, and what you're paying for right now doesn't get you much."

He eyed the half-filled juice glass. "I seem to be getting exactly what you're worth."

Just to be mean, she leaned far enough forward to shoot him a view of her well-supported cleavage. "You have no idea what I'm worth, bucko."

He took his time looking, leaning back in his chair and not even bothering to be subtle about it. In the end, she was the one who got uncomfortable, and she used her oatmeal as an excuse to straighten back up, which he found too darned amusing for words.

"You should be careful how you showcase your wares, Sugar Beth. I might think you want to expand your job duties."

"You couldn't be that lucky."

"Perhaps now is the time to tell you that I have a weakness for agreeable women."

"Well, that sure does leave me out."

"Exactly. With agreeable women, I'm unendingly considerate. Gallant even."

"But with tarts like me, the gloves are off, is that it?"

"I wouldn't exactly call you a tart. But then, I tend to be broad-minded."

She suppressed the urge to dump her *porridge* in his lap.

He turned his attention to his eggs, which gave her a chance to look him over, not exactly hazardous duty. He wasn't a pretty boy like her first two husbands. Darren had been a dazzler, and Cy had posed for Mr. January in the stuntman calendar. But there was something about Colin Byrne . . .

Lethal cheekbones, lips too carnal for that long blade of a nose. His feet were huge but not clunky, because they were so narrow. She studied his hands. They should have been slender and elegant, but they looked as though they'd been designed to dig ditches. A dangerous bolt of heat shot through her. He might be the demon personified, but he was also too sexy for her peace of mind. Apparently, she hadn't gotten rid of all her old suicidal instincts when it came to unsuitable men.

Her gaze returned to those blunt, competent fingers. She blinked. "You're the one who put that chain across my driveway."

"You knew that."

"No, I mean you did it yourself. You didn't hire anyone. You poured the concrete and set the posts."

"It's hardly brain surgery."

"I wasn't even gone for two hours. And when I saw you afterward, you were wearing Armani."

"I believe it was Hugo Boss."

"You actually know how to do manual labor?"

"How do you think I supported myself after I lost my teaching job?"

"With your writing." If she made it sound like a statement, maybe it would be true.

"I'm afraid my ability to write anything worth reading was put on hold after you had your fun."

She lost her appetite.

"My father was a bricklayer," he said. "Irish. And my mother was English. Rather an amusing story. She came from an upper-class family that spent the last of its dwindling fortune making certain their only daughter could make a brilliant marriage. Instead, she fell in love with my father. Tears, threats, disownment. The stuff of great romance."

"How did it work out?"

"They hated each other within a year."

She knew what that was like.

"I got my love of literature and the arts from my mother, but I'm more like my father in personality. Mean, unforgiving bastard. Still, he taught me a useful trade."

"You worked as a bricklayer after you went back to England?"

"In this country, too. The novel I wrote before *Last Whistle-stop* wasn't quite the best-seller I'd hoped it would be. Luckily, I enjoy working with my hands, and I had no trouble supporting myself."

But he shouldn't have had to do it laying brick, and some of the starch went out of her. "You aren't ever going to forgive me, are you?"

"Let's just say I'm in no hurry." He flicked his hand toward the door. "Run along and find something degrading to do."

The telephone rang. He reached out, but she was pissed again, so she beat him to it. "Byrne residence."

"Give me that."

"A freebie," she whispered.

"I need to speak with Colin," the woman at the other end said.

He held out his hand for the phone, clearly expecting the worst from her. It was tempting to give it to him, but she had a point to make, so she turned her back. "Mr. Byrne is working now. May I take a message?"

"Tell him it's Madeline." The woman on the other end made no attempt to hide her displeasure at being put off. "I'm sure he'll take my call."

"Madeline?" She turned back to Byrne. He vigorously shook his head. She settled back on the arm of the couch and reclaimed her oatmeal, finally beginning to enjoy herself. "I'm sorry, but I have orders not to interrupt him."

"He won't mind. I promise you."

"I'll make certain to deliver your message."

"I'm afraid you don't understand. I'm Madeline Farr."

Sugar Beth vaguely recognized the name of a New York socialite and put a little more magnolia into her accent. "Are you really? My, this certainly is an honor. I can't wait to tell all my friends I've spoken with you in person. Let me have your number."

She took a bite of oatmeal while an irritated Madeline reeled off a telephone number Sugar Beth didn't bother to write down. "Got it," she said when the woman paused for breath.

"It's very important for Colin to call me back by the end of the day."

"I'll tell him the minute I see him, but he still has messages backed up from last week, and he's been working so hard he barely comes out of the office, the poor ol' sod." She gave Colin a thumbs-up, making the point that she could talk his lingo anytime she pleased.

The corner of his mouth twitched.

"Do your best," the woman snapped.

"I sure will," she replied. "So lovely talkin' with you, Ms. Farr."

She hung up and regarded Byrne with satisfaction. "Note that I didn't tell her to go screw herself, even though she's obviously a bitch. I remained polite, fawning almost. At the same time, I didn't commit you to anything. In case you're not *bright* enough to figure it out, there's a real upside to having a sinner like me answer your phone. I lie, and your conscience stays clear." She rose from the couch. "Now, about that raise . . ."

He took a sip of coffee, unaffected by her outburst. "I'm having a dinner party in ten days to thank some of the people from the university who helped me with my new book. My agent and editor are flying in. A few others will be here, maybe thirty total, I'll let you know. The caterer's phone number is on your list. See what you have to do to get the house ready. And you'll need to serve, of course. After that, we'll discuss how much you're worth."

"You bet your sweet heinie we will."

She grabbed her oatmeal and headed out the door.

Colin listened to the taps of her ridiculously inappropriate heels retreating down the hallway. His writer's imagination could be a blessing or a curse, and right now he was cursed with the image of those tight black slacks hugging her bottom, and that little turquoise butterfly bouncing between her breasts. He needed to look for a uniform company as soon as possible.

It was ironic. When he'd arrived at Parrish High, he'd been twenty-two, in the throes of his own hormonal overload, and it had taken all his self-control to keep his eyes from lingering too long on so many short skirts and supple breasts. But Sugar Beth had never tempted him. So how was it that now, older and infinitely wiser, he found himself bombarded with mental images of her lying naked and feisty in his bed?

He knew better. Painful experience had taught him to keep his sexual relationships uncomplicated, but he still sometimes had to fight that instinctive part of him that was attracted to dramatic women. This was clearly one of those occasions. Still, age had taught him how to control his old weakness, and he wouldn't let it worry him.

He'd inherited his foolish romanticism from his mother. When he was a boy, it had made him far too caught up in dreams of slaying dragons and rescuing princesses for his father to tolerate, and after a few beatings, Colin had learned to confine that part of himself to the stories he wrote in his head. Still, it had taken his disastrous five-year marriage to a deeply neurotic American poet with raven hair, milky white skin, and haunted eyes to make him understand that he could never again express that secret part of himself anywhere but on paper. He'd loved Lara desperately, but there hadn't been enough love in the world to satisfy her kind of neediness.

One rainy New Orleans night nine years ago, she'd run their car into a concrete abutment, ending her own life and taking the life of their unborn child. It had been the worst time of his life, a black hell that had swallowed him whole for nearly two years. He'd vowed never to put himself through anything like that again.

Once again, he considered the wisdom of having the ultimate high-maintenance female working in his house, but the opportunity for revenge had been too sweet to resist. Still, he wouldn't let her distract him again. From now on, he'd direct every bit of his energy where it belonged. Into his new novel.

He heard the faint sound of running water in the kitchen. Last night it had taken him nearly an hour to come up with that overloaded list of things for her to do today. The dinner party had been in the works for a month, so that was pure serendipity. He smiled and checked his conscience to see if he was ashamed of himself, but the romantic boy who'd once dreamed of slaying dragons and rescuing princesses had developed the heart of a cynic, and his conscience didn't say a word.

Sugar Beth tossed aside Colin's list long before she got to the end and concentrated on the essentials. As she'd expected, his freezer was stuffed with frost-encrusted casseroles from the good women of Parrish, but the rest of his refrigerator was nearly as empty as hers. He'd tossed a pile of clothes destined for the dry cleaner on the couch, and a package addressed to a New York literary agency needed to go to the post office. He'd also left a note about some books waiting to be picked up at the bookstore. If she got enough done, maybe she'd be able to start searching the house this afternoon.

She polished off her coffee, set her oatmeal bowl in the sink to soak, then grabbed the keys to his Lexus. No way was she using her gas to run his errands. As an afterthought, she tossed the keys to her old Volvo on the counter, just in case he had an emergency. She was nothing if not considerate.

His Lexus smelled like designer cologne and a portfolio of tax-free municipal bonds. She set her purse on the seat. Inside was the envelope he'd left her with a hundred dollars in petty cash and a note saying he wanted a receipt for every penny. Suspicious bastard.

As she came out of the dry cleaner, she met Sherry Wilkes, a former classmate, who backed her into a corner and filled her in with a description of all her health problems, which included acid reflux, eczema, and early-stage endometriosis. Sugar Beth supposed she should be grateful that someone female wanted to talk to her, but the encounter only made her think about how much she missed the Seawillows. So far she hadn't run into any of them, but that wouldn't last forever. She wasn't looking forward to being cut dead by the women whose friendship she'd held so cheaply.

She found the town's new bookstore catty-corner across the street from Winnie's antique shop. Hand-painted African animals formed a border around the plate-glass window, which displayed current best-sellers, biographies, and a wide selection of works by African American novelists. A toy train surrounded a display of autographed copies of *Last Whistle-stop* designed to attract the tourists. In the center of the window, the store's name, GEMIMA BOOKS, was printed in bold brown letters outlined in black. Beneath that, a smaller inscription read *All people with free hearts are welcome here.* The only sign Sugar Beth could remember from Parrish's former bookstore had read NO FOOD OR ICE CREAM.

She heard the sounds of Glen Gould playing Bach's *Goldberg Variations* as she entered. Two elderly women chatted by the cookbooks, and a mother with a toddler browsed through the parenting section, aided by a clerk with curly blond hair. Sugar Beth used to believe nothing smelled better than the perfume aisles of a department store, but that was before she'd discovered the companionship of books. Now she breathed in the smell of the store.

A tiny woman, her head shaved to reveal the elegant shape

of her skull, came toward her. She wore a close-fitting saffron, long-sleeved top, wooden beads, and a slim, calf-length wrap skirt made of kente cloth. She had a dancer's body, what little there was of it, and she smiled as she slipped behind the cash register.

"What can I do—? Well . . ." She lifted her eyebrows. "Well, well, well."

They were probably close to the same age, so they might have gone to school together, but Sugar Beth didn't recognize her. There'd been little social interaction between the black and white kids, although they'd been expected to get along together, thanks to the influence of her father's hiring policies at the window factory. Although Griffin Carey had been a Southern traditionalist in many ways, he'd held liberal social views, and he'd used his economic clout to enforce them. Modern-day Parrish, with a relatively prosperous African American community and a forty-year history of racial cooperation, had reaped the rewards.

Sugar Beth braced herself for the worst. "I'm afraid you have me at a loss."

"I'll just bet I do. I'm Jewel Myers."

"Jewel?" She couldn't believe this beautiful woman was Jewel Myers, the scruffy tomboy daughter of Diddie's housekeeper Ellie. "I—uh—didn't recognize you."

"I grew up while you were gone." She seemed amused. "I became a radical lesbian feminist."

"No kidding. Interesting career path for a Mississippi girl."

A customer interrupted with a question, giving Sugar Beth a chance to reorient herself before Jewel turned back to her. She took her time looking Sugar Beth over. "I used to wear your hand-me-downs. Mom made them over so they'd fit."

"I don't remember."

"You never said a word about it. Year after year I'd show up at school in your old clothes, but you never once made fun of me."

"I wasn't entirely evil."

"Honey, you were the biggest bitch in school. If I'd been a threat like Winnie, you'd have taken out an ad in the school newspaper. I gotta say, though, you didn't bother the black girls much. Not unless somebody got in your face. Now how can I help you, Miz Sugar Beth Carey?"

Sugar Beth couldn't keep the wistful note from her voice as she gazed around her. "You could give me a job. I love bookstores."

"Afraid I don't need anyone. Besides, I only hire lesbians and other persecuted minorities." She grinned and took in Sugar Beth's black lace top. "You're not a lesbian, are you?"

"I haven't been in the past. Which doesn't say I wouldn't consider it for the right employment opportunity."

Jewel chuckled, an amazingly big sound coming from someone so petite. "So you're looking for a job?"

"Technically, no. But my current employer is a heartless bastard, and I'd drop him in a second if something better came along."

"The rest of us like Colin."

"News travels fast."

"A lot of people are holdin' their sides laughin'. Even I, a fair-minded person with no overt reason to hate you, find it amusing. Did you know that Colin's the one who helped me get a college scholarship? The counselors couldn't be bothered."

"He's a real saint, all right." Sugar Beth cast another wistful glance around the store. "I'm supposed to pick up the books he ordered. He said to put it on his account. And toss in some of Georgette Heyer's regency romances while you're at it."

"Not Colin's normal reading taste."

"He's broadening his horizons."

Sugar Beth followed Jewel as she headed for the best-seller aisle. Gemima Books was both cozy and well stocked. Index cards dangled from the shelves with Jewel's handwritten comments recommending a particular book. Comfortable chairs welcomed customers to sit and browse. Only the children's section seemed neglected. "This is a great store."

"I'm lucky. Even with all the tourists the community association has attracted, Parrish is too small to interest the big chains."

"Where did the name come from? Gemima Books?"

"Jewel is a gem."

"But Gemima?"

"I like reinterpreting African American female icons. Originally I was going to call it 'Mammi's' with an *i*, but my mother had a fit. Thanks for that note you wrote when she died, by the way."

They talked about books for a while. Jewel's preferences ran toward socially relevant fiction, but she wasn't a snob about it, and Sugar Beth could have followed her around all day. More customers entered the store, and Jewel greeted all but the tourists by name. She pointed out a book by a Hispanic author she said Sugar Beth should read, and a new commercial women's fiction author destined to be a bestseller. It felt so good being with someone who wasn't hostile that Sugar Beth had to resist the urge to throw her arms around Jewel and beg her to be her friend. Which just went to show how far loneliness could drag you down.

Jewel rang up her order and gave Sugar Beth an impish smile as she handed over the package. "Tell Colin to enjoy those Georgette Heyers."

"I sure will." She toyed with the strap of her purse, then shifted the package from one hand to another, trying to be casual about it. "If you get bored sometime and want to grab a cup of coffee, let me know."

"Okay." Jewel's response wasn't exactly enthusiastic, but it wasn't entirely unfriendly either, and Sugar Beth had heard that miracles did happen, even if they never seemed to happen to her.

She glanced at her watch as she got back into the car. She

had more errands to run, but she'd stayed away longer than she should have, and she'd better put off the rest until tomorrow.

A good decision, as it turned out, because trouble lurked at the ducal estate. His Grace, it seemed, had grown restless waiting for the return of his lowly housekeeper . . .

"You are shameless!" he said angrily.
"Nonsense! You only say so because I drove
your horses," she answered.

GEORGETTE HEYER, *The Grand Sophy*

Chapter 7

*W*here the devil have you been?"

Colin stalked into the kitchen with Gordon padding at his heels, just as Sugar Beth set the last of the grocery sacks on the counter. "Running your errands, your lordshit."

"You took my car."

"Did you expect me to walk?"

"I expect you to take your own car."

"I like yours better."

"Undoubtedly." He loomed over her. "Just as I liked that brand-new red Camaro you used to drive in high school. Nevertheless, I didn't take it upon myself to run off with it, now did I?"

"I bet if I'd left the keys lying around, you would have. That junker you drove was a major embarrassment."

"Which was the only reason I could afford to buy it." He swept his keys from the counter and pocketed them. "Where's my lunch?"

"I thought famous writers drank their lunch."

"Not today. It's two o'clock, and all I've had is coffee and cold poached eggs."

"They wouldn't have been cold if you'd eaten them right away like I told you."

"Spare me the stereotype of the sassy servant."

"Fine." She slammed a box of rice on the counter. "Leave me the hell alone, and I'll bring your lunch as soon as I get to it."

He regarded her glacially. "Hostility already?"

"Hostile or sassy—it's all I've got. Take your pick."

"Let me remind you that one of your duties is to prepare my lunch, which I expect to have served at something approximating lunchtime." He turned his back on her, effectively ending the discussion, but instead of going back to his office, he wandered into the sunroom and threw himself in the big chair by the windows, all long, lithe grace and surly attitude.

She studied him as she put away the perishables. He drummed his fingers on the arm of the chair, then crossed and uncrossed his ankles. By the time she'd tucked the onions in the pantry, she decided something more than her attitude was bothering him. She picked up a grocery sack that had fallen to the floor. "You probably didn't know this, but in addition to being a stuntman, the late, and pretty much unlamented, Cy Zagurski fancied himself a songwriter."

"You don't say."

"Bad country western. Cy was generally sweet, even when he was drunk, which, I'll admit, tended to be most of the time. But drunk or sober, the minute he had trouble thinking up his next lyric, he'd start yelling at me."

"In what part of this conversation am I supposed to express interest?" He sounded snooty as hell, but he didn't make a move to get out of the chair, and as she set more oranges in the bowl, she congratulated herself on having acquired at least a little insight into human nature. "So tell me about your new book."

"Which one?"

"The one that's making you act like a prick, bless your heart."

He leaned his head against the back of the chair and sighed. "That would be all of them, at one time or another."

"All?" She peeled the cellophane from a two-pack of Twinkies, took one out, and wandered into the sunroom. "I know about *Last Whistle-stop,* and you said you'd written a novel a long time ago. Anything else?"

"The sequel to *Last Whistle-stop.* I finished it in July. It's called *Reflections,* if you must know."

Last Whistle-stop had ended in 1960, and if *Reflections* was a sequel, it stood to reason that her parents would be major characters. Considering Byrne's feelings for Diddie, Sugar Beth decided she needed to get her hands on a copy as soon as she could. "When's it coming out?"

"In about two months."

"I'm guessing from the title that my parents and the Carey Window Factory might be major players."

"Without the factory, Parrish would have died out after the 1960s like so many other small Southern towns. Is my lunch ready yet?"

"Just about." She took a bite from her Twinkie and played with danger by sitting on the edge of a small rattan slipper chair near him. "What have you been doing since July?"

"Some traveling. Researching a novel." He rose and walked toward the windows, his big frame blocking the sun. "A family saga. I've had it in mind for years."

She remembered the crumpled paper scattered over the floor in his office. "So how's it going?"

"Beginning a book is always difficult."

"I'm sure."

"This one is roughly based on my own family. The story of

three generations of an upper-class British family set against the same three generations of a poor Irish one."

"With everybody meeting up when the upper-class daughter falls in love with the bricklayer's son?"

"Something like that."

"Writing a novel is a big change."

"Just because I've become known for nonfiction doesn't mean that's all I can do."

"Absolutely not." She wasn't surprised that he sounded defensive. He'd been wildly successful writing nonfiction but failed at his early attempt at fiction. "You don't seem to be brimming with confidence."

He gazed at her Twinkie. "Is that organic?"

"I'm guessing not." She went after a dab of filling with the tip of her tongue.

He grew very still, and the way his eyes lingered on her mouth told her he was reacting to her, whether he wanted to or not. She used to be mystified by women who didn't know how to turn men on, since she could do it so easily herself. Then one day she'd realized that intelligent women relied on their brains to get ahead in the world, instead of sex. And hadn't that been a real *well, duh* moment?

Still, sometimes you had to use what God gave you, and she continued to make oral love to the Twinkie, nothing even close to blatant—that would be too tacky for words—only a few slow swirls of her tongue to show this arrogant Brit he didn't intimidate her. Or not much anyway.

His gaze stayed on her mouth. "You do enjoy playing games, don't you, Sugar Beth?"

"Us tarts like to keep ourselves amused."

He gave her an enigmatic smile, then turned away from the window. She expected him to head back to his office, but instead he walked into the kitchen and began examining the groceries she hadn't finished putting away. "Apparently you didn't read my instructions about buying organic food."

"Dang, you were serious. I thought that was some kind of

test to see if I could think for myself instead of being a blind follower of the ridiculous."

Another of those arched eyebrows. She polished off the Twinkie and headed back to the kitchen.

"I believe I mentioned fresh produce, organic when possible. Whole grains, fish, nuts, yogurt." He picked up a bag of cherry Twizzlers. "Your diet is abominable."

"I had oatmeal for breakfast."

"Undoubtedly your first decent meal since you got here. And you mainly ate the brown sugar."

"I need to keep up my strength. My boss is a slave driver."

He caught sight of the sack from Jewel's store and lost interest in the groceries. Unfortunately, he pulled out one of the Georgette Heyers first. She grabbed it from him. "A perfect example of that miscellaneous pilfering from the help you were talking about to justify being a cheapskate."

He glanced at the receipt. "So I see."

He flipped open one of his new research books. She watched him for a moment. "If you need any help with that chapter you're trying to write—the one that's responsible for your chipper mood—let me know. I have lots of ideas."

"I can imagine."

She should have stopped right there, but she still hadn't learned to curb her tendency toward excess. "For example, I'm positive I could write a great sex scene."

"I'll keep that in mind."

"You are planning to have lots of sex scenes, aren't you? You can hardly expect to sell fiction without them."

His eyes drifted from her collarbone to her breasts. This man could find his way around a woman's body. "You know a lot about writing a novel, do you?"

"Not lesbian scenes, either. I know how much you men like them, but women buy most of the books in this country, and that's not a big turn-on for most of us." She thought of Jewel. "Although I suppose sticking one in wouldn't hurt."

"*Sticking one in?* Interesting turn of phrase."

"I've always had a gift for the spoken word." She toyed with her turquoise butterfly. "Personally, I'd like somebody to write a scene with one woman and two men. Oh, heck, make it three."

"I believe that's why they invented porn."

"As if all those lesbian scenes you want to write aren't porn."

"I don't want—"

"I understand." She waved a dismissive hand. "Heterosexual men get all threatened when there's more than one man in bed. But as long as you keep the woman in the middle, I don't see what the big deal is."

"Speaking from personal experience?"

"I'd ruin the mystery if I told you." She beamed him her beauty queen smile. "Now, run along so I can get my work done."

He didn't rise to the bait. Instead, he eased down on a stool at the counter and opened one of his books. Dirty pictures began to flash through her mind, pictures of herself naked in bed with Colin. She added George Clooney, then tossed in Hugh Jackman just for fun. She played with the image a bit, letting the filmstrip unwind in her head, but then she realized she didn't like what she was seeing. Instead of paying attention to her naked body, George and Hugh were talking *football*. She tried to refocus the film, but they were real sports fans, and the next thing she knew they'd abandoned her for a Chargers game. Which meant that she and Colin were alone. And naked.

Her nipples tightened. Luckily, he seemed to have lost himself in his book and didn't notice.

It had only been a year since Emmett's health had failed, and here she was having a sex fantasy about a man who hated her guts. Typical. Just when she'd thought she'd developed sense, all her old masochistic habits came banging at the door trying to get back in.

Promise me, Sugar Beth, that you won't waste time mourn-

ing me. You've been living like a nun for more years than I want to admit to. It's gone on long enough.

But it hadn't been nearly long enough. She thought of him lying in bed all those months, his powerful body wasted, and the old anger-washed love filled her. *Why'd you have to up and get sick on me, you old coot? Let alone die. I need you, don't you know that?*

He'd been the love of her life, and some days she didn't think she could bear the pain.

Colin rose and returned to his office. She threw together his lunch, a turkey sandwich on whole wheat bread, and—as further punishment—a big handful of organic bean sprouts. He was back at the keyboard, so she left the tray on the corner of his desk without interrupting him.

Colin's treatise on her job responsibilities noted that he had a weekly cleaning service, but that she was supposed to tidy up after him, which included making the ducal bed and straightening the imperial bathroom. Since both activities gave her an excuse to explore, she headed upstairs. Gordon had grown bored with the writing life, and he padded after her.

Smoke-colored paint had replaced Diddie's pink floral wallpaper, and modern copper wall sconces framed the windows on the landing. When she reached the top of the stairs, she glanced to the right and saw small changes: paint and moldings, different lighting, a slender steel sculpture resting on a block of frosted glass. To the left, however, everything had been reconfigured. Instead of a hallway leading to Diddie's and Griffin's separate bedrooms, a neoclassic arch framed a niche holding a set of double doors. She couldn't believe it. The old attic door had been located at the end of a hallway that no longer existed!

She dashed into the master bedroom suite, a vast space with arches, art, and sleek furniture that included a king-size bed with four twisted metal posts. The nearest door led to a cathedral-size bathroom. The second door opened into a luxurious, cedar-scented, two-room closet complete with a teak bench. She looked everywhere but couldn't find any access to the attic, and she headed for the other wing.

Her former bedroom, along with the old sewing room, had been converted into a state-of-the-art home gym. Another guest room held a small, book-lined study, while a third had been luxuriously refurbished for company. She poked into closets, peered behind chests, searched everywhere she could think of.

The attic door had vanished.

Ryan didn't fall asleep until after midnight, but he awakened before five. He had an OSHA meeting scheduled for that day, and he wanted to be sharp, but he'd been having trouble sleeping for a couple of weeks. He should be sleeping like a baby. He had a wonderful life—a family he loved, a job that challenged him, a beautiful house, good friends. He was the luckiest guy in the world.

Winnie gave a soft sigh in her sleep and curled against him. She smelled faintly of the perfume she'd dabbed at the base of her throat before he'd come home from work. She always did things like that, made sure her hair was combed, her makeup fresh. Other men complained about their wives letting themselves go, but Winnie grew prettier all the time. She was perfect in every way: smart, kind, loving. So different from Sugar Beth, who'd been demanding, temperamental, vain, and spoiled.

But she'd also been glorious, an out-of-control thrill ride sending him from ecstasy to despair and back to ecstasy again in the wink of an eye. When she'd broken his heart, he'd thought the pain would kill him, and the adoration in Winnie's eyes had been a salve to his young man's wounds.

She draped her hand over his thigh in her sleep. She was naked. She slept that way a lot. Willing. Available. He still couldn't get over how lucky he was. Sometimes, maybe, he wished she wouldn't try quite so hard, but that was only because he felt guilty knowing she gave more to their marriage than he did. But what could he offer when she'd already thought of everything?

He wasn't going to fall back asleep, so he slipped out of bed, and Winnie's radar kicked in as usual. "'S anything wrong?"

"Going for a run." He tugged the blanket over her bare shoulder and pulled on his sweats. It was still too dark to run. He'd catch up on some paperwork first.

As he let himself out into the hallway, he saw that Gigi had hung another poster on her door, even though she was supposed to keep them in her room. She'd begun asking questions about Sugar Beth. Gigi called her She Who Must Not Be Named after the evil Voldemort in the Harry Potter books. Wiseass.

They'd never tried to hide the truth from her, so she'd always known about the blood relationship between Winnie and Sugar Beth, but the complexities behind that relationship were beyond a thirteen-year-old's comprehension. He supposed it was only natural for her to be curious, but she'd been so rebellious lately that her questions had begun to make him uneasy. She was perfectly capable of accosting Sugar Beth on the street and asking her the same questions she'd been asking him. He'd finally told her she was forbidden to have any contact.

Now, if only somebody would do the same for him.

By the time he got to work, Ryan felt back in control again. The refurbished three-story Art Deco lobby with its great sweep of CWF windows greeted him. He'd never quite gotten over the fact that, at thirty-three, he was COO of the company where his parents had spent their working life, his mother as a file clerk, his father as a painter. He'd earned his position, along with the respect of the employees, through hard work and dedication, and he never took it for granted.

The factory had a good safety record, and his OSHA meeting was going well when his secretary pulled him away from the plant tour he was conducting to tell him the principal at Gigi's school was on the line. Eva never called him, and he quickly excused himself to take the call in the loading dock office. "Eva, it's Ryan. What's wrong?"

"I have Gigi here. I need you to come in."

"Is she hurt?"

"She's fine. But Chelsea Kiefer has a broken wrist. Gigi pushed her into a locker."

"Gigi wouldn't push anyone." He rested his hip on the corner of the desk and gazed through the window onto the loading dock. Craig Watson, one of his senior VPs, had taken over the tour, but Craig wasn't up to speed on all the new safety regulations, and Ryan needed to get back. "Chelsea's Gigi's best friend. I'm sure there's been a misunderstanding. Call Winnie. She'll take care of this."

"She's in Memphis for the day. You'll have to come in."

He'd forgotten Winnie had a buying trip. He shifted his position to get a better view through the window. "I can't leave right now, but one of us will be there around five." If Winnie hadn't gotten back by then, he'd juggle his schedule. An inconvenience, but he could manage it.

"This isn't going to wait that long. Gigi is being belligerent, and Chelsea's mother is furious. She's talking about filing a police report."

"A police report?"

"Yes, Ryan, a police report. Get in here right away."

Gigi had never seen her dad so mad. His knuckles were white on the steering wheel, and the muscle at the corner of his jaw jumped up and down. He'd never hit her, but she'd never done anything this bad, and she thought he might want to.

He hadn't said a word to her since they'd left the principal's office. Part of her wanted him to start yelling, so they could get it over with, but the rest of her wanted to postpone it as long as possible. It wasn't like she'd meant to break Chelsea's wrist.

Just thinking about it made her stomach ache. Chelsea had been acting like a bitch all week, maybe because she'd been fighting with her mom, but that still hadn't been any reason for her to say that Gigi had started acting all stuck up again because she was rich. Gigi'd finally gotten so mad that she'd told Chelsea she was getting fat, which was totally true. Chelsea had yelled back that she hated Gigi just like everybody else, and then Gigi had sort of pushed her, not to hurt her, just to push her a little, except the door to her locker was open, and Chels had fallen against it and broken her wrist. Now everybody was blaming her.

The piece of cafeteria pizza she'd had for lunch rose up in her throat. She kept hearing the sound Chelsea had made when her wrist broke, this choky little scream. Gigi swallowed hard to push the pizza back down.

When her dad had finally walked in the office, Gigi had been so scared about Chelsea's mom saying she was going to file a police report that she wanted to throw herself in his arms and cry like she used to when she was little. But he hadn't even looked at her, just like he wasn't looking at her now.

Mrs. Whitestone had suspended Gigi for the rest of the week and sent her outside to wait on the office bench so the adults could talk. Chelsea's mom had always liked Gigi's dad. She'd even kind of flirted with him, which Gigi'd always thought was creepy, but was probably a good thing, because she'd finally stopped yelling. When he'd come out of the office, though, his face had looked like he wanted to kill somebody, and Gigi didn't think it was Chelsea's mom.

The other kids always told her she was lucky to have such young parents because they remembered what it was like to be a teenager, but her dad didn't look like he remembered anything about being a teenager right now. Resentment gnawed at her. In high school, her dad had been named most popular boy. She'd seen it in his yearbook. And her mom never got into any trouble. Well, Gigi wasn't like them.

She couldn't stand the quiet in the car for another second, and she reached for the button on the radio.

"Leave it alone." Usually, they listened to music together, but now he sounded like he wouldn't ever listen to music with her again.

"Chelsea started it."

"I don't want to hear it."

"I knew you'd be on her side."

He shot her a cold look. "I suggest you keep your mouth shut."

She tried to, but everything was so unfair, and she hated that he wouldn't put his arm around her and give her one of his bear hugs and say everything was going to be all right. "This is all because I'm not perfect like you and Mom used to be!"

"This has nothing to do with your mother or me. This has to do with the fact that you've been acting like a brat for months now, and today you physically assaulted someone. You're lucky her mother decided not to file charges against you. Actions bring consequences, Gigi, and, believe me, you're going to face some serious ones."

"You broke a guy's collarbone once. You told me that."

"It was a football game!"

"That didn't make it right."

"Not one more word!"

That night after her mom got home, they made her sit down in the living room. Her dad did most of the talking, going on about how disappointed they were in her, and how serious an offense this was. She kept waiting for him to say that, even though she'd done something wrong, he loved her anyway, but he didn't.

"We're taking away your telephone privileges for two weeks," her mom finally said. "You can't watch television, and you can't leave the house unless one of us is with you."

"That's so unfair! You don't even like Chelsea. You think she's a bad influence. But you *love* Kelli Willman!"

Her dad ignored her outburst. "You're also going to be doing a lot of studying to make up for the classes you're missing while you're suspended."

As if she couldn't catch up in about three seconds.

"And you have to apologize to Chelsea," her mother said.

Gigi jumped up. "She has to apologize to me first! She started it."

"This isn't negotiable. You broke her wrist."

"I didn't mean to!"

But neither of them would listen. They just started in again, not understanding that Gigi already felt like shit, and she didn't need to hear any more about how evil she was. Her parents totally forgot what it was like to be a teenager, but everybody hadn't hated them the way the kids hated Gigi. Her parents had been *perfect*. Well, Gigi wasn't perfect. She wasn't like them. She was . . .

She was like her aunt.

The word rolled around in her head like a big shiny marble. *Aunt.* She didn't have a lot of relatives: Grandma Sabrina and Nana Galantine, her Uncle Jeremy, but he was a lot older than her dad and wasn't ever getting married. That left only one other person. Maybe Sugar Beth Carey was only a half aunt, but still . . .

The Seawillows talked about her a lot when they didn't think Gigi was listening and how everybody had totally kissed her butt in high school. One time she'd heard Colin say that Sugar Beth had also been one of the smartest kids in her class, but the Seawillows hadn't believed him, since she got crappy grades. Still, Colin had seen everybody's test scores, so he should know, even though he wouldn't tell any of them what their scores were.

Sugar Beth would totally understand what Gigi was going through. But Gigi's dad had forbidden her to talk to her. He'd said if Gigi saw her someplace, she couldn't even say hello because he knew how Gigi was, and she wouldn't stop at hello, and nobody wanted old history dredged up again.

But this wasn't old history. This was Gigi's life. And she had to talk to somebody who'd understand. Even if she got grounded for the rest of her life.

"You now belong to me—body and soul."

GEORGETTE HEYER, *These Old Shades*

Chapter 8

Colin's voice slid over Sugar Beth like a trickle of cold water. "What are you doing in here?"

"I'm making your bed."

"Well, make it somewhere else."

"You forgot to put on your happy face again, didn't you?" She stretched her legs, balancing her weight on the toe of one foot, cocking her other knee, and leaning far enough across the bed to make him appreciate her bottom-line assets. This was the only weapon she had left, and she'd been using it as frequently as possible in the nine days she'd been working for him. So what if her sexual shenanigans were also making her more aware of him than she wanted to be? He didn't know that. Or did he? That was the thing about sexual games. You could never be completely sure who was getting to who.

To *whom*. It was a bitch living with your old English teacher, especially when your old English teacher wasn't old at all, and he had exactly the kind of body that most appealed to her, tall and lean, broad in the shoulder, narrow at the hip. Then there was his brain. It had taken her a lot of years to find that particular part of a man appealing, but she'd finally gotten in the habit, and she couldn't seem to give it up.

She took her time arranging the last pillow. His dinner party was scheduled for tomorrow night, and the rental company's truck would be arriving soon. Although the dining room at Frenchman's Bride was large, it wasn't big enough to seat the thirty people he'd invited, and she'd rented smaller tables to set up throughout the downstairs. His agent and editor were flying in from New York, but he'd done a lot of research at Ole Miss, and most of the guests would be driving from Oxford.

But not all of them.

"How many locals did you say you'd invited?" He hadn't shown her the official guest list, and she couldn't relax about this party until she knew she wouldn't be forced to wait on anyone she wanted to avoid.

"I already told you. Two of the local librarians—you don't know them. And Aaron Leary and his wife."

Aaron was Parrish's current mayor. She'd gone to high school with him, but since he'd been president of the chess club and black, they'd moved in different circles. She remembered him as a sweet, studious kid, so she probably hadn't tried to screw him over. Being forced to wait on a classmate was degrading, but since he was the mayor, she could handle it. "What about his wife?"

"Charise. A lovely woman."

"Stop being difficult."

"We've already had this conversation."

She fussed with the corner of the duvet. "The name Charise doesn't ring a bell."

"I believe she's from Jackson."

"Why didn't you tell me that in the first place?"

"I'm sorry. Have I given you the impression that I want to make things easier for you?"

"It's just weird that you don't have more friends in Parrish. No, on second thought, it's not weird."

He slipped off his watch. "The party tomorrow night is business."

"I know. To thank the people who helped you with *Reflections*. But aren't there a lot more people here in town who helped with your research than in Oxford?"

"Your aunt is dead, Hank Withers is in the hospital, and Mrs. Shaible is visiting her daughter in Ohio. Are we done with this conversation yet?"

He began unbuttoning his shirt and taking his time about it. As the person responsible for his laundry, she already knew he didn't wear undershirts, just as she knew he favored jewel-toned designer boxers. She knew *way* too much.

"You could at least wait until I'm finished straightening up in here to undress." She sounded testy, but she didn't like the way his presence had encouraged her inner slut to come out of her coma.

"Is this bothering you?" The erotic peep show continued, one button giving way to another, his eyes watching her.

"Only because I saw that book you've been reading."

His shirt fell open. "Which book would that be?"

"*The Erotic Life of a Victorian Gentleman.* Some gentleman. All-around dog is more like it. There are entire chapters devoted to masters and servant girls."

He slipped a thumb into the waistband of his slacks, looking arrogant and dangerous. "You think I might be getting ideas, do you?"

"I *know* you're getting ideas. You were using a Hi-Liter."

He chuckled and disappeared into the closet. She loved it in there, the extravagance of the polished cherry shelves and pewter fixtures, the tidiness of the drawers, racks, and compartments, the way it smelled of imported fabrics and stuffy attitude. "It's research," he said from inside. "And what were you doing poking around in my office?"

"Picking up your crap." And looking for the manuscript of *Reflections,* although she didn't intend to tell him that. She straightened a lamp shade. "The chapter on auctioning off virgins is disgusting."

"My, my, we have been snooping, haven't you?"

"I need intellectual stimulation. This job's more boring than dirt." He hadn't closed the closet door, so she wandered over and looked in. "I don't think you're doing research at all. I think you're just being pervy."

"Such a harsh word. Where are my gym shorts?"

He still wore his trousers, but the shirt was gone. She wondered how that skinny chest she remembered from high school could have turned into something so magnificent. He set his hands on his hips, and she realized he was waiting for a response.

She licked her lips. "Beats the heck out of me." His gym shorts were on the shelf where he'd left them, but she tried not to make his life any easier than she had to. She spotted his belt draped over the teak bench in the middle of the closet. He liked things tidy, and she had a feeling he worked hard not to pick up after himself. "I thought you exercised in the morning."

"In the afternoon, too, when I feel like it."

"And you're feeling like it today because you're stuck again, aren't you?"

"Don't you have something filthy to scrub?"

"You're throwing away so many pages that I need to buy you a second wastebasket for your office."

"Would you mind turning around so I can take my pants off?"

"This is pretty much my only job perk, so yes."

An outsider would have had a hard time telling whether the slight curling at the corner of his mouth was an expression of amusement or contempt, but she liked to tell herself that he found her a lot more diverting than he wanted to. She leaned against the edge of the door. "So tell me why you're blocked. Normally I'd recommend a sex scene—you might remember I have a fondness for them—but after what I read in that book this morning, I'm leery about encouraging you."

"It's a complicated story, and I'm trying to introduce a new character. She's giving me a bit of trouble, that's all."

"Cherchez la femme."

"Precisely." He picked up the belt he'd abandoned for no other apparent reason than to make her nervous. "Fannie is pivotal to the book. She's young, well bred, but strangling on the conventions of Victorian society."

"I can identify with— Hey, that's my name!"

For once she seemed to have caught him by surprise. "What are you talking about?"

"My real name. Frances Elizabeth Carey."

"I didn't know that."

"Of course you did. Nobody ever calls me Frances, but it was on all my school records."

"I'm sure I've forgotten it long ago."

"I'm sure you haven't."

He slid the belt through his fingers. "Go back to work. You're annoying me."

"She'd better not be a beautiful blonde with impeccable taste."

"These pants are coming off, whether you're looking or not." He abandoned the belt, unzipped, and dropped his trousers.

She caught a glimpse of firm, long-muscled thighs just before she turned away. A shiver passed through her, and she reminded herself that she had more important things to think about than his body.

She went into the bathroom and pressed one of his wet towels to her face before she hung it up. Nine days had passed, and she still hadn't been able to find a way into the attic. Twice she'd asked him about the door, making the question casual so he didn't get suspicious. The first time, the phone had rung before he could answer. The second time, Gordon had gone ballistic over a squirrel and stopped the conversation cold. A squirrel, for God's sake! She hated that dog.

The dinner party gave her a good excuse to bring it up a

third time, and she returned to the bedroom, speaking just loudly enough so he could hear her in the closet. "I called the florist again this morning. I told her what you said about not wanting the arrangements to be too girly because you don't want to keep feeding those lingering rumors that you're gay. She's a Christian, so she understood completely."

She thought she heard him sigh, and she smiled to herself as he emerged from the closet wearing a pair of gray cashmere gym shorts and carrying a navy T-shirt.

"Fascinating," he drawled, "but I don't remember saying a word to you about the flowers."

She dragged her gaze away from his chest. "If you'd show a little more interest in football, I'm sure those rumors would die a natural death. Plus you need to stop talkin' like a sissy."

His lips twitched, which irritated her, because she wanted to aggravate him, not entertain him. She put a hand on her hip, fingers pointed backward, a bored look on her face. "The party's tomorrow night, and I'm thinkin' Diddie's Spode might still be in the attic. I'll go up this afternoon to check." She held her breath.

He pulled his T-shirt over his head. "Don't bother. The caterer is bringing dishes."

"As a foreigner, you can't be expected to know this, but in Mississippi, using caterer's china instead of perfectly lovely family heirlooms is considered tacky."

"Whatever family heirlooms were in the attic are long gone."

"What do you mean? What happened to everything?"

"Winnie sold whatever was up there before I moved in." He didn't make any attempt to soften what even the most insensitive person would know had to be a blow to her.

"Sold?" There it was again. That alarming sense that she'd lost everything. She conjured up an image of Delilah's big smile to hold herself together.

"She had the right," he pointed out.

"Yes, I guess she did." She made a fist behind her back and

dug her fingernails into her palm. "Still, she might have over-looked some of the serving platters. Diddie had her hiding places."

But he was already walking out.

The steady cadence of the treadmill usually calmed him, but it felt too tame today. He needed to be outside. Do something with his hands. Fighting off Sugar Beth's sexual allure was difficult enough without having to fight off her charm, too, especially since he knew it was calculated. He didn't like it. Just as he didn't like that wicked sense of humor she was as likely to turn on herself as on him. Or the sharp intelligence that kept surfacing beneath her good ol' girl demeanor. He'd known it was there, of course, but he'd never expected her to discover it, too.

And where had she found her grit, not to mention that quirky, but nonetheless impressive, competence? She produced acceptable meals, better than what he made for himself, and while she ignored most of his instructions, they were generally the ones he'd conjured up to antagonize her. Somehow she winnowed out the sensible from the nonsensical and got things done. No, he didn't like it at all.

He wiped the sweat from his eyes and punched the treadmill up a few notches. She'd shown up in another of her shrink-wrapped tops today, this one the same silvery blue as her eyes. And the heart-shaped neckline dipped just low enough so he could see that bloody turquoise butterfly flitting from the swell of one breast to the other. He should have followed through on his threat to buy her a uniform, but somehow he'd never gotten around to it.

His old resentment burned away. Bringing her to her knees wasn't proving as simple as he'd thought, but then he hadn't played his ace yet, either. He imagined those beautiful blue eyes filling with at least a few tears of honest regret. Finally, he'd be able to turn the last page on this very old, very tiresome chapter of his life.

"I wish your mum could see her precious boyo now. Comin' back home with his tail between his legs."

He turned the treadmill higher and picked up his pace, but it didn't help. His hands craved the familiar feel of brick and stone.

Gordon wasn't entirely useless. Even before the carriage house doorbell rang, he began to bark. Sugar Beth set aside the book that she'd swiped from Colin's amazing library. It continued to surprise her that Gordon trotted home with her every evening instead of staying with his beloved Colin. True, he generally managed to trip her as they walked across the yard, but he came along nonetheless, and the carriage house felt a little less lonely.

She reluctantly rose from the couch. Even when life was going well, good news didn't generally show up at the door at ten o'clock at night. As she made her way across the room, Gordon continued to bark. She pulled the curtain back from the sidelight and saw nothing more ominous than the outline of a young girl. "Quiet, Gordon."

She flipped on the porch light. As she opened the door, Gordon trotted out and took a few exploratory laps around the girl's ankles. She was maybe thirteen or fourteen, thin, coltish, and beautiful. But it was an awkward beauty, still in its infant stage, and probably making her miserable. She'd tucked her shoulder-length straight brown hair behind her ears. Her clothes were awful—a pair of shapeless pants at least two sizes too large and a ratty man's windbreaker that came to her hips. Her face was round and delicate, her wide mouth a little large for such fragile cheekbones. Even in the weak porch light, Sugar Beth could see her eyes, a pale blue, almost eerie with that dark hair.

Gordon trotted off the porch to poke in the bushes. The girl stared at Sugar Beth as if she were a ghost. Sugar Beth waited for her to say something and, when she didn't, finally spoke herself. "Can I help you?"

The girl licked her lips. "Yes, ma'am." She rubbed one of her thick-soled shoes over the vamp of the other. Her voice had a husky note that made her sound older than she looked.

There was something unsettling about her, almost familiar, although Sugar Beth had never seen her. She waited, even as she felt a ripple of apprehension.

The girl's throat worked as she swallowed. "I'm . . . uh . . . sort of . . . your niece."

"Niece? I don't understand."

But she did.

"I'm . . . Gigi Galantine."

Her name sounded so odd combined with his. *Gigi*. Ryan's daughter.

Longing, sharp and bittersweet, squeezed her heart. Ryan's child. The daughter who could have been hers. How was it that she'd managed to lose the only good men she'd ever loved? She'd lost Ryan through stupidity, and Emmett . . . Maybe as a punishment for what she'd done to Ryan.

But this girl was also Winnie's child, and that stopped her cold. No wonder she looked so familiar. Griffin Carey's silver-blue eyes had found their way into the next generation.

Gigi's hands flew from the windbreaker pockets. "I mean, I know this is really rude and everything, to show up like this, but I thought maybe you didn't know about me. And I know I'm not supposed to be here or anything, but I just wanted to say hi."

It had been a long day. Colin and his bare chest. The dinner party. Then she'd had an upsetting call from Delilah, who was bereft because Sugar Beth couldn't come to Family Day. She didn't need any more emotional complexity, which was exactly what this pale-eyed child promised.

"Aren't you out a little late?"

"Yes, ma'am. My dad'll kill me if he finds out."

Sugar Beth couldn't imagine even-tempered Ryan killing anyone, but then he was still only eighteen in her mind, lying next to her at the lake on a bright red beach towel telling her how—once they got married—they'd leave Parrish and go live in Atlanta.

"Maybe you'd better get home before that happens."

She looked down at her shoes, stubbed the chunky heel against a splintery floorboard. "I was sort of hoping maybe we could talk." Her head came up, a trace of defiance in her eyes. "Because you're my aunt and everything."

"I don't think your parents would be too happy about that."

"They're not the boss of me."

Sugar Beth took in the mulish set of her jaw, suppressed a sigh, and stepped back to let her in. Sooner or later, there'd be hell to pay for this, and sure as anything, Sugar Beth would be the one standing at the cash register.

"Really? I can come in." She nearly knocked Sugar Beth over in her eagerness to get inside.

Gordon hopped back up on the porch and followed her. "Just for a few minutes," Sugar Beth said as she shut the door. "I'm sure you have homework to do."

"No, ma'am. It's Friday night. And I was suspended."

Sugar Beth couldn't imagine Ryan and Winnie having a daughter who'd do anything serious enough to get suspended. Ryan had never gotten into any trouble, and Winnie wouldn't even turn in homework late. "I imagine your parents are thrilled."

"They hate me."

Despite her defiance, Sugar Beth thought, she looked lost. "I sincerely doubt that."

"Maybe not hate exactly, but they're really mad."

"I'm not surprised."

"You *can't* take their side!" Her small fists knotted at her waist. "You just can't."

Sugar Beth studied her more closely. Her face was flushed, her brow furrowed with tension. She looked as though Sugar Beth had betrayed her.

Her empty bed beckoned, and Sugar Beth took the path of least resistance. "All right. I'm on your side."

Gigi bit her lip, her silvery eyes filling with anxious hope. "Really?"

"Why not?"

"I knew you would be."

Terrific. Now what? "You want a Coke?"

"Yes, ma'am. If it wouldn't be too much trouble."

Good Southern manners beneath that angry defiance.

Sugar Beth headed into the kitchen where she extracted two cans of Coke from the refrigerator. As an afterthought, she unwrapped a Devil Dog and dropped it on one of Tallulah's Wedgwood plates. She considered the matter of glasses but decided late-night hospitality had its limits.

Gigi followed her into the kitchen, then crouched down to rub Gordon's stomach. He splayed his legs, ears flopping on the linoleum, his expression one of basset bliss. "You have a very nice dog." She rose as Sugar Beth set the cans on the table. Gordon hopped up, too, and rubbed his head against the girl's ankles, the friendliest pet on the planet. Gigi gazed back toward the living room. "You have some very nice antiques, too."

"They were my Aunt Tallulah's."

"I know. Mom used to bring me here sometimes. She didn't like kids very much."

"Tell me about it." She gestured toward the chair across from her.

Gigi moved a little awkwardly, as if she still hadn't quite gotten used to the new growth in those long legs. "It's hard to believe she was the object of Lincoln Ash's passion."

Sugar Beth smiled. "You know about that?"

"Everybody does." She settled at the table and began fiddling with the Coke can. The Seth Thomas clock ticked away in the next room. She reached down to scratch Gordon's head.

"How old are you, Gigi?"

"Thirteen."

Sugar Beth remembered thirteen. She'd grown real breasts

that year and made Ryan Galantine realize there was more to life than sports and Donkey Kong. She pushed the plate with the Devil Dog across the table. Gigi broke off a corner but didn't put it in her mouth.

"So how did you get suspended?"

"I never got suspended before, if that's what you're thinking."

"I wasn't thinking anything. I don't know you."

"It's sort of complicated." The Devil Dog disintegrated into a pile of crumbs as the story spilled out, slowly at first, then gathering momentum. Kelli Willman's betrayal. Gigi's friendship with Chelsea . . . The argument . . . The locker . . . The broken wrist . . . Gigi had a disconcerting way of mixing teenage slang with adult word choices. Her mother's daughter. As she wound down, she looked both miserable and defiant. She knew she'd done wrong, but she wasn't ready to cop to it.

If Sugar Beth had knocked somebody into a locker when she'd been thirteen, Diddie would have blown a smoke ring and said that well-bred young ladies didn't push people into lockers, even girls who deserved it. A lady simply walked away, threw a divine party, and neglected to invite the offending party.

Thanks a big heap, Diddie. Really useful advice.

This was as good a time as any to see what Gigi Galantine was made of. "I'll bet Chelsea's sorry she called you stuck-up."

Gigi liked that, and she nodded vigorously. "I'm not stuck-up. I mean, it's not my fault we're rich."

Sugar Beth waited. Gigi began chewing on her lip again, no longer looking quite so self-satisfied. "I wouldn't have said Chelsea was fat if she hadn't already been mean to me."

"But Chelsea is fat, right?"

"Her mom lets her eat a lot of junk."

Sugar Beth suppressed the urge to hide the Devil Dog under her napkin.

Gigi took another sip of Coke and kept her eyes on the can as she set it back down. "My mom drove me over there and made me apologize, but Chelsea wouldn't even look at me. Her wrist was in this cast."

Sugar Beth shoveled a little more dirt into the grave Gigi had dug for herself. "I guess people get what they deserve."

Gigi looked less certain. "I don't think she was feeling too good that day. And she doesn't have as many, you know, advantages as I have. Like a dad and being affluent and everything." Another storm cloud formed. "But her mom's like her best friend. *Her* mom understands things."

Unlike Gigi's mom who apparently didn't . . . "So what are you going to do?"

Gigi lifted her head, and Sugar Beth's skin prickled. For an instant, she felt as if she were looking into her own eyes.

"That's why I came here. So you could tell me."

"Honey, I'm the last person anybody should turn to for advice."

"But you're the only one who knows what it's like. I mean, we're sort of the same, aren't we?" Once again her words rushed out. "You were the richest girl in town, too, and I bet everybody thought you were stuck-up and egotistical. All the other kids' parents worked for your dad, just like they work for mine, and they must have said things you didn't like behind your back. But nobody ever messed with you like they do with me. And I want to be like that. I don't want people to mess with me. I want to be, you know . . . powerful."

So that was it. Sugar Beth bought some time by taking a sip of Coke. Gigi thought they were alike, but they weren't. This child didn't have Diddie telling her that she was better than everyone else, or letting her believe that unkindness was acceptable. Unlike Sugar Beth, Gigi had a decent shot at growing up without having to learn everything the hard way.

Her niece. Sugar Beth had gotten used to thinking of Delilah as her only family, but she and this child shared blood. She turned the idea over in her mind. "So you want me to tell you how I did it, is that right? How I manipulated people so they'd do what I wanted?"

Gigi nodded, and one part of Sugar Beth felt like applauding. *Good for you, baby girl. You're after your share of power in the world. And even if you're not going about it the right way . . . good for you.* She tucked an ankle under her hip. "You're sure about this?"

"Oh, yes," Gigi replied earnestly. "All the Seawillows say you were the most popular girl in school."

So Gigi knew about the Seawillows.

"They were my very best friends, but I don't see them anymore." Sugar Beth let that sink in for a moment. "I miss them."

"But you've got a lot of other friends. Important friends you made when you lived in California and Houston. It's not like you need the Seawillows anymore. I mean they're not important or anything."

A traitorous tightness gripped her throat. Her emotional rope felt frailer every day. "Real friends are always important."

It wasn't the answer Gigi wanted to hear, and Sugar Beth could see her quick brain getting ready to launch another battery of arguments. Before she had the chance, Sugar Beth said, "It's late, and I'm tired. I'll bet you are, too."

Gigi looked crushed. Sugar Beth reminded herself that she already had more trouble than she could handle. But she understood this child a lot better than she wanted to, and as she rose from the table, she heard herself say, "I have some time off on Sunday. Maybe we could talk then."

Gigi perked up. "I could get away in the afternoon. My parents have a concert."

Sugar Beth remembered the posters she'd seen in town. *The Ryan and Winnie Galantine Concert Series . . .*

"I don't think sneaking around's a good idea."

"My dad's pretty strict. It's the only way I can see you."

Sugar Beth could understand Winnie forbidding Gigi to see her, but Ryan? Exactly what did he think Sugar Beth would do to her? "All right." She rose from the table. "Sunday afternoon it is."

Gigi's face broke open in a smile. "Thanks!"

Sugar Beth couldn't send her home alone this late, so she got her jacket. "I'll walk with you."

"You don't have to."

"Yes, I do." She opened the door and followed Gigi outside. Gordon dashed ahead, naturally choosing to trot beside Gigi instead of his rightful owner. There were no sidewalks on Mockingbird Lane, so they walked in the street.

"My dad was your boyfriend, wasn't he?"

"A long time ago."

"And you and my mom didn't get along, right? Because of her being illegitimate and everything."

"It's complicated."

"I guess." She tilted her head and gazed up at the sky. "When I leave Parrish, I'm not ever coming back."

That's what we all say, honey.

Lights shone through the windows of the old brick French Colonial that would have looked at home on the Vieux Carré. Gigi stopped before they got too close. "You don't have to come any farther. My bedroom is over the back porch, and the railing's pretty easy to climb. It's real safe."

"I'll bet." She should make her go in the door and take her punishment, except she wasn't Gigi's parent, and she didn't have to do the right thing. "I'll watch just to make sure."

"Okay, but don't get too close. We have landscaping lights. Win-i-fred's idea."

Sugar Beth heard the scorn in Gigi's voice and issued a strict warning to herself. *No piling on, no matter how tempting.* She pushed away the image of Diddie's pearls encircling Winnie's neck. "I won't."

Moments later, she watched Gigi climb the wrought-iron post on the small back porch. It offered easy footholds, and before long she'd swung her leg onto the narrow roof. Just before she'd slipped open the window at the back, she turned and waved.

Sugar Beth stood too far in the shadows to be visible, but she waved back all the same.

I've brought your daughter home, Ryan. Safe and sound.

She sighed and gazed down at Gordon. "Come on, pal. Time for us to head for bed. We have a big day tomorrow."

The Duke was always magnificent, but tonight he had surpassed himself.

GEORGETTE HEYER, *These Old Shades*

Chapter 9

Colin finished shaving and made his way to his closet. Gordon usually accompanied him when he was getting dressed, but he'd been banished to the carriage house for the evening. The best thing about Sugar Beth was her dog.

A crash echoed from the vicinity of the kitchen. The caterer again. Or maybe Sugar Beth had dropped something. She'd been flying around the house all day: answering the door, rearranging flowers, arguing with the caterer. *Throwing herself heart and soul into her own comeuppance.*

He cursed as he stubbed his toe on the closet bench. He had no reason to feel guilty. There was a brutal simplicity about what would happen tonight, and since revenge wasn't anything he cared to devote his life to, this would be the end of it. A clean break. He pulled a shirt from a cedar hanger. Once the evening was over, he'd write her a big severance check and never think about her again. Which, admittedly, wouldn't be easy.

He'd just flipped the toggles on a pair of Bulgari cuff links when he heard a knock. "Go away."

She stormed in, just as he'd known she would. She was

conservatively dressed—for her at least—in black slacks and a white blouse with a V neck. If the angle was just right, as it was now, he could catch a glimpse of a lacy white bra. He missed those towering stilettos she'd shown up in, even though he was the one who'd made her change. He'd pointed out that she'd be on her feet all evening, but they both knew the truth. Guests wore dressy stilettos, not the staff. The staff also didn't pile its hair up and let long, unruly locks fall every which way—over the curve of a flushed cheek, along the nape of a slim neck, in front of small ears where a tiny pair of gold hearts swung—but he'd let that go.

"I'm fixin' to come to blows with that caterer," she exclaimed, the gold hearts bobbing. "The minute he said he was from California, I should have told you to find somebody else. He's usin' tofu in an hors d'oeuvre. And he didn't even deep-fry it!"

She was in full good ol' girl mode, something he was beginning to suspect she did when she was on the defensive, which seemed to be most of the time. The flush in her cheeks made her look healthier than when she'd arrived in Parrish, but her wrist bones were still frail, and the tracery of blue veins in the back of the hand she planted on her hip might have been a road map of all the disappointments life handed out to aging beauty queens.

"He just broke that new pitcher I bought you. And did you know he was plannin' to use disposable aluminum pans on the buffet table? I had to remind him this was a dinner party, not a fish fry."

As she ranted on, he wanted to order her to stop putting so much energy into a party that wasn't hers. Right from the beginning, he'd told her she'd be waiting on his guests, but she hadn't blinked. He'd even driven the point home by instructing her to dress appropriately. Surprising how easy it was to play the bastard once you set your mind to it. If only she'd bow those proud shoulders just once and concede defeat, he could let this go. But she wouldn't. So here they were. And, now, he simply wanted the whole thing done with.

". . . make sure you take the cost of that pitcher out of his check when you pay him tonight."

"I'll do that." The caterer had probably broken the pitcher because he was staring down her blouse.

"No, you won't. Except for me, you're Mr. Big Spender. Even with that incompetent West Coast weasel of a caterer."

"Such prejudice from someone who once lived in California herself."

"Well, sure, but I was drunk most of the time."

He caught his smile just in time. He wouldn't give in to that seductive charm. Her self-deprecating sense of humor was another manipulation, her way of making sure no one else threw the first punch.

"Is that all?"

She eyed his dark trousers and long-sleeved grape-colored shirt. "If only I hadn't sent your dueling pistols to the cleaners."

He'd promised himself he'd stop sparring with her, but the words came out anyway. "At least I still have my riding crop. Just the thing, I've heard, for disciplining an unruly servant."

She liked that, and she flashed him a wide smile on her way out the door. "You can be funny for a stiff."

The word *stiff* hung in the air behind her like the scent of sex-rumpled bedsheets. If only she knew . . .

So far, so good, Sugar Beth thought to herself. The house looked beautiful with flowers everywhere and candles glowing. In the foyer, the flames of a dozen white tapers reflected off the shiny black finish of the baby grand. The young woman Colin had hired to play looked up from the keyboard and smiled. Sugar Beth smiled back, then took a last glance at the living room. Creamy pillar candles nested in the magnolia leaves she'd arranged across the fireplace mantel, and clusters of cut-glass votives flickered on the smaller tables she'd positioned here and in the sunroom.

Keep moving. Don't think.

Not all the changes Colin had made to the house were bad. Without the fussy wallpaper, the downstairs had a more spacious feel, and the efficient new kitchen was a definite improvement over the old cramped one. She also liked the way the sunroom kept the back of the house from being too gloomy. But she still missed the sight of her father's keys tossed on a table and the scent of Diddie's perfume permeating every room.

In a few hours, it'll be over.

She headed to the dining room to make certain the caterer hadn't moved anything. The pepperberry sprays she'd wound through the arms of the chandelier made the room homier, and the centerpiece of pale orange Sari roses and deep gold Peruvian lilies glowed against the mocha linen tablecloth just as she'd known they would. She'd already dimmed the hallway chandelier, and now she did the same in the dining room. The old walls embraced her. *You should have been mine,* she thought. *I don't deserve you—I didn't even want you—but you should have been mine all the same.*

She wanted to believe she'd worked so hard on this party to prove to Colin that she wasn't a screwup, but it was more than that. She'd needed to see this house shine again. And she'd needed to keep herself so busy she wouldn't brood over the part she'd play tonight.

For a moment she let herself pretend she was still the daughter of Frenchman's Bride, that tonight's guests were the ones she would have invited if she hadn't worked so hard at ruining her life: the Seawillows; Ryan; batty old Mrs. Carmichael, who'd died ten years ago but used to tell everyone that Sugar Beth was just as sweet as her name; Bobby Jarrow and Woody Newhouse; Pastor Ferrelle and his wife;

Aunt Tallulah, even though she'd disapprove of Sugar Beth's arrangements.

Where are your grandmother's cheese straws? Bless your heart, Sugar Beth, even you know you can't have a party at Frenchman's Bride without Martha Carey's cheese straws.

The imaginary guest list evaporated. The last thing she wanted to see tonight was a familiar face. Glassware tinkled as Renaldo, the college boy who'd be serving drinks, headed toward the bar in the living room with a tray of empty champagne glasses. "Ernie says he needs you in the kitchen."

"All right. Thanks." *Don't think about what's coming. Just do your job.*

Ernie, the hapless caterer, looked like a demonic Porky Pig with his pink face, bald head, and bushy eyebrows. He'd forgotten toothpicks for the hors d'oeuvre trays, so Sugar Beth dug some out. She'd just handed them over when the doorbell rang. Her stomach pitched.

Oh, no you don't. You're not wimping out now. She straightened her shoulders and made her way to the front door.

Colin had gotten there first. He stood in the entrance hall with two men and a woman whose chic black outfit had New York City written all over it. One of the men was fiftyish and swarthy, the other a trim Ivy Leaguer. This could only be Colin's agent, his agent's wife, and Neil Kirkpatrick, his editor. Colin had met them for lunch at the Parrish Inn, where they were spending the night, but this was the first Sugar Beth had seen of them.

The woman's eyes widened as she took in the sweeping staircase and candlelit foyer. "Colin, I wasn't prepared. This is incredible."

Sugar Beth absorbed the compliment as if it had been given to her. Frenchman's Bride wasn't the last whistle-stop on anybody's nowhere line.

The soft ballad coming from the piano, the marble floor glowing in the velvety light from the chandelier, the candles shimmering . . . Everything so beautiful. The house swept her up in its spell, and she imagined she caught a whiff of Diddie's perfume. It made her smile. She walked toward the guests. Extended her hand. "Welcome to Frenchman's Bride."

The woman cocked her head. The men looked confused. Sugar Beth realized what she'd done, and her fingers convulsed as she snatched back her hand. Colin stepped forward, his voice quiet. "Take Mrs. Lucato's coat, Sugar Beth."

Her face burned with embarrassment as she forced herself to reach out again. "Of course."

She couldn't look at him, couldn't bear knowing he was watching her. In the space of a few seconds, she'd undone ten days of wisecracks and pigheadedness, ten days of never once letting him see how much it hurt to be a servant in the house that should have been hers.

Somehow she made her way to the laundry room where she'd set up a rack for coats. She'd been ready to introduce herself to them all, just as if she had the right. Her skin felt hot. She wanted to run away, but she was trapped. Trapped in this house, this town. Trapped with a man who wished her nothing but harm.

The doorbell rang again, faint but audible. She thought of Delilah, put steel to her spine, and went to answer it.

This time Colin's guests were an elderly couple. She managed to admit them with nothing more than a polite nod. After that, the arrivals came more quickly until Mayor Aaron Leary and his wife arrived.

"Why, Sugar Beth . . . It's been a long time," he said.

"Yes, it has."

"This is my wife, Charise."

The model-slim woman at his side hadn't come from Parrish, and she looked confused about why her husband was presenting her to the maid.

"It's nice to meet you, Mrs. Leary." She wouldn't make the mistake of overstepping the bounds of familiarity again, not when Colin stood close by waiting for her to do just that.

Several couples arrived from Oxford, professors, she gathered. Everyone greeted Colin as if he were one of them, which he'd never be, not in a thousand years. She felt him watching her every move. He wanted this to be horrible. It was his payback. She knew that, made herself accept it.

Jewel Myers showed up, along with the curly-haired blonde who'd worked for her at the bookstore. Sugar Beth remembered how Ellie used to send Jewel out to the veranda with a pitcher to serve Sugar Beth and her friends.

"This lemonade isn't pink, Jewel. Take it back and tell Ellie we want pink."

Jewel studied Sugar Beth's black slacks and white blouse. "Well, well . . . The world gets more interesting all the time."

Only last week, Sugar Beth had been hoping for a friendship with Jewel. Now she realized how impossible that was. "Would you like me to take your shawl?"

"I'll keep it for now."

Voices from the past echoed in her head. *"I don't want ham, Jewel. Tell Ellie to make me peanut butter and honey."*

"Yez'm, Miz Scarlett."

Jewel had actually said that to Sugar Beth, and Sugar Beth wanted to believe she'd laughed, but that was probably only wishful thinking.

In the living room, Colin stood with his head tilted toward one of the professors, but she knew it was merely a pose. Every bit of him was focused on her. *Payback time.*

"I don't think Meredith wants to keep her coat," Jewel said, amusement dancing in her eyes.

Sugar Beth welcomed the chance to escape, and as she hung up the coat, she sent out a little prayer. *Okay, God, it's time to ease up, all right? I get the fact that I was horrible. But I've tried to mend my ways. Some of them, anyway . . . So could you back off now?*

God, however, had better things to do than listen to the prayers of a tarnished Southern belle, because the next time she opened the door, the Seawillows were standing on the other side.

Not all of them. Only Leeann and Merylinn. But they were enough. Sugar Beth stared into their faces, so familiar, yet changed, and she remembered how Colin had danced around the truth. She should have known they'd be here. Part of her must have known.

Leeann and Merylinn stared back, not surprised, because they'd been expecting exactly this. Leeann's eyes sparkled with malicious delight. "Why, Sugar Beth. We heard you were back in town."

"Imagine running into you here of all places," Merylinn said.

Once the two of them had been her closest friends. But she'd gone to Ole Miss and forgotten them. Leeann was a nurse now and a good twenty pounds heavier than her high school weight. She'd been one of the best athletes in the senior class. She wore a bright yellow silk sheath more suited to July than early March. Merylinn's ribbed-knit tangerine suit fit her tall, large frame, but she still had too heavy a hand with makeup. Tallulah had said she taught high school math. It was hard to imagine Merylinn, Sugar Beth's favorite companion in mischief, as a teacher.

Sugar Beth realized she was blocking the doorway and stepped aside. For the first time, she noticed the men. Deke Jasper, Merylinn's husband, had lost some of his auburn hair, but he was still square-jawed and good-looking. He'd always been a soft touch, and she thought she saw a flash of sympathy in his eyes. Leeann's date was a small neat man who wore too much cologne.

"Hey, Sugar Beth. Remember me? Brad Simmons."

He'd been one of those boys who hadn't fit into any particular crowd. At the eighth-grade spring dance, he'd asked her to dance, and she'd almost wet her pants laughing because he was short and she was Sugar Beth Carey.

She sensed Colin standing a few feet away, waiting to see if she'd fall apart. She bit the inside of her lip and began to close the door, only to see two more couples making their way up the front sidewalk. Heidi and Amy, along with their husbands. She should have known. Where there was one Sea-willow, there were bound to be more.

Just that morning, she and Colin had smiled at each other when Gordon had trotted into the kitchen with one of his ears turned inside out and an empty cracker box in his mouth. Now she hated him for that smile.

Heidi Dwyer—Pettibone now—still had big hazel eyes and unruly curly red hair. A sterling silver teddy bear hung from a chain around her neck, and her bright purple sweater was appliquéd with a bouquet of kites flying in the March breeze. Sugar Beth imagined a bureau stuffed full of sweaters appropriate to every season and holiday. In the old days, Heidi had made clothes for their Barbies.

Heidi's husband, Phil, had played football with Ryan. He was as thin as he'd been in high school, but now he had the tanned, wiry look of a distance runner. During the summer between junior and senior year, all of them had spent their weekends at the lake making out and drinking the beer that one of the busboys at the Lakehouse had smuggled to them. Phil and Heidi had been going out then, but Phil had tried to kiss Sugar Beth. She hadn't wanted to spoil his friendship with Ryan, so she'd never told him about it, but she'd told Heidi and made her cry.

Amy still didn't wear makeup, and the gold cross visible in the open neck of her matronly pink dress was a larger version of the one she'd worn in high school, when she and Sugar Beth had taken over Ellie's kitchen to bake cookies. The brown-haired man in glasses must be her husband.

"Hi, Sugar Beth." Amy was too religious to walk past her. But just because Amy had forgiven the sinner didn't mean she was obligated to forgive the sin, and she neglected to introduce her husband. Instead, she headed straight for Colin, and her warm greeting made no secret of where her loyalty lay.

Leeann waved at someone in the living room. She'd been Sugar Beth's oldest friend. They'd met in nursery school, where, according to their mothers, Leeann had tried to take a play telephone away from Sugar Beth, and Sugar Beth had conked her over the head with it. When Leeann had started to cry, Sugar Beth had cried along with her, then handed over her new Miss Piggy watch to make her stop. Of all the Seawillows, Leeann had felt the most betrayed when Sugar Beth had turned her back on them for Darren Tharp.

"Colin, sweetie." She plastered herself against the teacher who'd nearly flunked her because she wasn't smart enough to b.s. her way through his essay questions. But the fact that Leeann probably still thought Beowulf was a WWE wrestler didn't seem to bother him now. As he gave her a warm hug, he didn't even try to look down her dress.

Sugar Beth finally let herself notice what she hadn't wanted to see. Leeann was wearing a coat.

It was a jacket, really. Quilted brown wool that was too heavy to wear inside. Something the maid would be expected to hang up. Leeann quivered with delight as she shrugged out of it and tossed it to Sugar Beth. "Be careful with that. It's my favorite."

A dozen insults skipped through Sugar Beth's head, but she didn't utter a single one of them because she'd turned her back on her oldest friend for a worthless shortstop named Darren Tharp.

All of them watched her as she made her way across the foyer. The jacket on her arm weighed a thousand pounds.

The bell rang again. She kept moving. Didn't let herself hear it. Almost made her escape.

"Get that, would you, Sugar Beth?" Colin said quietly.

Dread curled in her stomach. *Where there was one Seawillow, there were bound to be more.*

The walk back to the door took forever. No more Seawillows lived in Parrish. All the rest had moved away. But some of their boyfriends had stayed . . .

She opened the door.

He looked as familiar as if she'd seen him just that morning, yet the years had left their mark, and as she gazed into his eyes, she knew the teenage boy she remembered was a mere shadow of the man he'd become. He was even more handsome than she'd imagined he would be, confident and polished, his blond hair a shade darker but his eyes the same warm caramel. His black-and-white-herringbone sports coat was perfectly coordinated with a subtly striped shirt. Both pieces were beautifully made and very expensive. But despite his astounding good looks, she felt no pangs of passion. None of the hot rush of desire that Colin Byrne aroused. Instead, she experienced a mixture of nostalgia and bone-deep regret.

Leeann's wool jacket burned her arm. The pianist began playing a Sting ballad. Ryan's family had been poor compared with her own. Their house was small and cramped, their cars old, but she'd never cared about that. Even when he'd been a boy, she'd seen his worth. For that, at least, she could give herself credit. Then again, maybe it had just been sex.

"Hello, Sugar Beth."

She tried to get his name out, but it stuck to the roof of her mouth, and all she could manage was a nod. She stepped back awkwardly to let them in. Because, of course, Ryan hadn't come alone.

Winnie had replaced Diddie's pearls with a bezel-set diamond, and matching studs glittered through her dark hair. She wore a slim-fitting basil green pantsuit with an emerald sequin camisole. The color would have washed out Sugar Beth, but Winnie had Griffin's olive tones, and she looked stunning.

She didn't show any of the spiteful delight that Leeann and Merylinn had shown. As their eyes met, she exhibited only a deep, fierce dignity. Let all the world see that the lumpy outcast had turned into a very beautiful, very wealthy swan.

Ryan slipped his arm around Winnie's shoulders. Sugar Beth got the point.

Colin stepped forward. Winnie looked small and feminine

standing between the two men. Sugar Beth had forgotten how petite she was. She and Colin exchanged a social kiss.

"Winnie, you look smashing tonight. But, then, you always do." His smile told Sugar Beth that, however fond he might be of Leeann and the other Seawillows, his friendship with Winnie ran deeper.

"I was afraid we'd be late. Ryan had an emergency at the plant."

"Equipment trouble with one of the lines," Ryan said. "But we're up and running again."

"Glad to hear it." Colin and Ryan shook hands in the easy way of men who were comfortable with each other. They were a study in contrasts: Ryan fair and fine-featured. Colin dark, brooding, and enigmatic. She fled.

By the time she reached the laundry room, she was shaking. Nothing would make her go back out there. She was leaving and never coming back. Her purse? Where had she left it? Where—

I love you, my Sugar Beth. And you love me, too, don't you?

Delilah . . . Just for a moment, she'd let herself forget. Preserving her pride wouldn't put a stop to the bills that were coming due for her stepdaughter's care. Once again she'd reached another of life's turning points. Emmett would have called tonight a golden opportunity to show what she was made of.

Glass, my darling. Just like one of Daddy's windows.

Quitcher bitchin', love, and do what has to be done.

Easy for you to say. You're dead.

But you're not, and Delilah depends on you.

She stabbed a hanger into the sleeves of Leeann's jacket. She could almost taste the sweetness of revenge on Colin's tongue. He expected her to run—wanted her to run—and the longer she locked herself away back here, the more satisfaction she was giving him.

She turned to the door and drew a deep breath. It was time to test herself. Again.

"There is something excessively vulgar about persons under the sway of strong emotions."

GEORGETTE HEYER, *The Corinthian*

Chapter 10

𝒞olin watched as Sugar Beth came into the living room, carrying a tray of canapés and a stack of cocktail napkins. The Seawillows lifted their heads, carrion birds spotting their prey. They'd flocked together, leaving their husbands to fend for themselves. Winnie, the former outcast who'd become their leader, shone in their midst like the diamonds she wore. She took a sip from her wineglass, neither ignoring Sugar Beth's presence nor staring at her as the others were doing.

Ryan stood in the archway, separated from the rest, but discreetly watching Sugar Beth. Colin tried to tap into the sense of righteousness that had fueled him ever since she'd returned to Parrish, but he couldn't find it. Watching her being forced to take Leeann's coat had been more than enough to satisfy his need for revenge. Now he simply wanted the evening over so he could put Sugar Beth and all the mayhem she caused behind him.

The color burned high in her cheeks as she crossed the room, but instead of avoiding the Seawillows, like any sensible person, she headed straight for them. Colin could feel their bad will creeping toward her like radioactive waste. She'd hurt them all, and they hadn't forgotten. As she forged ahead, he wished she had at least a little ammunition to defend herself: the black stilettos he'd forced her to abandon, one of her shrink-wrapped tops, the turquoise butterfly.

She held out the tray to Leeann. "Shrimp?"

Leeann touched a finger to her chin. "Give me a minute, will you? I'm trying to imagine what Diddie would think if she could see her Sugar Baby now."

Instead of wiping the smirk from Leeann's face with one of her cutting remarks, as the old Sugar Beth would have done, the tall blonde with the shrimp tray didn't say a word. She just stood there and let them look her over as if she'd grown fungus.

Colin hated this. Why didn't she cut her losses and walk away? Did she need that painting so badly? He could think of no other reason she'd be so willing to trade in her self-respect.

"Are the shrimp fresh?" Heidi asked, nose in the air.

As a host, he should have been offended, but this didn't have anything to do with him or the shrimp. He willed Sugar Beth to launch a counterattack, but she didn't.

"I'm sure they are."

Heidi took a shrimp, and Leeann, full of self-righteousness, reached for Winnie's half-full glass. "Winnie's champagne needs refreshing. Get it for her."

He'd been the evening's architect, so how could he blame them for such naked displays of delight? When he'd made his plan, he'd seen this as the perfect way to settle scores. A gentleman's revenge, if you will—straight to the point but without bloodshed. Now, however, his old bitterness seemed like a grainy piece of film that had played too long in his head.

Sugar Beth slipped the napkins into the same hand that balanced the tray, and took the flute.

His thirst for revenge turned to ashes in his mouth, and the old, destructive desire to slay dragons took over. He moved to her side. "I'll take care of that."

She pulled the glass away before he could touch it. "Don't you trouble yourself, Mr. Byrne. I'm more than happy to get it." She set off for the bar, chin high, posture erect, a queen with a shrimp tray in her hand.

"Well, la-di-da." Leeann frowned, disappointed that she hadn't gotten more of a reaction. "She's still a snot."

Heidi craned her neck to watch Sugar Beth at the bar. "Did you see her face when Leeann gave her Winnie's glass? I don't know about y'all, but this is the best party I've ever been to."

Amy looked worried. "I shouldn't be enjoying this so much."

"Have a ball," Merylinn retorted. "You can beg Jesus for forgiveness tomorrow."

"She just wrote us out of her life," Heidi said. "The minute she got to college, it was like we didn't exist anymore."

"Plus what she did to Colin," Amy added.

"She swore it was true," Leeann said to him. "But we never believed her."

Colin had heard this before, and he didn't want to hear it again. "Water under the bridge and all that. Let's let it go."

They stared at him, but before they could pounce, Sugar Beth returned with Winnie's glass. Winnie took it without looking at her, just as if Sugar Beth were invisible. He should congratulate himself. This was drawing-room justice at its finest.

"I finished reading that Chinese author you recommended," Winnie said. "You were right. I enjoyed the book enormously."

Colin felt a stab of irritation. Winnie, more than any of them, knew what it felt like to be an outcast, and he wanted better from her. The hypocrisy brought him up short. Was he now going to blame Winnie for what he'd put in motion?

Sugar Beth disappeared toward the kitchen, and he let himself relax a bit. Maybe she'd come to her senses and leave. The old Sugar Beth certainly would have. He gamely plunged into a discussion of the Chinese author. He sounded pompous, but he didn't let that stop him. And, blast it, he wasn't pompous, no matter what Sugar Beth said. He simply liked encouraging people to talk about books.

"Unless there's a naked man on the cover, I prob'ly won't read it," Merylinn said. "Maybe they'll make a movie."

All of them laughed, except Winnie. He followed her gaze and saw that Sugar Beth had come back from the kitchen, and this time she was heading straight for Ryan.

Ryan enjoyed parties with good music and great food, parties where old friends could mix with enough new people to make it interesting, but he hadn't wanted to attend tonight. At the same time, he'd barely been able to think of anything else. Finally he'd see her again.

"Colin's gonna rub her nose in it, just you wait and see," Leeann had crowed the last time they'd all been together. "He wouldn't be human if he didn't."

The others had chirped in with their opinions, while only Winnie remained silent.

He didn't have to see Sugar Beth to know she was coming toward him. It had been that way in high school, too. Even before he'd turned a corner, he knew she'd be standing on the other side.

Luv U 4-Ever.

He shut out that rusty whisper. They'd hardly been Romeo and Juliet. More like Ken and Barbie as they'd so often been teased. He'd lapped at her ankles like a lovesick pup, and she'd been exactly what she was now, a woman born too beautiful and too rich to worry about a small thing like integrity.

"Hey, there," she said, her voice huskier than he remembered. "I've got some mediocre bruschetta waiting for a man with an appetite, but stay away from that other stuff. It's tofu."

He turned slowly.

Even though she was more plainly dressed than the other women, she'd managed to outshine them just by the way she held herself. As he studied her, he saw that she'd left behind the fresh beauty of her girlhood. She was too thin, drawn around the eyes. Maybe she looked a little used. Not used up. Just no longer new. At the same time, nothing could hide her thoroughbred's pedigree.

She held out the tray she was carrying. "Look at you," she said softly. "Mr. Big Shot." She didn't speak sarcastically but fondly, more like a proud mother than a faithless former girlfriend.

He felt oddly deflated, and he bristled. "No complaints. I'm right at home in your father's office."

"I'll bet you are." If anything, her smile grew more generous, which only provoked him.

"You never know when life's going to throw you a curveball, do you, Sugar Beth?"

"You sure don't."

A pang pierced him, along with a flood of emotions he couldn't quite interpret. He didn't like the affection in her eyes. He wanted something more dangerous, something more satisfying. A little anguish over what she'd turned her back on, maybe. A few remnants of leftover lust to soothe his ego, although, considering his teenage clumsiness, that wasn't too likely.

"Take it out, Ryan. I changed my mind. It hurts. Take it out."

But it had been too late. *"Oh, God, I'm sorry."*

She'd laughed. *"It's okay. Let's do it again."*

And they had. Again and again until they'd finally gotten it right. They'd done it in her Camaro. On blankets at the lake. Next to the furnace in Leeann's parents' basement. And still it hadn't been enough. When they got married, they promised, they'd do it at least three times a day. *Luv U 4-Ever.*

"Sugar Beth, I'd like to speak with you for a moment."

He hadn't heard Colin approach, and he felt an unexpected

surge of protectiveness as Sugar Beth's smile faded. "Sorry, boss. No time for chitchat. I have to serve these horse-doovers before they get soggy."

"Forget that."

But she'd already taken off.

The pianist switched to a Faith Hill song. Colin glowered at her retreating back. Ryan took a sip of beer and shook his head. "What the hell did you think you were doing?"

Colin sighed. "It seemed like a good idea at the time."

"It wasn't."

"Tell me something I don't know."

Colin's sense of foreboding grew stronger as he watched Sugar Beth move around the room with her tray. Ted Willowby couldn't keep his eyes off her, and the kid at the bar was making an idiot of himself whenever she stopped for refills. She offered a napkin to the head librarian at the university and fetched a drink for Charise Leary. Then she slipped on her mask of cool indifference and headed right back to serve the Seawillows.

The scotch he'd been drinking sloshed in his stomach. She'd break before she bent an inch. He wanted to drag her from the room and kiss the stubbornness right out of her.

"She still thinks she owns the world," Ryan said.

Except Sugar Beth wasn't the toxic teenager they remembered. He thought about saying as much to Ryan, but since he'd only begun to understand that himself, he kept silent.

He heard a soft gasp and turned his head just in time to see Merylinn tip her glass of red wine right down the front of Sugar Beth's blouse.

Sugar Beth fled to Colin's bedroom. She wasn't going to let them make her cry. She'd cried enough self-pitying tears in her life to drown a goat, and all it had gotten her was a big fat nothing. Wine soaked her blouse like blood from a fresh kill. She made herself take a deep breath, but it didn't help break the traffic jam in her throat. Might as well call a spade a spade. That traffic jam came from shame. There was a big difference between knowing people still hated your guts and seeing it in their faces.

She found tissues in the bathroom to blow her nose. She wasn't running away. The Seawillows could take all the bites out of her they wanted, but she refused to go anywhere. She was like a kid's punching toy. Knock her down as many times as you wanted, and she'd still get back up, right?

But she didn't feel like getting up as she pulled off her blouse and swabbed her chest with Colin's washcloth. The wine had left a red blotch on her bra, and she couldn't do much about that. Truth was, she couldn't do much about anything. As she headed for his bedroom, she felt as fragile as the spun-sugar castle that had once decorated her eighth birthday cake.

Colin walked in.

"Get out," she said, marching into his closet.

He didn't mention that this was his room. Instead, he stood just inside the closet door, the same place she'd stood a few hours earlier while he'd been dressing. "I want you to go back to the carriage house right now," he said with a gentleness that stung more than the hostilities downstairs.

"Do you now?" She flipped through his shirts.

"Enough is enough."

"But I haven't bled yet." She whipped one of his white shirts from the hanger and shoved her arms in the sleeves.

"I don't want your blood, Sugar Beth."

"You want every last drop. Now get out of my way." She started to push past him, but he grabbed her arm, forcing her to look up.

Normally she liked looking at him, but now those arrogant jade eyes had softened with a compassion she hated. "Hands off, bud."

He eased his grip, but he didn't release her, and his words fell over her, as cool and light as snowflakes. "Do I have to throw you out?"

She fought the urge to bury her face in his neck. If he wanted to go all sensitive on her, that was his problem because she wasn't having any of it. "You betcha, suckuh." She pulled away. "Throw me out because that's the only way I'm leaving."

"This isn't a battle."

"Tell them. Better yet, tell yourself." She worked furiously at the buttons.

"I made a mistake," he said. And then, in that same Father Caring voice, "Go home now. I'm firing you. I'll be over first thing in the morning to write you a check."

A big one, she'd bet anything. "You and your pity money can go to hell, Your Grace. The guest of honor doesn't leave in the middle of her party."

"I planned this party before I hired you."

"But you hadn't planned the entertainment. You waited till I came along for that."

He didn't deny it. Whenever she'd asked who he'd invited, he'd danced around the truth. "Let me." He pushed her hands away from the buttons. "You're making a muddle of it."

"I can do it myself."

"Right. Just like you do everything." She tried to back away, but he held her fast. His hands began moving along the row of buttons, unfastening the ones she'd gotten wrong, refastening. "You don't need anybody, do you?" he said. "Because you're the biggest badass in town."

"Believe it."

"Armed and dangerous. Letting everybody know how tough you are."

"A hell of a lot tougher than a weasel like you," she countered.

"Undoubtedly."

"You're such a wuss."

He cocked an eyebrow. "I like to think I have a certain female sensibility."

"I'll bet you wear lace panties."

"I doubt they'd fit."

He reached her breasts, and the backs of his fingers brushed the curve of flesh, sending little feathers of sensation skittering across her skin. The feeling scared her more than the idea of going back downstairs. He exuded exactly the kind of male power that had brought her down in the past.

But not this time. No matter what.

She pulled away and began knotting the shirttails at her waist. "I sure haven't seen any women around here. How long since you've had a date? With a female, that is."

"I'm on sabbatical."

"That's what they all say right before the closet door bangs them in the ass."

"Go home, Sugar Beth. You've already shown them what you're made of. You don't have anything left to prove."

"Now why would I leave a party just when it's getting fun?"

"Because this particular party is ripping your heart out."

"You couldn't be more wrong, bucko. I've buried two parents and a pair of husbands. This isn't bothering me at all." She pushed past him and headed for the door. This time he didn't try to stop her.

Colin hadn't thought things could get worse, but he was wrong. Sugar Beth refused to back down. With the mask of polite detachment fixed on her face, she continued fetching drinks and passing hors d'oeuvre trays. When he couldn't stand watching her any longer, he grabbed the last tray away from her and earned a syrupy smile and a laser-hot put-down for his efforts.

As she'd stood in his closet, her white bra stained with wine, even his desire for her couldn't mask his self-disgust. He began moving around the room, trying to concentrate on his duties as a host. Everyone here had helped him with *Reflections* in one way or the other—the librarians, the historians. Winnie had critiqued his manuscript when he'd needed a fresh perspective. Jewel and Aaron Leary had given him entrée to the town's African American population and made him understand the mind-set of its older members. The Seawillows had helped him sort out fact from gossip.

Colin saw Winnie standing next to one of the small tables that had been set up in the sunroom. She was gazing out into the darkness beyond the windows. On the other side of the peninsula that divided off the kitchen, Sugar Beth and the caterer were adding the final touches to the serving platters. Ryan and the Seawillows had drifted into the sunroom, along with a few of the other guests, but Winnie had separated herself from all of them. She looked small in comparison to Sugar Beth, but not as defenseless.

"A memorable party," she said as Colin approached her.

He made a futile attempt to distance himself from the cruelty he'd set in motion. "I planned it before she came back to Parrish."

"I know."

Unlike so many other women, Winnie wasn't afraid of conversational lulls, but tonight her silence made him edgy, and he was the one who finally broke it. "Merylinn shouldn't have dumped the wine on her."

"You're right. But I loved it, Colin. I'd be lying if I pretended I didn't enjoy every drop."

He understood, and he only felt angrier with himself.

His editor had drifted into the sunroom. The goodwill of a publishing house wasn't to be taken lightly, even by one of its mega authors, and Colin should go over and talk with him. Instead, he watched Sugar Beth carry a salad bowl toward the dining room. "It happened such a long time ago," he said. "When it comes right down to it, we were all kids. Do you ever think about just letting it go?"

He knew he'd botched it even before he heard her quiet intake of breath.

"She's getting to you, isn't she? Just like she gets to every other man who flies too close to her web."

"Of course not."

Her look of betrayal said she didn't believe him. He didn't believe it himself. He remembered the rush of heat he'd felt as he'd buttoned the shirt Sugar Beth had taken from his closet.

"I always thought you were the one person who'd be immune," she said.

"We all have a lot of rubbish in our pasts. Having her here has simply made me realize that, at some point, we need to step over the piles and get on with it."

She fingered the diamond solitaire at her throat. "You think I haven't gotten on with it?"

"I'm only talking about myself," he said carefully.

"More power to you, then, if you're ready to step over being accused of sexual assault. Me, I'm not that evolved."

"Winnie . . ."

"She made my life a nightmare, Colin. Do you know I used to throw up before school, then stuff myself with junk food to try to feel better? She never passed up a chance to humiliate me. In junior high I plotted which hallways to walk down so I wouldn't run into her. All she had to do was look at me, and I'd start tripping over my feet. If one of the other girls showed any signs of seeking me out, she'd zero right in on her and tell her only losers hung out with Winnie Davis. She was vicious, Colin, and that kind of viciousness doesn't go away. It's part of a person's character. So if you think she's changed, then I feel sorry for you. Now, excuse me. I haven't had a chance to speak with Charise."

He suppressed the urge to go after her. On Monday, he'd stop by her shop and smooth the waters. By then he'd have gotten over his urge to defend Sugar Beth. By then, he wouldn't be tempted to point out that it couldn't have been easy for her either, being forced to go to school with her father's illegitimate child and having someone like Diddie as her role model. Maybe Sugar Beth had fought back in the only way she'd known how.

More of his guests drifted into the sunroom, drawn by the

smell of food. The Seawillows cornered Neil, and he over-heard them asking if he knew any good diet books, and was he personally acquainted with Reese Witherspoon? Sugar Beth came up to him, but he wasn't fooled for a moment by her deference. "Excuse me for interrupting, Mr. Byrne, but dinner's ready. Your guests can help themselves to the buffet."

She'd emphasized her servitude by wrapping one of the caterer's aprons around her waist, and he wanted to rip it off her, wanted to rip everything off and carry her back into his closet. "You've worked hard enough. Get a plate and join us."

The Seawillows heard. Their heads circled like vultures. Winnie's back stiffened, and Ryan headed for the bar. But the wintry bonfires that blazed in Sugar Beth's eyes told him not to expect a thank-you note anytime soon. "Now aren't you the dearest thing takin' such good care of the hired help, but I've about stuffed myself already on those hors d'oeuvres. I swan, I couldn't eat another bite."

Dear God, he'd exhumed Diddie.

"Is there anything else you need?" she cooed, her eyes daring him to take this any further. "I'll be more than happy to get it for you."

She was dismissing him like one of her ex-husbands, and the Irish stubbornness he'd inherited from his father rose up to bite him. "You can get rid of that bloody apron and join us for dinner."

The out-of-town guests who overheard looked puzzled, but the Seawillows understood, and hisses of displeasure came from their beaks. By tomorrow, his betrayal would be all over Parrish. Hell, sooner than that. Their fingers were itching to whip out their cell phones so they could be the first to pass the word that Colin Byrne had crossed over to the dark side.

Sugar Beth had the gall to pat his arm. "You got your med-ications mixed up again, didn't you, bless your heart. We'll call your shrink tomorrow and straighten it out." She reached for Aaron Leary's empty wineglass. "Let me take that, Mr.

Mayor, so you have both hands free for the buffet." And off she went, little drops of Colin's blood trickling from her sparkly fangs.

Neil came up next to him. "The ongoing drama of life in a small Southern town. You should write a book."

"Smashing idea."

Neil gazed toward the dining room. "She's just like you described her. Why didn't you tell me she'd come back?"

"It's been complicated."

"Maybe we could get a trilogy out of the Parrish books after all."

Colin had no trouble interpreting his hopeful expression. *Last Whistle-stop* had been the most successful book in Neil's editorial career, and *Reflections* would do even better. Neal wanted a third book about Parrish instead of a lengthy generational novel about Irish and English families.

Neil balked as Colin began to steer him toward the buffet table in the dining room. "Not yet. The Seawillows just went in. They're very scary women."

"Imagine what they were like when Sugar Beth led them."

"I don't have to," Neil said. "I've read *Reflections.*"

But no one else had, and once again, Colin found himself wondering how the citizens of Parrish were going to react to the second book about their town when so many of its featured players were still around. He gazed toward the dining room.

The Seawillows chose to eat at the smaller tables in the sunroom. After all his guests were served, Colin disguised his lack of appetite by making the rounds of the other tables. Eventually, he returned to the sunroom and propped himself at the counter with a plate of food he had no interest in eating, futilely hoping that his higher vantage point would, in some mysterious way, allow him to control what was happening.

"I forgot to pick up a napkin," Heidi cooed. "Get me one, Sugar Beth."

"I want another of those delicious rolls. Make sure it's warm."

"Take this dirty plate. I'm done with it."

As soon as she'd returned from one errand, the Seawillows sent her off on another. And she let them do it. She didn't rush, but she didn't tell them to bugger off, either.

"Get me a damp towel. I've got something sticky on my hands."

"See if you can find the pepper mill. I'm sure there's one somewhere."

Even Amy couldn't resist finding her own way to join in, and he heard her whisper, "Jesus can wash away anybody's sins, Sugar Beth, even yours. Throw yourself on his mercy."

Colin pushed aside his plate, intending to put a stop to the nonsense, but Sugar Beth detected the movement and shot him a look that challenged not only his manhood but also his very right to exist on the planet. With a sense of resignation, he sank back down and braced himself.

"I do not think," said Lord Bromford, having considered the matter gravely, "that one should sacrifice one's principles to gratify a female's whim."

GEORGETTE HEYER, *The Grand Sophy*

Chapter 11

$\mathcal{W}$innie offered Ryan a taste of her kiwi tart right before she made her move. As Sugar Beth began to pick up the empty plates, Winnie raised her voice, ever so slightly. "Oh, dear, I accidentally kicked my fork under the table. Let me move out of the way, Sugar Beth, so you can get it for me." She rose from the table and took one small step to the side.

Colin understood at once. Winnie had chosen something small, unimportant, something almost insignificant that symbolized everything. To retrieve the fork, Sugar Beth would have to drop to her knees at Winnie's feet.

He had no idea whether Sugar Beth would do it, didn't wait to see. Instead, he shot off his stool only to realize that Winnie's husband had beaten him to it.

"Let me," Ryan said quickly.

The edges of Winnie's mouth collapsed, and for the first time that evening, she seemed more vulnerable than Sugar

Beth. Sugar Beth met Ryan's eyes for a fraction of a second before she took a small step back. Slowly, he dropped to one knee at his wife's feet, reached under the table, and withdrew the fork that Winnie had undoubtedly kicked there.

Colin gazed from one woman to the other. He'd always been fascinated by literary archetypes, but if someone had asked him, right at that moment, which of these women was plucky Cinderella and which the wicked stepsister, he'd have been hard-pressed to come up with an answer.

The evening ground on. He might be miserable, but his guests seemed to be enjoying themselves, and it was past eleven before they finally began to trickle away.

Winnie's hands weren't quite steady as she slipped into her skimpy black lace teddy. It was one of several she owned in various colors. Ryan came into the bedroom without his sport coat. He'd undoubtedly tossed it over a chair downstairs. It would still be there when they got back from church tomorrow. He didn't expect her to pick up after him. He just failed to notice how many of his things he left lying around.

"Look at this." He held out a rumpled wall poster showing a bare-chested hunk sporting a pair of nipple rings while a woman's hand reached through his legs to cup his crotch. "She had this hanging on the back of her door when I went in to check on her."

"She knows how much we hate her posters. That's why she keeps putting them up."

"If she's this rebellious now, what's going to happen when she's sixteen?"

Winnie didn't voice her deepest fear, that genetics would somehow play out, and Gigi would end up like Sugar Beth: self-centered, spiteful, and sexually active at too young an age.

Ryan tossed the poster in their trash basket and headed for the closet. He didn't remark on her imported black teddy, but why should he? She had a vast collection of sexy sleepwear, and he saw her in or out of one of the pieces nearly every night. Sometimes she wanted to throw them all away and head to Wal-Mart for a set of comfy cotton pj's.

As he went about his bedtime routine, she slid under the covers and opened the book she'd left on the table, but she didn't even pretend to read it. Instead, she gnawed over the ugly memory of Ryan kneeling at Sugar Beth's feet. What a terrible miscalculation she'd made. She'd forced her husband to choose sides, and he'd chosen the wrong one.

She was sick of her jealousy. All evening he'd watched Sugar Beth. He'd been discreet about it, but you couldn't live with a man for so long and not know what he was thinking. Tonight Winnie had to make love with him until he was so mindless he forgot about Sugar Beth. *Give it to me, babee . . .* Just like a third-rate porn star. But the thought of the gyrations, the moaning, the mess, made her feel exhausted and resentful.

Ryan finished in the bathroom and slid naked into bed. He turned on his side so he was facing her. She only had to brush against him and he'd be hard. He reached out and stroked her hair, then ran his finger under the strap of her teddy to graze her nipple.

Give it to me, babee . . . She owed him everything, but she put her book on the nightstand as an excuse to turn away. Then she said the most extraordinary thing.

"I'm not feeling well. I think I'll sleep in the guest room tonight."

His golden brown eyes filled with concern. "What's wrong?"

"A little stomach upset." She pushed back the covers and dropped her legs over the side of the bed. "I don't want to wake you if I have to get up."

He reached out to rub the small of her back. "I don't mind."

"We'll both sleep better this way."

She slid out of bed without giving him a good-night kiss. She was appalled with herself. Tonight, of all nights, when she most needed to be seductive, she couldn't bring herself to kiss him. She was sick of him. Sick of his good looks, his flawless manners, his endless solicitude. She was sick of always feeling second-rate. And most of all, she was sick of pretending to like him when she didn't. Love him, yes. She loved him with all her heart. That would never go away. But right now she couldn't stand the sight of him.

She gathered her robe from the foot of the bed. "Gigi's going to raise a stink in the morning about going to Sunday school. I'll let you deal with her."

He'd propped himself on his elbow, gazing at her quizzically. "All right."

She told herself not to say another word, to go to the guest room and shut the door before she did any more damage. "I'm going to buy some pajamas."

"I don't wear pajamas."

"For me."

He gave her his patented sexy smile. "I like what you have on right now."

"That makes one of us."

His smile faded. "You're tired."

Sick and tired. And he knew why. But he wouldn't say it. He would ignore the ghost that had hovered over them for fourteen years, just as she would, because their marriage was fragile as an eggshell, and neither of them wanted to risk cracking it.

"Tired. Yes." She managed a shaky smile. "I'll make you pancakes in the morning." As if a stack of pancakes would fix what was wrong between them.

She turned off the light and walked to the door.

"Do you want me to rub your back?" he said.

"No. No, I don't want that at all." She let herself out of the room.

*   *   *

Colin came into the kitchen and saw Sugar Beth standing on a stool, putting away a tray in the cupboard over the cooktop. It was one in the morning, the caterer had left, and she was clearly exhausted, but she still hadn't finished proving that she could take anything Colin threw at her. What kind of man tried to snuff out a spirit like this? "You're dead on your feet. Go home."

She gazed at her dog. "What's Gordon doing here?"

"I went over to the carriage house to let him out, and he followed me back. He chewed up one of your shower thongs."

"He hates me."

"Dogs don't hate their masters. It defies the natural order of the universe."

"Says you." She climbed off the stool, and as she picked it up to tuck it away, he saw shadows like bruises under her eyes.

"Put that bloody thing down. I can take care of whatever's left tomorrow."

She cocked the stool against her hip and eyed him with open mockery. "Look at you. Guilt oozing from every pore. You're not going to start crying, are you? Because, frankly, that's more than I could stomach."

"I'll attempt to keep my tears in check. Now, go to bed. I'll write you a check in the morning."

"Darn right you will. And you're paying me double for overtime. But then two times zip is zip, right? God, you're cheap. Maybe if you didn't spend so much money on fancy perfume and Barbra Streisand records, you could pay me what I'm worth."

"My dear, even I don't have that much money."

That stopped her cold. He had the satisfaction of seeing her blink, then frown, as she searched for the hidden insult. He pressed his advantage. "I know this will disappoint you, but tonight was the end of it. We're even. I've officially been avenged for your teenage treachery."

She rolled her eyes, back in the game. "Are you telling me

that little bit of guilt is all it takes to make you tuck your tail between your legs? And you call yourself a man."

He'd been reading too much Victorian erotica because he wanted to bend her over a chair and . . . do something quite nasty.

She settled on a stool at the counter and hooked a stockinged heel over the rung. "I guess I never told you about this." She leaned her chin on the back of her hand in a parody of dreamy reminiscence. "The night I made up my lie about you . . . I cried real tears."

"You don't say." She was hurting herself—he could feel it—but he didn't know how to stop her. Besides, his days of attempting to rescue wounded women were behind him.

"See, I'd had an accident with my Camaro that day—stop signs still bring out the rebel in me—and I was afraid Daddy would take my car keys. So it wasn't only the fact I hated your guts that made me lie."

"It's late, Sugar Beth, and you're tired."

"It was funnier than hell. The minute I told Diddie that you tried to feel me up, she forgot all about the dent in the side of that car, and so did Daddy. They didn't even dock my allowance for the repairs. I still laugh thinkin' about it."

She didn't look like laughing. She looked soul weary and worn out. He walked toward her. "You were a kid, and you'd been spoiled rotten. Stop being so hard on yourself."

He should have known empathy would be a mistake because she came up off the stool hissing. "Aren't you just all Christian charity? Compassion and forgiveness pourin' out of you. Well, I don't need your pity, Mr. Byrne. I don't need—"

"That's enough!" In one swift motion, he scooped her off her feet and carried her from the kitchen. He was done fighting with himself. All night it had been building up to this, and now he was taking her upstairs, dumping her in his bed, and making love with her until neither of them could think straight.

"Well, well, well . . ." She gazed up at him, all tired eyes and provocative drawl. "This is more like it, big guy."

That stopped him cold.

"What's the matter, your lordship? Having second thoughts?" She mocked him with her weary coquette's pout. "Maybe you're afraid you can't get it up for a girl."

Sex and sass were the only weapons she had left. He understood that, just as he understood his solicitude must feel like slow poison to those proud veins, and this was the only way she had left to pay him back.

He was a cynical man aroused beyond bearing, but he'd once had the spirit of a romantic, and somehow he found the willpower to ease her to her feet. Then, because he deserved something for his restraint, he kissed her deeply and thoroughly.

She responded like a temptress—full tongue, breathy moans, hips rubbing against his, all of it phony, designed to let him know what he could do with his pity. Even so, blood throbbed in his groin, and his body demanded more. He needed all of his self-control not to lose patience with her, but he kept his lips soft and coaxing, giving her time to work out her anger. Gradually, the writhing stopped, and her tongue retreated into her mouth. She curled soft and warm against him. He sipped at her lips. They tasted like velvet.

Sugar Beth felt the gentle pull of Colin's mouth and knew he'd disarmed her, but she was too exhausted to struggle any longer. He was fully aroused, and it startled her to realize she was, too. Beneath her bone-deep weariness, her body had come to life.

He tasted of health and vigor, of the kind of male potency she'd nearly forgotten existed. His kiss deepened. She felt the ropey muscles, the tensile strength of his body. Her lips parted, and he slipped his tongue into her mouth. She let her arms drift around his neck. He dallied and stroked. She heard herself sigh as he abandoned her mouth to pick her up again.

But instead of heading for the stairs, he carried her across the foyer, then shifted her in his arms so he could open the front door.

"This may very well be the hardest thing I've ever done"—he was clenching his teeth—"but when we make love—and believe me when I tell you we're going to—it will be about pleasure, not some bloody contest to see who's still standing at the end."

It was cold outside. She rested her cheek against his shirt-front. He wasn't even breathing hard as he carried her across the yard with Gordon leading the way.

"Furthermore," he went on, "you will be rested. And"—he gripped her tighter—"*sweet-tempered.*"

"You had more to drink than I thought." She yawned and closed her eyes. "Go ahead and admit it. You're afraid of me."

"Terrified is more like it."

She burrowed deeper into his chest. "I'm a handful, all right."

"My worst nightmare."

The carriage house door stuck, and he had to put her down to open it. Once he got her inside, he kissed her again, but just the lightest brush of his lips, as if he didn't trust himself to do more. That was when she realized he wasn't fooling about leaving. She didn't want him to, but she couldn't come up with a way to tell him she was lonely, lost, and needed him to stay.

"You have no idea what this is costing me," he said as he headed for the door, "so don't expect me to be pleasant when I come to see you in the morning."

"Who said you were invited?"

"Who said I need an invitation?"

This time when he left, he took her dog with him.

She barely dragged herself upstairs. She dropped her clothes in a heap and somehow managed to brush her teeth, but summoning the energy to sort through her jumbled feelings was too much to ask, and she fell into bed.

Just as she drifted off to sleep, she heard them.

"Sugar . . . Sugar . . . Sugar . . ."

At first, she thought she was dreaming, but as she rolled to her back, their calls grew louder.

"Sugar . . . Sugar . . . Sugar Pie . . ."

Cubby Bowmar and his drunken friends were out front, baying for her just like in high school.

You're going to be a woman for the ages, Diddie had said.

Sugar Beth pulled the pillow over her head and went to sleep.

Winnie awakened to the sound of Ryan showering. Not long after, she heard him rousing Gigi for Sunday school along with her predictable protest.

"I was suspended, Dad. Remember?"

"Not from church."

"Where's Mom?"

"She isn't feeling well."

"Me either."

"Get dressed."

Winnie drifted. She caught the faint scent of coffee . . . dishes clattering in the kitchen . . . a door slamming . . . a car driving away . . . the world going on without her. Finally, she roused herself enough to get out of bed.

She stepped over the black teddy she'd shed last night in favor of an old T-shirt of Ryan's and a pair of pink sweatpants she'd stashed in the closet for the church collection box. She made her way to the bathroom and managed to brush her teeth, but a shower was beyond her. She gazed at herself in the mirror: puffy-eyed, pasty-faced, hair smashed to one side of her head. Her life was unraveling like the seat of the pink sweatpants, one thread at a time.

"Feelin' better?"

She jumped as Ryan's reflection appeared in the mirror over her shoulder. He was wearing khakis and the Old Navy rugby Gigi had bought him for Christmas. "I thought you left."

"I was worried about you, so I asked Merylinn to take Gigi to church with them. How are you doing?"

"All right." The isolation of the guest room bed called out to her—a place where she couldn't hurt either one of them. She wanted to creep back in and bury herself under the covers.

"The concert's this afternoon. The reception. Are you going to be up for all that?"

"I'll be fine."

He crossed his arms and leaned against the doorjamb. She knew why he'd stayed home from church. He wanted to make up for what he'd done at the party. Everything had always been so effortless for Sugar Beth: her beauty, her charm, her ability to hypnotize the most decent of men, even Colin. As for Ryan . . . One look at Sugar Beth was all it had taken for him to be run down by a whole truckload of the might-have-beens.

Winnie's anger choked her. She'd sacrificed the very essence of who she was in a futile attempt to compete with the ghost of a spoiled eighteen-year-old girl. She was so sick of herself she couldn't bear it.

Ryan glanced at his watch. "Gigi won't be back for a while. Let's—"

"Don't you ever think about anything but sex!" The words erupted from her as if they'd been shot to the surface by some prehistoric geyser.

He couldn't have looked more shocked if she'd slapped him. The geyser sputtered, then retreated as remorse swamped her. "I'm sorry. Oh, dear, Ryan, I'm so sorry. I didn't mean that."

But no easy apology would fix this. His warm brown eyes had grown wintry. "I was about to suggest you throw on some clothes so we could drive to the bakery and get some of the cherry fritters you like."

The unfairness of her attack sickened her, but the simmering anger wouldn't go away. All her life she'd believed she didn't deserve anything better than everyone's emotional leftovers, and she was tired of it. She breathed hard, choked the anger back down. "I'm sorry."

"Contrary to what you seem to believe, sex isn't all I think about."

"I know that. I'm just . . . out of sorts." She pressed her hands to her waist, trying to hold the bubbling geyser in. "Let me get cleaned up, and I'll go with you."

"Forget it. I have some paperwork to do." He took a step, then stopped. A slash of morning light threw his face into shadow, and for a moment, he looked like a stranger. "If you're mad about last night, why don't you just come out and say it instead of going through all this drama?"

The geyser rumbled. "I'm not."

"Sugar Beth deserved the cold shoulder, but what happened went beyond that. You all behaved like children, and I won't have any part of it."

"Of course you won't." The geyser churned inside her, searching for a weak place to push through her skin.

"When are you going to let the past go?"

"Like you have?"

"Damn right I have."

"You couldn't take your eyes off her! All night. Every time I looked at you, you were watching her."

"Stop right there." His hand shot out. "We'll talk about this when you're ready to make sense."

His dismissal cut through what was left of her self-control, and the geyser erupted again. This time it brought everything with it, including the secret she'd kept locked away for so many years. "I can't do this!"

He began to walk away.

"Don't you dare walk away from me!"

He kept going.

She rushed after him, a wild-eyed harridan, shrieking, hysterical, out of control. "I got pregnant on purpose!"

"Settle down."

"I lied to you!"

He stopped at the top of the stairs and turned back to her. For the first time, he looked genuinely alarmed. "Winnie, stop this."

"I got pregnant on purpose so you'd marry me!"

"I know."

She pressed her fingers to her lips, swallowed her bile, tried to breathe, couldn't. "You *know*? You *know,* and you never said anything?"

"What was the point?" He thrust a hand through his hair. "There's no reason to talk about this."

"I trapped you!"

"I don't feel trapped. Gigi's more precious to me than my own life. Now go take a bath. You'll feel better."

As if a bath could wash away her sin.

"Ryan . . ."

But he was already disappearing down the stairs.

She slumped against the wall. Her darkest secret . . . and he didn't want to talk about it.

Numbly, she returned to the bathroom and sank down on the side of the tub. She'd never planned to trap him. But then one night she'd heard herself say that she was on the pill, and he didn't have to worry. Since she was Winnie Davis, he'd believed her.

She had responsibilities, so she turned on the faucets. The concert was this afternoon, the reception. If only she could be like Sugar Beth—callous and self-centered, utterly without conscience. She began to cry. How long did a person have to pay for old sins? Her lie had made Gigi, so she couldn't regret it. Why, then, did she keep hating herself?

Maybe because Ryan had never done the job for her.

Sugar Beth smelled coffee. And bacon. She loved bacon. She rolled over, saw that it was nearly eleven, and headed for the bathroom. Twenty minutes later, she was on her way downstairs wearing clean underwear, a black satin Victoria's Secret robe she'd had forever, and her oldest pair of cowboy boots. She'd washed her hair, but she hadn't taken the time to dry it. She also hadn't bothered with makeup. After yesterday, Colin Byrne didn't deserve more than clean hair and a little moisturizer.

Her muscles ached from hard work and righteous indignation, but more than that, she felt relief. Whether Colin knew it or not, he'd finally forgiven her. The burden she'd carried for so long had been eased at last.

He stood at the stove in the small kitchen, his back turned to her, his presence dominating the small space. Just looking at him made her want to rip off his clothes and drag him upstairs.

"I was getting ready to wake you up."

She wished she'd stayed in bed longer and let him do it. That ol' black magic—falling for the wrong man. Except she wasn't so stupid now. It might have taken her awhile, but she finally knew the difference between lust and love. "Good Lord, are you really wearing jeans? Give me some coffee fast."

"They're custom made," he said as she pulled one of Tallulah's Wedgwood cups from the shelf and helped herself. "French. They cost over three hundred dollars a pair, but I think they're worth it."

She studied the way the denim conformed to his hips beneath the Gap label. "Those Frenchies sure do know something about making jeans," she said dryly.

"I heard your admirers last night."

"Cubby and the boys?"

"Celebrating their graduation from idiot school, no doubt. One egg or two?" He cracked two into the skillet.

"Tell me there's a box of Krispy Kremes hidden somewhere."

"You're lucky the toast isn't whole wheat." He took in her satin robe and the cowboy boots. "Fetching."

"You are the only man in Parrish with the nerve to use a word like that. Where's my dog?"

"Outside. He doesn't seem inclined to wander."

"Too obstinate." She carried her coffee to the kitchen table and sat. "I smell bacon, so why am I not seein' it?"

"I'll make you a fresh batch." He scooped her eggs onto a plate with surprising competency, added toast he'd already buttered, and set them on the table in front of her.

"What are you doing eating bacon? Your arteries have probably gone into shock."

"A moment of weakness."

"I sure know how that feels." The toast was cold, but he hadn't spared the butter, so she didn't complain. And the eggs weren't bad. The bacon sizzled as he tossed it into the skillet, every motion efficient. She spoke around her first bite. "I hope nobody finds out you're providing aid and comfort to the enemy."

"No doubt I'll survive."

"Are you making me breakfast because you're still working through your guilt, or are you just being nice so you can get to the goodies?"

"By goodies, I assume you're referring to those delectable parts of yourself tucked away beneath your robe."

"Those would be them, yes."

"Probably."

"Which one? Guilt or goodies?"

"I have to choose?"

"Never mind." She polished off the first egg. "Tell me about your wife."

"No."

"No talky. No goodies." He didn't pull his punches with her, and she wasn't going to do it with him. "How did she die?"

He stabbed at the bacon. "If you must know, she ran into a bridge abutment. Tragic enough under any circumstances, but she did it deliberately."

"Ouch."

"Exactly."

There was a whole world of pain hidden behind that impassive profile. "You know a lot more than I thought about guilt," she said. "Funny how you can misjudge people."

"I had no reason to feel guilty. I'd done everything I could to help her."

Sugar Beth knew way too much about recrimination to believe he was that clearheaded, and she lifted an eyebrow.

He looked away. "All right, she was pregnant, and it took me awhile. But sanity reigned, and I finally worked through it. Learned a bit about myself in the process."

"Such as?"

"That marriage isn't for me. Some people can make it work, but I'm not one of them."

"You haven't been tempted since then?"

"Hard for you to imagine, I'm sure, but not even once. I finally have my life exactly where I want it, and I've never been happier. But enough of my tedious past." He poured himself a fresh cup of coffee and turned to regard her. "Tell me if there was anything beyond the obvious that possessed you to marry a man forty years your senior."

"You wouldn't believe me."

"I'm becoming more discerning about sorting through your bullshit, so let me try."

She broke off a corner of her toast, but couldn't eat it. "I loved him."

"And why not? He was worth millions."

"Ordinarily you'd have a point, but I didn't find out how rich he was until he'd already worked his magic."

"He was seventy. How much magic could the man work?"

"You'd be surprised. He was a handsome son of a gun, looked fifteen years younger than his age, a Texas version of Anthony Hopkins, but without that scary dental appliance." Her throat began to tighten. "The most charming man I've ever known. Real charm, the kind that goes bone deep because it's born of kindness. He was the love of my life."

"Touching." His tone was caustic, his smile sympathetic.

She appreciated the combination. He pulled out the bacon. "I gathered from something you mentioned earlier that he was sick for quite a while."

"For two years. In a coma the last six months."

"And he died four months ago?"

She nodded and shook off her sadness. "So here we are. A grieving widow and a lonely widower staving off lives of quiet desperation with a well-intentioned, but badly prepared, breakfast. It's enough to make Hallmark cry. By the way, I'm fixing you grits next week. I've got a hankerin'."

He'd begun to pick up the plate of bacon, but now he set it back down, no longer looking cynical, just serious. "There's not going to be a next week for us, Sugar Beth."

She jumped up from her chair. "Oh, no, you don't. I haven't found that painting yet, and you are *not* firing me. I need the money, as paltry as it is."

He regarded her with his old haughtiness. "The job is demeaning. I only offered it to humiliate you."

"You're coming closer all the time. Another few weeks, and I know you'll get it right."

He lifted his eyes. She sat back down. "Please, Colin, don't be a prick."

"Exactly what I'm trying not to be. You can't stay in this town any longer. I've written you a check that'll tide you over for a while. Go back to Houston. You can support yourself a lot better there than you can here."

Supporting herself had never been the problem. It was paying Delilah's bills she couldn't seem to manage. "I'm not leaving without that painting."

"You don't even know if it still exists." He loomed over her. "And whatever luxuries you could buy from selling it aren't worth giving up your dignity."

"Easy for you to say. You weren't born shallow."

"Bloody hell, Sugar Beth! Look at you. You're skin and bones. You don't look like you've slept well in weeks. Top that off with the fact that people are spitting at you in the street, and you're doing nothing to stop them. It'll only get worse, you know. Make no mistake, Winnie has power in this town."

"I'm not afraid of Winnie Davis."

"I'm sure you're not. But Winnie Galantine is a different kettle of fish. *She's* Diddie, Sugar Beth. Get that through your thick head. Winnie has all the power your mother used to have."

"But none of the charm."

"Then there's the issue of the two of us." He scowled. "Last night more than satisfied my blood lust, but I still don't exactly wish you well. That said, I find it particularly ominous that we're on the verge of having sex. More than on the verge, if I have my way about it."

"Which you may not. I'm still making up my mind."

"Liar. We're throwing off so many sparks the walls are smoking."

"Sparks caused by faulty wiring. We're the two most mismatched people in the universe."

"Which only makes it more alluring, doesn't it?" His eyes burned her. "I avoid high-maintenance women with a vengeance, and they don't come any more high-maintenance than you."

"I pride myself."

"You thrive on men who worship you, and that won't happen with me."

"I love the way you sweet-talk."

"The sexual attraction of opposites."

"You're making a good point, except I've got this sneaky feeling you'll be a major disappointment in the sack."

His voice descended to a single ominous note. "And why is that, may I ask?"

"You know."

"Do share."

"The prissy thing. My body isn't neat like yours. It's female. It gets all musky. Wet. You're fastidious. I just don't think you're going to like it that much." She tried to figure out exactly what she thought she was doing other than scaring herself to death.

"You, my dear, are the very incarnation of evil."

She beamed at him. "I know."

"Eat." He slapped the plate of bacon in front of her. "Not hungry? Fine. Let's go upstairs."

"If I do, I get to keep my job."

"This doesn't have anything to do with keeping your job, and you know it." Gordon howled at the front door just as he began to reach for her. "That bloody cur."

"You've finally seen the light."

He let in her dog, who headed for his water bowl. She gazed down at the bacon, but she'd lost her appetite. Until she'd come back to Parrish, grief and anxiety had pretty much taken care of her sex drive. Then she'd met Colin Byrne again. Why did he have to be the man who'd jarred her out of her uncomplicated limbo? He hadn't exactly been blowing hot air when he'd said he didn't wish her well.

"Tell me you're not coming to your senses," he said, gazing down at her.

"Stupidity is hardwired into my DNA."

"Thank God."

She knew that she was going ahead with this. At the same time, she needed to make sure he understood this was all fun and games. "Let's get it on," she said, rising from the table to head for the stairs. "And you'd better not be a dud because, if you are, I'll make sure the whole town finds out about it."

"And you, my dear, had better be more than talk, something I'm beginning to doubt."

"Is that so?" She stopped right there on the third step from the bottom, unfastened her robe, and let it drop.

He took in her white bra, black thong, and the cowboy boots. "I'm dumbstruck."

She trailed the tip of her thumb down her belly. "And you haven't even seen the good stuff."

"You couldn't be more mistaken." The corner of his mouth quirked, and in three long strides, he'd covered the distance between them. "Although I'll admit I'm more than a little anxious to see the rest."

"Okay, but I get to keep my job."

"Shut up, will you?" He snaked an arm around her waist and pulled her off the step, hard against him. The toes of her cowboy boots banged against his calves as she looked down at him. She dipped her head, his lips parted, their mouths met, and he kissed her with a thoroughness that should have been foreign to such an elegant man.

Without breaking their kiss, he walked her backward to the couch. His arm reached behind her, and he tugged open her bra. "You are magnificent," he whispered as he tossed it aside.

"I know."

He chuckled and massaged her breasts, then kissed her again with that same thoroughness. As good as it felt, she wanted more. She wanted his mouth on her breasts, his tongue there, too, his teeth—

Gordon barked.

And she wanted privacy.

"Get rid of him," she groaned.

"He's a dog." Colin nibbled at her lip. "He won't tell."

"He'll watch."

Colin cursed and shot Gordon a commanding look. "Stay."

He grabbed her wrist and pulled her up the stairs to her bedroom, the dog following along. When Colin kicked the door shut, Gordon began to howl. Despite her need, Sugar Beth smiled, then laughed out loud at the vaguely murderous look on Colin's face. "Don't you move," he snarled as he shot back out the door.

Still smiling, she sank down on the side of the unmade bed

and pulled off her boots. Colin either found a doggie treat or some rat poison because things stayed quiet when he let himself back in. She looked up at him.

"Lovely," he said, taking her in.

She wore only her thong and a pair of purple socks with a Powerpuff Girl on each side. She'd bought them for Delilah, who hadn't liked them because she was going through a pink phase. "I do know my lingerie."

"No argument there." He stood in the center of the faded old floral rug and began tossing aside his clothes. When only his jeans were left, she rose and walked toward him. "Let me." She hooked a finger over the fastener and began toying with it.

"Need help?" His voice caught in a husky rasp.

"No, thanks." His skin warmed the backs of her fingers. She trailed her thumb over his zipper. He was thick, hard, and—another of his surprises—very large. Nose. Hands. Feet. She should have been prepared.

Her need was as urgent as his, but she couldn't bear the idea of having this over too quickly . . . or of making it too important. "You should never have given me a D on my Charlotte Brontë paper."

He expelled his breath in a warm hiss against her neck. "Perhaps we could discuss this later."

"I don't think so." She fiddled with his zipper tab. "I worked real hard on that paper."

"And turned it in a week late, I'm sure."

She lowered the zipper half an inch, then stopped to pout. "Still . . ."

"I'll change it to a C. I promise."

She released the tab. Ignoring the sweet lethargy in her limbs, she took a step back and regarded him sulkily. "I want an A."

She wasn't the only person in the room who knew how to play games.

"*That* you'll have to earn." He gestured toward her feet. "Give me one of those socks."

"Only one?"

"I'm nothing if not reasonable."

"I guess." She propped her foot on the edge of the bed and leaned slowly over her thigh. She drew the Powerpuff sock off as if it were a fishnet stocking, then stuck it in the waistband of his jeans.

"Very nice, indeed. I'll take that thong now."

"An A plus."

"For your body alone."

That was nice, especially since they both knew she was too thin and her thighs hadn't been near a StairMaster in forever. Still, long legs counted for a lot with men. "Only if you kiss me first."

"My pleasure, indeed."

This kiss was even slower than the others, more intense, world-class. He tunneled his fingers in her hair. His jeans abraded her flesh. She could feel herself reaching the breaking point even before he hooked his thumbs in her thong, pushed it down, and went on his knees.

She let her head fall back as he buried his face. He inhaled her in the way good men did. And bad ones, too, for that matter, but no need to worry about that when she was the only sinner in the room. He pushed open her thighs. One of his hands cupped her bottom.

He devoured her.

Her legs lost their strength, but he held her in place with his massive palm, keeping her right where he wanted, open and accessible.

Her orgasm caught her by surprise. She let out a strangled cry.

He stayed with her through the waves, then laid her on the bed as if she were a doll. He got tangled in his jeans, and his unusual clumsiness made her lips curve in a slumberous smile. He'd come prepared, she noticed, as he dragged a thoughtful, but unnecessary, condom from his pocket.

Finally naked, he pushed her to her back and trailed his mouth from nipple to belly and then below. Who could have predicted such earthy generosity from so fastidious a man? She dug her hands into his thick hair, rough silk under her fingers. He toyed with her, bringing her to the brink again, but never quite letting her tumble over. She rolled to her side to return the favor.

Drunk on sensation they explored—touching and tasting, trading sweet smut and breathy groans, making themselves crazier and crazier. She tried to close her legs so she could torture him more, but he would have none of it.

"Don't even think about it."

He caught an ankle, the one still wearing the sock, and pressed it high on the bed. Then he clasped her opposite knee, pushed it wide, and thrust himself deep inside her, not being brutal about it—he was too big for that—but not being all that careful either. Just as if he could read her mind.

She wrapped her legs around him, and their bodies locked in the rhythm of longtime lovers. The muscles in his back quivered beneath her hands. He angled his hips, cupped her bottom, found a new spot to please her.

She arched, cried out. Their gazes locked. For one startling moment, a shock of recognition passed between them, something soul deep and very important. But before it could find a name, the cataclysm swept them away.

"I declare, I could kill Vidal! It is so unthinking of him to ravish honest girls . . ."

GEORGETTE HEYER, *Devil's Cub*

Chapter 12

Sugar Beth rolled to her side. "I'm done with you. You can go."

His breathing hadn't yet returned to normal, so she was probably rushing him, but she was a lot more shaken by what had just happened than she intended to let him see. Meaningless sex was allowed to feel good, but it wasn't allowed to feel important, and that's what might have happened if she hadn't kept up her guard.

She felt Colin watching her as she walked naked across the room. She remembered his threat to fire her and told herself not to entertain even the possibility that he'd stick to his guns.

"That was only a warm-up, my dear," he said, in his royal family drawl. "I'm definitely not done with you."

"No man ever is. But I have things to do, and, alas, none of them involves you."

"Is that so?"

Just looking at him propped against her pillow, chest damp with sweat, that dramatic dark hair even more rumpled than usual, made her want to climb right back in and let him work his magic all over again. But she needed to get her barricades back in place, so she picked up his jeans and tossed them on the bed. "You were fabulous. Inspired, even. Go home and recuperate. I'll see you in the morning."

His languor faded, and he raised one knee beneath the sheet that had fallen low on his hips. "I believe we already discussed this."

"Don't make me bargain for my job with more sex. You'll only feel tawdry."

"God, you're full of it."

He was right about that, but before he could drive his point home, she tried to make a dash for the bathroom only to have him catch her long before she got to the door and drag her back to bed. "Not so fast. There's an interesting perversion I stumbled across in my research recently."

"What kind of perversion?"

He slipped his hand between her legs, and the way his fingers moved made her forget that she didn't have her defenses back in place. "I'm sure it would be too much for you."

She nipped at his shoulder. "Maybe if you're extra gentle?"

"Or maybe not."

And that was the last either of them said for a very long time.

Much later, when she emerged from her second bath of the morning, her bed held only a disgruntled basset hound. The time she'd spent in the tub had sobered her, and she sank down on the edge of the mattress. Gordon inched over and propped his head on her thigh. One long, floppy ear fell across her knee.

She dropped her head and fought back the tears. All morning she'd tried not to think about Emmett, but the ghosts could only be kept at bay for so long. She'd just severed another tie with him. Which was the thing about watching a loved one die a slow death. There was no clean break, no single moment of overwhelming grief, just an endless strand of losses. She rubbed Gordon's head. Clasped her knees.

Being with Colin had felt too good. But she couldn't blame herself for what she'd done, not after going for so long without a man's touch. At the same time, she had to make certain her old needy habits didn't come creeping back. She'd never let herself depend on another man for her happiness, and definitely not anyone as emotionally aloof as Colin Byrne.

The clock chimed downstairs, and she remembered this was Sunday. Colin was going to the concert, and she'd told Gigi she could visit this afternoon. She was in no shape for an angst-ridden teenager, but she could hardly ring Gigi up and tell her not to come, so she blew her nose, pulled on her jeans, fixed her makeup, then headed downstairs to clean up the breakfast mess.

Colin's kiss-off check lay on the counter. She picked it up. Two thousand dollars. His guilt ran deep, and she tore it up. She thought of Delilah. Once again, she considered the possibility of having her stepdaughter live with her, and once again she rejected it. Delilah enjoyed their shopping expeditions and restaurant lunches together, but after a few hours away from Brookdale she got agitated and begged to go home.

She was staring at the wall when Gigi arrived, wearing another of the ratty, oversize outfits that must be giving her parents fits. She bent down to give Gordon the attention he demanded. When she rose, she looked awkward and nervous. "I was supposed to go to the concert with them this afternoon, but I talked back to my dad."

"How convenient."

"Do you . . . uh . . . want to make some cookies or something?" She flushed, deciding too late that her big-city aunt was too worldly for cookie baking. Sugar Beth repressed a sigh. She couldn't deal with her own insecurities, let alone this child's.

"No flour," she said.

"That's okay. Making cookies is lame."

"Think so?" Sugar Beth could have told her she loved baking cookies nearly as much as she loved eating them, but she didn't want to encourage any more bonding.

"Maybe you could show me how you do your eye makeup? It's pretty cool."

Sugar Beth took in her baggy cords and faded T-shirt. "Aren't you afraid it'll clash with that trendy outfit?"

"I don't always dress like this."

"No?"

Gigi examined her thumbnail. "It's better this way."

"Better for who?"

A shrug.

Sugar Beth didn't have the energy to probe deeper. Eye makeup was safe. And it would be better for Gigi to learn makeup tricks from Sugar Beth than from her stick of a mother, or, God forbid, Merylinn, although Merylinn did have a nice touch with lip liner. She started to lead Gigi upstairs, then remembered the sex-rumpled sheets. "I'll bring the stuff down here. The light's better."

"Okay. And then I sort of have a list."

"Of what?" Sugar Beth asked warily.

"Some questions I want to ask you."

Her head began to throb. She abandoned the eye makeup plan and made a beeline for the kitchen. "I need coffee."

"I drink coffee."

"Sure you do."

"I do!"

Fine. Let Ryan worry about caffeine addiction. She set up the coffeemaker, flicked the switch, and turned to see that Gigi had seated herself at the table and was dredging a piece of paper and a pencil stub from her pocket, all ready to take notes. "First, do you think it's better to be smart or popular? I think popular."

"They're not mutually exclusive."

"They are in Parrish."

"Not even in Parrish."

"You were smart," Gigi said, "but you got crappy grades, and it made you popular."

"I hate to disillusion you, but I got crappy grades because I had my priorities screwed up. And I would have been popular even if I got good grades."

"How?" Gigi abandoned her notes. "That's what I don't understand. How did you do it? You were rich like me. Didn't all the kids hate you for it?"

Sugar Beth was tired of letting the world watch her bleed, and she didn't want to talk about this now. Or ever, for that matter. But Gigi deserved an answer. "I was born with a false sense of superiority," she said slowly, "and I managed to manipulate everybody so they bought into it. It was great short-term, but you might have noticed it hasn't done zip for me long-term."

Gigi hadn't gotten the answer she wanted. "How exactly did you manipulate them?"

Sugar Beth glanced longingly toward the coffeemaker, but it hadn't finished brewing. She needed caffeine now, and she grabbed a Coke from the refrigerator. "Want one?"

"No, thanks. I prefer coffee."

"Of course you do." She popped the top. Gigi waited, all big eyes and eager ears. Sugar Beth tried to think of what to say that would make sense to a thirteen-year-old, or even to herself. "The goal isn't to be popular, Gigi. The goal is to be strong."

"I don't feel strong," she said miserably.

Welcome to the club, kiddo. "Nobody does when they're thirteen. But thirteen is a great time to start accumulating power. The right kind."

Gigi's face lit with interest. "That's what I want. I want to be powerful."

"But you want to be powerful right now, which isn't going to happen."

"You were powerful when you were thirteen."

Sugar Beth repressed a bitter laugh. "My power was an illusion. All the tricks I used to acquire it ended up backfiring on me as I got older. You want power that lasts. And you don't get it by being less than you are."

"I don't know what you mean."

"In your case it means pretending you're poor by disappearing inside ugly clothes, then blowing off schoolwork and hanging out with the wrong kind of kids."

Gigi looked outraged. "Just because Chelsea isn't rich . . ."

"This doesn't have anything to do with money. It has to do with brains, and from what you told me, Chelsea wasn't blessed with a full set. You, on the other hand, have more than your fair share, but you don't seem to be taking advantage of them."

"I'm not hanging out with geeks like Gwen Lu and Jenny Berry, if that's what you mean."

Sugar Beth remembered Winnie trying to make herself invisible as she walked down the school hallways. "Because you don't like them, or because you're afraid the other kids will make fun of you if you do?"

Gigi waited too long to respond. "Because I don't like them."

"Do you want real power or not?" Even as she asked the question, Sugar Beth wondered how she could pretend to have an answer.

"Oh, yes," Gigi said with a wistful sigh. And then her face clouded. "You're going to tell me to study, aren't you? And be nice to Gwen and Jenny."

"Respecting other people and trying to understand how they feel about the world gives you power." Sugar Beth hoped that was true. "It also makes you kinder. And people are drawn to kindness. That doesn't mean you forget to stand up for yourself. But you don't do it by trampling on other people, unless they need to be trampled on, in which case you do it in an up-front manner, with no snotty remarks about being fat."

Gigi slouched into her chair and looked sullen.

Sugar Beth rolled the Coke can between her palms. She unconsciously waited for the click of her wedding ring, but she'd made herself take it off last month. Gigi gazed up at her. She was going to be a real beauty before long, but Sugar Beth hoped with all her heart it didn't happen too soon. Beauty at too young an age got in the way of developing character.

She drew a deep, unsteady breath and tried to think of how to say what Gigi needed to hear. "Maybe it's time you came up with a plan for your life. A really ambitious plan. Without holding back. Even if it means deciding to be president of the United States. Your plan will probably change as you get older, but that might be even better, because, while you're preparing yourself for one goal, you'll be learning things that help you meet another goal. That's what real power means— not spending your time being bitchy because you're worrying about what somebody might be saying behind your back." She was shocked by the rush of anger that hit her. Why couldn't Diddie have said something like this when Sugar Beth was thirteen? But her mother had been incapable of thinking beyond the boundaries of her own narrow vision.

Sugar Beth leaned back in the chair and dredged up what she hadn't, until that moment, realized she understood. "People will always try to steal your power. When you do well, they'll say it's only because you're rich and your parents are big shots. People who care about you will try to steal your power, too, but they'll go about it differently. When you fail at something, they'll try to make you feel better by saying that nobody's good at everything, and you shouldn't be so hard on yourself. They might tell you not to feel bad about screwing up a math test because math's hard for girls. Or they'll say you shouldn't worry so much about injustice in the world because you're only one person. And even though they mean well, they'll be making you less than what you can be." Her chest felt tight, and she tried to ease it with another breath. "One way to grab your power is to learn when you need to step up to the plate and admit you're wrong, and when you need to dig in your heels because it's the right thing to do."

"How do you tell the difference?"

Sugar Beth shrugged. "Figuring that out is what life's all about."

"Have you? Figured it out?"

Only a thirteen-year-old could ask such a question. "Not yet. But I'm working on it."

Gigi nodded, as if she were thinking it all over, then planted her elbow on the table. "Let's talk about sex now."

Sugar Beth had no intention of being dragged into that discussion, but she welcomed the change of subject. "Coffee's ready." She hopped up from the table.

"I mean, how do you know when you're ready to have sex?"

She thought about the rumpled sheets upstairs. "Unless this is a pressing issue, which I sincerely hope it's not, why don't we postpone that discussion for another time?"

"Okay." Gigi's satisfied smile made Sugar Beth suspect she'd been manipulated into agreeing to another visit. "Could we do makeup now?"

"Why not?"

Sugar Beth's headache eased as they experimented with the contents of her cosmetic case. They talked about avoiding mascara smudges, obtaining power, setting goals. Sometimes Sugar Beth felt like a hypocrite, but not always, and as she contoured Gigi's eyelids, she wondered if she'd acquired at least a smattering of wisdom to pass on to the next generation.

Gigi said her parents were due back around four, and a little before three-thirty, she reluctantly headed to the door. "You don't have to come with me," she said as Sugar Beth followed her outside, leaving an unhappy Gordon behind. "I'm not a baby."

"And you're not climbing up that railing unless I'm there to make sure you get to the top."

"Like that's a big challenge."

"Sarcasm steals your personal power."

"You're sarcastic."

"Which is how I know this."

Gigi giggled.

Sugar Beth smiled at her. "We're all works in progress, honey. And believe me when I tell you that I've had to work harder than most."

"I think you've done a good job."

Sugar Beth shouldn't have felt so good about winning the approval of a thirteen-year-old, but she did.

As they neared the Galantine house, she ducked into the strip of woods at the side so she could watch Gigi climb the rail. Before she made it to the top, she started to goof around, leaning back and waving her arms and legs, deliberately trying to give Sugar Beth a heart attack and not doing a bad job of it. Sugar Beth forced herself to spoil the fun by turning away.

A branch cracked. Something moved in the woods in front of her, and Ryan stepped out of the trees.

He looked as shocked to see her as she was to see him and no happier about it. He was dressed in a navy sports coat, light blue dress shirt, and muted tie, an outfit she couldn't imagine anyone, except maybe Colin, wearing for a walk in the woods. "Sugar Beth? What—"

His head jerked as he caught sight of Gigi doing her acrobatics on the balcony post. "Gigi!" He rushed toward the house. "Get down from there right now!"

Gigi grabbed the post. Even from across the yard, Sugar Beth could see that she looked stricken. In a rush of memory, Sugar Beth recalled too well what a father's disapproval felt like. Gigi inched down the railing, moving as slowly as she dared, but not slowly enough for her father's anger to cool because the moment her feet hit the ground, he grabbed her arm and gave her a little shake. Sugar Beth instinctively rushed forward, but by the time she'd reached them, he'd let her go.

"What are you doing outside? And where have you been? Your mother and I've been looking everywhere for you."

"I took a walk," Gigi said stubbornly. "You weren't supposed to be back yet."

"We left the reception early, and you were told not to leave the house."

"I was suffocating," she cried, with all the drama of a soap star.

Ryan turned back to Sugar Beth, his expression hard. "I don't know what kind of game you're playing, but I don't ever want you around my daughter again."

It shouldn't have hurt so badly, but this was Ryan, and they'd watched *Scooby-Doo* together.

"Sugar Beth didn't do anything!" Gigi exclaimed. "I ran into her while I was walking. It was an accident. We didn't even talk. I don't even know her."

It had been a long time since anybody had tried to protect her, and Sugar Beth was touched. She gave Gigi a wry smile. "I'm afraid the jig's up."

"No, it's not! It's—"

"Ryan?" Winnie rushed around from the front of the house. Like her husband, she was dressed up, but her hair was windblown, her expression tense. "Ryan, what—" She froze. Her gaze flew from her daughter to Sugar Beth, then to her husband.

"Get inside right now," he snapped at Gigi.

In the kind of blatant miscalculation only a thirteen-year-old could make, she turned mulish. "I didn't do anything wrong."

Ryan's face flushed with anger, and Sugar Beth took a quick step forward. "Gigi . . ."

"Get inside!" he roared. "Go to your room. And stay there, do you hear me?"

Gigi turned on her parents, her hands in fists, eyes flooding with tears. "I knew this would happen. You're stealing my power! Just like Sugar Beth said you would!"

Oh, boy . . . Sugar Beth winced.

Winnie looked ashen, Ryan furious, but Gigi wasn't done. "I'm not going to let you! I'm not letting anybody steal my power."

Ryan's fist punched the air. *"Get inside right now."*

Gigi gave Sugar Beth a beseeching glance, but there wasn't a thing Sugar Beth could do that wouldn't make the situation worse.

Gigi stomped off toward the front door. A moment later, Sugar Beth heard it slam. She wished she could go to her room, too. She braced herself for Winnie's attack, but Winnie focused only on Ryan, who was looking at Sugar Beth as if he hated her. "She's only a kid," he said. "How could you have done this? You know we don't want you around her."

Gigi was in too much trouble already for Sugar Beth to rat on her. "She's my niece. I was curious."

Winnie came out of her daze. "Don't you *ever* come near her again. Do you hear me? I won't have it."

Sugar Beth ignored her to concentrate on Ryan. "Exactly what do you think I'm going to do to her?"

"We don't care to find out," he said pompously.

"You can't protect her from life."

"We can protect her from you."

Sugar Beth couldn't bear his self-righteousness and her temper flared. "You're too late. I already told her everything I know. How to smoke a joint. Steal money from her dad's wallet. Get *laid* in the back of a Camaro." It was a low blow, and Sugar Beth was ashamed of herself. Or at least she would be soon. "Go to hell, both of you."

Winnie watched numbly as Sugar Beth strode away from them, moving with her familiar long-limbed grace. Panic welled inside her. What if Sugar Beth stole it all? Her husband and her daughter?

"If we hadn't left the reception early—" Ryan broke off. "I'd bet this was Gigi's doing. She's been curious about Sugar Beth for weeks."

He was going to defend his old lover. Heartsick, Winnie turned away and headed back into the house.

Upstairs, they had the predictable scene with Gigi, who stood in the corner of her room, an ink-stained Laura Ashley pillow clutched to her chest, and proceeded to blame Winnie for everything. "I needed somebody I could really talk to. Sugar Beth listens to me. *She* understands me."

"I'm your mother, Gigi. I understand you. And you can talk to me whenever you want."

"No, I can't! You just want me to do everything your way."

Winnie found herself wondering who this demon child was living inside her precious daughter's body. "That's not true."

"At least Dad *listens* sometimes!"

Ryan stepped in. "This isn't about your mother. This is about you. And you gave away something precious today. You gave away our trust."

Gigi tucked the pillow under her chin.

"Why don't you think about that?" he said, curling his fingers around Winnie's arm. "And about how long it's going to take you to get it back."

He drew Winnie from the room and closed the door behind them. They heard the mattress squawk and Gigi's sobs. She was Daddy's little girl, and Ryan hesitated for a moment.

"Leave her," Winnie said. "She needs time to think."

They walked downstairs together and into the family room. Winnie felt sick to her stomach. Ryan tossed aside his sports coat and loosened his tie. "Sooner or later we'll have our daughter back." But he didn't sound convinced.

Upstairs, rap began blaring from Gigi's room. Winnie snatched up the sections of the Sunday paper he'd left everywhere. "When did I turn into the enemy? I have no idea. One morning I woke up, and there it was."

"This isn't about you. It's about her."

"It doesn't feel that way."

He unbuttoned his collar and slumped into the burgundy leather chair she'd bought at an estate auction. "I should have known she'd find a way to meet Sugar Beth. She gave me enough clues."

"What do you mean?"

"She asked a lot of questions. I forbid Gigi to contact her, but she's so damned hardheaded. I might as well have waved a green flag in front of her."

"You didn't say anything about this to me."

"You're not exactly rational where Sugar Beth is concerned."

"And you are?"

He came out of the chair. "Don't start this again."

"Why not? Shoving it under the rug isn't working."

"You're so completely out of line."

"I don't care. I'm sick of it."

His lips thinned. "You know what I'm sick of? I'm sick of having to walk on eggs around you, afraid I'll say the wrong thing and hurt your delicate feelings."

"Then stop doing it."

A muscle ticked in his jaw. He reached for the remote. "You need to get hold of yourself."

She knocked the remote from his hands and sent it skidding across the carpet. His eyes widened in shock. She turned on him. "You need to be honest! If you want Sugar Beth so badly, go get her!"

He looked stunned. "Is that what you think of me?"

"I'm tired of pretending."

"I've been faithful to you for fourteen years."

"Let me find a medal."

"I married you, goddammit! I knew you'd gotten pregnant on purpose, but I never once threw it in your face."

"You wouldn't. You're too decent for that. I was the liar."

"You said it, not me."

"Because you've never had the guts to."

"You are *not* turning this back on me. It's your guilt that's making you overreact to everything. This is your problem, Winnie, not mine."

Her fury turned to despair. She sank down on the edge of the couch. "I saw the way you looked at her last night."

"You saw what your imagination created. You're paranoid."

An eerie sense of calm came over her. Her hands fell limply in her lap, and she pressed her fingers together. "I'm jealous. I'm so jealous I can't see straight. But I'm not paranoid. After all these years, you still haven't gotten over her."

"That's bullshit. For God's sake, I married *you.*"

"You wouldn't have if I hadn't gotten pregnant."

He hesitated for a moment too long. "Of course I would have."

The pain cut deep.

"I would have," he said, as if repeating the words would make them true.

She drew a deep, unsteady breath. "I don't know who I am anymore. Maybe I never did. All I know is that I've worn myself out trying to be worthy of you."

"That's garbage."

"I don't think so." She stood up, gazed around at the antiques she'd collected. She loved this room, this house. She loved being surrounded by objects that spoke of the past. "I'm going to move into the apartment over the shop for a while." Her voice came from far away. She hadn't planned this, hadn't even thought of it until that very moment. But the idea beckoned like a shady grove.

His voice hit a low, dangerous note she'd never heard. "You're not going anywhere."

"We need some time."

"You need counseling, not time."

"I know you're angry."

"Anger doesn't begin to describe what I'm feeling right now. What do you expect me to tell Gigi? That her mother has up and left her?"

"I don't know what you're going to tell her."

"Just dump the whole thing on me, is that right?"

"Yes," she whispered. "Yes, that's right. For once, I'm dumping everything on you." She rose from the couch, walked to the door.

"Don't you leave this house, Winnie! I mean it. If you leave, you're not going to like the consequences."

She pretended she didn't hear him.

"... she had ample time to observe her sister's lover."

GEORGETTE HEYER, *Devil's Cub*

Chapter 13

Colin answered the door. Ryan stood on the other side, which wouldn't have been unusual except it was ten o'clock on Monday morning, and he looked like hell. "You look like hell."

"Thanks."

Colin hadn't spoken with Ryan since Saturday night. The lapse had been deliberate, since he'd had a fairly good idea of what direction their next conversation would take. Ryan was Colin's best friend. Their old relationship of teacher and student had happened so long ago that neither of them thought much about it anymore. They played in a basketball league together, occasionally jogged on weekends, and Ryan helped him coach the boys' soccer team.

"Has the plant burned down?" Colin said. "I can think of no other reason you'd abandon your customary workaholic habits."

"The plant's fine. We need to talk."

Colin wished he could avoid this particular tête-à-tête. Sugar Beth had appeared on schedule this morning, predictably ignoring the fact that he'd fired her, and then she'd made herself scarce while he'd holed up in his office, staring at his computer screen. He couldn't stop thinking about her. Making love with her yesterday had been better than anything he could have imagined, which, considering what he'd been reading lately, was fairly astonishing. She'd been bawdy, spontaneous, thrilling, and unpredictable. Afterward, she'd shown no interest in engaging in a postcoital examination of their relationship, which should have relieved him. Instead, he'd experienced this unhealthy compulsion to make her spill her secrets. Although he knew who she'd been, he didn't entirely understand who she'd become, and the mystery enticed him. Maybe this was why so many men had fallen under her spell. She issued a subtle, irresistible challenge that lured them to their deaths.

But the image of Sugar Beth as a cold-blooded man-killer wouldn't take hold.

Ryan gazed down at Gordon. "Where did the dog come from?"

"Just showed up one day." He gave in to the inevitable. "Would you like some coffee?"

"Why not? I might as well make the hole in my stomach even bigger."

"You should switch to a low-acid organic coffee."

"And give up all that stomach pain? No, thanks."

Gordon followed them into the kitchen, then waddled over to the sunroom and lay on the rug. Ryan pulled out one of the counter stools, only to push it back and begin to pace. "Look, Colin, you deserved some payback, no question about it, but this situation with Sugar Beth is out of hand. Now other people are being hurt, and you have to get rid of her."

The faint sound of water running overhead pressed home the need to get rid of Ryan, and Colin only filled the mug halfway before passing it over. "Winnie's upset, is she?"

"Winnie's way past upset. Sugar Beth's been seeing Gigi."

News, indeed. Still, nothing Sugar Beth did could surprise him.

"Yesterday while we were at the concert, Gigi sneaked out of the house to meet her. Sugar Beth probably encouraged it. I don't know how it happened. Gigi won't talk about it."

Colin silently cursed Sugar Beth. Did she go out of her way to create trouble? "I suppose it's only natural for them to be curious about each other."

"I can't believe she's involved Gigi in all this."

"What do you think Sugar Beth will do to her?"

"You know what she's capable of."

"Sugar Beth isn't eighteen any longer."

"Let's get real," Ryan retorted angrily. "She's floated through three marriages—the last one made her a certified gold digger. Now she's broke. Desperate, too, or she'd have told everybody to go to hell on Saturday night and stormed off. Call me overprotective, but I don't want a woman like that around my daughter."

Colin hated being dragged into other people's messes, but he couldn't see a way to sidestep this one. "Things aren't always what they seem where Sugar Beth is concerned."

"You're defending her?"

"I'm being objective." Now there was a laugh. Even before yesterday, he'd lost his objectivity where Sugar Beth was concerned.

Ryan's eyes narrowed. "You've gotten suckered in by her, haven't you?"

"I haven't gotten suckered in by anybody."

"Then fire her."

"I already did."

"You did?" Ryan looked surprised, then relieved. "The first good news I've heard this weekend. Sorry, pal, I underestimated you. Do you know if she's left town yet?"

"As to that . . ."

"I should have trusted you. But . . . I'm a little keyed up right now." He gazed into his coffee mug. "The truth is . . . Winnie's moved out of the house."

"What?"

"She's left. Moved into the apartment over the store."

Colin was stunned. Ryan and Winnie had the best marriage he'd ever seen. If they couldn't make a go of it, no one could. "I'm sure it's only temporary. You and Winnie are the genuine article."

"Apparently not. It's like Winnie's possessed. You know how rational she always is, but lately . . . She thinks I'm still hung up on Sugar Beth. After all these years. And she started talking about not knowing who she was, all that Oprah bullshit. I feel like I don't know my own wife anymore."

Colin remembered the way Ryan's eyes kept straying to Sugar Beth on Saturday night. By making it possible for her to stay in Parrish, Colin had inadvertently hurt the two people whose friendship he most cherished.

"I've tried to reason with Winnie, but she won't listen. She didn't even talk to Gigi before she drove off. She left that little task up to me."

"How did Gigi take it?" Colin asked, not really wanting to know.

"Oh, she's taking it fine. I said that her mother was stressed out because she had so much work to do at the shop, and she'd decided to settle in there for a few days to get things cleared up without any distractions. Gigi bought it, but she's a smart kid, and it won't take her long to figure out what's really going on."

"I'm sure Winnie will come to her senses before then."

"It'll happen a lot quicker if Sugar Beth is gone. I've never believed in throwing my weight around, but if I find out somebody else has hired her—"

"Hey, Ryan . . ." Sugar Beth waltzed into the kitchen, a bottle of drain opener in her hand. Colin wanted to strangle her. She couldn't have stayed upstairs until Ryan left. Oh, no. In her screwed-up head, that would have been a sign of cowardice, and how could she let a day pass without giving a hard time to as many people as possible?

"Your shower's running great now, Colin. Add the sixty bucks a plumber would have charged you to my paycheck."

Coffee slopped over the edge of Ryan's mug as he slammed it on the counter. "You said you fired her!"

"I did. Unfortunately, Sugar Beth still doesn't listen well."

"It gets in the way of my self-serving lifestyle." She headed for the sink, where she bent down to put the drain opener away.

Colin tore his eyes from her bottom, clad this morning in a pair of deep purple cigarette pants. "Exactly the sort of remark that makes people line up to hate you, Sugar Beth. But then you know that very well."

"You think?"

He refused to play her game. "Ryan stopped by to tell me that Winnie's moved out. Because of you."

She straightened and smiled. "No kidding. Now that just about makes my day."

Ryan's mouth hardened. "That's low, even coming from you."

Colin wouldn't let her weasel out of this with wisecracks. "Sugar Beth doesn't mean it. She's deliberately antagonizing you."

"I sort of mean it," Sugar Beth said. "You and Winnie pissed me off royally yesterday with Gigi."

"You were way out of line," Ryan said.

"In my humble opinion, you both need to lighten up with her."

Colin cut in before there was blood. "I'm sure Ryan isn't interested in hearing any of your opinions on child rearing."

"His loss. I know a hell of a lot more about headstrong teenage girls than he does."

Colin gave her his most quelling look. "You're baiting him again."

Ryan studied first one of them and then the other. "What's going on with you two?"

"Nothing."

Unfortunately, they spoke together, automatically making them look like liars. Sugar Beth recovered first and handled the situation in her own way. "Relax, Ryan. Colin's done his best to get rid of me, but I'm blackmailing him with some unsavory facts I've unearthed about his past, which may or may not involve the ritual deaths of small animals, so if my body ends up in a ditch somewhere, tell the police to start their interrogations with him. Plus you might warn everybody to be careful with their cats."

Amazing. Sometimes her cheek surprised even him. Ryan, however, had lost his sense of humor. "You still don't care how many people you hurt as long as you get what you want."

Sugar Beth liked to sting, but she didn't have much appetite for genuine hurt, and all the amusement vanished from her eyes. "I don't like being the bearer of bad news," she said quietly, almost gently, "but your marriage was already in trouble or my showing up wouldn't have sent your wife out the door."

"You don't know a thing about my marriage."

"I know that Winnie's moved out." She regarded him sympathetically. "And you seem to think all you have to do to get her back is see the last of me. But I doubt it's going to be that easy. Now if you'll both excuse me, I have some errands to run."

Sixty seconds later, she was out the door.

By the time Colin got rid of Ryan, the house had closed in on him. How had a man who cherished his privacy let everything get so far out of hand? Nothing he'd written so far that morning was worth keeping, so he grabbed a jacket and headed out the back door.

He'd thought about this long enough. It was time for action.

Everybody in the lunchroom was watching her, or at least it felt that way. Gigi's clammy hands gripped the plastic tray as she gazed around for somebody—anybody!—she could sit with. She should have spent lunch period in the library, but she'd told herself she was claiming her power today, no matter how scary it was and no matter how much her parents hated her. Now, though, she decided she was too young to claim her power. She should have waited till ninth grade. Or maybe tenth.

Until now, she'd been feeling pretty good about her first day back in school. Nobody'd said too much about her getting suspended, and Jake Higgins told her she looked cool. Jake had acne and was like four feet tall, but still . . . Before she'd gone to bed last night she'd painted her fingernails with black polish and borrowed this black T-shirt her mom never wore because she said it was too small. This morning, she'd put on an old pair of black jeans that were tight and too short, but, with black socks, she didn't think anybody noticed, and she'd found a choker necklace she'd strung in seventh grade with brown beads. It wasn't the best Goth look she'd ever seen—she needed a cool belt with silver rivets or a black skirt with black-and-white tights—but it made her feel sort of strong and reckless.

Win-i-fred had spent the night at the store so she could get an early start on her inventory, and her dad had been in a crappy mood, so Gigi'd waited till she got to school before she ducked into the rest room and put on some really dark eye makeup. It made her light eyes look spooky and mysterious, which was cool. Her parents couldn't get any madder at her than they already were, so tonight she intended to cut some choppy layers in her hair around her face and maybe put red streaks in if she could find a red marker. It felt good getting rid of her old baggy clothes.

A seventh grader bumped into her, and her bean burrito nearly slid off the tray. She couldn't keep standing here. Chelsea was at their old table, throwing her dirty looks. She was sitting with Vicki Lenson, who Gigi knew for a fact had done oral sex so she'd be popular with the boys. Just the thought of oral sex totally grossed out Gigi. She'd never *ever* do that, not even if she was married.

Kelli Willman and all the girls Gigi used to hang out with were sitting near the front. There was an empty seat, but Gigi didn't feel powerful enough to take it. The thought of eating lunch by herself made her armpits sweaty. Only total losers sat by themselves.

Somebody laughed at Gwen Lu's table. All the geeks were there. Gwen and Jenny Berry. Sachi Patel and Gillian Granger. Which would be worse? Sitting by herself or sitting with the geeks? Somebody really powerful would admit that Gwen Lu and Gillian Granger were the most interesting girls in eighth grade and nice, too. But if she sat with them today, she couldn't turn her back on them tomorrow. That would make her as bad as Kelli.

Panic hit her. She didn't want everybody thinking she was a geek, but she couldn't keep standing here. Her feet began to move. She didn't know exactly where she was going until she found herself standing next to Gwen's table. Her tongue stuck in her mouth. "Can I sit with you?"

"Okay." Gwen moved her tray a little to give her room, but she didn't make a big deal out of it. Gigi sat down and unwrapped her burrito. Gwen and Sachi were talking about their science fair projects. Finally, Gwen asked Gigi what she was going to do.

"Something about cows and why everybody should be a vegetarian." Gigi opened her bag of chips.

"Gillian's thinking about being a vegetarian," Gwen said, talking a little too loud. "But I like meat too much. I couldn't ever do it."

"I think it'd be cool," Jenny said. "I love animals. But I talked to my mom about it, and she freaked. She said I need protein."

Which led to a big and very interesting discussion about how parents didn't ever want you to do anything unique. Then Gigi said she thought they all needed to make sacrifices for the planet, and she knew Gwen was starting to think about it because she didn't finish her hot dog.

Gigi was surprised what a good time she had at lunch—nobody even asked her about being suspended—and she was sorry when the warning bell rang. After they took their trays up and got rid of their trash, Gwen and Gillian left for gym class. Gigi had English, and she headed for her locker to get her notebook. She'd just closed it back up when she saw Kelli and Heather Burke coming toward her. She started to put her head down and pretend she didn't see them like she'd been doing all year, but she changed her mind and walked up to them instead.

Kelli looked so surprised that she stopped chewing her gum, and Heather's cheeks got sort of red, like she was afraid something embarrassing might happen. Gigi pulled her books tighter to her chest and spoke fast before she chickened out. "Kelli, I want you to know you really hurt my feelings when you said all that stuff about me behind my back, about me being a rich bitch. I think if people are really friends and they have problems with each other, they should just be honest, so I guess we weren't as good friends as I thought. And if I was acting stuck-up, I'm really sorry. I don't feel stuck-up anymore."

Kelli sort of hunched her shoulders, like she only knew what to say about people behind their back and not to their face. Gigi felt kind of sorry for her because Kelli didn't know about claiming her power.

"It's not my fault," Kelli finally said, sounding really immature. "Nobody liked you."

Gigi felt herself starting to get mad all over again, but she knew she'd be giving up her power if she lost her temper. "I was being immature," she said, which totally surprised Kelli because she wasn't used to total honesty.

Heather spoke up for the first time. "I think maybe we were being immature, too."

Kelli didn't say anything, she just looked down at the floor, and Gigi walked away. She didn't know if she and Kelli could ever be friends again, or if she even wanted them to be, but when she got to English class, she answered every question.

* * *

Sugar Beth couldn't believe what she was hearing. "A job? You're offering me a job?"

"I'm desperate, and at least you read." Jewel set a stack of books on the counter near the register. "Meredith quit without giving me notice. One phone call from an old lover, and she was on her way to Jackson."

It had been evident at Colin's dinner party that Meredith was more than an employee, and Jewel's offhandedness didn't fool her. "I'm sorry. Not about the job; I couldn't be happier. But a broken heart isn't any fun."

Jewel shrugged her small, graceful shoulders. "I'll get over it. We weren't right for each other. We both knew it. But we were lonely, and, let's face it, the pickin's are slim in Parrish for girls who like girls."

Sugar Beth had to say it. "You understand, don't you, that hiring me could hurt your business?"

Jewel smiled for the first time since Sugar Beth had walked into the store. "Are you kidding? After what I saw on Saturday night, customers are going to line up just to get inside and torture you."

Unfortunately, she was probably right. Still, Sugar Beth accepted the job.

On her way back to Mockingbird Lane, she told herself this would make everything so much simpler. It wasn't good for her to be around Colin so much. She flipped on the radio and hummed along with Lucinda Williams as she sung a needy-woman song, but that didn't help shut down her thoughts. She had to stop overdramatizing and put things in perspective. Yesterday had been nothing more than a hot fudge sundae. She'd gone without one too long, so the craving had built up until she hadn't been able to think about anything else. But now that she'd given in and eaten her fill, she wouldn't need another for a long time.

She turned the volume louder. She should be thinking about how she could get into the attic instead of about hot fudge sundaes. Jewel wanted her to start the day after tomorrow, which meant she had to accomplish her goal right away. Her stomach grew queasy at the thought.

When she returned, she found the door to Colin's office shut, but she couldn't hear his keyboard clicking. She was beginning to realize that the writing life would be a lot more glamorous if writers didn't actually have to write. Ryan's coffee mug sat in the sink. Sugar Beth didn't like the pain she'd seen on his face, and fair or not, she blamed Winnie for it. What kind of spineless woman ran out on her husband just because an old girlfriend showed up?

A movement outside distracted her. She gazed through the sunroom windows and saw a workman digging at the far end of the backyard. As far as she knew, no one was scheduled to—

Her eyes widened. She shot to the door, bolted across the yard, and came to a dead stop next to him. He propped a wrist on the handle of his shovel and regarded her with his customary hauteur. She held up her hand. "For the love of God, don't say anything until my heart starts pumping again."

"Perhaps you should put your head between your knees."

"I was only teasing when I told everyone you had a drug problem. If I'd thought for one minute . . ."

"You will let me know when you're done caterwauling, won't you?"

He wore the raunchiest pair of Levi's she'd ever seen— threadbare in the right knee, a hole in the butt—an equally ratty gray T-shirt, worn work gloves, and scuffed, dirt-encrusted brown work boots, one of which had a knot holding the shoelace together. An honest-to-God smudge ran up alongside that gorgeous honker of a nose. And he'd never looked more irresistible. She scowled. "Even your hair's a mess."

"I'm sure a quick trip to my stylist will set it right again." He pushed the shovel back into the ground.

"I'm not kidding, Colin. If the Armani people see you like this, you're going to get blacklisted."

"Horrors."

She wanted to drag him into the pecans, wrap her arms around his neck, and make love with him until they were both senseless. So much for one hot fudge sundae being enough to satisfy her.

Dark patches of sweat stained his T-shirt, and the muscles bunched in his arms as he drove the shovel in again. He tossed a square of turf into the wheelbarrow at his side. He was digging some kind of trench. Or maybe a shallow grave . . .

He knew she was curious, but he kept digging for a while before he condescended to explain. "I've decided to build a stone wall. Something low that defines the property. It's warmed up enough to get started."

"Does this have anything to do with how quiet your computer's been lately?"

"I've been thinking about doing this for a while," he said with a trace of defensiveness. He pointed toward the west, where the property dipped toward a small ravine. "I'm going to build some terracing back there. I want everything to conform to the landscape. Then I'll extend the wall up the sides of the property."

"It's going to be a lot of work."

"I can do it at my own pace."

Although the front of Frenchman's Bride had been exquisitely landscaped, no one had ever paid much attention to the back. He dug up more turf. There was something about a man with a shovel, and the sweat on his neck might as well have been chocolate sauce. It wasn't fair. Brains and brawn should be two separate categories, not bundled into one irresistible package. She needed to pull herself together before she went after him with a spoon. But where to start?

"I have to get into the attic. I heard something scampering around up there while I was in your bathroom."

"I haven't heard anything."

"If you'd been upstairs you would have."

He stopped what he was doing and propped both hands on the shovel to study her. "You've been trying to get into the attic ever since you started working for me."

"I'm a housekeeper. It's part of my job."

"You're not that good a housekeeper."

Time to make her getaway. "Fine. If you want squirrels nesting over your head, I'm sure I don't care." She flipped her hair and turned away. Unfortunately, she wasn't fast enough because he threw down his shovel and stepped in front of her.

"This new book has distracted me more than I thought, or I'd have caught on faster. You think your painting's in the attic."

Her stomach sank.

"All those stories you've come up with . . . Squirrels, looking for dishes. They were excuses."

She tried to see a way out, but every exit was blocked, so she stuck her nose in the air. "Call it what you like."

"Why didn't you just come out and ask me?"

She tried to think of a polite way to explain that she didn't trust him not to claim the painting for himself. He was a smart man. Let him figure it out.

Except he didn't.

The bridge of his nose furrowed. He cocked his head and waited. Right then, she had one of those blinding realizations that told her she'd made a gross miscalculation. She tried to save the situation.

"It occurred to me that you might . . . The house is yours, after all, and . . ." Her voice faded. She licked her lips.

Another few seconds passed before he finally got it, and then outrage took possession of his dirty, elegant face. "You thought I'd take the painting from you?"

Her reasoning had been sound. Surely he could see that. "You do own the house. And I didn't have enough money to hire a lawyer to figure out what my rights were."

"You thought I'd take your painting." It was no longer a question but a cold, hard accusation.

"We were enemies," she pointed out.

But she'd offended his honor, and he was having none of it. He leaned down and snatched up the shovel.

"I'm sorry," she said as he rammed it back into the ground with enough force to sever a spinal column. "Really. A miscalculation on my part."

"This conversation is over."

"A gross miscalculation. Come on, Colin. I really need your help. Show me how to get into the attic."

Another clump of turf flew into the wheelbarrow. "What if your painting's there? Aren't you afraid I'll steal it?"

He sounded sulky now, and sulky she could deal with. "See, this is the problem with having so many character flaws. I assume everybody else does, too."

That chipped a bit of ice from his offended British dignity. "You don't have that many character flaws. But you *are* an idiot." He pronounced it like an American so she'd get the point.

"Does this mean you'll show me your attic?"

"There's nothing up there. Winnie cleaned everything out before I moved in. She might have put some of it in storage. I'm not certain."

"Maybe you don't know where to look. For example . . . there's a hidden cupboard." She could see that he wasn't entirely mollified, but she also detected the first hint of curiosity. She pushed her bottom lip forward, going for a pouty, adorable look. "I really am sorry I offended your honor."

He saw right through her, but he didn't call her on it. She held her breath.

"All right," he said begrudgingly. "Let me get cleaned up, and we'll have a go at it. But don't say I didn't warn you."

She wanted to tell him not to get cleaned up, that his grungy self was perfectly fine with her—more than fine—but she held her tongue.

Half an hour later, the sweaty stonemason had traded in his jeans for Dolce & Gabbana. He led her down the hallway to the upstairs study. "The door to the attic had to be moved for the renovation. But I didn't want to lose wall space, so the architect got creative." He headed for the built-in bookcases.

She'd already noticed that the center unit stuck out farther than its mates, but she'd assumed it had been built that way to accommodate ductwork. As Colin pushed on the edge of a shelf, however, the whole thing came forward a few inches, then slid to the side. Behind it, a narrow flight of stairs led to the attic.

"I'd never have found this."

"Prepare to be disappointed."

She followed him up the new set of stairs, then came to a stop at the top.

The attic was empty. The last time she'd been up here, her family's dusty relics had filled the place, but now Colin's footsteps echoed off the bare wooden floor and bounced against the faded green beadboard walls. The odds and ends of three generations of Careys had been wiped out. The Christmas boxes were gone, along with her grandmother's steamer trunk and her grandfather's golf clubs. Diddie's ugly wedding china and the zippered plastic bags holding her old evening gowns had been swept away. A nail still protruded from the old paneling, but Griffin's fraternity paddle no longer hung from it, and the basket holding Sugar Beth's precious Care Bears collection was nowhere in sight. Everything erased. Winnie Davis had thrown away all the pieces of Sugar Beth's history.

Dust motes swam in the shafts of sunlight coming through the small windows, and the floorboards creaked as Colin wandered toward the middle of the attic, the place where a Rubbermaid bin had once overflowed with her old dance recital costumes. "Nothing here."

He had his back to her, which made it imperative to find her voice. "Yes, I see." As he turned, she somehow managed to pull herself together. "The old house has a few secrets, though."

The attic was filled with nooks and crannies from chimneys and dormers. She headed for a corner just to the left of the main chimney where she and Leeann had built tents from two broken chairs and an old stadium blanket.

Diddie had shown her how to open the cupboard long ago, but also made sure Sugar Beth wasn't tempted to do it herself. *"See, precious. Nothing's in there except great big bugs and hairy spiders."*

Sugar Beth knelt in front of a two-foot-wide section of the old beadboard paneling and felt along the base. "My grandfather lived in terror of a return to Prohibition. He said that knowing this was here let him sleep at night." She felt for the concealed latch and released it. "There's another latch above the ledge at the top."

The expensive fabric of Colin's trousers brushed her shoulder as he moved closer. "I have it."

The paneling had warped over the years, and she pushed hard on the sides to loosen it. Colin stepped in front of her and lifted it away.

The cupboard was too small to hold one of Ash's larger, mounted canvases—she'd known that all along—but he might have left Tallulah a smaller work. Or a larger one could have been rolled up. She'd dreamed of the moment for weeks, but now that it had come, she was afraid to look. "You do it."

He peered inside. "It seems to be empty, but it's hard to see." He turned his shoulders and crouched so he could reach along the floor. "There's something here."

Her mouth went dry, and her palms felt clammy.

He withdrew a dusty old liquor bottle. "My God, this is fifty-year-old Macallan scotch."

Her spirits crashed. "It's yours. See what else is there."

"Be careful with that," he exclaimed as she jerked the bottle away from him and set it on the floor with a hard thud. He reached into the cupboard again. "This definitely isn't scotch."

She gave a soft cry as he pulled out a fat tube about three feet long wrapped in ancient brown paper tied with string.

He straightened. "This doesn't feel like—"

"Oh, God . . ." She pulled it from his hands and rushed toward one of the windows.

"Sugar Beth, it doesn't seem heavy enough."

"I knew it was here! I knew it."

The string broke easily, and the brittle craft paper fell apart in her fingers as she peeled it away. But underneath, she found only a fat roll of paper. Not canvas at all. Paper.

She slumped against the window frame.

"Let me look," he said softly.

"It's not the painting."

He squeezed her shoulder, then opened the roll. When he finally spoke, his voice held even more awe than he'd shown toward the scotch. "These are the original blueprints for the window factory. They were drawn in the 1920s. This is quite a find."

To him, maybe. She hurried back to the cupboard, crouched down, and reached inside. It had to be here. There was no place else to look. She felt along the floorboards and into the corners.

Nothing but cobwebs.

She sank back on her heels. Paper rustled as he set the blueprints aside. He knelt next to her, bringing with him the smell of cologne and sympathy. He pushed a lock of hair behind her ear, ran his thumb along her cheekbone. "Sugar Beth, you don't need the painting. You're perfectly capable of supporting yourself. Maybe not in the first lap of luxury, but—"

"I have to find it."

He sighed. "All right, then. We'll search the carriage house and depot together. Maybe I'll see something you overlooked."

"Maybe." She wanted to lean against him so badly that she pushed herself away. "I'd better get back to work."

"I'm giving you the rest of the day off."

That unbearable sympathy again. She rose to her feet. "I have too much to do. And I don't need coddling."

He'd only been trying to be kind, and she'd snapped at him,

but she couldn't manage another apology, and as she made her way to the stairs, she felt as blue as a person could get.

He stayed in his office the rest of the afternoon. Whenever she passed the door, she heard the muffled clatter of the keyboard. As evening approached, she put one of the mystery casseroles from the freezer into the oven, set the timer, and left him a note saying she'd see him in the morning. She felt too fragile to risk having him showing up at the carriage house later, so she added a P.S. *I have cramps, and I intend to do some serious self-medicating. Do not disturb!*

By the time she left Frenchman's Bride, she still hadn't told him she was quitting to take a job with Jewel, hadn't thanked him for his kindness in the attic, hadn't said anything to him she should have.

It had begun to drizzle again, and Gordon shot ahead. She let him in the house but didn't enter herself. Instead, she made her way to the studio. As she opened the lock and stepped inside, she tried to convince herself that what had happened today hadn't marked the end of her search. Colin had said he'd help. Maybe fresh eyes would see something her own had missed.

She flicked on the overhead bulb and gazed around at the workroom—the paint-encrusted ladder, the ancient cans and brushes. Even through the dirty plastic that protected it all, she could make out thick dabs of vermilion, splashes of pulsating green, curls of electric blue, and great sweeps of acid yellow. On the drop cloth that covered the floor, tacks and cigarette butts, a lid from a can of paint, other objects that weren't as recognizable had become encapsulated like beetles fossilized in amber.

Paint was everywhere, but the painting was nowhere. And the man who lived in Frenchman's Bride wouldn't leave her thoughts. She struggled to hold back her despair.

"When are you going to end this folly?"

GEORGETTE HEYER, *These Old Shades*

Chapter 14

The apartment above Yesterday's Treasures was cramped and dingy, filled with furniture that either hadn't sold or hadn't yet made its way downstairs. The living area had an exposed brick wall, two tall windows that looked down over the main street, and a sleeper sofa. A plastic shower stall occupied the corner of the old-fashioned bathroom, while the kitchen nook offered up an ancient refrigerator, a modern microwave, and an apartment-size harvest gold gas stove from the 1970s. The apartment couldn't have been more different from Winnie's house, and although she wasn't exactly happy here, she wasn't entirely unhappy, either.

She carried a cup of Sleepytime tea to the French café table she'd pulled from the display window so she'd have a place to eat, and gazed down on the dark, empty street below. It was nearly eleven, and the stores had closed long ago. The red neon sign for Covner's Dry Cleaning blinked in the light drizzle that had begun to fall, and a passing headlight reflected off the window of Jewel's bookstore. Winnie was thirty-two years old and living alone for the first time. Not that she'd been alone for long. It was only her second night.

"This is so dumb!" Gigi had exclaimed when she'd stormed into the shop after school today. *"Last night Dad made me do everything. I had to clean up the kitchen after we had pizza, and then I had to take the garbage cans out. He didn't even help; he just went in the study and shut the door. When are you coming home?"*

Winnie had been so taken aback by Gigi's black outfit and eye makeup that she hadn't responded right away. Her baby! As much as Winnie had yearned to see the end of her baggy Salvation Army clothes, she hadn't expected this. What would be next? Tattoos and tongue piercing?

She took a sip of tea. Not even the Seawillows knew she'd moved out, although Donna Grimley, the woman Winnie had hired as her new assistant, was getting suspicious.

On the street below, the traffic light flashed red, and the lone figure of a man came around the corner. He was tall, broad-shouldered, jacket collar turned up against the drizzle. It was Ryan, and her pulses quickened just as they used to when she was a girl. She felt a rush of sexual awareness she hadn't experienced in a long time and rose from the table so she could get closer to the window.

His steps slowed at the curb. He saw her looking down at him and tilted his head back to gaze up at her. She rested her cheek against the dirty glass and pressed the warm cup of tea between her breasts.

He made a sharp, upward gesture with his thumb. *Open the door, damn it, and let me in.*

Her breath made a cloudy circle on the window. Once, she would have drawn his initials inside that circle. Now, she pulled back just far enough to shake her head.

His anger spiraled up at her, the anger of an ill-used husband saddled with an ungrateful, hysterical wife. He made another jab with that furious thumb.

She shook her head again. At home, a spare key hung on the rack. Either he'd never noticed or it hadn't occurred to him he'd need it. Rain glistened in his hair, and his posture grew rigid. He stalked away, his angry strides devouring the wet pavement.

Long after she'd lost sight of him, she continued to stand at the window, cradling her teacup and waiting for the tears to come.

They didn't.

Sugar Beth overslept the next morning. Cubby and his cronies had shown up again last night—two nights in a row—and kept her awake with their hooting.

"Sugar . . . Sugar . . . Sugar . . ."

She hurried to dress, and when she arrived at Frenchman's Bride, she found a note from Colin saying he had business in Memphis and wouldn't be back until evening. At the end, he'd written, *I've made a dinner reservation for us tonight at the Parrish Inn. I'll pick you up at seven.*

Of all the dimwitted notions . . . He had a death wish. Why else would he want to do something so lamebrained? It was one thing for her to work for him—people liked that—but quite another for them to be seen together socially. She'd be leaving Parrish soon, but he'd planted roots here. And no matter how famous he'd become, he was still an outsider. If people realized he'd stopped dedicating himself to making her miserable, he'd lose all their hard-won respect.

She rose and tossed the note in the kitchen trash where it belonged, then gazed down at Gordon who'd just finished his breakfast. "I've been doing a con job on myself, haven't I? Nothing about this affair is going to work."

He paused in his postmeal stretch to give her his I-told-you-so look.

She grabbed a sponge and attacked the counter. Colin would refuse to sneak around like any sensible person. From his permanent mount on that moral high horse, he'd view the concept of seeing her only for sex as sordid. But who said sordid was always a bad thing? Sometimes sordid was simply practical.

She worked feverishly all day—stocking up on his groceries, cleaning out the refrigerator, straightening the closets. As she went into his office to sort through the household mail, she wished she'd told him yesterday that she'd taken a job with Jewel.

She also wished she'd been able to find a manuscript of *Reflections*. When she'd asked him if she could read it, he'd told her he didn't have a fresh copy. She'd said any old copy would do, but he'd put her off until she'd finally told him straight out that attacking Diddie after she was dead wasn't her idea of fair play. He'd ignored her, and all her snooping since then hadn't unearthed the manuscript, not even in his computer files. She spotted a printout of the first few chapters of his new book sitting on top of his desk. The red ink staining the pages reminded her of her senior year when that same critical handwriting had streaked the margins of every paper she'd written for him.

She returned to the kitchen and began making casseroles to freeze, just like all the other smitten single ladies in Parrish had done. Finally, she couldn't postpone it any longer, and she punched in the number of his cell phone.

"Frances Elizabeth here," she said when he answered.

"I did *not* know that was your name."

"Tell it to your shrink." She settled next to Gordon on the sunroom couch. "Where are you?"

"Almost home. How are you feeling?"

"Fine. Why?"

"Your cramps?"

"Uh . . . all gone."

But he'd heard the hesitation, and he was smarter than the average bear. "You lied to me! You didn't have cramps at all. I won't have it, do you hear me?" He sounded deliciously pompous and decidedly miffed.

"Sorry," she said, "I was tired last night, and I didn't want to bruise your ego by rejecting you. Men can be so sensitive. And don't forget that I have a long history of taking the easy way out."

"Why am I becoming increasingly apprehensive about this phone call?"

It was hard to put one over on Yogi Bear. "As a matter of fact, I do have a little news to share. But it's good news so don't worry. You might even want to pull over to the side of the road so you can do a happy dance." She stroked Gordon's fur, not feeling much like doing a happy dance herself. "As of tomorrow morning, I'm not working for you."

"What are you talking about?"

"Jewel hired me. She doesn't pay much, but neither do you, so the money's pretty much a wash. Not that I've forgotten about that two-thousand-dollar guilt check you wrote me, which, by the way, I tore up."

She waited for the explosion. It wasn't long in coming.

"This is completely unacceptable!"

"Why? You fired me, remember?"

"We renegotiated."

"When?"

"You know very well what I'm talking about."

"Don't tell me that you regard what we did in bed on Sunday morning as a labor negotiation."

"Stop being obstinate. Working at the bookstore will make you vulnerable to whoever walks in the door. You'll have no way of protecting yourself against whatever nastiness your old enemies decide to unleash on you. Jewel should have more sense."

"Quit it, Daddy, you're scaring me."

"Mock all you like. As long as you're working at Frenchman's Bride, you're protected. At the bookstore, you'll be a sitting target."

"I've known some unreasonable men in my time, but you

just shot to the head of the cafeteria line. You want to get rid of me, remember?"

Predictably, he ignored her. "Why didn't you discuss this with me?"

"No time. She didn't offer me the job until yesterday morning."

The slow, ominous monotone that rumbled over the phone line told her she'd made a strategic mistake. "You've known this since yesterday, and you're just getting around to mentioning it?"

"I had some distractions. Thanks, by the way, for being so nice in the attic. I should have thanked you yesterday, but you might have noticed I have a problem expressing gratitude."

"You have no problem at all expressing gratitude. And I'd very much appreciate it if you'd stop trying to control every conversation that makes you in the slightest bit uncomfortable by throwing out your imaginary character flaws."

He was a dangerous man, and she quickly changed the subject. "Don't you think it's about time you did that happy dance?"

"One of us has to look out for your best interests. Call Jewel immediately and tell her you've reconsidered."

"No."

"We have an agreement. I don't plan to let you back out."

"Hold it right there. The only agreement we ever had was that you intended to make me as miserable as possible, and I intended to courageously make the best of an intolerable situation like valiant Southern women have always done."

"We'll talk about this over dinner," he snapped, clearly reaching the end of a very short rope.

"As to that—"

He broke the connection before she could say more.

Colin was in a foul mood that night as he got dressed to take Sugar Beth to dinner. In her typically reckless fashion, she'd only made her life more difficult. By accepting the job at the bookstore, she'd be at the mercy of everybody who still held a grudge against her. He slipped his watch on. Her yowling admirers had shown up again last night. He'd been reading in the second-floor study, so he hadn't heard them right away, and by the time he'd gotten downstairs, they'd driven off, robbing him of the satisfaction of driving them off himself.

He gazed around at his bedroom. She'd made sure he had clean laundry, fresh sheets, and a supply of his favorite toiletries. He'd started to get used to having someone looking out for his comfort, even though he was perfectly capable of doing it himself. Still, the smaller touches tended to escape him, like the polished red apple resting on a white cloth napkin next to his bed. *One* apple. Maddening woman. He frowned and shot his cuffs.

As he made his way to the carriage house, he chastised himself for not specifically telling her she'd been rehired, but he doubted it would have made a difference. Sugar Beth liked to muck about with things. She'd been on his mind all day— the way she'd looked when they'd made love, her sharp edges smoothed out, those silvery eyes slumberous and utterly beguiling. Afterward, she'd snuggled in his arms and entertained him with her sass. The thing of it was, he'd never been a lighthearted person, but when he was with her, he at least felt the possibility of lightheartedness. Too late, he wished he'd thought to bring her flowers, something intrinsically Southern, full of spice. Something beautiful, complex, and as elusive as she was.

He approached the carriage house porch. Just the thought of seeing her again lifted the dark mood he'd been carrying around all day. And then he spotted the note taped to the door.

More cramps.

Sugar Beth nibbled on a sweet potato french fry and gazed through the Lakehouse windows. Beyond the docks, the water lay dark and mysterious, waiting for the Jet Skis and swimmers to return. In high school, they'd hung out at Allister's Point, where they'd drunk illegal beer, told dirty jokes, and made out. She wondered if Colin had ever made out on a beach blanket that smelled like beer and suntan lotion. She couldn't imagine it.

She pushed aside the uneaten half of her barbecue, a Lakehouse specialty, along with tamales, corn bread, and fried dill pickles. The weeknight crowd was sparse, but she'd still opted for the far corner table in the dining room, and even then she'd had to fight off Jeffie Stevens.

She'd been drawn to the Lakehouse tonight by nostalgia, along with a taste for the barbecue she'd grown up on. The rustic riverboat decor still looked much as she remembered: brass light fixtures with green glass shades, plank walls, gingerbread trim, wooden captain's chairs with vinyl cushions to protect against the wet swimsuits that were prohibited in the dining area—a rule that was conveniently forgotten from May into October, when the Lakehouse did most of its business. In the old days, green velour valances had topped the big windows that looked out over the water. Now the valances were red with gold ball fringe, and the wooden floor held a fresh coat of steel gray paint. A jukebox sat in the corner next to a tiny dance floor conveniently located by the doorway that led to the bar.

She reached for her Coke, then nearly knocked it over as Ryan stepped up to that very same bar. Just her luck. She'd come here to avoid being seen in public with Colin, and now she'd run into Ryan. Maybe he wouldn't spot her. But a long mirror ran along the wall in front of him, and as the bartender passed over his beer, Ryan's head came up.

She turned to gaze out the window, pretending not to notice him, but he was coming right toward her. He wore a gray suit, white shirt, and a tie loosened at the neck. Every eye in the dining room swung in their direction. She gazed down at her plate, spoke through tight lips. "You know better than this. Go away."

He kicked out the chair across from her and sank into it, beer bottle in hand. "I don't feel like it."

The teenage boy she remembered would never have taken a seat without being invited, but *that* boy had been a lot more polite than this hard-eyed captain of industry. She wanted her dog.

"I mean it, Ryan. Everybody's going to say I lured you out here, and frankly, I'm getting a little tired of being held responsible for the fall of all mankind."

His hair wasn't deliberately rumpled like Colin's. Instead, it looked as though he'd shoved his hand through it a few too many times, and the lines in his face seemed deeper-etched than they'd been four nights ago. His suit coat fell open as he stretched his legs and gestured toward her plate with his bottle. "Are you going to eat the rest of that sandwich?"

"Yes."

But he'd already pulled her plate toward him. As he picked up her untouched half, the past rushed at her so fast she felt dizzy. How many meals had he finished for her when they were in high school? She'd been a picky eater, more interested in fun and flirting than food, and he'd had a teenage boy's gargantuan appetite. Suddenly, she wanted it all back: the opportunities she'd squandered, the self-confidence she lost, the blissful arrogance that had made her believe nothing could ever harm her. She wanted her mother. The Seawillows. Most of all, she wanted the life she'd have lived if she'd stayed with her first lover, even though she hadn't loved him for a very long time.

The boy most likely to succeed polished off her sandwich and took a swig of beer. "Did you think about Parrish after you left?"

"I tried my best not to."

"Remember how we were going to leave here? Go to the big city and make our mark?"

"You were going to make your mark. I was mainly going to shop."

Colin would have enjoyed that, but Ryan barely seemed to hear her. Even as kids, they hadn't shared the same sense of humor. His had always been more literal. Like Winnie's. He peeled up the edge of the beer label with his thumb. "Did you ever think about me?"

Weariness from a long day caught up with her, and she sighed. "Go home, Ryan. Better yet, I'll go."

She tossed down her napkin and started to rise, but his hand shot across the table and grabbed her wrist. "Did you?" he said fiercely.

She was in no mood for this, and as she fell back in her chair, she jerked her hand away. "I thought about you all the time," she retorted. "When Darren Tharp slapped me across the room, I thought of you. When he screwed around on me, I thought of you. And the night I staggered into a Vegas wedding chapel with Cy, both of us so drunk we could barely say our vows, I thought of you then, too. One morning— And this happened *after* my divorce, mind you, because, unlike my loser husbands, I didn't screw around. One morning I woke up in a seedy motel with a man I could have sworn I'd never seen before, and, and, baby, you'd better believe I thought of you then."

A mixture of emotions played across his face: shock, pity, and the faintest trace of satisfaction that came from knowing she'd been punished for what she'd done to him. His all-too-human reaction quenched her anger, and she gave him a rueful smile. "Before you get too smug, I'd better tell you that I stopped thinking about you the day I met Emmett Hooper. I loved that man from the bottom of my heart."

Ryan's satisfaction faded, and she knew what was coming next. She held out her hand to put a stop it. "Don't bother jumpin' on the pity train for me. Emmett and I had more happiness in our short marriage than most couples have in a lifetime. I was very lucky."

He surprised her by going all starchy. "Winnie and I've been very happy."

"I wasn't making comparisons."

"All couples hit rough patches now and then."

She and Emmett hadn't. He'd died too soon.

"Anything I can get you, Mr. Galantine?" The waitress's eyes were bright with curiosity as she sidled up to the table. "Anything else, miss?"

"I'll have another beer," Ryan said, "and bring her some of that chocolate pie."

"Just my check," Sugar Beth said.

"Make it two pies," he said.

"Sure enough."

"I don't want pie," Sugar Beth told him, as the waitress left. "I want to go home. And since you're such a saint, apparently it hasn't occurred to you that Winnie's going to hear all about our little tête-à-tête here, and I'm guessing she won't take it well, so this might not be the best way to patch up your differences."

"I have nothing to feel guilty about."

He'd answered too carefully, and Sugar Beth studied him. "You want Winnie to hear about this."

"Hand me those fries if you're not going to finish them."

"I don't appreciate being used."

"You owe me."

"Not after Sunday."

He studied the ring his bottle left on the table. "You're talking about Gigi."

"Still as sharp as ever."

"I'm not apologizing for being upset."

"Then you're an idiot. You and Winnie managed to turn me into forbidden fruit, and you can bet that Gigi's already figured out a way to see me again."

Instead of an angry rejoinder, he traced the water ring with his finger. "You're probably right."

The waitress returned with the beer, two pieces of pie, and Sugar Beth's check. As she left, Sugar Beth stirred the last bits of ice in her Coke with her straw. "She's a great kid,

Ryan. Right now, she's asking the questions that most of us don't get around to until we're older."

"She hasn't asked me anything."

She arched an eyebrow.

"We have a great relationship," he said defensively. "We've always talked."

"Before she turned into a teenager."

"That shouldn't make any difference."

"You sound like you're ninety. You remember what it was like. I'm not her parent, and I'm also notorious, which makes me an irresistible confidante."

"What kind of questions is she asking?"

"Privileged information. You'll have to trust me."

He gazed at her for a long moment. She waited for him to say she was the last person he'd trust, but he didn't. "Colin's right. You have changed."

She shrugged. He fiddled with his beer bottle again. "Do you ever wonder what would have happened if we'd stayed together?"

"We wouldn't have. My self-destructive streak was a mile wide. If I hadn't left you for Darren Tharp, I'd have left you for somebody else."

"I guess you couldn't help it."

"Wait a minute. You're not going to wave the olive branch that easily, are you?"

"Your father was an insensitive son of a bitch. If he'd given you a little affection, maybe you wouldn't have adopted your scorched-earth policy with men."

"Girls and their daddies."

He flinched.

"Ryan, it's not going to be that way with Gigi. She knows you love her. She'll come through. Just give her some room to make a few mistakes."

He switched directions before she could see it coming. "Don't zero in on Colin, Sugar Beth. He bleeds like the rest of us, and he still has a lot of wounds from his wife's suicide."

"Worry about yourself." She pushed her pie across the table. "And don't use me again as a pawn in your problems with Winnie."

"Is that what you think I'm doing?"

"Yes."

He leaned back in his chair, looking her square in the eye. "What if I said I still thought about you?"

"I'd believe you, but I wouldn't attach any importance to it. There's not a single spark left between us."

"You're still a beautiful woman."

"And you're a gorgeous man. Ken and Barbie all grown up. We look real good together, but we don't have a lot to say to each other."

That made him smile, and she thought she felt something ease between them. Before it went away, she gathered up her purse and pushed her check across the table. "Thanks for dinner. And good luck explaining this to Winnie."

The house felt abandoned as Ryan entered. No wife waiting for him with a glass of wine and a smile. No rock music blaring from the upstairs bedroom. He tossed his suit coat over the back of a kitchen chair, on top of the sweater he'd left there yesterday. His *Sports Illustrated* lay open on the table. The counter held a litter of advertising flyers mixed in with bills and brokerage statements he hadn't taken the time to sort through. He'd always thought of himself as being well organized, but when he'd gotten dressed this morning, he couldn't find either his good black belt or his nail clippers. He tried to imagine Winnie's reaction when she heard he'd been with Sugar Beth. Maybe this would finally shake enough sense into her to bring her home.

The front door banged.

"Dad!"

Gigi sounded frantic. He dropped the newspaper. She'd eaten dinner tonight with Winnie at the Inn, and as he rushed into the foyer, images of disaster flashed through his head.

She stood just inside the front door, her eyes pools of misery, her chest quivering. She looked so young and forlorn. He pulled her into his arms. "Honey? What's wrong?"

"Dad?" She shuddered against him. "Dad, Mom's left us."

Winnie gripped the steering wheel. She hadn't been able to keep Gigi in the dark any longer. Maybe she and Ryan should have told her together, but that would have made it seem too serious, and she hadn't wanted to scare her. Besides, she doubted Ryan would have agreed to talk to Gigi with her. He was too angry.

When she'd spoken with him a few hours ago on the phone, he'd been hostile and sarcastic, playing the long-suffering husband saddled with a crazy wife. And maybe he was right. What sane woman walked out on her husband because he didn't love her enough? Still, she wasn't sorry she hadn't let him come up last night.

Ironically, she and Gigi had been having a good time at dinner once Winnie had gotten over the shock of her daughter's hair. Not only had she added red streaks, but she'd also chopped chunks in it around her face, cutting too far in on one side. Still, she'd seemed happy with it, so Winnie had managed a compliment. And she hadn't uttered a word about Gigi's eye makeup or too-tight black outfit. After some initial awkwardness, Gigi had started to chatter away about how girls gave up their power, a topic that had first reared its ugly head after her clandestine meeting with Sugar Beth.

". . . like when a girl does something goofy in class just to make some stupid boy she likes laugh. Or when the girls let teachers ignore them, even the women teachers. Mrs. Kirkpatrick calls on the boys a lot more than she calls on the girls because the boys are always jumping out of their seats, and she wants to keep them quiet. Today I raised my hand about six thousand times, but she still wouldn't call on me. Finally, I jumped out of my seat, too, and started waving my arms until she got the point."

"I remember getting passed over, too."

"Because you were quiet."

Winnie had nodded. "Not by Colin, though. He was the worst teacher in some ways, the best in others." She'd put on her fake British accent. *"Jasper, keep your bum in that bloody chair till I call on you. Winnie, speak up! I was terrified of him."*

Gigi had giggled, and for a few moments, it felt like old times. Then Gigi's strawberry shortcake had arrived, and Winnie had known she couldn't postpone telling her any longer.

"There's something I wanted to mention before you hear it from someone else and get the wrong impression." She'd made herself smile a little, as if what she was about to announce were no more unpleasant than a dental appointment. "I've decided I need a little time to myself. No big deal, and definitely nothing for you to worry about. But I'm going to stay at the store awhile longer."

At first, Gigi hadn't understood. "This is so lame! It's not fair. You're at the store even more now than before you hired Donna."

Winnie'd tried again, speaking carefully. "It's not entirely about work. There are some things I need to sort out. Dad and I got married when we were very young, but as people grow older they change a little. I want to think some things through. A few weeks maybe. A month. It's nothing serious—I don't want you to think that—but you're also getting older, and it's not fair to keep you in the dark."

The petulance in her daughter's expression had been replaced by dawning realization and then horror. Within seconds, Gigi made the leap to the ultimate disaster. "You and Dad are getting a divorce!"

"No! No, sweetheart, nothing like that." Winnie hoped her own creeping doubts didn't show. "Dad and I aren't getting a divorce. I just need some time away, so I can figure a few things out."

A vulnerable little girl replaced the sullen teenager, and Gigi began to cry. "You're getting a divorce."

Winnie knew then that she shouldn't have chosen the Inn's dining room to break the news, but she'd thought a public setting would make it seem less important. Once again, she'd been wrong.

"It's me, isn't it?" Gigi's nose had started to run. "Because I've been such a bitch."

"No, sweetie. No. This doesn't have anything to do with you." She didn't add that Gigi's behavior hadn't helped. Instead, Winnie hustled her into the ladies' room, where she'd hugged her, cleaned up the smeared eye makeup, and done her best to reassure both of them that this was only temporary.

She was still shaking as she climbed the stairs and let herself into the dingy apartment that had become the living quarters of the richest woman in Parrish, Mississippi. After she'd slipped into a T-shirt and her new blue-and-white-checked pajama bottoms, she settled down to do some paperwork, but she couldn't concentrate. She picked up *Southern Living* and thumbed through the recipes, only to realize she had no idea who she might be cooking them for. The phone rang. She knew it would be Ryan. By now, Gigi had told him about their conversation, and he'd be furious. If she ignored his call as she wanted to, she'd only make things worse. "Hello."

"Winnie, we're all in the alley." It wasn't Ryan, but Merylinn. "Come down right now and unlock this door."

She'd hoped a few more days would pass before the Seawillows learned that she'd moved out. "I'll be there in a minute." As she made her way downstairs, she considered the odds of convincing them she was only staying here so she could get an early start on inventory. Not good at all.

They looked as though they were dressed for a come-as-you-are party: Leeann in faded capris and a man's work shirt, Merylinn in yellow J-Lo sweatpants with a matching tank and zipper jacket, Heidi in jeans. Amy must have gone to church that evening, because she wore a rose-colored suit with a white shell. They swarmed upstairs, bringing with them the scent of strong perfume and interference.

"We have sustenance." Merylinn pulled a bottle of vodka from her tropical tote along with a silver cocktail shaker. "Thank God for Amy's bladder infections. You always know where you can find cranberry juice."

"I've been doing better with them." Amy took the Ocean Spray from a sack and a couple cans of Coke, because she didn't drink alcohol.

"If you'd pee right after you and Clint have sex, you wouldn't get so many." Heidi headed for the kitchen and began opening the cupboards, looking for glasses.

"I do pee," Amy retorted. "It doesn't help."

Heidi waved a tumbler at her. "Right after? Or do you mess around some more first."

"Depends."

"I pee," Merylinn said, "and I still get 'em sometimes."

Trying to stop the Seawillows once they'd set themselves in motion was like trying to stop kudzu. Winnie sank down on the room's saggy couch and let them do their work. Leeann pulled a box of Cocoa Puffs from a Radio Shack sack. "This was the only chocolate I had in the house. The kids got into my Hershey's."

The last time there'd been a Seawillows emergency involving vodka, cranberry juice, and chocolate, Leeann had ended up divorced. Winnie crossed her legs. "What's all this about?"

"Sue Covner, among other people." Leeann dumped the Cocoa Puffs in the bowl Heidi passed over. Sue was a notorious busybody and the wife of the owner of Covner's Dry Cleaners across the street from Yesterday's Treasures.

Merylinn headed for the kitchen. "Don't anybody say another word till I get our drinks ready."

The Seawillows were used to working together, and it didn't take long for them to settle around the couch, glasses in hand, the French café table moved closer to hold the Cocoa Puffs, accompanied by some Skittles Heidi dredged from the bottom of her purse.

"Y'all can tease me if you want," Amy said, "but this is serious business, and we're startin' off in prayer." She grabbed Winnie's and Leeann's hands. "Lord Jesus, we're here in the spirit of friendship to help Winnie and Ryan in their time of trouble. We ask you to give them forgiving hearts, so they can deal with their problems, whatever they might be. Remind them how much they love each other. And what you've joined together, Lord Jesus, don't let anybody, and we mean *anybody*, pull apart. We pray in your name. Amen."

"Amen," they all replied.

Winnie took a sip of the cranberry juice–laced vodka—lots of vodka, very little cranberry juice—and watched as Merylinn sat forward in her seat. "All right, everybody, let's get down to business." Her forehead crumpled. She reached over to touch Winnie's knee. "Honey, Sue Covner called me this afternoon. She said the lights have been on over your store for the past two nights, and that she thinks you're sleeping here." She took in Winnie's sleepwear. "I told her she was surely mistaken, but apparently she was right."

"Sue Covner should mind her own business," Winnie retorted.

"She's too busy minding everybody else's." Leeann grabbed a handful of Cocoa Puffs and tucked her feet under her on the couch.

"Deke called Ryan at work today," Merylinn continued. "He said Ryan sounded awful."

"Good," Winnie retorted, surprising herself almost as much as she surprised them.

Heidi cradled her glass and looked at the others. "Y'all know how intuitive I am. I said I thought they might be having problems."

Over the years, Heidi's intuition had proved even less reliable than the local weather forecasters, and Winnie wished

she could have found another time to get it right. "We're going through a bumpy patch," Winnie said carefully. "It's
nothing serious, I don't want to talk about it, and this is just a
waste of good vodka."

Merylinn gazed at the others, and Winnie felt a stir of uneasiness as she watched some kind of silent communication
pass among them. Amy picked up Leeann's glass and stole a
sip. Leeann turned to Winnie. "Honey, we're thinkin' it might
be more than a bumpy patch. That's why we're here."

"What makes you think that?" Winnie said slowly.

"Sue called me twice, the second time not much more than
an hour ago." Merylinn waved a helpless hand in the air. "Oh,
shit, I'm gonna cry."

Amy patted Merylinn's arm, but she kept her eyes on Winnie. "Sue's daughter called her from the Lakehouse." She fingered her cross, looking like the mother of all sorrows.
"Ryan was there. At the Lakehouse." She took a long, slow
breath. "And he was having dinner with Sugar Beth."

They all began talking at once.

"I'm so mad at him I could spit . . ."

"We had to get here first and warn you . . ."

"You know Ryan would never look at another woman. If it
weren't Sugar Beth, nobody'd even think twice about it."

"I just hate her. I can't help it. She's not going to get away
with this."

Winnie's first thought was to blame herself. If she hadn't
left home, this wouldn't have happened. If she'd let Ryan
come upstairs last night . . . If she'd been more conciliatory
on the phone . . . Acid burned in her stomach. At least they
were no longer in limbo. "Ryan's a big boy," she heard herself say. "He's strong enough to fight her off if he wants to."

"But what if he doesn't want to?" Leeann blurted out.
"What are we going to do then?"

Not *you*. *We*. Whether it was vodka or fear, Winnie's heart
filled with love for these women.

They started poking and prodding. What exactly had Ryan

done? How long had they been having problems? Who did Sugar Beth think she was? Winnie polished off her drink, told them how much she loved them, and refused to answer a single question.

"We're your best friends," Merylinn protested, refilling her own glass. "If you can't talk to us, who can you talk to?"

"Obviously not that bastard I'm married to."

The novelty of hearing the Golden Boy of Parrish, Mississippi, called a *bastard* made Heidi snort, which sent a little vodka up her nose, and they all started to giggle, even Winnie. Eventually, they settled down. Heidi drank a Cocoa Puff that had somehow made its way into her glass. Amy polished off Leeann's drink. Merylinn refilled the cocktail shaker. Leeann picked at her nail polish. Their friendship enfolded Winnie like a warm blanket.

Leeann slipped back into her shoes, all the laughter gone from her eyes. "Ryan's a very special man, and the sad fact is . . . if you're not careful, Sugar Beth's going to steal him from under your nose."

"Leeann's right," Merylinn said. "Ryan is special. You can't let her take him away from you. You have to fight for him."

"I'm special, too," Winnie heard herself say. "And I think it's about time Ryan Galantine fought for *me*."

They all stared at her, but Winnie was claiming her power, and she didn't flinch. "As a matter of fact, I think it's long past time."

"You can't keep me at arm's length forever, my little beauty. I want you. Will you come to me?"

GEORGETTE HEYER, *Devil's Cub*

Chapter 15

Sugar Beth let herself inside the carriage house, flicked on the light, and screamed.

"Welcome home, my dear." Colin slouched in the darkest corner of the room, one hand draped over the arm of the wing chair, the other clasping a crystal tumbler of scotch. The collar of his dress shirt was unbuttoned, and Gordon lay at his feet, one ear flopped over the toe of a polished black Gucci loafer.

"Don't you ever scare me like that again!"

"I warned you about locking your door."

She dropped her purse on a chair and shrugged off the jacket she'd tossed over a sweater and a short denim skirt. "You could at least have turned on a light."

"I wanted to brood."

"Well, stop it."

He crossed his ankles, disturbing Gordon's comfortable perch. "Come now, you must be accustomed to finding angry men on your doorstep. We had a date."

"You had a date. I wasn't asked."

"I believe I left you a note, and we also spoke about it when we talked on the phone."

"A one-way conversation."

"I'm not going to sneak around." He set down his drink with a thud and rose. "That's what this is about, isn't it?"

"You're the one who has to live in this town, dawg."

He rose to his feet so he was looming over her. "This is your bizarre idea of protecting me."

"No matter how much the good citizens of Parrish fawn over your famous self, you're still an outsider, and the welcome mat can be snatched away at any minute."

"That's my concern. I won't have it, Sugar Beth. Any of it."

"You sound like one of your Victorian ancestors."

"I don't need anyone's protection," he said, advancing on her with slow, menacing steps. "And I especially don't need the protection of a woman whose life plan seems to start and end with selling a painting she can't find."

"And aren't we being supportive tonight?"

"Believe it or not, you can live a decent life without diamonds and furs."

"Thank you, Mr. Gucci." She moved away.

He curled his hand over the back of the wing chair. "I enjoy the luxuries my money buys, but I don't need them, and I sure as hell wouldn't sell my soul to get them."

"Once again proving you're the better person."

"Sugar Beth . . ."

The low note in his voice suggested the time had passed for another wisecrack. "I'm not a total idiot," she said. "I've never intended to support myself with the painting. I'm going back to Houston and get my real estate license." It had been such a good idea—it still was—but she needed to work hard to inject any enthusiasm into her voice. "I have a lot of contacts there, and I want to sell high-end real estate. But that's hard to do without an impressive car and a decent wardrobe."

"You? Sell real estate?"

"What's wrong with that?"

"Not a thing. It's a perfectly respectable career. But I can't see you doing it."

"I'll be terrific at sales."

"Until some demanding client pisses you off."

"I can be tactful."

He crossed his arms over his chest. "Ah, yes, you're a master of tact, all right."

"Thanks for the vote of confidence."

"I'm simply pointing out what you seem determined to ignore, but then I believe we've already discussed your difficulties staying in touch with reality. Witness your lamebrained idea to work at the bookstore."

"I'm not talking to you about that anymore."

"Then let's go back to your plan to sell minimansions." He was getting steamed up again, and she gave him an uneasy glance as he moved away from the chair. "You need a realistic method of supporting yourself, not some scenario based on finding a painting that was probably destroyed."

"I know! I'll go to auto mechanic school."

"That does it." With no more warning than the flare of those aristocratic nostrils, he backed her right against the wall. He looked ferocious as he pulled her into his arms and growled, "God help me, I've never wanted to do violence to a woman, but we're either going to make love or I'm going to beat you."

That finally made her smile. "I choose door number one."

He muttered a dark curse, then crushed her lips with his kiss. At the same time, he shoved his hands under her denim skirt . . . and she didn't do a thing to stop him.

Within seconds, her hose and panties were gone. He clasped the backs of her thighs and lifted her against him. A china vase crashed to the floor near Gordon's head, sending him scurrying into the kitchen. She wrapped her legs around Colin's hips. He fumbled with his clothes. Shoved himself inside her.

She was ready for him.

He thrust deep, then groaned and began to withdraw. "No condom."

She pushed against him, not letting him go. "It's all taken care of."

"Thank God."

He pressed her back to the wall, his fingers digging into her bottom. She took his mouth and gave herself up to the hot, wet rub . . . the sounds and scents . . . his fierceness . . . his care.

She was falling in love with him.

The knowledge had been there for days, but she'd refused to examine it, and now she couldn't, not when his eyelashes lay in tough dark spikes against his cheekbones, and he felt so good inside her. She sucked at his bottom lip. He moaned, drove deeper, and she abandoned herself to the tumult.

After it was over, she let him pull her upstairs where they took off the rest of their clothes and made love again, this time more slowly and with a tenderness that nearly undid her. She was losing her battle to keep the barriers between them in place.

When they were finally satiated, they took a bath together. She fastened her hair on top of her head. He sat behind her, his big knees bent, an elbow propped on the edge of the tub. "What did you mean about the condom?" His soapy hand stroked the curve of her breast. "When you said it was taken care of?"

The rosy glow from Tallulah's ancient red Christmas candles made the old bathroom seem like a place out of time. If only that were true. She didn't want to answer his question, but he had the right to know. "I had an ectopic pregnancy when I was twenty-two, a few other problems. I am, you'll be pleased to know, incapable of mommyhood."

He pressed his lips to the side of her neck. "You can't catch a break, can you?"

He'd stirred dark waters, and she couldn't manage a reply.

He stroked her other breast, gave her time to recover. Eventually, he tucked a lock of wet hair behind her ear. "How long has it been for you?"

She drew a spiral in the soapy water on his knee. "Emmett got sick two and a half years ago."

"You hadn't had sex in nearly three years?"

"Not with another person."

He chuckled. One of the candles sputtered. He shifted his leg to a position that was only marginally more comfortable, dabbled with her earlobe. She rested the back of her head against his shoulder. Falling in love wasn't exactly a red-letter event, since she'd done it so many times before. It was her old weakness, but she'd believed she'd gotten past the point where she didn't feel alive unless she fancied herself in love. Apparently not. At least she was smarter now, and she knew exactly what she had to do about it.

"We need music," he said. "Bach, I think." But instead he began singing "Ain't She Sweet" in a surprisingly mellow baritone, which made her smile despite her mood. When he was done, he caressed her shoulder. "Promise me you'll tell Jewel you changed your mind, darling. Promise me you'll stay at Frenchman's Bride."

Men had called her a lot of things over the years—*honey, sweetie, babe, bitch*—but never *darling*. "My days at Frenchman's Bride are over, Your Grace."

"Why, pray tell?"

In spite of herself, she had to smile. "Being a kept woman and all that."

"You're hardly a kept woman. You work for me."

"Sleeping with the boss and all that."

"You're determined to be difficult. Fortunately, I'm in an exceptionally fine mood."

"You should be after what I did to you tonight."

That managed to distract him for a couple of minutes. Not long enough, though, because he soon returned to the subject at hand. "We're going to approach this rather amazing chemistry we have in a logical fashion."

"Okay, but I'm having my lawyer draw up an ironclad prenup to make sure I get Frenchman's Bride after our divorce."

Instead of scaring him to death, she'd amused him. "You won't put me off that easily."

"You should be shaking in your boots. Except for one thankfully short-lived period during the worst of my drinking days, I tend to marry my lovers."

"Now, however, you are a wiser, more mature woman."

"Not that wise, dawg, and I've got a powerful hankering for you."

"Stop toying with me. I'm not so easily frightened. I'll admit that what's happened has been fairly astonishing. We seem to be one of those odd flukes of nature . . ."

Easy for him to talk about flukes of nature. He didn't have a neurotic compulsion to fall in love with everything in pants.

". . . and I believe I've come up with a rather tidy solution to our dilemma."

"I don't have to write a term paper, do I?"

"Not unless you plan to make it highly erotic." His thumb found a tight muscle in the back of her neck, and he gently kneaded it. "What we most need is time, a chance to let this thing between us run its natural course."

"Colin, you only like low-maintenance women, remember?"

"I like you well enough."

"Be still, my heart."

She sensed his smile.

"You really are an extraordinary woman."

"And I'm not even at the top of my game." Her defenses weren't as strong as they should be, and it was time to take harsher measures. She fumbled for the plug with her toe. "You might remember that I've caused you nothing but trouble since I got here. And, forgive me if I'm hurting your feelings, but I've lost my taste for getting involved with the wrong sort of man. Or any man, for that matter."

"Nonsense. I'm exactly the right sort. No one could be safer for you than me."

The naked, workingman's body pressed hard against her didn't feel the least bit safe. "How exactly do you figure that?"

"We understand each other perfectly. I'm sarcastic and unpleasant. You're headstrong and manipulative."

"Bless our hearts." She located the ring on the plug and tried to work it free.

"Exactly. Neither of us entertains any fantasies about the other, so we're not in much danger of letting things get messy, now are we?"

The plug gave. "I've been married three times. Messy's my middle name."

"Which is exactly your problem. You get married. With me, that pressure will be off you from the beginning."

Something ached inside her—not the fact that he didn't want to marry her; she'd never go down that road again—but the knowledge that she was incapable of the uncomplicated, loving relationships that came so easily to other women. The time had come to play it straight, but she couldn't do it with his body pressed so close, and she rose from the tub before she spoke.

"Making love with you has been the first thing that's felt really good in a long time, but no matter how much I've been rationalizing it, this was a backslide for me."

The hand sliding up her leg stilled at her calf, and he went all haughty on her. "I'm not some bloke you picked up in a bar."

She stepped out of the water and wrapped herself in a towel. "You may find it hard to believe, but I do know how to take care of myself, and having an affair with you isn't the way."

"A little late to decide that."

"You were more temptation than I could resist."

He looked more thunderous than appeased.

"The worst part is, I'm just starting to realize we've screwed up a nice friendship."

"Nonsense. We haven't screwed up a thing." Water sluiced over the hard planes of his body as he rose, and the gleam of candlelight over those ropey muscles made her want to sink back in the tub with him. "It's possible to be both friends and lovers. Preferable, actually."

"Not in the Universe of Sugar Beth." She put more distance between them as he stepped from the tub. "It tends to be all or nothing with me, Your Grace, and the fact that I'm standing here without my panties four months after my husband died means I'm pretty much back to my old tricks." Her voice faltered. "Which is a lot more depressing than even you can imagine."

"He was in a coma long before he died. And from what you've said about the kind of man he was, I can't believe he'd have expected you to live the rest of your life in mourning."

"You're missing the point. This isn't good for me."

"It was bloody well good enough for you half an hour ago."

He refused to understand, which made it time to hit him with her full arsenal. "I don't tend to separate sex and the illusion that I'm falling in love."

The instant wariness in his eyes told her she finally had his attention. "Sugar Beth, you don't honestly believe . . ."

"That I'm falling in love with you? Why not? Look at all the practice I've had. And if that's not enough to send you running for the hills, it's sure enough to make me grab for a pair of Nikes." She took in a little air so she could get through the rest. "That's why I'm dumping you."

His concern faded, and indignation took its place. "Like hell. I'm not one of your toy boys, Sugar Beth. You can't toss me aside just because you're having one of your snits."

"Have you listened to what I've said?"

"Every word. And all of it twaddle. You're far too accustomed to having men roll over at your command. Well, this man doesn't roll."

"I'm sure your brain will kick in any minute now."

He wrapped the threadbare towel low on his hips, spoiling a magnificent view. "There's no need for all this drama."

"Let me make it a little clearer. I've been involved with enough painful relationships to last a lifetime, and I'm not doing it again. Ever."

"Agreed. Pleasure only."

"You're either stone-deaf or the stupidest man on earth."

"Stop being so stubborn."

She clutched the towel tighter and headed for her bedroom. "If you want to be an idiot, go ahead, but you're taking that long walk to the gas chamber all by yourself. This affair is over."

His voice drifted over her shoulder, low and full of purpose. "That, my dear, is what you think."

"You have played fast and loose with my affections, ma'am. I could laugh at myself for having been so taken in. To be sure, I should have known what to expect from a member of your family."

GEORGETTE HEYER, *Devil's Cub*

Chapter 16

$\mathcal{R}$yan waited until Winnie's assistant left for lunch before he approached Yesterday's Treasures. The bell over the door rang as he stepped inside. Winnie was alone, standing near the counter, arranging a display of antique dolls in a wicker carriage. She looked up, a welcoming smile fixed on her face until she saw who it was, and the smile disappeared. That made him so furious he flipped the sign on the door so it read CLOSED, twisted the lock, and shot her a look that had *badass* written all over it.

He was rewarded with the first sign of wariness on her part, a small, almost imperceptible step backward. Good. He was tired of being the only one on edge.

"I'm expecting a delivery," she said.

"Tough."

"This isn't a good time, Ryan. If you have something to discuss, we'll do it later."

"I have something to discuss, all right. And I don't want to do it later."

His bad temper came from too much caffeine and not enough sleep. He should be at his desk now, eating a ham sandwich from the cafeteria while he caught up on a stack of unread reports and a P & L he'd intended to finish three days ago. But his concentration was shot.

Nearly forty-eight hours had passed since he'd seen Sugar Beth at the Lakehouse, and Winnie hadn't said a word about it, even though they'd spoken twice on the phone. He knew for certain that she'd heard the news. Deke had called to tell him that the Seawillows had flown off for an emergency powwow on Tuesday night. Too late, he wished he'd stopped at Gemima's to fan the fire, but he'd walked right past without re-membering that Sugar Beth had started working there. The truth was, he'd barely thought about Sugar Beth since Tuesday. He'd been too consumed with his resentment toward Winnie.

Her hair looked longer than he remembered, which was crazy, since she'd only left home four days ago. A tiny, jew-eled clip, barely the size of his thumbnail, held her bangs back from her face on one side. She didn't seem much older than Gigi, but she looked far less innocent.

He'd never paid much attention to her clothes. Her wardrobe was stylish, conservative, and at first glance her ivory-colored wrap dress seemed that way, too. Surely he'd seen her wear it before, so why had he never noticed the not-so-subtle way it clung to her body? She always complained that her legs were too short, but even without that ridicu-lously sexy pair of open-toed heels, they were more than long enough for his taste. Exactly long enough to wrap around his hips.

A flood of lust shot straight through him, not the familiar lust a husband feels for his wife, but something more sordid that evoked seedy motels and broken wedding vows. *All you ever think of is sex!* He'd been indignant when she'd thrown that at him, but he'd have a tough time defending himself now.

"Ryan, I really don't have time to talk."

"And I really don't care."

Her wariness increased. "Is there something specific . . ."

"How about the fact that my wife's moved out, my daughter alternates between clinging to me like a burr and refusing to come out of her room, and I haven't been worth a damn all week at work. How about that?"

"I'm sorry." She might have been offering sympathy to a stranger, and the pit of his stomach burned. He'd been so sure that hearing he'd had dinner with Sugar Beth would have shaken her up enough to realize she couldn't keep doing this, that it was time to start fighting for her marriage instead of running away. Fighting for her *husband*. He'd at least wanted to frighten her into coming back to the bargaining table. It hadn't occurred to him that she might not care enough to make the trip.

He was overcome with a watershed of unpleasant emotions—anger, fear, guilt, and something primitive that had to do with antiquated notions of possession. He concentrated on his anger, the one he could most justify. "You're not sorry about anything. If you were sorry, you'd fix this."

She had the audacity to laugh, a dark, brittle sound. "Oh, yes, sir, let me just do that, right away, sir."

"God, I hate it when you're sarcastic."

"Only because you're not used to it."

"What do you expect me to do?"

"Be honest."

He could feel himself losing it, and he gritted his teeth. "What the hell's that supposed to mean? Tell me what you want from me?"

She dropped her eyes, and for a moment he thought she was embarrassed. But when she lifted them, she didn't look embarrassed at all. She looked tough and determined. "I want your heart, Ryan."

Her quiet dignity spoke of intelligence, of decency, of qualities that made *him* feel like the guilty party, which was something he didn't deserve, so he struck back hard. "This is a great way to go about getting it."

She didn't flinch. Instead, she took a few steps toward him. She looked young, innocent, very beautiful. "I want your heart, and I want your forgiveness."

Her words should have pacified him, but they only made him angrier. "This is bullshit."

She gave a weary sigh, as if he were the unreasonable one. "Go back to work. You're still too angry to talk."

His sense of being ill-used had eaten away at him for days. No. Longer than that. He'd had plans for his life, and none of them had included being a twenty-year-old husband and father. She'd stolen his dreams. She'd stolen his *future,* but he'd swallowed his resentment. Not in one big gulp—that would have been too much to ingest—but in queasy sips— sips so small and far apart he'd never managed to get to the bottom of the glass.

"If you want my forgiveness," he heard himself say, "you're going to have to wait a hell of a long time for it."

Her head came up. He told himself to leave it at that, but he hadn't been sleeping well, and he knew he'd taken too much for granted, taken *her* for granted, and that she was right—he had held something back—but he no longer cared about fair. "I hate what you did to me. I've always hated it, do you hear me?"

Her face grew as pale as Gigi's two nights ago, her eyes as wide and just as stricken. Tough. For fourteen years, he'd swallowed his resentment, and for what? So she could run away and upset everything?

"Ryan—"

"Shut up!" He whipped her with his words, blasted her with everything he'd stored up. "You said you wanted me to be honest. Here's some honesty! You stole my fucking life!" His arm shot out, and he caught a display of glassware with the back of his hand. She gasped as the pieces flew, shattered, just like his marriage, but that didn't stop him. He bore in, said what he'd barely let himself think. "You took away my choices when you decided to get pregnant. You didn't care what I wanted. All you cared about was what you wanted. I hate what you did to me, goddammit. And hell, *no,* I don't forgive you. I won't *ever* forgive you."

Shocked silence fell between them. Her face was ashen, her lips trembling. His lungs constricted, and he felt as if he were choking. Broken glass lay everywhere, wine and water goblets, shattered pitchers. Shards slicked the floor, brutal ice, the glittering debris of a fractured rainbow life.

He waited for her to fall apart, wanted her to fall apart like he was. Instead, she met his eyes, and through the trembling in her voice, he heard a lifetime of sadness, right along with a toughness he'd never expected. "All right," she whispered. "All right, then."

The reality of what he'd said hit home. He didn't want this. He didn't want his life broken. He wanted his marriage back, his wife, the woman who'd once looked at him as though he hung the moon and stars. Everything he'd said was true, but where was the relief he should feel at finally getting it off his chest? Where was his old bitterness? He needed it back. He needed to gnaw over the righteousness of his anger so he could justify the broken glass, the shattered marriage.

But he'd waited fourteen years too long to tell her how he felt, and his bitterness had no taste left.

Her breasts rose and fell beneath the soft fabric of her dress. She'd given him everything he'd wanted, everything he'd dreamed of, and instead of treasuring it, he'd just thrown it all back at her.

"I'm so sorry," she whispered. Her expression was full of compassion and understanding—pain, too, but not the sharp agony he felt. "I'm so very sorry."

He knew then that he'd screwed everything up, and he had no idea how to make it right. His secret resentment had been the bedrock of their marriage, responsible for her eagerness to please, for his subtle, punitive detachment. But now that resentment had gone up in flames, and he wanted to tell her he loved her. Except she'd never believe the words after everything he'd just hit her with.

His eyes stung. He had to get out of here. He made his way to the door and fumbled with the lock.

She didn't say a word to keep him with her.

As Sugar Beth came out of the bookstore's back room, she saw a little boy staring at the Nightingale Woods mobile she'd hung a few hours earlier, part of a promotion for the newest book in the *Daphne the Bunny* series. The boy was around five, dressed in jeans and a striped T-shirt, and he had the slightly broadened features that signaled Down syndrome.

He was the first child who'd ventured into the dimly lit and awkwardly positioned children's section all morning. "I know I should give it the same attention I give the rest of the store," Jewel had said when Sugar Beth had asked her about it as they opened up the store that morning. "But I don't have any passion for selling children's books. Besides, they haven't been profitable for me."

"Not surprising. It's hardly the most appealing part of the store."

Jewel had stuck her small nose in the air. "Fine. If you think you're so smart, you're the new manager of the children's book department."

"There isn't a children's book department."

"And don't let it interfere with your other work."

Sugar Beth had grinned down at her diminutive employer. "Only my third day on the job, and I've moved into management. I knew I'd be a star."

Jewel snorted and walked away.

Sugar Beth had to fight the urge to pick up the phone and call Colin with the news. She couldn't do that kind of thing any longer. The fact that she'd dumped him didn't prevent him from calling her, however. Generally he used Gordon as an excuse—he'd insisted on sharing custody. Sometimes he called with a question. Did she remember if she'd renewed his *Atlantic Monthly* subscription? Had she taken his tweed sports coat to the dry cleaner, because he couldn't find it? She missed him desperately, and sometimes she wished he'd press her for a dinner date, but he seemed to be biding his time, a hungry wolf on the prowl, waiting for a moment of weakness so he could pounce. Maybe his strategy was working because this morning she'd had to resist the urge to run over and make him breakfast before she headed to the bookstore.

She couldn't start brooding again, so she turned her attention to her small customer. She was alone in the store, and Jewel would expect her to assist the parent who'd come in with the little boy, but she didn't. Instead, she followed the direction of his gaze to the fanciful mobile. "Do you like the Daphne books?"

He gave her a wide smile. "Like Benny!" He pointed toward the cardboard figure of a mischievous-looking badger wearing goggles and an aviator's scarf. "Benny's my friend. Read book!"

She grinned. How could she resist all that enthusiasm? The boy grabbed one of the earlier books in the series from the display she'd just set up. She took it from him. "What's your name?"

"Charlie."

"Come on then, Charlie." She sat cross-legged on the floor, deciding right then that they needed to add some small chairs or at least a few pillows. She patted the space next to her, and Charlie settled close.

"Daphne Takes a Tumble, by Molly Somerville." It was probably Colin's influence, but shouldn't children be trained from the beginning to recognize authors and titles? *"Daphne the Bunny was admiring her sparkly violet nail polish when Benny the Badger zoomed past on his red mountain bike and knocked her off her paws . . ."*

"I like this part." Charlie climbed into her lap, and by the third page, he'd wound his fingers through a lock of her hair.

". . . Benny pedaled faster and faster. In the road ahead he saw a great big puddle." She heard the front bell chime and fervently hoped Jewel had returned so she could wait on the other customers because Sugar Beth wasn't going anywhere. Charlie reached over and turned the page. "This is a really good part."

"Benny laughed and pretended the puddle was the ocean. The ocean! Splashhhh!"

"Splash!" he mimicked.

They finally reached the end of the book, and he turned up his face to give her another of his heart-melting smiles. "You a very good reader."

"And *you* a very good listener."

She sensed a movement off to her right and looked over to see Leeann standing at the end of the biography section watching them. Sugar Beth gently set Charlie aside and rose. Leeann wore slacks and crepe-soled shoes, so she must be on her way to the hospital or coming off her shift.

"Mommy!" Charlie ran to her. "I like Benny and Daphne!"

"I know you do, punkin'." Although Leeann spoke to her son, her eyes stayed on Sugar Beth.

"I want book. Please, Mommy."

"You already have that book."

"Don't have that one." He raced for the display, snatched up the newest book in the series, and carried it back to her. "What's this say?"

"Victoria Chipmunk and Her Bothersome Baby Brother."

"Don't have that one."

"How much is it?" Leeann asked.

Sugar Beth was so disconcerted it took her a moment to find the price. Leeann rubbed Charlie's head. "If you get a new book, you can't buy a toy the next time we go to Wal-Mart."

"Okeydoke."

"All right. Take it to the register. I'll be there in a minute."

He ran off, sneakers thumping on the carpet.

An awkward silence fell. Leeann fidgeted with the clasp on her purse. "Charlie's my youngest. I had an amnio before he was born, so we knew from the beginning he had Down syndrome."

"That must have been tough."

"We had some problems. Money's always been tight. My ex—Andy Perkins—you didn't know him. He grew up in Tupelo. Anyway, Andy gave me an ultimatum. Either have an abortion or he'd leave me."

"And you told him not to let the door hit him on his way out?"

Leeann gave a weak smile. "I thought about it long and hard, though. And it hasn't been easy."

"I'm sure it hasn't. Charlie's adorable. Smart, too. He knew just when to turn the pages."

"It was a good trade." She ran her thumb along the edge of a shelf. "You didn't know he was mine, did you?"

"No."

"Thanks for reading to him."

"Anytime."

She slid her purse to her other hand. "I gotta go."

"I'll ring up the book for you."

"Jewel'll do it."

Still, she didn't move, and Sugar Beth couldn't stand it any longer. "Just spit it out, Leeann. Whatever's on your mind."

"All I want to say is that you've hurt a lot of people, and you're still doing it. Stay away from Ryan."

Sugar Beth thought about trying to defend herself, but Leeann was already walking away. Sugar Beth set *Daphne Takes a Tumble* back where it belonged and looked up at the mobile. As she blew softly on the cardboard animals, she wished she could live in Nightingale Woods. Just for a little while.

The rest of the afternoon passed so quickly that Sugar Beth had no chance to get back to reorganizing the children's department. She decided to do it after they'd closed. Unfortunately, that meant calling Colin.

"Would you keep Gordon until nine or so? I'm working late."

"Doing what? The store closes at six."

She knew he was trying to keep her on the phone, but she couldn't resist sharing her news. "I'm management now. Jewel's put me in charge of the children's section."

"She didn't want to do it herself, then?"

"That would be one way of looking at it."

"Do you know anything about children's literature?"

"Heaps."

"That bad, is it?"

"Luckily, I'm a quick study."

"Good news, old chap." Colin's voice faded as he turned his head away from the receiver. "Mummy's coming home late tonight. It'll be just we guys, so we can get drunk and watch porn."

She snorted. "*We* guys."

"Predicate nominative."

"You're such a tool." As she hung up, she reprimanded herself for sparring with him. Typical addictive behavior.

Catty-corner across the street, she watched Winnie closing up for the evening. In the past few days, Sugar Beth had caught glimpses of her entering and leaving the store. Once she'd seen her changing the display in the window. Winnie had a good eye for design, she'd give her that.

Gigi had stopped by the store to see Sugar Beth yesterday, but she'd been subdued and uncommunicative, even when Sugar Beth had asked her about her new baby-Goth fashion statement. Sugar Beth suspected her parents' separation was weighing on her. Around lunchtime that same day, she'd seen Ryan walk into Yesterday's Treasures. For Gigi's sake, she hoped they'd worked out their problems, but now, as she watched the lights go on in the apartment above the store, she suspected it wouldn't be that simple.

Sugar Beth's call shot Colin's concentration. He played the piano for a while and, as he ran his hands over the keys, invented a game for himself in which all her mystery was gone. He'd seen every secret part of her, hadn't he? He'd touched and tasted. He knew the sounds she made, the feel of her. She loved being on top, but her orgasms were more explosive when she was beneath him. She liked having him turn her head to the side and hold it in place while he tormented her neck with his kisses. Her nipples were as sensitive as flower petals and having her wrists pinioned excited her.

But for every mystery he'd uncovered, a thousand more waited to be discovered. And there was so much they hadn't done. He'd never had her in his own bed or in a shower. He wanted her on a table, legs splayed, heels propped on the edge. He wanted her turned bottom up over the arm of a chair. Oh, yes, he definitely wanted that.

He pushed himself away from the piano. He needed something more physical than Chopin to occupy him tonight. He needed to make love with her again.

The foyer had grown dark. He flicked on the chandelier, then turned it off again. He'd been taken aback on Sunday when she'd talked about falling in love with him, but now that he'd had some time to think it over, the idea no longer seemed quite so terrifying. It was simply Sugar Beth being overly dramatic as usual. Her shortsightedness in trying to put an end to their affair frustrated him. He wasn't insensitive to her grief. She'd lost her husband only four months earlier. But Emmett Hooper had been in a coma for six months before his death and ill for months before that, so she was hardly being unfaithful to his memory. He understood she was frightened—he wasn't calm himself—but if she'd consider the situation logically, she'd realize this was something they needed to see through.

He didn't like how empty the house felt without her. His writing hadn't been going well at all. In the old days, he might have talked with Winnie about it, but she had enough to cope with now. Besides, she tended to be too tactful. Sugar Beth, on the other hand, had an amazing ability to cut through to the essential, and she'd give him her unvarnished opinion.

That morning he'd called Jewel, ostensibly to order another book but really to check up on her new employee. "Sugar Beth's a gold mine, Colin," Jewel had said. "She loves selling books. You wouldn't believe how well-read she is."

He'd believe it, all right. He'd already noticed the diversity of the books she'd swiped from his shelves. "So she's working out, then?"

"Better than I could have hoped. Everybody in town's found an excuse to drop by the store these past couple of days. Since they don't want to look nosy, they all buy something. I try to wait on the women—they're giving her a hard time—but I leave the men to her. She can hand-sell the boys just about anything, even the ones I swear can't read a lick."

"Glad to hear it," he'd growled.

He headed for the kitchen to see about dinner. Sugar Beth had left his freezer well stocked, and he grabbed a casserole. She, of course, would be so wrapped up in reorganizing the kiddie section that she'd forget to eat. Or if she did remember, she'd grab a candy bar and call it dinner. Her dietary habits were abominable. She had no regard for her health, and while she might not be the best cook in town, she was far from the worst, and she needed to take better care of herself.

He thrust the casserole in the microwave and slammed the door, ignoring the fact that he was behaving very much like a man bent on slaying dragons and rescuing princesses. *Dumping him, indeed.* Did she really think it would be so easy?

The phone rang, and he snatched it up, hoping she'd called again so he could give her his opinion of fainthearted women.

But it wasn't Sugar Beth . . .

Somebody banged on the door. The store had closed two hours ago, and Sugar Beth frowned as she heaved the last bookcase into place. By repositioning some of the standing bookcases, she'd made the children's section more accessible. Unfortunately, she'd had to steal a little floor space from Jewel's beloved poetry section, which would mean some fast-talking in the morning.

She brushed off her hands and headed to the front. Her short, one-piece coral knit sweater dress had a dirt mark on it. She hoped she could get it out because working at the bookstore was stretching the boundaries of her slim wardrobe.

"Coming!" she called out as the door continued to rattle. She passed through the biographies and saw a man standing on the other side of the glass. Big, broad-shouldered, wearing Versace and a thunderous expression. Her pulses kicked like a teenager's. She fumbled with the lock and opened the door. "Your Grace?"

He pushed past her into the store, leaving behind the faintest trace of brimstone. "Who's Delilah?"

She swallowed. "My cat."

"Fascinating. Your *cat* wants to know why you haven't called her in two days."

Sugar Beth could have kicked herself. She'd left Colin's phone number as a backup in case her cell conked out, and she'd forgotten to change it. The number had been only for emergencies, but Delilah could be wily, and she must have wormed it out of someone in the office.

"Did you scare her? I swear, Colin, if you said one thing to upset her . . ."

He slapped a foil-covered casserole on the counter. "Why would I upset her when I was conserving my energy to upset *you*?"

"What possible business is this of yours?"

"She called you her mummy."

"*Mommy.* You're living in the home of the red, white, and blue, buddy boy. We speak American here."

But she couldn't distract him. He leaned his hips against the counter, crossed his arms over his chest, tapped the toe of an exquisitely polished loafer. "She did not sound like anyone's little girl. She sounded like an older woman."

"Delilah is my stepdaughter. Now, I have work to do, so *ta-ta.*"

"She told me she was forty-one."

"Numbers confuse her. She's not."

His gaze was a lot steadier than her heartbeat. "She's the reason for those whispered phone calls I used to overhear, isn't she?"

"Don't be silly. I was talking to my lover."

"She told me she lives at a place called Brookdale. After I hung up, I did a little research on the Web. Your talent for obfuscation continues to amaze me."

"Hey, I haven't obfuscated in weeks. Makes you go blind."

He lifted an imperious eyebrow. She grabbed the casserole he'd brought, and peeled back a corner of the aluminum foil. Her lasagna. He'd stuck a fork in the top. She'd barely eaten all day, and the smell should have made her mouth water, but she'd lost her appetite. "It's no big deal. Delilah is Emmett's daughter. She was born with some mental disabilities. She's fifty-one, if you must know, not forty-one, and she's lived at Brookdale for years. She's happy there. I'm all she has. End of story."

"Brookdale is an expensive private facility."

She carried the casserole she didn't want toward a reading nook with a table and two chairs. As she sat, she extended the fork. "Normally we don't allow food or drink in here, but we're making an exception for you."

He advanced on her. "This finally begins to make sense."

"All right, I'll eat. But only because I'm famished." She forced herself to dig in.

"I know you loved the man, but what kind of father wouldn't make provisions for a dependent daughter?"

She'd never betray Emmett by revealing her own frustration with his lack of planning. "His finances were complicated." She forced herself to take another bite. "I make good lasagna, if I do say so myself."

"This explains why you've been so obsessed with finding that painting. This is the missing piece. You were never interested in buying yourself diamonds. I should have figured that out."

"No kidding. I think this is the best casserole I ever made."

He braced his hand on a bookcase. "You need the money so you can keep her at Brookdale. You're not the villain in this piece, are you? You're not the viperous blond bitch-goddess who only cares about herself. You're the poor, unselfish heroine willing to sacrifice all to help the less fortunate."

"Seriously, don't you want some of this?"

"Why didn't you tell me?"

She couldn't head him off any longer, and she jabbed the fork into the casserole. "I had no reason to."

"The fact that we're lovers didn't factor in?"

She shot out of her chair. "Past tense. And I do what I have to so I can take care of myself."

"By building a wall that's so thick nobody can see through it? Is that your idea of taking care of yourself?"

"Hey, I'm not the one spending all my spare time laying stone in the backyard of Frenchman's Bride. You want to talk about your basic symbolism . . ."

"Sometimes a wall is just a wall, Sugar Beth. But in your case, putting up barriers is a permanent occupation. You don't *live* life. You *act* it."

"I have work to do." She headed for the counter only to have him follow.

"You've created this alternate persona—this woman who's so tough that she doesn't care what anybody thinks of her. A woman so tough that she's proud to announce all her character defects to the world, except—and make note of this, because here's where your true brilliance lies—those faults you hang out for everyone to see don't have anything to do with who you really are. Applause, applause."

She concentrated on straightening a display of bookmarks. "That's not true."

"Then why didn't you tell me the real reason you needed to find the painting? Why did you shut me out?"

"Why should I let you in? What possible advantage could there be in it for me? Should I have stripped myself bare just because still another man has walked into my life? Another man to destroy my well-being? Thanks, but no thanks. Now get out."

He gazed at her in a way that made her feel as if she'd failed another of his exams. But she was living her life the best way she could, and if that didn't suit him, then too bad.

He came toward her, and as he looked down into her face, tenderness replaced his customary haughty expression. "You are . . . ," he said softly, ". . . the most amazing woman."

She wanted to melt into him like the needy ex–homecoming queen she was. Instead, she kept her spine straight and arms at her sides. "I have work to do."

He let her go with a sigh and walked to the door. With his hand on the knob, he turned back and regarded her imperiously. "It's not over, my dear. Whatever you may think."

She waited until he disappeared to rush to the door and throw the lock. Her chest felt tight, but she absolutely refused to start crying over another man. She grabbed the casserole and paced around the store, eating a few bites here and there, missing Delilah, missing Gordon, missing the man she was determined to lock out of her heart. By the time she finally got back to work, the pleasure had faded, and at ten o'clock, she began turning off the lights. When she reached the front of the store, however, something across the street caught her attention. At first she thought it was an illusion, an odd reflection from the streetlights, but then she looked more closely and gave a soft gasp.

Smoke was trickling from the second-floor window above Yesterday's Treasures.

"'Tis no wonder we grew up like snarling dogs."

GEORGETTE HEYER, *These Old Shades*

Chapter 17

Sugar Beth watched the smoke trailing from the window. The lights were on. Winnie was up there.

She dove for the phone and called 911. After she'd given the dispatcher the information, she hung up, thought for a moment, then grabbed the stapler from the counter, unlocked the door, and rushed across the street.

Smoke was still coming out. *"Winnie!"* she yelled up toward the window. "Winnie, can you hear me?"

There was no response. She peered through the front window but couldn't see any smoke on the first floor. She rattled the knob and, when it didn't give, stepped back and flung the stapler at the door. The safety glass shattered into a thousand round pebbles.

The faint smell of smoke hit her as she stepped inside. "Winnie!" She made her way to the back of the store. "Winnie, are you up there?" The smell of smoke grew stronger. She saw a narrow wooden staircase leading to the second floor. It had *death trap* written all over it.

"Winnie!"

She heard a thud, then an un-Winnie-like curse. "Call the fire department!"

"I did. Come down!"

"No!"

She strained to hear sirens, but there hadn't been enough time. Reluctantly, she grabbed the handrail and made her way up the stairs.

Three rooms opened off the dingy hallway at the top, with a smoky haze coming from the center one. She headed toward it. "Winnie?"

"In here!"

The room was long, high-ceilinged, and old-fashioned, a combined living area and kitchenette. Smoke poured from the area near the stove. Winnie was beating at the cupboard next to it with a bath towel. Although Sugar Beth couldn't see any leaping flames, the situation was far from under control, and Winnie should be getting out.

"I was making fried chicken, and—" She glanced over her shoulder and started to cough. "What are *you* doing here?"

"Do you want me to leave?"

"I don't care what you do."

"I should let you burn."

"Then get out."

"Don't tempt me."

Winnie gasped as a stack of paper napkins sitting on the counter burst into flames. While she swung the towel at them, Sugar Beth snatched a scatter rug from the floor and began beating at a wisp of flame licking at a wall calendar. She heard the sound of a siren. Her eyes were stinging, and it was getting harder to breathe.

"This is stupid. The fire department's coming. Let's leave while we can."

"Not till they get here. I can't let this spread downstairs."

The store held irreplaceable antiques, and Sugar Beth

could almost understand. *Almost.* She slapped at the cupboard door. "Say, 'Pretty please, Sugar Beth. Stay and help my *stupidass* self.'"

"The towel!"

Sugar Beth spun around in time to see a dish towel drop to the floor in flames. She smothered it with the scatter rug, coughed. "You're giving me back Diddie's pearls, or I swear to God I'll lock you up in here."

"Bite me."

The smoke was getting thicker, the sirens closer, and Sugar Beth decided Winnie had pressed her luck for long enough. She tossed down the scatter rug, took a quick step forward, and threw a hammerlock around her neck.

"What are you *doing*?"

"Putting an end to negotiations."

"Stop it!"

"Shut up. The trucks are almost here." Sugar Beth pulled her toward the door.

"I'm not going anywhere!" Even though Sugar Beth was taller, Winnie must have been working out because she was strong as an ox, and she started to break away. Sugar Beth used a neat trick she'd learned from Cy Zagurski and dragged her into the hallway.

"Ouch! That hurts. You're twisting my arm off."

Sugar Beth began maneuvering her down the steps. "Play nice, and I won't break it."

"Quit it!"

"Save your breath."

They were nearly at the bottom when she made the mistake of easing the pressure. Winnie immediately tried to bolt back up the stairs, but she'd breathed in just enough smoke to slow her reflexes, and Sugar Beth put her in another choke hold. "Quit being an idiot!"

"Let me go!"

She wasn't certain how much longer she could have held on to her if the first fire truck hadn't pulled up in front of the store just then. Winnie saw it, too, and finally stopped struggling. Through the broken door, Sugar Beth watched people getting out of their cars and realized a small crowd had begun to form.

She also realized she'd just been handed a golden opportunity. Granted, it was the kind of opportunity a more honorable person would resist. Colin, for example, wouldn't think of it. Neither would Ryan, and certainly not Winnie. But the fire didn't seem too serious, and none of those stuffed shirts had Sugar Beth Carey's particular gift for enjoying the moment.

The firefighters jumped from the truck and rushed toward the broken door, but before they could get there, Sugar Beth stuck out her foot and tripped Winnie. Since she was a naturally considerate person, she made sure she caught her before she fell into the broken glass.

"I've got her!" she called out to the pair of firemen who'd just broken into the store. "I didn't think I was going to be able to carry her all the way down the stairs—she weighs a ton—but the Good Lord was watching over both of us."

"What do you think—"

She plastered her hand across Winnie's mouth. "Don't try to talk, honey. It'll make you cough again." She waved the fireman toward the stairs. "She's fine. I'll get her outside."

One of them began to break away to come to her aid, so she took her hand off Winnie's mouth just long enough for her to start to sputter again. "See! She's breathing fine. But it's a mess up there."

He joined the others, and as they stormed past, Sugar Beth dragged Winnie out onto the sidewalk, not an easy task, since Winnie was fighting mad. "You're going to be okay now, honey," Sugar Beth announced just loudly enough for the small group of onlookers to hear. "I'd have died myself before I left you up there to burn. And I'm no heroine, so don't you dare thank me again."

The EMTs rushed up and grabbed Winnie, which was a good thing, because she was starting to bite. Sugar Beth hurriedly backed away. Dulane Cowie, who looked a lot better in a cop's uniform than he'd looked picking his nose in fourth-period study hall, rushed up to her.

"Sugar Beth? Did you carry Winnie out by yourself?"

"It's amazing what you can do when a person's life is at stake," she said modestly.

Winnie had begun arguing with the EMTs, and a woman Sugar Beth recognized as an older, chubbier version of Laverne Renke waved from just behind the police line. "Hey, Sugar Beth, what happened in there?"

"Hey, Laverne. I saw smoke when I was leaving the bookstore and ran over to see if I could help. Winnie was being so brave trying to fight the fire by herself. I'm just glad I was around to help."

"I'll say," Laverne replied. "It looked like she was unconscious when you carried her out."

Winnie heard that, and she stuck her head around the EMT to shoot Sugar Beth a furious glare.

"Probably just breathed a little too much smoke," Sugar Beth said quickly.

Dulane gazed toward the second story. "She was lucky you were there."

"Anybody would have done the same thing."

The EMTs still had Winnie, and the smoke had begun to clear from the upstairs window. Sugar Beth watched along with the crowd. Before long, one of the firemen emerged and headed toward Winnie. Sugar Beth decided this was an excellent time to make herself scarce, but just as she began to head to her car, a tan BMW screeched to a stop behind the fire trucks and Ryan leaped out, barefoot and dressed in jeans and a gray T-shirt.

He ran for Winnie and pulled her to his chest. Since they were barely eight feet away, Sugar Beth could hear every word. "Are you all right?" he said.

"Yes, I—I was frying chicken—Charise has been sick,

and . . . The phone distracted me. The oil got too hot. It was stupid."

"I'm so sorry." The emotion in his voice made Sugar Beth suspect he might be talking about something more than the fire. She'd seen a lot of men in love, and Ryan fit right in.

She lost the thread of conversation for a few minutes as she convinced another EMT that she hadn't suffered any harm. When she finally got rid of him, she saw Ryan push a lock of hair from Winnie's grimy cheek and search her face. "What I said yesterday . . . I didn't mean any of it."

Winnie gave a wobbly nod.

A young fireman Sugar Beth didn't recognize came forward. "You've got a lot of smoke damage, Mrs. Galantine, but it could have been worse." He turned to Ryan and indicated Sugar Beth with his thumb. "It's a good thing the lady over there showed up. She carried Mrs. Galantine downstairs. Your wife could have been seriously hurt."

Winnie had temporarily forgotten about Sugar Beth, but the fireman's praise brought it all back, and her eyebrows slammed together. Ryan spun around. "Sugar Beth?"

Winnie opened her mouth, all ready to blast her, only to have Ryan pull her to his chest again. "My God . . . Are you sure you're all right?" He seemed to be having a hard time breathing. "You have to come home now. It's over, Winnie. You don't have any choice."

He didn't gloat, and he wasn't even the tiniest bit smug, but Sugar Beth could see Winnie withdrawing. Looking deeply unhappy, she took a small step backward and tucked a lock of hair behind her ear with sooty fingers. "Not yet. Not until we're both sure."

"I'm sure," Ryan said, his voice thick with emotion. "I've never been more sure of anything."

"I'm glad for you." Winnie reached out and touched his cheek tenderly. "A little longer."

Even from where she was standing, Sugar Beth could feel

Winnie's love for him, but Ryan didn't seem as perceptive. Instead of relaxing and giving her the room she needed like any person with half a brain would do, he continued to press. "You have to come home. You don't have anywhere else to go."

Winnie got all starchy, and Sugar Beth found herself thinking that even the best of men could be stupider than dirt.

"I'll stay at the Inn," she said.

"Aaron's hosting the chamber of commerce conference right now, remember? Everything's been booked for weeks."

"I'd forgotten." Winnie began to look cornered. "I'll—I'll work something out."

"You can work it out later. In the meantime, I want you to come home."

"Ryan, please . . ."

"It's the only thing that makes sense."

"If I come home now, we'll never get fixed!" she cried.

"We aren't broken," he insisted. "Not anymore."

"We're still damaged," she said more quietly. "And we need to make it right."

But he wouldn't back down. "Just for tonight, then."

Winnie looked like an animal caught in a trap, and the same impulse that had made Sugar Beth trip her now suggested she do something else entirely, something not nearly as much fun. Something not fun at all.

She ordered herself to walk away, but instead, she heard herself speak. "You could . . ." *Shut up, you dummy.* "You could . . . you know . . ." She started to cough and patted her chest. "Smoke."

Don't say another word. Not one more word. Just walk away.

Their impatient expressions made her feel like a child who'd interrupted the grown-ups' important business. She pressed her hand to her throat. "You could . . . uh . . . stay with me, Winnie. Just for tonight . . . Tomorrow, maybe, if you have to, but . . . Not more than . . . Whatever, damn it!"

"With *you!*" Ryan laughed. "That's a good one. Save your breath. Winnie is *not* going to stay with you."

The bigger they were, the dumber they were.

"All right," Winnie said slowly, her expression remote. "Yes, thank you. I will."

Ryan looked as though somebody'd knocked him in the head with a two-by-four. "Are you out of your mind? That's Sugar Beth!"

"I'm well aware of who it is." And then, with a completely straight face: "She did save my life."

Sugar Beth tried her best to look humble. "It was nothing."

"Believe me, I'm the best judge of that," Winnie said, tight-lipped.

Ryan gazed at them both, as if they'd lost their minds. "I don't understand any of this."

"You can come by as soon as you're done here," Sugar Beth said to Winnie. "I'm going home to hide the knives."

An hour later, after Ryan had checked on Gigi to make sure she was still asleep, then downed a stiff drink, he called Colin and told him what had happened. "You're sure they're both safe?" Colin asked for the third time.

"From the fire, yes, but who knows about tonight. Go over and check on them, will you? I'm so upset with Winnie right now, I don't trust myself to get near her."

"Forget it. I'd do anything else for you, but as long as I know they're safe, I'm not going near that house. They'll have to work this out for themselves."

"Sugar Beth doesn't want to work anything out. This was pure spite on her part. She's scheming to keep Winnie from coming home."

Colin sincerely doubted that. At the same time, who knew what was going through her mind. "You say Sugar Beth saved Winnie's life?"

"That's what they're telling me. God knows, I'm grateful, but— Why did it have to be her? Everything's so screwed up. One minute I had life by the balls, and now it's got me."

"Things'll look better in the morning, no doubt."

"I'd like to believe that."

After they hung up, Colin had to keep reminding himself that Sugar Beth wasn't hurt, so he didn't rush over to the carriage house. His presence would make her feel as if she had two battles to fight instead of one. As he gazed out the window, he saw Winnie's Benz parked by the house. He turned away only to be greeted with the sight of his unmade bed. He wanted Sugar Beth there—naked, legs twined through rumpled sheets, arms reaching out for him.

Now that he knew about Delilah, all the parts of her that wouldn't fit together had snapped into place. She was a woman of strong principles and sterling character, the kind of woman who, in days of yore, had driven ordinary men to scale castle walls or sent a prince door-to-door with a glass slipper in his pocket.

Who could have imagined a hardheaded realist like himself would have fallen under the spell of Sugar Beth Carey? But fall he had, and now he needed to figure out exactly what he intended to do about it.

Sugar Beth was fairly certain Winnie wouldn't go home to pack a suitcase, so she set out a toothbrush, along with a change of clothes, in the small bedroom. She was in no shape to deal with her natural-born enemy tonight, so after a quick bath, she went to bed.

Unfortunately, she couldn't avoid her the next morning. A little after eight, she heard Winnie coming downstairs. Sugar Beth shut off the kitchen faucet and spoke to her without turning around. "I've got Fruity Pebbles or Doritos. Take your pick."

"I'll get something on my way to the store."

"Good choice." Sugar Beth glanced at her over her shoulder, then snorted. She'd known Cy's old *Matrix* T-shirt and her own ratty gray sweatpants wouldn't look good on Winnie, but she hadn't been prepared for quite how oversize they'd be. "Nice outfit."

Winnie, as usual, was the better person and didn't rise to the bait. "It's fine," she said stiffly. Gordon slithered from under the table to check out the new houseguest, bared his teeth at her, and headed for the living room. "I appreciate your letting me sleep here last night."

"It was the least I could do. After saving your life and everything."

That set Winnie off. "You could have *hurt* me when you tripped me like that."

"No risk, no reward."

"It was *my* risk."

"Exactly what made it irresistible."

"You always have to be the center of attention, don't you?"

"Let's just say I seize my opportunities."

"And everybody else's while you're at it."

"Has anybody mentioned that you have no sense of humor?"

"Everything isn't a joke."

"Is *anything* a joke to you? Or do you look like you're sucking on prunes all the time."

"Lemons. The expression is 'sucking on *lemons.*'"

"You should know." Gordon started barking in the living room. *"Quiet!"* And then Sugar Beth realized he was barking because somebody was banging on the front door. With a hiss of exasperation, she stalked off to answer it and found Gigi wearing a sweater and jeans that actually fit. Even with her mangled hair, she looked pretty cute.

"Were you guys yelling?"

"Hey, kiddo."

Winnie shot out of the kitchen. The teenager rushed over and gave her an awkward hug. For a moment Winnie closed her eyes and simply held her. When she finally let her go, Gigi looked embarrassed and knelt to greet Gordon. "Hey, boy. Missed me?"

Gordon rolled on his back to let her scratch his stomach. As she rubbed, the dog cast a hostile eye toward Winnie. Gigi took in her mother's outfit and wrinkled her nose. "Gross."

"Not mine. You're up awfully early for a Saturday."

"I think I might have had a premonition that something was wrong." She gave Gordon a last pat and rose. "Dad told me what happened. He said I could come here."

"Want some cinnamon French toast?" Sugar Beth asked, moving back into the kitchen.

"Sure."

Winnie immediately got pissy. "You offered me Doritos."

"Dang, I must have forgotten about the French toast."

Hope flickered in Gigi's eyes. "Are you guys friends now?"

Sugar Beth occupied herself with the eggs and let Winnie answer that one. "Not friends. No."

Gigi's forehead crumpled. "You still hate each other, don't you?"

"I don't hate anyone," Mother Teresa replied, pouring herself a cup of coffee. Sugar Beth hid another snort by cracking an egg.

"If I ever had a sister, I wouldn't hate her." Gigi sat on the floor by the door so Gordon could snuggle up to her.

"We aren't regular sisters," Winnie replied, taking a seat at the table.

"Half sisters. You had the same father."

"But we weren't raised together."

"If I found out I had a half sister, even if we weren't raised together, it would make me happy. I hate being an only child."

"As you've mentioned at least a hundred times."

Gigi gave her mother a reproachful look. "I don't understand why you have to hate her so much."

"Gigi, this isn't any of your business."

The temporary truce between mother and teenager came to an end, and silence fell over the kitchen, broken only by the soft, contented moans of a basset having his ears rubbed. Sugar Beth tapped the whisk against the sides of Tallulah's old spongeware bowl. Gigi intended to cast her mother as the bad guy, with Sugar Beth as the injured party, which meant it was time to come clean. She consoled herself with the reminder that she owed Winnie one after the trick she'd pulled last night. All right. She owed Winnie more than one.

"The truth is, cupcake, I pretty much made your mother's life miserable."

Gigi abandoned Gordon's ears to gaze up at Sugar Beth. "What did you do?"

"Everything I could think of." Sugar Beth concentrated on dredging the bread so she didn't have to look at either one of them. "Your mother was shy, and I used that to my advantage to make her look bad in front of the other kids. Whenever somebody wanted to be her friend, I found a way to break it up. I made fun of her behind her back. I even found this diary she kept and read it out loud to everybody."

"I don't believe you," Gigi replied, too loyal to abandon faith in her new aunt so quickly. "Even Kelli Willman wouldn't do something like that."

"Believe it." Sugar Beth threw a slab of butter into the skillet. She'd forgotten to turn the burner on, so it sat there in a hard lump. She picked up a tea towel to wipe her hands, then turned to face them both. Winnie had the coffee mug cradled in her hands, her expression unreadable.

"My senior year, I did the worst thing to her I've ever done to anybody." Sugar Beth looked at Gigi because she didn't want to look at Winnie. "Your mom was in a show at school—"

Winnie rose from her chair. "There's no reason to go into this."

"It's my shame, not yours," Sugar Beth shot back.

To her credit, Winnie sat down again. Maybe she realized, as Sugar Beth did, that the time had come to drag the old ghosts out into the sunlight.

"She had paint all over her," Sugar Beth said, "so I knew she'd have to go to the locker room to get cleaned up when it was over. I waited till she had time to get into the shower, then I sneaked in and hid all her clothes. I hid the towels, anything she could use to cover up with."

She half expected Winnie to make another protest, but she simply cradled her mug and gazed straight ahead.

"That wasn't as bad as reading her diary to everybody," Gigi said.

"I haven't finished."

Gigi drew Gordon's head farther into her lap while Winnie sat stone-faced.

"I was with some boys," Sugar Beth said, "and I dared them to go into the locker room. I made a big joke out of it. They didn't know your mom was in there, so they went along with me." She fiddled with the tea towel. "Your dad was one of those boys."

The muscles worked in Gigi's throat as she swallowed. "Did he see her?"

Sugar Beth nodded. "Yes. And she had this huge crush on him. Otherwise, it wouldn't have been so bad. But she liked him so much, and she was humiliated."

"Why would you do something so mean?"

Sugar Beth gazed at Winnie. "Maybe you'd like to explain this part."

"How can I explain it when I never understood it myself?" Winnie said stonily.

"Sure you did."

"There was no reason for it," Winnie retorted. "You had everything. You were legitimate. You had a real family."

"And you were popular, too," Gigi said. "So what did you have to be jealous of?"

Winnie knew, but she wasn't going to say it.

"My father loved your mother, but he didn't love me," Sugar Beth said. "The truth was, he could barely tolerate me. I giggled, I got lousy grades, and I made too many demands on him."

"I don't believe you," Gigi said. "Dads love their kids, even when they screw up."

"Not all dads are like yours. Mine didn't hit me or anything. He just didn't like being around me. But he loved being with your mother, and that made me hate her." Sugar Beth turned back to the stove and flipped on the burner, aware of how much the past still hurt. "Whenever I saw them together, he looked happy with her in a way he never looked with me. I couldn't punish him for it, so I punished her."

Gigi swallowed hard, trying to make the best of it. "Teenagers do dumb things. I don't see why it should still be a big deal."

"You're right," Sugar Beth said. "It shouldn't be."

Winnie continued being unhelpful by taking another sip of coffee and not saying a thing. Sugar Beth concentrated on the French toast. Finally, Gigi set Gordon aside and rose to her feet, a little furrow in her brow. "Did you take my dad away from my mom in high school?"

"Now *that* I didn't do."

"He was your boyfriend for a long time, right?"

"Until we went to college. Then I dumped him for another guy. A guy who wasn't half as nice as your dad. But you have to admit that turned out to be a good thing because, if I hadn't cheated on him, your dad and mom wouldn't have gotten to know each other, and you wouldn't have been born."

"They had to get married. Mom got pregnant."

Sugar Beth glanced at Winnie, but she had that miles-away expression she used to wear sometimes in school.

"I'd never be stupid enough to get pregnant if I wasn't married," Gigi said.

"That's because you're not going to have sex until you're thirty," Sugar Beth replied.

Something that might have been a smile caught the corner of Winnie's mouth, but Gigi didn't see the humor. "Are you, like, going to try to take him away from her again?"

"No!" Winnie smacked her hand so hard on the table her mug rattled. "No, Gigi. She's not going to do that."

Gigi moved to her mother's side, relaxing almost imperceptibly.

Sugar Beth tossed the bread into the skillet. "Honey, I couldn't take your dad away from your mom even if I tried. He loves her. He doesn't love me."

Still troubled, Gigi gazed at her mother. "I don't understand how you could let her do so many bad things to you. Why didn't you stand up for yourself?"

"I was a wimp," Winnie said, looking surprisingly formidable in her oversize clothes.

Gigi nodded with the wisdom of the ages. "You didn't claim your power."

"I didn't know I had any. You should have seen her, Gi. She was so beautiful, so confident. Her hair was perfect, her clothes perfect, her makeup always right. And she had this amazing laugh that made everybody want to laugh with her. Nothing was ever boring when Sugar Beth was around. When she walked into a room, you couldn't look at anybody else."

"She's still kind of like that," Gigi said. "People pay attention to her."

"Hey, I'm standing right here, in case you've forgotten," Sugar Beth said. "And nobody outside of Parrish even notices me."

"I seriously doubt that," Winnie said. "You're just so used to it you don't see it anymore."

Gigi got her mulish look. "I think you should say you're sorry, Sugar Beth. And, Mom, I think you should forgive her because she's not like that now."

"It's not that easy," Sugar Beth replied, so Winnie didn't have to be the bad guy. "I am sorry, but there've been too many years of animosity."

Winnie's expression held the hint of a smile. "Griffin Carey did love me more."

"Mom! That's mean."

"Well, he did," Winnie replied. "But I was still jealous because Sugar Beth had Diddie."

"You had Grandma Sabrina."

"Believe me, there was no comparison. Diddie was like a movie star. She was beautiful and glamorous, and she had this amazing laugh. She and Sugar Beth were more like girlfriends than mother and daughter. If Sugar Beth wasn't with your dad or the Seawillows, she was with Diddie. Everybody knew not to schedule meetings for Saturday mornings because they always watched *Josie and the Pussycats* together. When they were out in public, they'd whisper secrets to each other, and if you walked by Frenchman's Bride, you'd see the two of them sitting on the front porch, drinking sweet tea and gossiping. All Grandma Sabrina and I ever did was get on each other's nerves."

"Grandma's nicer now."

"Old age mellowed her. When I was growing up, she only had room in her life for one person, and that was my father."

Sugar Beth flinched to hear Griffin referred to that way. At the same time, she acknowledged that Winnie had the right.

"So what are you going to do?" Gigi said. "Are you going to keep hating each other? Or do you think you could be friends, now that you've talked out your problems."

"Not likely," Sugar Beth said. "Or at least not until somebody's handed over somebody else's pearls."

Gigi looked at her mother for an explanation.

"I have Diddie's pearls," Winnie said. "They should be Sugar Beth's, but they aren't, and I'm not giving them back."

"That's pretty mean."

"As mean as what happened in the locker room?"

"No, not that mean." Gigi returned her attention to Sugar Beth, a pint-size secretary of state trying to negotiate a treaty between warring nations. "I think Mom should keep the pearls to make up for what you did, even if they look dumb on her."

"They don't look dumb on me," Winnie said, "which is why I wear them *all* the time."

"You should be glad Mom's keeping them. They'd look dumb on you, too."

"That's not the point," Sugar Beth said. "The point is . . . Oh, never mind. I know where this is leading, Gigi, and don't waste your breath. Your mother and I will never act like sisters, no matter how hard you push. The best we can hope for is politeness."

"I guess. But, Sugar Beth, did you ever think . . ." Gigi touched her mother's shoulder. "Me and Mom are the only two people in the world that have the same blood as you."

Sugar Beth got that old tight feeling in her throat and did her best to shrug it away. "Them's the breaks, kid."

"Can I take Gordon to see Dad?" she said abruptly.

"Leaving us alone together won't work," Sugar Beth said.

"I just want Gordon to meet Dad."

"What about your French toast?"

"I'll take it with me." She grabbed a piece from the plate, called to Gordon, and a few moments later, they were out the door.

Winnie rose and headed for the coffeepot. "I knew you were jealous of me. I guess I never quite realized how jealous."

"You don't have to look so happy about it."

"Life doesn't hand you too many perfect moments. I'm savoring." She smiled, transferred a piece of French toast to her plate, then regarded it critically. "This was supposed to have cinnamon on it."

"I got distracted humiliating myself in front of your daughter."

Winnie squeezed out a dab of syrup, then picked up a knife and fork. Still standing at the counter, she began to eat, but she no longer looked quite so full of herself. Finally, she said, "I'd like to stay here for a few more nights if it's all right."

"You'll have to deal with him sooner or later."

"Later." She took another bite. "What's going on with you and Colin?"

"I'm toying with him."

Winnie laughed as she set down her plate. "You're nuts about him."

"Says you."

Winnie headed for the living room and picked up her purse. "It's going to be so much fun watching you get dumped."

"Yeah? We'll just see about that."

Winnie snickered, and the door shut with a firm thud.

Sugar Beth lunged for the maple syrup. "And isn't it nice having our old animosity behind us."

Chapter 18

All that day Sugar Beth kept her eye on the comings and goings at Yesterday's Treasures. Despite the CLOSED sign taped to the boarded-up front door, the place was a beehive of activity. Ryan and Gigi showed up around nine-thirty. Later, the Seawillows began dropping by. Shortly before noon, a paneled truck appeared, and Ryan, who was dressed in jeans and a work shirt, stood on the sidewalk for a while, talking to the men before he led them inside. Later, Gigi slipped out, then returned with a pizza. Winnie's family had circled its wagons. Maybe all was finally well in the Land of Galantine.

Which meant that Winnie wouldn't be coming back to the carriage house tonight. Not that Sugar Beth had exactly been looking forward to it. Still, there was something about their confrontation that morning she hadn't entirely disliked.

Her thoughts were interrupted as a thinly built woman with a square jaw approached the register. "You remember me, don't you, Sugar Beth? Pansye Tims, Corinne's big sister."

"Yes, Pansye, of course. How've you been?"

"Gettin' over a sinus infection." She leaned closer. "Everybody in town's talking about last night. Imagine what could have happened to Winnie if you hadn't been there to carry her out. She's such a special person. Parrish wouldn't be the same without her. I just want you to know how grateful we all are."

Sugar Beth shifted uncomfortably. Pansye was at least the twentieth person who'd stopped in the bookstore already to thank her. Why hadn't Winnie outed her? "As a matter of fact, Pansye, the story's gotten a little exaggerated. I really didn't carry Winnie out. I—"

"Oh, stop now. You're a heroine."

Jewel popped up next to the register like an evil elf. "That's right, Sugar Beth. I even heard talk about you getting the mayor's Good Citizen Award."

She glared at her employer, who knew the truth. When Sugar Beth had come in that morning, she'd told her exactly what had happened. But Jewel had merely laughed. After Pansye left, Sugar Beth confronted Jewel in the self-help aisle. "This whole thing was supposed to be a joke. I only did it to entertain myself and aggravate Winnie. She's deliberately not telling people the truth because she knows I'm expecting her to."

Jewel chuckled. "I swear, Sugar Beth, hiring you was the best move I ever made, and not just for your entertainment value. You've brought more business into the store than I ever dreamed."

"Based entirely on deception."

"Whatever works." Jewel got distracted by her shrunken poetry section. Her smile faded, and her forehead crumpled in outrage. "Where's all my Langston Hughes? He's—"

"Dead," Sugar Beth retorted. "I needed his floor space for the children's department."

"Well, Nikki Giovanni's not dead." She poked a finger toward the shelf. "And if she walks into this store, I don't know how I'm going to face her."

"I doubt Parrish, Mississippi, is at the top of Nikki's

dream travel destinations. And we don't need to display three copies of everything she wrote."

"Says the white girl."

Jewel didn't stop grumbling until late afternoon, when she realized Sugar Beth had sold out the new *Daphne the Bunny* book, along with half a dozen other titles. "All right," she said begrudgingly. "I'll leave you alone. But if you even *think* about touching Gwendolyn Brooks, you're the one who's gonna be dead."

As closing time approached, Sugar Beth realized she was still waiting for Colin to call. He had to have heard about the fire by now. Wasn't he the slightest bit concerned? Apparently not.

"Dinner at the Lakehouse tonight," Jewel said. "My treat."

"Okay. But just so there are no awkward moments, I'm not putting out on our first date."

"Don't flatter yourself. This time around, I'm looking for a sister."

"You could at least give me a chance."

"Some things were not meant to be."

By the time they reached the Lakehouse and placed their order, their conversation had turned more serious. They spoke of books they loved, of old dreams and new insights. Sugar Beth ignored Jewel's nosiness about Colin but told her a little of what had happened that morning with Winnie.

When she finished, Jewel regarded her sympathetically. "You're upset because she's not staying with you longer."

"Not exactly."

"Exactly."

It was true, Sugar Beth realized later as she drove home and parked in her empty driveway. Somehow she'd hoped her encounter with Winnie might be the basis for some new kind of . . . whatever.

Gordon didn't knock her down to get outside, which meant Colin had brought him over recently. She resisted the temptation to trump up an excuse to bang on his door and pick a fight. She loved fighting with him. The freedom of it. No worries about getting slapped or thrown across a room. No fears of inducing a fatal heart attack. When they were together, she felt alive again. But that was her old pattern, wasn't it? Only feeling alive when she could see her reflection in a man's eyes? No more. She was smarter now, although wisdom hadn't driven the loneliness away.

Everything that was wrong with her life settled over her. She was tired of keeping her head up when she wanted to bury it under the covers, tired of pretending she didn't care what other people thought, tired of the neediness that made her keep falling in love. And she only knew one way to numb the pain. By getting drunk.

She headed for the kitchen, hoping chocolate would do the job instead.

Ryan cursed under his breath as he saw Sugar Beth's Volvo sitting by itself in the carriage house drive. Winnie wasn't there. And he'd brought her white tulips. Granted, ten o'clock was a little late to deliver them, but Gigi had joined the Spanish club's outing at Casa Pepe, and he'd ended up with car pool duty.

He stared at the Volvo's bumper and tried to ease the knots in his back, but they refused to budge. He'd thought maybe Winnie had forgiven him for that ugly scene at the store on Wednesday, but he'd been kidding himself. Just because she hadn't been openly hostile when he'd helped her clean up from the fire mess at the store today didn't mean she'd forgotten or forgiven. Every time he'd tried to get her alone, she'd dodged him, and she'd blown him off when he'd invited her back to the house.

She'd been all smiles when she'd talked to everybody else, laughing when Gigi tried on old hats, chatting with the workmen doing the upstairs cleanup, joking with the Seawillows. She'd only smiled at him once, and his mouth had gone dry. Until today, he'd never paid much attention to Winnie's smiles. Now he knew they started out slow, then gradually took over her whole face.

She hadn't thanked him for helping out today, and she hadn't fussed over him even once. The old Winnie would have told him not to bother helping with the cleanup. Naturally, he'd have insisted, and then she'd have been all over him, stopping what she was doing to get him coffee, asking if he wanted something to eat, and generally irritating the hell out of him. But this new Winnie wasn't nearly that sweet. Instead, she was hardheaded, confident, and so tantalizing he could think of little else but making love with her again.

He realized today was the first time he'd spent more than a few minutes at the store. Even though he'd known how much she loved antiques, he'd secretly thought of the shop as a rich woman's diversion. Today, however, as he'd watched her handle the objects and talk to Gigi about them, he'd realized how good she was at what she did, and he'd felt ashamed.

He left the tulips on the seat and got out of the car. He couldn't imagine anything stranger than asking Sugar Beth if she knew where Winnie was, but he refused to call the Seawillows. Once again, he wondered what had happened between Winnie and Sugar Beth that morning. Gigi knew, but when he'd tried to worm a few details out of her, she'd clammed up.

He changed his mind about the tulips and retrieved them from the car. Maybe leaving them would soften her up a little. He needed to start courting his wife, and to his surprise, the idea didn't displease him. He'd always liked challenges. He'd just never expected to find one with Winnie.

Sugar Beth came to the door. She was bare-legged, wearing a man's T-shirt that fell below her hips. Those endless legs, tousled blond hair, and pouty expression had *Homecoming Queen Gone Wild* written all over them. She was still the most provocative woman he'd ever known, but all he felt now was regret for the fourteen years he'd wasted thinking about her when he should have been paying attention to his wife.

She grabbed the tulips from him. "*Pour moi?* How sweet."

"They're for Winnie, and don't even think about telling her I brought them for you. I mean it, Sugar Beth. None of your fun and games. You've done enough damage to my marriage as it is."

"Uh-oh, somebody's transferring blame again."

She was right.

She curled her fingers around his wrist and pulled him into the room, looking at him as if he were a big ol' box of candy. "You, my man, are exactly what the doctor ordered. I need a distraction."

"Find it somewhere else." He turned to leave, but she stepped around him and pressed her back to the door, blocking the way. "Please, Ryan." She didn't say the words so much as purr them, and the hair on his arms stood up. "I've been doing battle with the demon rum. Just stay for a little while."

"Are you drunk?"

"Sober as a judge . . . if you don't count a serious sugar high. But I'm not feeling too confident about staying that way."

"Look, Sugar Beth, all I want to do is see Winnie."

"And all I want to do is forget how much I need a drink."

"Have one."

"Unfortunately, one's never enough, and before I know it, I'm dancing on the bar in my underwear."

"There's no bar here, so I wouldn't worry about it."

She slipped her arms around his waist. He jerked back, but she held on tight. "Then how 'bout I just show you my underwear without the drinking?"

Her scent drifted up to his nostrils as she pressed against him. He caught her shoulders, and his voice wasn't quite steady. "What are you trying to do?"

"I just need a little comfort, that's all. It's been a shitty month. A shitty year." She rested her cheek against his chest, slid her bare foot along the inner slope of his calf. "Remember how it used to be, Ryan? The two of us. Remember when we couldn't get enough of each other."

His chest felt tight. "A long time ago."

She gazed up at him through the same silver-blue eyes as his wife's. "Don't push me away. Please."

He'd dreamed of this moment—Sugar Beth throwing herself at him—begging him to take her back.

"I'm not going to tell if you won't," she whispered. "Just for tonight. What's the harm?"

He was hard. How could he be anything else with the way she was rubbing against him? Hard. But not tempted. Not even for a moment.

He gripped her shoulders and firmly set her aside. "I love my wife. That's the harm."

"Well, aren't you the noble one?"

"Nobility doesn't have anything to do with it. She means everything to me. I'd never betray her."

"Then get the hell out of here."

He felt a flash of pity for her, an urge to tell her she was too old for games like this. But he wasn't the person to offer advice, and with a brief nod, he turned away and let himself out.

The March wind rustled his hair as he made his way down the front steps. When he got to the bottom, he drew a deep breath, tilted back his head, and gazed through the tree branches toward the sky. Maybe it was his imagination, but he couldn't remember the last time he'd seen such bright, perfect stars. He smiled.

Inside the carriage house, Sugar Beth dove for the half-empty bag of Oreos she'd left on the couch. As she munched, Gordon trotted downstairs, followed by Colin and then Winnie.

"Was that entirely necessary?" Colin inquired, nostrils flared with distaste.

"Ask her." Sugar Beth jerked her head toward Winnie and stuffed another Oreo in her mouth.

Winnie gazed at the door, her expression bemused. "You upset him."

"Not to mention what you did to me." Colin thrust a pointed finger in her face. "You're a lunatic. Someone should lock you up. Bloody hell, *I'll* lock you up."

Sugar Beth ignored him so she could turn her wrath on Winnie. "This is *it*!" she exclaimed through the Oreos. "Tonight's mortifying little escapade stamps *Paid* on whatever debt I still owed you. That man loves you. He doesn't give a damn about me, and as far as I'm concerned, we're even. If you don't see it that way, I don't really care. Got it?"

Winnie gave a distracted nod.

She'd shown up barely ten minutes earlier with Colin in tow. She'd told Sugar Beth that the window in her bedroom was stuck and she needed him to open it. Sugar Beth hadn't believed her for a minute. Winnie had brought Colin here simply to cause trouble. Apparently the two of them had enjoyed a cozy pizza dinner at Frenchman's Bride. And didn't that just warm the ol' heart cockles?

"You were completely shameless," Winnie continued, staring at the door. "You threw yourself at him."

"I wrapped around him like a snake. And, believe me, he noticed."

"Uhm . . ."

Sugar Beth waited for Winnie to grab her purse and take off after Ryan. Instead, she picked up the pot of white tulips and floated toward the stairs, a dreamy smile on her face.

Sugar Beth shook her head as she disappeared. "That woman is playing some serious hard-to-get."

"Come into the kitchen," Colin said. "I'll make you a cup of hot chocolate."

"There's not enough chocolate in the world to satisfy me tonight." She followed him anyway.

"Do you need a drink that badly?"

She thought about it as he opened the refrigerator. "No. I'm just tired. And frustrated."

"Nobility's a bitch." He gave the milk a suspicious sniff before he poured it into a saucepan, then extracted an ancient tin of cocoa from the cupboard. "Were you truly an alcoholic or is this another of your exaggerations?"

"Let's just say I looked forward to getting drunk a little too much. The day I ordered my first club soda was the day I started liking myself."

"How long ago was that?"

"Right before I met Emmett. Until then, drinking was the way I coped with crisis."

"Now you do it with sugar."

"And grease. Don't forget the grease."

He adjusted the burner, then turned to inspect her, and the lazy sweep of his jade eyes made her skin prickle. "Are you wearing anything underneath that jersey?"

"Sure."

He lifted an inquiring brow.

She told herself not to be a smart-ass, but she was born to be bad. "Tallulah's White Gardenia."

She should have known better than to toy with a master. Those lips curved in a thin smile, and his visual inspection continued, lazier than ever. It sent little shock waves skidding through her. While he was enjoying himself, she deliberately turned away to locate the mugs and sugar bowl. She hadn't been entirely truthful about the White Gardenia. She also wore a pair of blue bikini panties with questionable elastic.

Colin divided his attention between the saucepan of milk and her legs. The tension grew with the silence in the kitchen, but she seemed to be the only one bothered by it. Why didn't he just go away? Even knowing Winnie was upstairs didn't make her feel safe, and by the time he'd poured the hot chocolate, she was ready to jump out of her skin. She nearly did when he finally spoke.

"Everyone in town is talking about how you saved Winnie's life last night."

"More like I tripped her when she got to the door, then dragged her outside so everybody'd think I'd saved her."

He smiled and lifted his mug in a toast. "Well done."

"You've been hanging out with me way too long."

"Interesting that Winnie never mentioned it to me."

"Too devious. She's storing up more ammunition against me."

"That would explain it, then." He pulled his cell from his pocket. She frowned as he punched in a number. He waited, listened. She heard the muted beep of an answering machine. "Ryan, Colin here. Winnie's staying with Sugar Beth tonight, but she left her car at my place. I'll talk with you tomorrow."

As he hung up, Sugar Beth frowned at him. "You're going to tell him I set him up, aren't you?"

"Tempting, but I believe I'll let Winnie do that." Once again, he took in the sweep of her legs.

"Stop it."

"You're determined, then, to dump me?"

"Absolutely." She heard a queer little catch in her voice.

He took a step closer. "I hope it goes without saying that I wouldn't think of trying to press you to change your mind." Another step. "British rules of fair play and all that."

"Colin . . ."

"Of course, I am an American now." He slid his hands along her arms, leaving a trail of sensation in their wake. "And we Yanks are an aggressive lot."

"Oh, Colin . . ." She didn't get a chance to say more because he was kissing her again, and she was letting him, kissing him back, taking his tongue and giving him hers in return. He used his knee to separate her thighs, cupped her under her shirt.

"God, Sugar Beth," he murmured against her lips. "You feel so good."

The warmth of his hand penetrated her skin through her panties. She was overcome with a need for him that made her weak. That *was* weak. She simply couldn't do this any longer. "No." She pushed him away. "I won't let you turn me into some kind of sexual challenge. I meant it, Colin. I'm not an obstacle for you to conquer just to prove you can."

His eyes grew hooded and the lips that, only seconds earlier, had been soft, tightened. "Is that what you think of me, then?"

She rubbed her arm, tunneled a hand through her hair, slowly shook her head. "No. You're aggressive, but you're not a predator. You don't mean to hurt me."

"Exactly. Why should I go to the bother when you're doing such a good job of it by yourself? I can only hope you'll be in a better mood when we get together in the morning."

"The morning?"

"I promised to help you search the depot and the carriage house. Surely you haven't forgotten. Shall we say ten o'clock?"

Spending the morning with him was the king of bad ideas, but she needed his help. And no matter what he had in mind, she wouldn't let him bulldoze her with any more kisses. "All right," she said. "Ten o'clock."

Gigi didn't usually like church too much. Sometimes the sermons were okay—Pastor Mayfair was pretty cool, and Sunday school had been sort of interesting today—but she wasn't too crazy about the Bible, in general, which had way too many depressing parts and, in her opinion, should be R-rated for violence. This morning, though, she didn't even mind John the Baptist getting his head chopped off because her mom had slipped into the pew next to her right before the worship service began.

Gigi wished she could think of a way to change places, so

her mom was in the middle, next to her dad. Still, they'd looked at each other across her and smiled, although Gigi couldn't tell if they were real smiles or just-being-polite-for-the-sake-of-the-child smiles. As the sermon went on, she fought the urge to lean against her mother's shoulder and close her eyes like she used to when she was a little girl.

She'd even put on a totally lame Bloomingdale's skirt and blouse because she wanted to make her mother happy. She still hadn't figured out what she was going to wear to school next week, but she'd started thinking about giving up her Goth stuff. Yesterday Sugar Beth had told her it was an excellent eighth-grade look, but the way she'd said it had sort of made Gigi feel like she was only copying everybody else instead of being an individual.

Last night she'd gone to the Spanish club dinner with Gwen and Jenny, but her parents were so wrapped up in their own problems they still hadn't asked her about it. Mostly, she was glad they'd stopped poking their noses in her business, but it'd be nice if they showed a little interest. Especially her mom. Gigi was starting to realize that maybe her mom wasn't as perfect as she'd thought. And what she'd gone through in high school was a lot worse than anything Gigi was going through.

After the service, her parents hung around for a while to talk to their friends, but they didn't talk much to each other. When they finally began walking to the parking lot, Gigi hung back on purpose.

"Thank you for the tulips," she heard her mother say.

Her dad had given her mother flowers?

"When I saw them, they made me think of you," he said.

Way to go, Dad.

"Really? Why?"

Uh-oh. He was going to say something dumb.

"Because they're beautiful. Like you."

She was going to hurl. Right here in the parking lot.

But her mother wasn't as critical, and she looked like she

was blushing. Her dad took advantage and moved right in. "Would you like to have dinner tonight at the Inn? Maybe around seven? If you don't have other plans."

Gigi forgot to breathe.

Her mother took a moment to reply. "The Inn would be nice."

Yes!

"It'll be just the two of us, is that all right? Gigi has a project due."

In two weeks.

"Oh. Yes. All right."

"If you want her to come along . . . maybe she could work on her project this afternoon."

Gigi prayed her mother wouldn't be a dope.

"No, that's all right."

Way to go, Mom!

Her dad held the door of the Benz open, and her mother slid in. Gigi wished she'd come home with them, but her dad didn't try to talk her into it. He just smiled, shut the door after her, and waved.

As they rode home in his car, Gigi thought about what had happened, and the more she thought, the more worried she got. Finally, she turned down the radio. "Ask her about the store?"

"What?"

"When you go out tonight, ask her about the store. She likes to talk about it. Not about how much money it's not making, either. Ask her how she decides what she's going to put in the window, and how she knows what to buy. Stuff like that. Stuff that shows you're interested."

"All right," he said slowly.

"And whatever she's wearing, don't ask her if it's new. You always do that. She'll put on something she's worn a million times, and you'll say, is that new?"

"I don't do that."

"You do it all the time."

"Anything else?" he said, starting to sound sarcastic.

"She likes to talk about books. And tell her she looks beautiful again. She really liked that. And maybe you should say she has nice teeth."

"You say that about a horse, not a woman."

"I'd like it if a boy told me I had nice teeth."

"All right. I'll compliment her teeth. Are you done yet?"

"Don't ask her about Sugar Beth, Dad. They still have issues."

"Believe me, I won't."

She knew he was curious about what had happened yesterday morning, and she thought about telling him she knew about all the stuff in high school, but it was too embarrassing.

They got ready to turn into Mockingbird Lane just as Colin's Lexus passed them in the opposite direction. Gigi waved. "Hey, Sugar Beth's going somewhere with Colin."

"And may God have mercy on his soul."

"Richard, I could hit you!" she declared.
The smile grew, allowing her a glimpse of
excellent white teeth. "I don't think you could,
my dear."

GEORGETTE HEYER, *The Corinthian*

Chapter 19

Sugar Beth looked like a diet Pepsi ad, one of those TV commercials shot at a gas station in the desert. As she sauntered toward his car in her pipe-stem jeans, bare midriff top, and straw cowboy hat, she led with her hips, a gorgeous genetic freak of a woman, too tall, too thin, too leggy. Her straight blond hair floated in slow motion at her shoulders. Her arms swung in graceful arcs at her sides, and a denim jacket dangled from her fingertips. Long before they'd reached the depot, he'd started to sweat.

"You're quiet this morning."

"Not a bloody thing to say." He slammed the car into park, climbed out, and stalked across the crumbling asphalt toward the door, where—since she had the key—he had to stand cooling his heels while he watched the whole thing all over again. The careless, undulating walk, leggy grace, lithesome tilt. Her stretchy top rode up as she hit the steps; the waistband of her jeans dipped and played peekaboo with her navel. By the time she opened the lock, he'd been swept up in a conflagration of lust. *"Let me do that!"*

"Jeez, what's eating you?"

Since every reply that sprang to mind was salacious, he ignored the question. Instead, he slapped a pair of work gloves into her hands and pointed toward the rear of the depot. "We're going to do this systematically, starting in the back."

"Whatever you say."

When she'd arrived in Parrish, she'd looked worn out, but she didn't look that way now. Her complexion had regained its glow, her hair its bounce. He wanted to believe his lovemaking had revitalized her, that he'd filled her with a magic elixir that had restored her bloom. He could almost hear her scoff at the notion. *The lies you men tell yourselves.*

"Are you gonna stand there all day, Your Grace, or could you help me move this crate?"

"Damn it, Sugar Beth, I'm concentrating!"

"On what? You've been staring at that wall for five minutes. Either tear the son of a bitch down or come over here and help me."

"You curse far too much."

" 'Son of a bitch' isn't a curse. It's a figure of speech."

Colin had been sullen all morning, but since he understood buildings and construction, Sugar Beth couldn't let him off the hook. She needed him to find what had eluded her, and if they came up empty today, then she needed his sarcasm to console her.

"This place isn't as bad as it looks." He pushed the crate to the side. "It needs a new roof, and there's water damage, but the structure's basically sound. Tallulah was right. Someone should restore it."

"Don't look at me. I can't even afford to get the dent taken out of my fender."

"Why don't you talk to Winnie about the depot? The planning council should at least consider it."

"I'm the last person the planning council would listen to."

"Restoring it would take serious money, that's for certain."

"It's a mess." But even as the words left her mouth, a picture sprang into her mind of a children's bookstore, complete with a miniature caboose, model trains, signal lights, and a trunkful of dress-up costumes. She sighed.

"What's wrong?"

"I wish Jewel cared more about selling kids' books. Wouldn't this make a fantastic children's bookstore? Not that she could afford to renovate it even if she were interested."

"It's a great location. But it has more square footage than a specialty bookstore needs."

"Not with a coffee shop next door." She didn't know where the idea had come from, and his eyebrows rose as he studied her more closely. She turned away and headed for the back. Some things were too impractical even for daydreams.

Colin tapped walls, investigated storage areas, and took every opportunity to snarl at her. Eventually, he announced that he was going up into the loft.

"I didn't know there was one."

"Exactly what did you think was above the ceiling?" he inquired with the same scathing tone she remembered from high school. *"Did you imagine you would absorb this information through osmosis, Miss Carey, or could you open your text?"*

She followed him into the ticket office, where he climbed up on the old desk and pushed aside a splintery access panel above his head. As she watched how effortlessly he pulled himself through the opening, a rush of desire swept through her. First his chest disappeared, then the rest of him, all in one effortless motion. She wanted to feel that strength pressed against her once more, inside her. She stepped away.

He reemerged five minutes later, looking dirtier and more withdrawn. "Nothing. Let's get out of here."

She'd hoped Winnie would be at the carriage house to act as a buffer while they searched its rooms, but only Gordon greeted them at the door. Colin continued to snap her head off, and by the time they reached the studio, she'd lost patience with him. "Forget it! I'll do the rest myself."

"Right. Since you've done so well already." He pulled away the plastic. She gritted her teeth and watched. He moved the ladder to the side, looked under the drop cloth, and studied a pair of paint-splattered cracked leather boots she'd found during an earlier exploration.

"He wouldn't have left them here if he hadn't planned to come back," she said.

"Who knows?"

As he returned the boots to their place under the workbench, Sugar Beth thought of Tallulah and the bitterness that came over women who defined their lives only through their relationships with men.

Finally, there was no place left to look, nothing to do but lock up. "I'm sorry, Sugar Beth."

She'd been counting on his sarcasm to sustain her, and now she had to fight to keep her composure. "*C'est la vie,* I guess."

"Give me a couple of days," he said, more softly. "I'll think of something."

"It's my problem, not yours."

"Nevertheless."

She didn't hang around any longer. Instead, she left him standing on the path and made her way back into the house. As she shut the door, she reminded herself that finding the painting today had always been a long shot. She shouldn't have let herself hope.

Barely five minutes passed before Winnie appeared, her arms full of grocery bags. Gordon snarled at her as she sidestepped him. "Is that dog dangerous?"

Sugar Beth mustered the energy to reply. "So far, you and I are the only ones he doesn't like."

"Why would you keep an animal like that around?"

"A lesson in humility."

Winnie glared down at Gordon, who was still growling. "Stop it right now."

He backed away just far enough to block the doorway to the kitchen so that she had to climb over him. "I picked up some groceries," she said. "I told Gigi to come over for lunch. I hope that's all right."

"Sure. I *like* Gigi."

The implication didn't bother Winnie one bit. She hummed as she began unpacking the groceries. Sugar Beth surveyed what she'd bought. All that green stuff and not a carton of mint chocolate chip in sight. She emptied the wastebasket, then lined it with a new trash bag.

"You look upset," Winnie said.

"Broken fingernail."

"It's the painting, isn't it? Colin said he was going to help you look for it today. You must not have found anything."

"Not unless you count spiders."

"What are you going to do now?"

"I don't know. Talk to Tallulah's canasta club again, maybe. Try to figure out if she had any other confidantes."

"Not that I know of. She was so critical most people avoided her. I can't believe someone like Lincoln Ash could have fallen in love with such a sourpuss."

"I don't think she was always like that. My father said she was funny when she was a girl."

"*Our* father. Just once, Sugar Beth, I'd like to hear you say it."

"Maybe you'd better check the weather report. Last time I looked, hell hadn't frozen over."

"Doesn't being a bitch get exhausting after a while?"

"You tell me."

"I believe in deferring to the experts."

They continued like that for a while, trading insults and, in general, keeping themselves entertained, which was a welcome distraction after Sugar Beth's dismal morning. So many years of being a respectable, law-abiding citizen made Winnie's jabs clumsier than Sugar Beth's, but she compensated by delivering them with the zeal of the newly converted. Eventually, however, she calmed down and concentrated on her salad.

Sugar Beth went upstairs to wash off the dirt and phone Delilah. Afterward she gazed over at Frenchman's Bride. Colin had said he intended to write today, but he was outside working on his wall.

When she returned downstairs, she heard the humming of a happy little kitchen elf. "Orzo." Winnie gazed cheerfully into Tallulah's spongeware bowl. "Hard-boiled eggs, tomatoes, pine nuts, an avocado coming up. Gigi's going to love this salad."

Sugar Beth decided to distract herself by picking another fight. "It wouldn't kill you to thank me for what I did last night. If I hadn't gone that extra mile, you'd still think your husband was nuts about me."

But Winnie chose her own battle turf and struck back with a zinger. "You're sleeping with Colin, aren't you?"

"Yeah, that's exactly the kind of information I'm gonna share with my worst enemy."

"I knew there was something going on between the two of you the night of the cocktail party. But you've met your match. Colin is one man who has his head screwed on straight."

"Right now, mine is screwed on a lot straighter than his."

"I sincerely doubt that." Winnie stabbed a tomato. "No matter how you try to manipulate him, he'll never marry you."

"I don't want him to."

"If that man dangled a diamond in front of you, you'd rip his arm off to get to it."

Sugar Beth shrugged. "Whatever you want to believe."

By turning serious, she seemed to have taken the fun out of the game. Winnie set down the tomato, wiped her hands on a paper towel, and leaned against the counter. "You mean it, don't you?"

She nodded.

But if she'd expected Winnie to back off, she was mistaken because real anger flashed in her eyes. "You're trying to collect another scalp. You don't care about hurting him. You just want to add him to your collection. And he's so smitten he doesn't see what's coming."

"He sees it, all right. I've been trying to dump him since Tuesday night, but he won't stay dumped."

That threw Winnie off stride. "I don't believe you. Why would you want to dump him? He's rich, successful . . . brilliant. He *owns* Frenchman's Bride. And except for Ryan, he's the sexiest man in Parrish. Colin Byrne has more character than all of your ex-husbands put together."

"Two of them, anyway. When did you say Gigi would be getting here?"

"Don't try to tell me you're not attracted to him. I've seen the way the two of you behave when you're together."

"Just drop it, okay."

"My, my. Have I hit a tender spot?"

All Sugar Beth could do was nod.

That gave Winnie something to think about, and she turned away to concentrate on the salad. Sugar Beth took a sip of cold coffee. A minute ticked by, and then another. Finally, Winnie set down her knife. "I got pregnant with Gigi on purpose."

Sugar Beth nearly choked on her coffee. "That's definitely not something you should share with your worst enemy."

"Probably not." She cracked a hard-boiled egg against the side of the bowl. "I spent fourteen years trying to make it up to him. I didn't think he knew, but he did. And he never said anything. He just let his resentment eat away." A piece of eggshell fell to the floor, but she didn't notice. "What a pair we've been. He suffered in noble silence, and I fed my guilt by overcompensating. Then I blamed you for everything that was wrong in our marriage. So when it comes to you and me, Sugar Beth, which one of us is the biggest sinner?"

"Beats me. I'm not good at making moral judgments."

"You seem to have made a few about yourself."

"Yeah, but that's easy."

Winnie fished a piece of eggshell from the bowl, a distant expression on her face. "Gigi would say that I gave up my power."

"You're doing one heck of a job getting it back."

Winnie smiled. "Ryan asked me out to dinner tonight."

"Just because a boy buys you a steak doesn't mean you have to put out for him."

"I'll remember that."

Gordon began to bark as Gigi arrived. This time she wore jeans and an Ole Miss T-shirt. "Dad's really mad at Sugar Beth again. He didn't want me to come down here. What'd you do?"

"Come see what I've got in the salad," Winnie said before Sugar Beth could reply.

Gigi patted Gordon, who was worshiping at her feet, then walked over to examine the salad. "Orzo! That's so cool. And avocado. Don't put any chicken in, okay." She plucked out a piece of tomato with dog-slobber fingers and nearly gave Winnie apoplexy.

Sugar Beth rinsed out her coffee mug. "I'll leave the two of you to your own devices."

"Don't go," Gigi said.

"I have things to do." She was trying to give them some time alone together, but Winnie got her snippy look.

"Now you can see exactly how inconsiderate your aunt really is, Gigi. I've made a nice lunch for us, but does she care? No, she doesn't."

Sugar Beth didn't want Winnie to guess how good it felt to be included. "Okay, but I'm going to switch plates at the last minute, so don't try any funny stuff with food poisoning."

"You guys act so weird."

Ten minutes later they were settled at the drop-leaf cherry table in the living room with the salad, rolls, and Tallulah's pressed-glass tumblers filled with sweet tea.

"Did you decide what you're going to wear on your date tonight?" Gigi asked her mother.

"It's not a date. Your father and I are having dinner together, that's all."

"I think you should borrow something from Sugar Beth."

"I'm not meeting your father in Sugar Beth's clothes!"

"Just a blouse or something. He won't know. Hers are sexier than yours."

"Good idea," Sugar Beth said. "I'll trade you a slinky little number I bought at Target last winter for that Neiman's cashmere sweater set I saw you in last week."

"She's trying to get you upset again, Mom."

Sugar Beth hid a smile. "If you keep spoiling my fun, kid, you're out of here."

Gigi leaned closer. "He's picking her up at seven. Do her makeup, Sugar Beth."

"I'll do my own makeup," Winnie retorted.

"Sugar Beth does better eyes."

"That's true. I do know my eyes." She gazed at Gigi. "Hair, too. What do you say I even up your new do a little?"

"I guess."

Their conversation moved on to other things, and without planning it, Sugar Beth found herself telling them about Delilah, leaving out only the financial troubles her stepdaughter was causing.

Gigi wrinkled her nose. "It's sort of gross, isn't it? Having a stepdaughter that old?"

Winnie smiled and touched the back of her daughter's hand. "Love's a strange thing, Gigi. You never quite know exactly when it's going to hit or how hard it'll strike."

On this, at least, Sugar Beth and her evil half sister were in total agreement.

Colin sat with his back to the wall of the lobby bar of the Peabody Memphis Hotel, trying to stave off his guilt by going about the business of getting seriously drunk. Southerners said that the Mississippi delta began in the lobby of the Peabody Hotel, but the place was best known for its ducks.

For more than seventy-five years, a small group of mallards had marched along a red carpet at eleven o'clock every morning to the sound of Sousa's "King Cotton March" and spent the day splashing in the lobby's travertine marble fountain. But it was evening now. The ducks had retired for the night, and the subdued lighting cast a sepia glow over the grandeur of the Italian Renaissance lobby with its marble floors, stained glass ceiling, and elegant, Old World furnishings. Driving sixty-five miles for the sole purpose of getting drunk wasn't something he'd normally do, but he'd always loved the Peabody, and after he'd spent a frustrating afternoon laying stone instead of writing, this had seemed as good a destination as any, so he'd packed an overnight bag and left Frenchman's Bride behind.

"Colin?"

He'd been so preoccupied with his self-loathing that he hadn't noticed the attractive redhead approaching. Carolyn Bradmond was one of those high-powered, low-maintenance women whose company he should most enjoy. She was intelligent, sophisticated, and too involved in her career to be emotionally demanding. Colin Byrne's ideal woman . . . So why hadn't she crossed his mind since he'd last seen her five months ago?

He rose to greet her. "Hello, Carolyn. How are you?"

"Couldn't be better. How's the new book coming along?"

It was one of the two questions people most frequently asked writers, and if he invited her to join him, it wouldn't take her long to get around to the other one. *"I've always wanted to know, Colin. Where do you authors get your ideas?"*

We steal them.

From extraterrestrials.

There's a warehouse outside Tulsa . . .

He had no energy for such a conversation, so he stayed on his feet and chatted with her until she took the hint and left. As the pianist at the bar's baby grand switched to Gershwin, he finished his third whiskey and ordered a fourth. Before

Sugar Beth had come banging on his front door, he'd taken pride in the way he'd confined his romantic inclinations to the printed page. But how did a man distance himself from a woman like her?

He couldn't let her leave Parrish. Not yet. Not until they'd had a chance to work through this bloody train wreck of a relationship. They needed time, but she didn't want to give it to them. Instead, she'd made up her mind to run as soon as she got the chance. And it was wrong.

He remembered her wistful expression as she'd gazed around at the depot and talked about making it into a children's bookstore. She belonged in Parrish. She was part of this town. Part of him.

His guilt settled in deeper. The pianist abandoned Gershwin for Hoagy Carmichael. Colin finished his drink, but the alcohol didn't offer the absolution he craved.

Today, he'd found Sugar Beth's painting, and he hadn't said a word.

Ryan had never been more attentive. He asked Winnie a dozen questions about the shop and seemed genuinely interested in her responses. He complimented her on her hair, on her posture, on her jewelry, on her *teeth,* for goodness' sakes. He didn't compliment her on her clothes, which interested her, since she was wearing Sugar Beth's trashy black stretch lace crisscross top and a midnight blue skirt that—in a moment of madness—she'd chopped off and hemmed to midthigh. There was a certain novelty in looking like a hooker, but she didn't necessarily want to look like this again, and she was glad he seemed just the slightest bit displeased with her plunging neckline and short skirt.

Considering his attentiveness, she should probably have been happier with the evening, but she wasn't, because the elephant still sat at the table between them, that beast created by her deceit and his resentment. Ryan ignored the animal, acting as if the angry, pent-up words he'd assaulted her with last week at the shop had never been spoken. And she was tired of always being their emotional archaeologist, so she didn't bring it up.

"Are your scallops good?" he asked.

"Delicious."

After what he'd said to Sugar Beth last night, she wanted emotion from him, passion, but he chatted with the waiter, waved to Bob Vorhees across the room, remarked on the wine, and talked to her about everything that didn't matter. Even worse, he didn't seem to be struck by any of those stunning little volts of sexual electricity that had begun plaguing her at the most unexpected times—when she heard his voice on the phone or caught sight of him behind the wheel of his car, or at church this morning when his arm had brushed hers during the doxology. And what should she make of that shocking, limb-melting rush of desire that had overcome her last night when he'd rejected Sugar Beth's enticement?

All you ever think about is sex!

They finished their dinner and ordered coffee. Someday she'd have to tell him that Sugar Beth had set him up, but not just yet.

He paid the bill, and the elephant followed them to his car. She'd known the patterns of their marriage were too deeply etched for easy changes, and she shouldn't have pinned so many hopes on tonight. She was always to be the pursuer, Ryan the pursued. She the adorer, Ryan the object of her adoration. But she'd lost the will to play her part.

He took a corner too sharply, and she realized they were headed toward the southern edge of town instead of Mockingbird Lane. "I want to go back to the carriage house."

He responded by hitting the automatic door locks.

She couldn't have been much more shocked if he'd slapped her. "What are you doing?"

He didn't reply.

His gesture was symbolic. She would hardly jump out of a

moving car. She started to ask him what he hoped to accomplish with his theatrics, but something about the tough set of his jaw made her decide to wait.

As they reached the highway, a blade of light thrown by the headlights of a passing car slicked across his face, and another jolt of lust shot through her. "I want to go back," she said, not meaning it.

He didn't reply. Courteous, accommodating Ryan Galantine ignored her, just as if she hadn't spoken.

They were heading toward the lake, but it was only March, and the season hadn't kicked in yet. She clasped her hands in her lap and waited to see what would happen. It felt odd to be so passive.

He drove past the road that led to Amy and Clint's cottage, then passed the entrance to Spruce Beach, where they all swam and picnicked. The bait shops were still closed for the winter. He ignored the boat launch and the Lakehouse. Ten minutes ticked by. They were approaching the less-populated southern side of the lake. She seldom came this far, but he seemed to know the road by heart.

She didn't see the narrow, unmarked lane until he'd begun to turn into it. She couldn't imagine where they were—

Allister's Point. This was the place where the Seawillows used to go with their boyfriends during high school to drink beer and make out.

"Oh, my God," she whispered.

She'd driven out here by herself not long after she'd gotten her driver's license, just to see what it looked like, but she'd never been here with a boy. She could hardly breathe.

The lane ended at a small promontory, which was protected on three sides by trees, with the open end overlooking the lake. At some point, the county had thrown down a little gravel, but not much of it was left. He turned off the ignition. She swallowed and gazed straight ahead. Moonlight dripped down the center of the lake like spilled milk.

"I tripped the safety locks," he reminded her.

She licked her dry lips and looked over at him. "I'm gonna tell my mom."

"No, you won't," he replied, leaning back into the seat and regarding her with cocky, half-lidded eyes. "She'll ask you what you were doing out here. How are you going to tell her you were lettin' Ryan Galantine feel you up?"

"Is that what I'm going to do?"

"I guess we'll just have to see, won't we?" He slipped his finger under the plunging stretchy black lace neckline. "Don't wear Sugar Beth's clothes again."

"You recognize this?"

"I'm not entirely unobservant. I was hoping for your blue silk blouse, the one that matches your eyes. Or that pink yarn sweater you can see your bra through. Or maybe the yellow dress you wore the last time we went to Memphis. I like the way your legs look in it."

The fact that he'd ever noticed anything she wore left her speechless, let alone how her legs looked in her yellow dress. He slid his arm behind her shoulders, leaned forward, and gave her a deep soul kiss.

Everything inside her melted. A few weeks ago she'd felt as though she'd never experience desire again. Now, she wanted to rip off her clothes and attack him.

Always the aggressor. Never the pursued.

"Take me home," she said. "I'm not going all the way with you."

"No?" He trailed his index finger from the base of her throat to the black lace. "You really think you can stop me?"

Her short skirt had ridden up on her thighs, and she did nothing to pull it back down. "I could scream if I wanted to."

"Then I'll have to make sure you don't want to." He hooked his finger deeper under the lace neckline, picked up a bra strap, and drew them both down, exposing one breast. His hair brushed her cheek as he leaned forward and sank his teeth into a spot just above her nipple. She let out a tiny exclamation of pain. He sucked hard on the place he'd bitten and blew softly. "Tell me something, Winnie Davis. How are you going to explain that to your mamma?"

She was going to die right here, dissolve into a steaming pool of lust. Her legs inched apart. Her breasts ached; her panties were wet. "If you don't stop that . . ."

"Oh, I'm not gonna stop."

He began kissing her again. Not married kisses, but deep, sloppy make-out kisses with spit and tongue. Her panty hose disappeared. Her panties. He was sweating under his shirt. The windows had fogged up. He grabbed one of her ankles, propped her foot on the dashboard, pushed his finger inside her. She moaned. He dipped his head. Feasted on her. Sent her thundering to her orgasm.

For a horny teenage boy, he knew his way around a woman's body, and the second time he sent her crashing with the heel of his hand. When she recovered, she drew her foot down from the dashboard and gazed over at him. He was breathing hard.

And he didn't even have his pants unzipped.

She made no move to change that. Instead, she pulled her skirt down. What a bitch she was. A tease.

The door locks snapped open, and his voice was hoarse. "Let's get some fresh air."

After what he'd just done for her—what she hadn't done for him—she should be agreeable. "It's too cold."

"You can have my sports coat. Believe me, I don't need it."

"I guess."

He leaned across her and pulled a flashlight from the glove compartment.

"You Boy Scouts," she said, doing her best to sound bored.

He climbed out. She had no panty hose, no panties. She slipped her bare feet into her shoes and waited like the good Southern girl she wasn't for him to open her door. As he did, she gazed directly at his bulging crotch. Poor baby.

He draped his jacket around her shoulders and took her arm. She was wearing heels and the ground was soft, so she balanced her weight on the balls of her feet. He drew her toward the woods. She smelled pine and the dankness of the lake.

He switched on the flashlight and played it over the trunks of the trees. "It's around here somewhere."

Under her skirt, the cool air tickled her bare bottom. If she kept on like this, she'd develop a reputation. Slutty Winnie Davis.

"Wait here."

He moved off without her, flashlight in hand, inspecting the tree trunks like some horny forest ranger. Finally, he found what he wanted. "Over here."

He'd stopped at the base of a big oak. She waddled over— high heels, short skirt, bare bottom, all-around bimbo.

He dropped the flashlight to his side, illuminating the toe of one of his loafers. "I don't see anything," she said.

He raised his arm and shined the light on the trunk in front of him.

She saw it then, the dim outline of a heart carved into the bark. The letters had grown gray and weathered by time, but they were still legible:

She reached out and traced the *R* with her finger.

"We heard a rumor that these oaks could live for a thousand years," he said, "and we believed it. Sugar Beth said that as long as our initials were in this tree, we'd love each other forever."

"Forever's a long time."

"Not so long." He smiled and drew out his pocketknife. With the flashlight in one hand and his knife in the other, he chipped away the *S* and the *B* and incised a deep *W* in their place. Then he turned the *C* into a *D*. The crooked letters of her freshly carved name stood out in the old wood. What a goof he was. She no longer cared about the initials two teenagers had gouged in a tree sixteen years ago, but he did, and that was nice.

He slipped his knife back into his pocket and caressed her cheek. "I'm not sorry for all those ugly things I said to you last week. Not one of them is true anymore, but they were true once, and I'm glad I said them."

"You should have said them fourteen years ago."

"I was afraid. You always seemed so fragile."

"Not too fragile to figure out how to trap you. I didn't have much self-respect."

"We were kids."

"I was needy and desperate, not a nice thing to remember."

"I remember that you were the sweetest girl I'd ever known."

She turned her face into his hand and kissed the palm. "A woman shouldn't idolize the man she marries."

That made him smile. "We sure don't have that problem now." With no warning, he took her hands and said the most astonishing thing. "Winnie Davis, will you marry me? I'd get down on one knee, but I don't want you fussin' at me for getting mud on my good slacks."

She laughed. "You're proposing to me?"

"I am. Of my own free will."

Blossoms of happiness unfurled inside her, and her smile took over her face. "Do I have to give you an answer right now?"

"I'd appreciate it."

"You're just doing this so I'll let you go all the way, aren't you?"

"Partly. You set me on fire, love."

She laughed again, looped her arms around his neck, and the flashlight fell to the ground as she kissed him.

He slipped his hands under her skirt and cradled her bottom. "I love you, sweetheart. You're everything to me. Please tell me you believe that."

"Convince me."

"Can I convince you naked, or do I have to write a poem or something?"

"Naked will do for right now, but a poem would be nice in the future."

He laughed, let her go, and headed back to the car where he retrieved a blanket. As he returned to her, she said, "You've done this before, haven't you?"

"Not like this. Not ever like this."

At that moment, standing in the damp leaves and matted pine needles with the smell of the lake in her nostrils, she felt the full force of his love for her. The elephant had disappeared; the ghosts had gone off to haunt someone else. They had a love that could be counted on. A love that wouldn't disappear at the sight of a less-than-perfect meal or fade away under the onslaught of a cranky mood. A love that could even handle a good fight.

She reached for the zipper of her skirt, then stopped. "Sometimes I don't feel like making love. Sometimes I just want to be by myself, to take a bath and read a magazine."

"All right." The corners of his mouth curled. "But please tell me this isn't one of those times."

She smiled and let her skirt fall.

"And if I do marry you, my lord? You'll let me go my own road? You'll not come near me unless I wish it? You'll not fly into rages with me, nor tyrannize over me?"

"I swear it," he said.

She came to him, her eyes full of tender laughter. "Oh, my love, I know you better than you know yourself!"

GEORGETTE HEYER, *Devil's Cub*

Chapter 20

W innie waited until they reached town before she told him. "You're not going to like this."

"Honey, there's not a single thing you could say to me tonight that I wouldn't like."

"I can't go home with you yet."

He hit the brake. "Okay. You found the *one* thing."

"I know it sounds crazy, but I need to stay with Sugar Beth for a while longer."

"Crazy doesn't begin to describe it." He pulled to the side of the road, turned off the ignition, and draped his arm over the back of her seat. She extracted a leaf fragment from his hair, just above his temple. He kissed her fingers, but he didn't look happy. "Sugar Beth is poison, Winnie."

She trailed the backs of her fingers along his jaw. "She's changed."

"That's what everybody keeps saying, but I'm here to tell you that you're wrong."

She rested her head against his arm. "We fight all the time, and I've said more rotten things to her in two days than I've said to everyone else in a lifetime. But she's not going to be around much longer, and this may be the only chance I have to figure things out with her."

He massaged the back of her neck with his thumb. "Honey, she doesn't have your best interests at heart."

"That's not entirely true."

"Believe me, it is." He withdrew his arm, tapped the steering wheel. "I wasn't going to say anything about this, but . . . She came on to me last night."

She smiled. "I know. I was there."

"What?"

"Colin and I were standing on the stairs. We heard the whole thing. Sugar Beth set you up."

"You and Colin stood there and listened to her throw herself at me?"

"We were weak. And we had a vested interest in the outcome."

"I don't believe this." He smacked the steering wheel with the heel of his hand. "She set me up?"

"She's a devil, all right."

"I don't like that admiration I hear in your voice."

"She's aggressive, but she's not mean-spirited—not the way she used to be. And she's great with Gigi. I want to know her better."

"You don't have to stay at the carriage house for that. You can meet her for lunch, for God's sake. Go shopping together."

"It wouldn't be the same. It needs to be just Sugar Beth and me, sink or swim, nobody else around." She kissed the corner of his mouth. "I have to do this."

"For how long?" he said begrudgingly.

"I'm not sure."

"What about us? Our marriage?"

"That's lookin' real good to me right now." She dabbled with his bottom lip. "Would you mind so much if we dated for a while?"

"Dated?"

"For a while."

"You want to date?"

"Just for a little while."

"Damned right I'd mind."

"Then we're going to have a fight about it, and as much as the idea appeals to me, can we wait until tomorrow to do it?"

"You want to fight with me?"

"Oh, yes."

He shook his head. "I know that someday I'll understand this, but right now I'm too wrung out from trying to satisfy your insatiable lust."

"Get used to it."

He laughed, started the car, and drove her back to the carriage house where he walked her to the front door and kissed her good night like a perfect Southern gentleman. With a pair of blue panties tucked in his pocket.

Sugar Beth didn't see Colin again until Wednesday morning. As she left for the bookstore, she spotted him pushing a wheelbarrow loaded with stone toward the tree line behind Frenchman's Bride. Gordon trotted off to join him, and Sugar Beth frowned. Colin should be writing.

When it was time for her lunch break, she carried her bag of taco chips and a Coke across the street to Yesterday's Treasures. The store had reopened for business the day before, and there'd been a steady stream of customers ever since, including the same busload of senior citizens who'd visited the bookstore a few hours earlier. She still couldn't get used to the idea of Parrish being a tourist destination.

She greeted Donna, Winnie's assistant, then headed for the back of the store where she found Winnie sitting at her desk looking starry-eyed and sleepy. Sugar Beth pulled up a straight-backed chair, propped her feet on the desk, and opened the taco chips. "I heard you sneak in again in the middle of the night. Why don't you just move back home?"

"I'm not done torturing you." Winnie yawned, then smiled. "Ryan and I had a *huge* fight last night."

"Ah, well, that explains the look of bliss."

"We never used to fight." She smiled as she reached across the desk to swipe some chips. "Fighting's wonderful."

"Each to his own. Although the two of you are such big pansies, I can't imagine it gets too dangerous."

"We yell," she said defensively. "Or at least he did last night. He really wants me to come home. He's trying to be understanding, but he's getting frustrated."

"Not from lack of sex, that's for sure."

Winnie actually giggled. "I never thought we'd have so much passion."

"You are a *lot* weirder than me."

Twenty minutes later, when Sugar Beth returned to work, Jewel passed over an envelope. "This came for *madam* while she was out."

Sugar Beth opened it and found a round-trip air ticket to Houston. She gazed at the date. The ticket was for tomorrow, her day off, a flight leaving in the morning and returning that same night. She pulled out a separate sheet of paper and found a confirmation number for a rental car.

She bit her bottom lip and gazed across the street at Yesterday's Treasures. It could have been Winnie who'd done this, but she was too preoccupied now to have thought of it. Sugar Beth pressed the envelope to her breast. Colin.

* * *

Less than twenty-four hours later, Sugar Beth stood in the doorway of the second-floor lounge at Brookdale and gazed at Delilah bent over a jigsaw puzzle. Her gray hair fell straight and smooth to just below her ears, and a headband printed with ladybugs held it back from her chubby face. Today she wore the pink jumper Sugar Beth had brought her several months ago, along with a lavender T-shirt. For a moment Sugar Beth simply gazed at her, then she spoke softly. "Hey, sweetheart."

Delilah stiffened. Her head came up slowly, her eyes already filled with hope. "My Sugar Beth?"

A moment later they were in each other's arms, with Delilah saying her name over and over again.

For the next half hour, she couldn't seem to stop talking. "I didn't think you'd ever come . . . You said you wasn't mad, but . . . And then I gave Henry my extra muffin . . . Dr. Brent filled my tooth . . . And Shirley knows you're only allowed to smoke outside . . ." As she spoke, she held Sugar Beth's hand, and she continued to hold it as they took a walk across the grounds. She chose Taco Bell for lunch, and afterward they went on a shopping expedition that finished off Sugar Beth's paycheck. She didn't let herself dwell on the fact that she had only six more weeks until the next payment was due.

Delilah's anxiety finally set in, and she wanted to go back to Brookdale. "Meesie gets worried if I'm gone too long." Meesie Baker was Delilah's favorite aide.

"I think it's harder on you bein' so far away than it is on her," Meesie said later when Sugar Beth caught her alone. "She misses you, but she's doin' fine."

Sugar Beth stroked Delilah's hair as they said good-bye. "I'll call you on Sunday. And I'll think about you every day."

"I know you will, my Sugar Beth. Because you love me so much."

"You got that right, ace," she replied, which made Delilah giggle.

On the flight back, Sugar Beth gazed out the window and

fought the lump in her throat. How many people were lucky enough to have someone in their lives who loved them so unconditionally?

As she drove home in the dark, she tried to figure out how she could thank Colin. In the end, she took the coward's way out and wrote him a note. Her first three attempts revealed too much and ended up in the wastebasket, but the version she stuck in his mailbox as she left for work on Friday morning did the job without the sentiment.

Dear Colin,

I saw Delilah yesterday. Thank you. Being with her meant everything to me, and I take back nearly every bad thing I've said about you.

Gratefully,
Sugar Beth

(Please do not mark for spelling and punctuation.)

Colin crumpled the letter in his fist and tossed it on the ground next to the wheelbarrow. He didn't want her gratitude, damn it, he wanted her company, her smiles. He wanted her body—he couldn't deny that—but also her quirky point of view, that irreverent humor, those sideways glances she gave him when she didn't think he was looking.

He threw down his shovel. Ever since Sunday, he'd been tense and irritable. He couldn't write, couldn't sleep. No big mystery why. Guilt wasn't a comfortable companion, and it was time he did something about it.

The phone call came at three o'clock on Saturday afternoon, an hour before the bookstore closed. "Gemima's Books," Sugar Beth said.

"If you want to see your dog alive again, be at Rowan Oak at five o'clock. And come alone."

"Rowan *Oak*?"

"If you call the police, the dog's . . . dog meat."

"I dumped you!"

But he'd already hung up.

She wouldn't do it. She wouldn't let him manipulate her. But not long after the store closed, she found herself on the highway heading toward William Faulkner's legendary home in Oxford. Colin had made it possible for her to see Delilah, and she owed him this. Still, she wished he didn't have to make everything so hard.

The house and grounds closed to the public at four o'clock, but someone obviously had important connections because a burgundy Lexus sat in the otherwise empty parking lot and the wooden gate was open. Having grown up in northeastern Mississippi, Sugar Beth had been to Rowan Oak many times—with a Girl Scout troop, church youth groups, the Seawillows, and during senior year, in a big yellow bus with Mr. Byrne's English classes. William Faulkner had bought the decrepit Greek Revival plantation in the early 1930s. At the time the house had no indoor plumbing or electricity, and Faulkner's wife was rumored to have spent her days sitting on the stoop crying while her husband began making the house livable. Until his death in 1962, Faulkner had lived here, gotten drunk here, frightened his children with stories of a ghost he invented, and written the novels that had eventually won him the Nobel Prize for literature. In the early 1970s, his daughter had sold the house and grounds to the University of Mississippi, and since then, visitors from all over the world had come to see the state's most famous literary landmark.

She approached the two-story white frame house through the imposing avenue of cedars that had been planted during the nineteenth century. Long before she reached the end of the old brick walk, she saw Colin leaning against one of the house's square columns with Gordon lying at his feet.

"Pat Conroy called Oxford the Vatican City of Southern letters," he said as he stepped off the porch.

"I didn't know that, but I do love the man's books." She scratched Gordon's head. "My dog's still alive, I see."

"I'm nothing if not merciful."

He wore a white sweater and an immaculate pair of gray slacks. The outdoor work had left him tan, and she was once again struck by the contrast between his masculinity and his elegance. He was a mass of contradictions, haughty and cynical, but also tender and a lot more sentimental than he let anyone see. How his wife's suicide must have devastated him. "What's this about?" she asked.

"I have something I want to give you."

"You've given me more than enough. That plane ticket—"

"Faulkner has always been my favorite American writer," he said, cutting her off.

"Not surprising. You share a fascination for the same literary landscape."

"We don't, however, share the same facility with language. The man was a genius."

"I suppose."

"Don't even contemplate saying anything disrespectful about William Faulkner."

"As long as I don't have to read another one of his books, I'll be completely respectful."

"How can you say that? Faulkner is—"

"He's a man, and I have a limited patience with dead white male writers. Or even living ones for that matter, you and Mr. Conroy being notable exceptions. Now Jane Austen, Harper Lee, Alice Walker, their books deal with things women care about." She let herself rattle on. "Margaret Mitchell isn't p.c. anymore, but that was one heck of a page-turner. Then there's Mary Stewart, Daphne du Maurier,

LaVyrle Spencer, Georgette Heyer, Helen Fielding—but only the first *Bridget Jones*. Nope, Faulkner just doesn't make my final cut."

"Your list is a little heavy on romance for my tastes."

"You try spending six months sitting at somebody's bedside waiting for them to die and then tell me that the happy-ending love story isn't one of God's good gifts."

He planted a quick kiss on her forehead, and the tenderness of the gesture nearly undid her. "Let's go inside."

He opened the door for her, and as they entered the empty house, she gazed at the foyer, where a set of stairs led to the second floor. "Can you get me into George Clooney's place, too?"

"Some other time."

They wandered through the hallways of Faulkner's home, gazing into each room but not entering. She couldn't resist pointing out the stack of paperback potboilers on display in Faulkner's bedside bookshelves, but Colin was more fascinated by his office. As he took in the old Underwood typewriter, he contemplated how modern word processing might have changed Faulkner's writing. Sugar Beth refrained from pointing out that Microsoft wasn't doing a thing for Colin's output, and the only work being done at Frenchman's Bride these days involved stone.

They left the house and walked around the grounds. Dusk was settling in, but she could still see the forsythia and wild plum blooming in Bailey's Woods behind the house. Before long, the dogwood would be in flower. Gordon waddled at Colin's side, occasionally stopping to investigate a shrub or sniff at a clump of grass. As they returned to the house, Colin took her hand. "I've missed you this week."

She felt the hard ridge of calluses on his palm and didn't want to draw away, but what was the point in torturing herself. "You're just horny."

He stopped walking and ran his finger along her cheek, regarding her with such tenderness that her heart missed a beat. "I want more from you than sex, Sugar Beth."

She had a saucy comeback all loaded and ready to fire, but she fumbled with the trigger. "You . . . you know I don't do windows."

"Please stop it, darling." The request was gently uttered, and the endearment, which would have sounded pompous coming from anyone else, fell over her like cherry blossoms.

She swatted an imaginary bug to give herself an excuse to move a few steps away. "What do you want?"

"I want you to give us time. Is that too much to ask?"

"Time for what? I'm a three-time loser, Colin. Four if you count Ryan." She tried to sound saucy, but she was afraid she'd merely sounded sad. "I feed off men. I lure them with my sexual tricks, then bite off their heads while they sleep."

"Is that how Emmett felt about you?"

"He was the exception that proved the rule."

"I'm not too worried about my untimely decapitation, so I don't see why you should be."

"Okay, I finally understand why you're being so persistent about this. You want to make me fall so desperately in love with you that I can't think of anything else. Then, when I've turned into a big bowl of mush, and I'm begging for a few crumbs of your affection, you'll laugh in my face and walk away. This is what you've been planning from the beginning, isn't it? Your ultimate revenge for what I did to you in high school?"

He sighed. "Sugar Beth. The romance novels . . ."

"Well, it's not going to happen, bucko, because I've spent way too much class time in the school of hard knocks. I'm past my obsessive need to center my life around another piece of beefcake."

"As much as I appreciate the description, I think you're just afraid."

Something snapped inside her. "Of course I'm afraid! Relationships do bad things to me." He started to respond, but the pain had gone on long enough, and she didn't want to hear it. "You know what I want? I want peace. I want a good job and a decent place to live. I want to read books and listen to music and have time to make some female friendships that are going to last. When I wake up in the morning, I want to know that I have a decent shot at being happy. And here's what's really sad. Until I met you, I was almost there."

His face set in hard lines. She knew she'd hurt him, but better this sharp, quick pain than a dull ache that never stopped. "I'm sick of this," she forced herself to say. "I told you I didn't want to see you anymore, but you wouldn't listen. Well, it's time to pay attention. I'm tired of you stalking me. Now get the message and leave me alone."

His face paled, and his eyes emptied of all expression. "My apologies. It wasn't my intention to *stalk*." He snatched up a manila envelope from behind one of the columns and thrust it at her. "I know you've been looking for this, and now you have your very own copy."

She watched him walk away, proud and haughty, his powerful stride devouring Faulkner's lawn. "Gordon! Come back here," she cried.

But her dog had a new master, and he paid no attention.

She heard the sound of his car driving away. Finally, she gazed down at the envelope and drew out what he'd brought her.

A copy of *Reflections*.

Colin was thirty miles outside Oxford when he heard the siren. He glanced at his speedometer and saw he was going eighty. Brilliant. He backed off and pulled over. Gordon sat up on the seat. The perfect ending to a miserable day.

A stalker. Was that how she saw him?

As he handed over his license, he thought about how much differently the evening had unfolded than what he'd planned. Getting Sugar Beth out of Parrish had seemed like a good idea, and Rowan Oak a convenient choice. He'd tried to impress her with a private tour, and he'd imagined the combination of a romantic setting and his personal charm would lull her enough so he could talk to her about *Reflections,* so he could explain. But he'd forgotten personal charm wasn't his long suit, and she'd undoubtedly grown immune to contrived romantic settings before her twenty-first birthday. He hadn't planned on throwing the book at her, that was for certain. He'd intended to lead up to it gradually, to explain how he'd felt when he'd been working on it and point out that he'd finished writing it months before she'd come back. Most of all, he'd planned to warn her. And then he was going to tell her about the painting.

"You're the author," the trooper said, gazing at Colin's license. "The one who wrote that book about Parrish."

Colin nodded but didn't try to strike up a conversation. He saw no honor in attempting to talk himself out of a ticket he deserved. But the trooper had a book-loving wife and a basset hound, and he sent him on with only a warning.

Colin reached the edge of town, but instead of heading directly for Frenchman's Bride, he drove aimlessly through the quiet streets. There'd been a fierceness about her tonight that scared him. She wasn't playing games. She'd meant every word she'd said. And he'd fallen in love with her.

The knowledge felt old and familiar, as though it had been part of him for a very long time. With his lifelong appreciation of the ironic, he should be amused, but he couldn't find a laugh anywhere. He'd misjudged, misplayed, and misbehaved. In the process, he'd lost something unbearably precious.

Sugar Beth wanted to be alone when she read *Reflections,* so she declined Winnie's invitation to join her for church on Sunday morning. As soon as her car pulled away, she threw on a pair of jeans, grabbed an old blanket, and set off for the lake. She'd have liked to bring Gordon with her, but he hadn't come back. It was beginning to look as though he never would.

She laid out the blanket in a sunny spot not far from the deserted boat launch and gazed down at the cover of the book. It was marked "Uncorrected Proof Not for Sale," which meant he'd given her one of the editions printed up for reviewers and booksellers before the real book came out in another month. She ran her hand over the cover and braced herself for what she was fairly certain he'd written about her mother. Diddie might have been high-handed, but she'd also been a force for progress, and if Colin hadn't acknowledged that, she'd never forgive him.

A church bell tolled in the distance, and she began to read:

I came to Parrish twice, the first time to write a great novel, and more than a decade later, because I needed to make my way back home.

He'd put himself in the book. She was startled. He hadn't done that in *Last Whistle-stop*. She rushed through the opening chapter, which told of his first days in Parrish. In the second chapter he used an encounter with Tallulah—*Your hair is far too long, young man, even for a foreigner*—to take the story back to the late 1960s, when the town's economy had begun to fall apart. His account of the near bankruptcy of the window factory read like a thriller, the tension heightened by funny, hometown tales such as the Great Potato Salad rivalry at Christ the Redeemer Church. As he moved into the 1970s, he personalized the human cost of the town's racial politics through Aaron Leary's family. And, as she'd suspected he would, he wrote of Diddie and Griffin. She didn't care so much about the portrait he'd painted of her father, but her cheeks burned with anger as he showed her beautiful, high-handed mother marching through town trailing cigarette ash and condescension. Although he didn't neglect her accomplishments, it was still a devastating portrayal.

With nearly a hundred pages left, she closed the book and

wandered down to the water. She'd assumed he'd end the story in 1982 when the new factory had opened, but there were three chapters still to go, and apprehension had begun to form a knot in her stomach. Maybe Diddie wasn't the only person she should have worried about.

She returned to the blanket, picked up the book again, and began the next chapter.

In 1986, I was twenty-two years old and Parrish was my nirvana. The townspeople accepted my oddness, my staggering shortcomings in the classroom, my strange accent and haughty pretensions. I was writing a novel, and Mississippi loves a writer more than anyone else. I felt accepted for the first time in my life. I was completely, blissfully happy ... until my Southern Eden was destroyed by a girl named Valentine.

At eighteen, she was the most beautiful creature anyone had ever seen. Watching her saunter up the sidewalk to the front doors of Parrish High was watching sexual artistry in motion ...

Sugar Beth finished the page, read the next, kept reading as her breathing grew shallow and her skin hot with rage. She was Valentine. He'd changed her name, changed the names of all of them who'd been teenagers at the time, but no one would be fooled for a moment.

Valentine was a teenage vampire, sipping the blood of her hapless victims along with her Chicken Mc-Nuggets after school. She didn't turn truly dangerous, however, until she decided not to limit herself to the plasma of teenage boys and began looking for older prey.
Me.

The sun dipped low over the lake, and the air grew cool. By the time she reached the end, she was shivering. She set the book aside and curled into herself. Her story took up less than a chapter, but she felt as if every word had been written into her skin, like the ink tattoos the boys punched in their wrists with ballpoint pens when they got bored in class. Everything was there—her selfishness, her manipulations, her lie—all of it exposed for the world to see and judge. Shame burned inside her. Anger. He'd known from the beginning. While they were laughing, kissing, making love, he'd known what he'd written about her, what she would someday read, yet he hadn't warned her.

She stayed at the lake until it grew dark, with the blanket pulled around her shoulders and knees drawn to her chest. When she returned, the carriage house felt empty and oppressive. Winnie had left a note on the table, but Sugar Beth walked past it. She hadn't eaten all day, and now the thought of food nauseated her. She went upstairs and washed her face, lay down on the bed, but the ceiling Tallulah had gazed at for forty decades felt like a coffin lid. Her aunt's life had been a dirge of regret and misery lived out in the name of love.

Sugar Beth couldn't breathe. She rose and headed downstairs, but even here, Tallulah's bitterness permeated everything. The shabby furniture, the faded wallpaper, the yellowed curtains—all of it stained with the anger of a woman who'd made lost love her life's obsession. Her head began to pound. This wasn't a home, it was a mausoleum, and the studio was its heart. She grabbed the key and made her way out into the night. She fumbled with the lock in the dark. When it gave, she pulled open the doors and flicked the switch on the bare, overhead lightbulb. As she gazed around at her aunt's pathetic memorial to lost love, she imagined Colin's explanations, his justifications. *The book was written long before you came back. What good would it have served if I'd told you earlier?*

What good, indeed?

She stepped into the chaotic heart of her aunt's dark spirit and began ripping away the dirty plastic. She would not live her life like this. Never again. She wouldn't be a prisoner to her own neediness. She'd strike a match to all of it, send this mad energy of paint and loss up in flames.

The colors swirled. Her heart raced. The frenetic dabs and splatters spun around her. And then she saw it.

The painting Lincoln Ash had left behind.

Chapter 21

The painting had been here all along, a ferocious web of crimson and black, cobalt and ocher, with angry trails of yellow and explosions of green. Not a drop cloth at all. It had never been a drop cloth. She gave a choked sob and went down on her knees next to the enormous canvas spread across the concrete floor, ran her hands over an encapsulated paint lid, a fossilized cigarette butt. These weren't objects dropped by accident, but relics deliberately left in place to mark the moment of creation. A strangled hiccup caught in her throat. There was nothing random about these dribbles and splatters. This was an organized composition, an eruption of form, color, and emotion. Now that she saw it for what it was, she couldn't believe she'd ever mistaken it for a drop cloth. She crawled around the perimeter, found the signature in the far corner, ran her fingers over the single word *ASH*.

She fell back on her heels. Even in the garish light of the single bulb dangling from the rafters, the painting's tumult spoke to the chaos in her own heart. She swayed. Let its angry rhythm claim her. Moved her body. Gave herself up to misery. Gazed into the painting's soul.

"Sugar . . . Sugar . . . Sugar Pie . . ."

A hoot. A whistle.

"Sugar . . . Sugar . . . Sugar Pie . . ."

Her head snapped up.

"Sugar . . . Sugar . . . Come out and play . . ."

She shot to her feet. Cubby Bowmar and his boys were back.

They stood on the small crescent of lawn in front of the carriage house—six of them—beer cans in hand, faces turned to the moon, baying for her. "Come on, Sugar Beth . . . Come on, baby . . ."

Hoots and howls.

"Sugar . . . Sugar . . . Sugar . . ."

They chanted and chugged.

"Sugar . . . Sugar . . . Sugar . . ."

Wolf whistles, yowls, drunken, piggish snorts.

She stormed toward them. "Cubby Bowmar, I'm sick of this. You stop it right now!"

Cubby threw out his arms and fell into Tommy Lilburn. "Aw, Sugar Beth, all we want is some love."

"All you're gonna get is a big fat piece of my mind if you and your sorry-ass friends don't haul yourselves off my property."

Junior Battles lurched forward. "You don't mean that, Sugar Beth. Com' on. Have a beer with us."

"Does your wife know you're here?"

"Don't be like that now. We're just havin' us a boys' night out."

"A morons' night out is more like it."

"You're the mos' beautiful woman in the world." Cubby tucked his free hand under his armpit and flapped it like a one-winged rooster as he began the chant again. "Sugar . . . Sugar . . . Sugar . . ."

Junior took it up. "Sugar . . . Sugar . . . Sugar . . ."

Tommy threw back his head, spewing beer and woofing.

"Oh, for Lord's sake *be quiet*." She spun on Cubby, ready to light into him, when, out of nowhere, Colin appeared like a dark avenger and launched himself at them.

Cubby let out a grunt of pain as Colin's shoulder caught him in the chest and brought him down. Colin went after Junior next, a sharp jab to the jaw that made Junior howl as he slammed into a tree. Carl Ray Norris tried to run away, but Colin threw himself at his back and brought him down, taking Jack McCall along for the ride. Eight feet away, Tommy dropped to the ground before Colin could touch him.

Gradually, Colin realized that nobody was fighting back. He cursed and rose to his feet. He stood with his fists on his hips, legs braced, waiting for Cubby or Junior, for Jack or Carl Ray. Moonlight glinted off his dark hair and gleaming white shirt. He looked like a pirate, the black sheep son of a noble family forced to earn his fortune plundering Spanish galleons and beating up rednecks.

He opened his palms, taunted them in a low, harsh voice. "Come on, boys. You want to play. You play with *me*."

Sugar Beth's eyes shot from Colin, to the men on the ground, to Tommy crawling on all fours trying to find his beer. The blood roared in her ears. "Isn't one of you going to *fight him*?"

Cubby rubbed his knee. "Dang, Sugar Beth, we're too drunk."

"There are *six* of you!" she shouted.

"We might hurt him."

"That's the idea, you *fool*!"

Junior rubbed his jaw. "It's Colin, Sugar Beth. He's a writer. Everybody'd get pissed off if we fought him."

"*I'll* do it, then, you worthless sons of bitches." And she hurled herself at him.

Colin staggered backward, taken by surprise. She swung at him, and he grunted as her fist caught the side of his head. She gave a hiss of pain—his head was harder than her hand—but didn't let that stop her. Instead, she shot out her leg and caught him behind the knee.

They went down together.

He gave an *oof* as her elbow sank into his midsection, then sucked in his breath. "What are you *doing*?"

"Kickin' your ass, you sneaky, rat bastard!" She tried to rise to her knees so she could swing again, but she slipped in the damp grass and came down hard across him, so she attacked his chest instead.

"You're going to hurt yourself!" He caught the waistband of her jeans and yanked on them, rolling her to the side, going with her, pinning her.

She gazed up at him.

His teeth glittered, and his eyes narrowed into slits. "Are you ready to settle down yet?"

She hit him as hard as she could.

He winced, grabbed her upper arms, and pinioned them. As she tried to free her knee, he anticipated the movement and trapped her under his thigh. She kicked out with the other leg and caught him in the calf. They rolled. Now she was on top. Instead of retaliating, he tried to contain her, which made her furious. "Fight back, you lying limey sissy!"

"Stop it!" He tried to snare her other leg. At the same time, he growled at the men, "Get her off me before she breaks something."

"She's doin' okay," Junior said.

"Watch 'at other knee," Carl Ray called out.

He was a few seconds too late, and Colin let out a bellow.

She'd missed the bull's-eye, but she'd caught him high enough on the thigh to hurt. He uttered a low, particularly vile curse and rolled her beneath him again.

You're going to be a woman for the ages, Sugar Beth.

The echo of her mother's words sent shame spiraling through her, and the adrenaline that had fueled her ran out. Another man. Another brawl. She felt sick.

Gradually, Colin realized she'd stopped fighting. The pressure on her chest began to ease. He rolled off.

She heard the pop of a beer can followed by Cubby's voice. "Looks like the fun's over, folks. Guess we better be on our way."

Feet began to move. "'Night, Sugar Beth."

Somebody's keys jangled. "'Night, Colin."

A belch. "Y'all take care now."

Moments later, she heard the sound of truck engines.

Colin stood, the sound of his breathing harsh in the night air, his chest heaving. He gazed down at her, then extended his hand to help her up.

She ignored him and made it to her knees by herself. Her elbow burned from a scrape, and she'd ripped her slacks. She felt something hot on her face, but it took her a moment to realize she'd started to cry.

Colin's heart wrenched as he gazed down at her and saw tears glistening on those beautiful cheekbones. He'd finally done it. He'd finally brought Sugar Beth Carey to her knees.

With a strangled exclamation, he sank down next to her and drew her close. She didn't fight him. He began kissing her eyelids, her cheeks, sipping up the moisture. His own eyes burned, and he blinked against the sting. He ran his hand down the fragile bumps of her spine. Kissed her temples. He was a man of words, but he couldn't think of anything to say except the ridiculous, which came out as a rusty whisper. "You've read my book, I see."

She nodded against him.

He pressed his forehead to hers. Breathed in as she exhaled. Tried to think of some way to make it all disappear, but he couldn't come up with a thing.

"I feel like I was raped," she whispered.

He winced.

Her breath fell soft on his face. "I know all of it was written long before I came back. And everything you wrote was true. I know that. I was fair game. More than fair game. And you could have written worse about me than you did. I even understand why you didn't tell me right away. What good would it have done, right? And now, at least I'll be prepared."

"Don't, my love," he whispered. "Don't try to justify something that hurts you so much." He cradled her face, kissed the damp trail on her cheek. "If I could do it again, I'd write it differently."

"Facts don't change."

"How we see them does."

He would have stayed there kneeling on the ground with her forever, but she pushed away from him and sank back on one calf in the wet grass. "I found the painting tonight," she said slowly.

Another sword through his heart. "Did you?"

"In the studio. The drop cloth. The drop cloth is the painting."

He told himself to get it over with quickly, but she was still talking. "When I was growing up . . . All those times I've searched the studio since I got back . . . I never saw it for what it was. Not until tonight."

The time had come to drive the final nail in his coffin. He rose to his feet. She did the same. Her hair tumbled over her cheek, and her hand trembled as she pushed it away. "No wonder my father always laughed when he talked about the painting. She hid it in plain sight."

Her top button had come unfastened, revealing the edge of her bra, which was creamy white, very much like her soul. "You have what you came for, then," he said.

She nodded. "The last Ash canvas this large sold at auction for four and a half million dollars."

"You'll be a wealthy woman. Independent."

"This canvas won't bring as much."

"No?"

"I want mine in a museum, not hidden away in a private collection. That'll limit the bidders. But all I need is enough to make Delilah secure."

"You'll have a lot more than that."

"I suppose."

"Our noble, self-sacrificing heroine." He didn't say it sarcastically, but she stiffened, and he cursed the part of him that was so terrified of the sentimental that he tainted everything with cynicism, even when he didn't intend it. He forced himself to utter the question he'd been dreading. "When are you planning to leave?"

"As soon as I make arrangements for the painting."

"That shouldn't take long."

"Maybe a week."

He touched her hair. "I love you, you know."

Her lips trembled and a tear caught on her lashes. "You'll get over it. Take it from one who knows. Love's not an emotion that lasts forever."

"Have you gotten over Emmett, then?"

"I must have, or I wouldn't have fallen in love with you so quickly."

Hearing her openly admit her feelings should have gratified him, but it only deepened his pain. "Do you have so little trust in yourself?"

"It's not a matter of trust. I'm being realistic."

"If that were true, you wouldn't leave. Everything you need is right here in Parrish."

"You're wrong."

"What about that children's bookstore you talked about? It doesn't have to be a dream now. This is your home, Sugar Beth, the place where you belong."

"No, it's your town now."

"And the place isn't big enough for both of us, is that it?"

"You know it wouldn't work."

"You need to be here. You have family." He drew a ragged breath. "And you have me."

Dismay darkened her eyes. "That's why I have to leave." Her lashes dropped, and she turned way. "I can't do this. I'm sorry."

"I found the painting last week."

She looked back at him.

"When we were searching the studio. I'd been in there at least a dozen times before, but . . . I was in a foul mood that day—knowing I was losing you—and you were standing next to it. I turned my head to snarl at you. Something about the colors, the violence of the paint . . . It grabbed me by the throat."

She nodded as though she understood, although even he didn't entirely comprehend the turbulent emotions that had claimed him right then.

"When were you going to tell me?" she asked.

"Every day this past week."

She didn't get angry as he expected. She didn't seem reproachful. Instead, she gazed at him with something that looked like understanding.

He sensed her getting ready to move away again, and he spoke before she could. "I want you to marry me."

Her eyes shot open.

His words should have rattled him—he'd never imagined saying them again—but they felt exactly right. He took a step closer and cupped her exquisite face. "I wish I had magnolias, or gardenias perhaps. Something to make the grand romantic gesture. I'm quite capable of it, you know."

She rested her cheek against his palm, but only for a moment. "I could never do that to you."

Her lack of courage maddened him. It felt too familiar, too

much like his past. "I won't beg, Sugar Beth. I begged a woman once in my life, and I'll never do it again. You're either strong enough to love me—strong enough to let me love you in return—or you're not. Which is it going to be?"

She dropped her head and said, in a whisper, "I guess what you see as lack of courage, I see as wisdom."

"There's nothing wise about running from love."

"There is when I'm involved."

And she walked away, leaving him alone in the damp spring night.

Sugar Beth moved numbly through the next few days. Other than catching an occasional glimpse of Colin's car turning out of the drive, she didn't see him. He'd even stopped working on his wall. Recognizing that she'd made the right decision for both of them didn't make it easier to accept the fact that she'd damaged someone she loved. As for the damage she'd done to herself . . . Sooner or later, she'd get over it. She always did.

As she waited on customers at Gemima's, she told herself Colin had been wrong when he'd accused her of cowardice. People who didn't learn from their mistakes deserved to be unhappy. She couldn't keep rushing from one man to another, handing out her heart helter-skelter, falling in love with love and then having it snatched away. Colin didn't understand that she was protecting him.

On Wednesday, the eager representatives from Sotheby's arrived to take away the painting. The studio seemed empty without it, but she wasn't sorry to see it go. She had enough disturbing emotions of her own to deal with, and she didn't need to see more of them on canvas.

The week ground on. She told herself she'd survive the public humiliation that awaited her when *Reflections* was published. She'd survived humiliation before.

She had no trouble securing a small loan from the bank to

hold her over until the painting sold. The Ash canvas was so much larger than she'd ever dreamed. Even after she'd set up a trust for Delilah, she'd have more than enough left over to open her children's bookstore. Colin had been right. She had no passion for selling real estate, not compared with the pleasure she felt introducing a child to a book. As soon as she got to Houston, she'd start looking for the perfect location, and she'd forget that she'd already found it in an abandoned train depot in Parrish, Mississippi.

She pushed away images of old brick walls with book-lined shelves and a reading area shaped like a caboose. She refused to picture a tiny outdoor café sitting on an abandoned loading platform or weed-infested tracks reclaimed with potted trees and tubs of flowers. Instead, she concentrated on her work.

Jewel advertised for a new clerk, but Sugar Beth didn't like any of the people she interviewed. "You owe it to the kids to find someone who cares about selling children's books."

"I did," her tiny boss replied. "I found you."

And right there, between Sandra Cisneros and Mary Higgins Clark, Sugar Beth began to cry. Jewel hugged her, but some things were beyond consolation.

Winnie announced she was holding a Reconciliation and Forgiveness Dessert on Monday evening so Sugar Beth could make peace with the Seawillows before she left town. "Frankly, I'm not sure how much Reconciliation or Forgiveness is going to happen," she said. "They're just getting used to the idea of having you back, and now you're leaving again. They're takin' it personally."

"You know I don't have any choice."

"I know you think you don't." And Sugar Beth saw in Winnie's eyes that she, too, felt betrayed.

At night, she barely slept. Instead, she stood at her bedroom window gazing over the hedge toward Frenchman's Bride and fighting the powerful force that urged her to run to him. How could he have asked her to marry him? Had he forgotten how to count? What kind of stupidity would make him volunteer to be her fourth victim?

Saturday was her last day at the bookstore. Word had gotten around that she was leaving, and half the town stopped by to say good-bye. At least this time they wouldn't think quite so badly of her. Late that afternoon, when things finally quieted down, she made her way to the children's section for the final time. She was putting the small chairs back in place when Winnie burst in.

"Ryan just called from Frenchman's Bride! Colin's leaving Parrish today."

"What are you talking about?"

"He's moving away. Leaving for good."

Sugar Beth's blood turned to ice. "I don't believe you."

"He's loading up his car right now. Colin told Ryan not to say anything to you until after he'd left."

"Colin loves Parrish! He wouldn't leave. This town means everything to him." Even as she said it, the opening sentence of *Reflections* flashed through her mind. *I came to Parrish twice, the first time to write a great novel, and more than a decade later, because I needed to make my way back home.* "Why would he leave?" she said weakly.

"I think we both know the answer to that."

"He believes if he leaves, I'll stay." She pressed her fingers to her mouth.

"He's planning to sell you Frenchman's Bride."

Sugar Beth stared at her.

"You're supposed to contact his attorney and make an offer."

She straightened. "He can't do this. I'm getting my keys."

"My car's already out front. Hurry."

They raced outside where Winnie's Benz sat at an awkward angle in a No Parking zone. The tires squealed as Winnie backed out. "You have so screwed this up." She blew through a red light.

Sugar Beth's shoulder hit the door as they shot around a corner, and she dug her fingernails into her palms. "My gift."

"You're supposed to be the great big expert at handling men," Winnie scoffed. "You're a national disaster, is what you are!"

"Don't start in on me again."

"You're perfect for him. That's what's so frustrating. I didn't see it right away—how could I, you being you?—but it's sure crystal clear now. You're the only woman strong enough to stand up to him. He intimidates everybody else. And he needs you. Yesterday, when I saw him, he said all the right things, but it was like part of him was missing."

Sugar Beth twisted her hands and stared dully ahead.

As they drew up in front of Frenchman's Bride, Sugar Beth saw his Lexus parked at the side and Colin setting something in the trunk. Ryan was carrying a computer box down the steps. She threw herself out of the car and rushed across the lawn. Gordon saw her coming and began to bark. Colin watched her for a moment, then frowned at Ryan as she drew near. "I asked you not to tell her."

"Things don't work that way around here," Ryan said. "You should know that by now."

Colin snatched the carton from him and rounded the car to set it in the backseat. Ryan moved toward Winnie, and Sugar Beth closed in on Colin. He looked haughty and remote, but he had a poet's soul, and his camouflage no longer fooled her. "This is crazy. What do you think you're doing?"

"You're the one who decided only one of us could live here," he said, reaching inside to move another carton.

"You!" she cried. "*You're* the one who's supposed to live here."

"Come now," he scoffed, as if his leaving were of no importance. "We both know Parrish is more your home than mine."

"That's not true. It's yours now. Colin, don't do this."

"We've made our choices. You've decided to be a coward, and I've decided to leave you to it."

"I'm not being cowardly. I'm being smart. You can't walk away from Frenchman's Bride. It's your home. You've put your heart and soul into it."

"No, Sugar Beth," he said quietly. "I put my heart and soul into you."

She flinched.

He leaned back into the car and repositioned a box of books. She saw Gordon's water dish on the floor. He emerged and shut the door, his mask of remoteness firmly back in place. "Talk to my attorney about the house. I'll get my things out as soon as I decide where I'm going to settle, but in the meantime, you're welcome to move in."

"I can't believe you're doing this." She gazed back at Winnie and Ryan, willing them to say something that would make him change his mind, but they looked as helpless as she felt. "Please," she whispered. "I ran you out of town once. Don't let me do it again."

"You're the one, my dear, who decided this place isn't big enough for both of us." He pulled something from his pocket and pressed it into her hand. As he moved away to shake hands with Ryan, she saw he'd given her the keys to Frenchman's Bride.

"Tell Gigi I'll call her tonight." He hugged Winnie. "Take care of yourself, Ms. Davis."

Winnie gave him a hard squeeze. "You, too, Mr. Byrne."

"No!" Sugar Beth shot forward. "No, I won't have it, do you hear me? This big sacrifice of yours doesn't mean anything because I'm leaving whether you go or not. I mean it, Colin. You're doing this for nothing. Next week I'm driving out of this town for the last time."

"That would be very foolish." He came to her then, tipped up her chin, and gently brushed her lips. It wasn't nearly enough contact, and she tried to embrace him, but he stepped away. "Good-bye, my love."

"Colin . . ."

He turned his back to her and walked around the car to the passenger door. "Come along, Gordon."

Gordon trotted over and hopped in, her awful, traitorous dog. Colin shut the door behind him. Gordon propped his front paws on the back of the seat and stared at Sugar Beth. Winnie moved to her side and took her hand.

"Don't do this," Sugar Beth whispered.

He gave her one last glance and opened the driver's door. But just as he began to climb in, Gordon shot across the passenger seat and hopped out.

"Gordon?" He snapped his fingers.

Gordon's head drooped. He slunk toward Sugar Beth, ears dragging on the ground. She crouched next to him, fighting the lump in her throat. "Go on, pal," she whispered, giving him a last pat. "You're his now."

But Gordon gave a miserable sigh and lay down in the grass at her feet.

"That's it, then." Colin spoke briskly, as if he didn't care, as if this desertion, too, had been inevitable. A moment later, he'd started the engine and begun to back down the drive.

"No!" Sugar Beth shot forward, ready to throw herself at the car, but Ryan caught her and pulled her back.

"Don't, Sugar Beth. Have a little dignity."

"Let me go!"

Too late. Colin Byrne had left the last whistle-stop behind forever.

Gordon began to howl, a mournful, heart-wrenching sound that came from the very bottom of his doggy soul. Sugar Beth's teeth started to chatter. She drew away from Ryan, and as she knelt by her dog she remembered his water bowl in Colin's backseat. Where would Colin be when he noticed it? At a gas station somewhere? Unloading a suitcase at a roadside motel? He'd endured so many losses: the father's love that should have been his birthright, the wife who'd betrayed him by not having the courage to live, the child he'd lost, Gordon . . . and her.

She looked up in time to see Ryan pull Winnie to his side. She curled against him, but he wasn't looking at her. He was gazing at Sugar Beth instead, and in those sympathetic golden brown eyes, she saw his big heart and his deep-rooted decency. She saw a man capable of fidelity, a man worthy of trust. A man who knew how to love . . . forever.

Something loud and shrill roared in her ears. Her heart thumped against her ribs. She sank back into the grass so hard she banged her tailbone.

Dear God, she'd done it again.

"Sugar Beth?" Winnie broke away from Ryan to rush to her side. "Are you all right?"

She couldn't breathe. Couldn't move. Once again, she'd turned her back on the love of a good man.

Winnie knelt next to her and rubbed her back. "It'll be all right."

Sugar Beth put her head to her knees. Colin had said he wouldn't beg, and he hadn't, but that had been grief talking, not pride. He wasn't leaving Parrish just so she could stay. He was leaving because he couldn't bear the pain of being around another woman with a cowardly heart.

All along, he'd been right. Rejecting him hadn't been an act of bravery. It was an act of fear. She'd sent him away because she hadn't been able to find the courage to give them a chance.

Gordon licked her cheek. She lifted her head to Winnie. "I'm too afraid," she whispered.

Winnie squeezed her shoulder.

The late-afternoon sun slid from beneath a cloud and struck Sugar Beth in the eyes. It felt like an electrical shock, and she jumped to her feet. "My purse! I need my cell. Where's my purse?"

"At the bookstore," Winnie said. "I'll get mine."

But Ryan had already handed his over. "For God's sake, don't screw this up, too."

Sugar Beth's heart pounded as she punched in Colin's number. She'd made a colossal mistake, the mother of all mistakes, and she had to set it right. She and Colin couldn't work this out unless they were together. She sank back down next to Gordon as it began to ring. Once, twice, three times. An automated recording kicked in.

"He's not answering." She disconnected and punched in the number again, but he still didn't pick up.

"He's licking his wounds," Winnie said. "He'll answer later. Let me drive you back to the store. Then we'll move your things into Frenchman's Bride."

Sugar Beth's head shot up. "I can't move into Frenchman's Bride."

Winnie regarded her evenly. "You're home for good now. You can't do anything else."

"Oh, dear, I wish to heaven I knew where he has gone, and what it all means!"

GEORGETTE HEYER, *The Corinthian*

Chapter 22

By dinnertime, Winnie and Ryan had resettled Sugar Beth at Frenchman's Bride, doing all the work themselves while Sugar Beth paced the house and made more fruitless calls to Colin's cell. With every call that went unanswered, her anxiety grew. He was tough. What if she'd only been given one chance and she'd blown it? Maybe he'd performed some sort of permanent exorcism when he'd driven away and cut her out of his heart forever.

She stood in her old spot just inside the door of Colin's closet and watched Winnie at work. The sight of her dismal wardrobe hanging among the expensive suits and sports coats Colin had left behind made her want to cry. "I'm just going to move everything back to the carriage house after you leave," she said.

"No, you're not," Winnie replied. "You'll feel better if you're here. This will help you understand where your life is supposed to be."

"How do you know that?"

"I just do."

Sugar Beth turned away. Gordon followed her downstairs, where Ryan was taking a break on the sunroom couch, drinking a beer and catching the end of a golf tournament. "I want my wife back," he said, flicking off the TV as she came in. "I know you're upset, and I know this isn't a good time for you, but I want her back tonight."

"You've had her for fourteen years. Can't I have her for a few more days?"

"No. I need her now."

"You think I'm being selfish, don't you? Keeping her?"

He smiled and set down his beer. "Always."

She wandered over to the sunroom windows. As she gazed out at the piles of stone still waiting to be laid, she prayed Colin would someday finish his wall. Why did he have to fly off like this? He should have given them more time, and when she finally reached him, she intended to tell him exactly that. "Why won't he turn on his phone?"

"Because he doesn't want to talk to you."

"I liked it better when you were nice."

"You didn't give him a lot of options."

Gordon rubbed her ankles. She leaned down and patted him, taking comfort in his sloppy warmth. "Do you remember Luv U 4-Ever?"

"We were kids," he said. "What we felt was real at the time."

"Ken and Barbie work a lot better in make-believe land than they do in real life."

He stretched his legs. "I don't think I've ever thanked you for dumping me."

"Don't mention it."

"It's easy to see now how badly matched we were," he said. "I'm too boring for you, and all your drama would have driven me nuts."

"Colin loves drama. It's how he makes his living."

He gave her his sweet Ken smile.

She sank down on the ottoman. "I should have been more flexible with him."

"Too bad you didn't have that epiphany a few days ago."

"I'm a drama queen," she said dismally. "I only learn things the hard way."

Winnie came in. "Ryan, I think—"

"No." He rose from the couch, his good humor fading. "No more. I mean it, Winnie. Either Sugar Beth comes first in your life or I do. Make up your mind."

"Don't you dare try to railroad me."

"You want to have everything your way. Well, I'm here to tell you that's not how it's going to work."

"Quit being an ass."

"If anybody's acting like an ass—"

"Oh, stop it," Sugar Beth said. "Wait until you're alone to start your foreplay." She rose from the ottoman, took a step toward the middle of the room, and froze. "Gigi!"

They gazed at her.

"Colin said he was going to call Gigi tonight. Hurry!" She raced from Frenchman's Bride, leaving Ryan, Winnie, and Gordon to follow in her wake.

She stormed into the Galantine house just as Gigi was coming downstairs. She'd abandoned Goth for a pair of cropped cargos that hung way too low on her hips and a sheer, pin-tuck shirt that didn't cover her rib cage. Yesterday when Sugar Beth had asked her about it, she'd gotten a calculating look in her eye and said she was exploring her sexuality. Even in Sugar Beth's emotionally impaired state, she'd known when she was being tested, and she hadn't risen to the bait.

"What did you do to Colin?" Gigi cried, ripping off her headset.

"What are you talking about?"

"He's gone!"

"How do you know that?"

"He told me."

Sugar Beth stiffened. "When?"

"A few minutes ago on the phone."

Sugar Beth sank down on the bottom step and dropped her head into her hands. "You've already talked to him."

"He sounded totally bummed," Gigi said accusingly. "You dumped him, didn't you?"

Sugar Beth couldn't muster a response.

It was one thing for Colin to leave. It was quite another for him to cut off all communication, and Sugar Beth didn't intend to put up with it. First thing Monday morning, she called his publisher and asked to speak with his publicist. When the woman answered, Sugar Beth adopted her best Yankee accent. "This is Frances Gordon calling. From the *Oprah* show."

"Gordon? I don't recognize the name."

"I'm new. This is very last minute, but Oprah wants to have Mr. Byrne on her show this week. I need to talk with him about it today if we're going to make that happen. Stephen King really wants the slot, and you know how pushy he can be."

"I don't believe Mr. Byrne is available."

"Of course, he's available. It's *Oprah*!"

"I'd feel more comfortable talking to my regular contact."

"Unfortunately, she was in an automobile accident this morning. Nothing too serious, but she'll be out for a while."

"Odd. I spoke with *him* less than ten minutes ago."

"Must have been while he was waiting for the ambulance."

The woman hung up.

Winnie had given in to Ryan's pressure and moved back home on Saturday evening. That didn't mean, however, that she believed in leaving Sugar Beth to her own devices, and she decided to hold the Reconciliation and Forgiveness Dessert at Frenchman's Bride. "It'll be more symbolic that way," she told her.

Monday evening arrived, and as Winnie stood at the sink rinsing off the chocolate-smeared dessert plates, she told herself she should be happy with the way things were unfolding. Sugar Beth was wound tight as a spring, so things had been a little tense at first, but the Seawillows had been prepared to forgive. Amy's absolution was a foregone conclusion, and Leeann had already been softened up by Sugar Beth's affection for Charlie. Heidi succumbed after Sugar Beth enthused over photos of her three-year-old, but Merylinn's resentment ran deep, and she didn't give in until Sugar Beth put her arms around her and said, "Either kill me or forgive me."

As for Colin . . . They said it was just like Sugar Beth to drive a man to do something like this, but they didn't turn against her, and Sugar Beth's manner grew a little less forced. By the time the last piece of Winnie's double chocolate cake had disappeared, Sugar Beth was once again a Seawillow. The leader of the Seawillows.

Winnie snatched up the last dish and shoved it under the running water. All five of them were clustered in the sunroom, giggling and sharing memories Winnie had no part of. She shouldn't feel as though they'd deserted her—she was the one who'd insisted on cleaning up the dishes—but she felt like she was sixteen all over again.

She grabbed the dish towel in disgust. She knew how much Sugar Beth had missed the Seawillows, and she should be happy that she'd brought them back together. But they were her friends, too, and Winnie liked being their leader. Until now, she'd been the one who had the final say on when they'd hold their get-togethers and on who'd bring what. She was the one who'd smoothed ruffled feathers and received confidences. And she'd been good at it. Now, however, everything would be different.

Unless Sugar Beth left Parrish.

The possibility brought Winnie to her senses. She didn't want Sugar Beth to leave. They were sisters now, and she wouldn't give that up, not even to hold on to her position as leader of the Seawillows. By the time she joined them in the sunroom, she was feeling a little better, but the conversation continued to go on without her.

". . . and remember when we were doing the moonwalk in Heidi's living room and we broke her mother's lamp?"

". . . and when Amy's dad caught us smoking?"

"What about that night we were out at the point and Ryan's car wouldn't start?"

"Remember how we all—"

"No, I don't!" Winnie said, shocking herself. "I wasn't a Seawillow then. I'm still not. And I'd appreciate it if you'd show a little sensitivity to my feelings by not spending the rest of the night talking about things I wasn't part of."

An awkward silence fell over the group. Merylinn brushed a speck of lint from her slacks. Heidi twisted her wedding ring. Only Sugar Beth seemed comfortable with the situation, and her fine brows arched in phony surprise as she surveyed the others. "You mean you never initiated her?"

"We never thought of it," Leeann said.

Merylinn tucked her legs under her. "You always took care of initiations."

"That's right, I did." Sugar Beth turned her attention to Winnie, who wasn't one bit comforted by the guile in those narrowed silver-blue eyes. "Winnie, leave the room while we vote."

"Vote?"

Sugar Beth regarded her haughtily. "Do you want to be a Seawillow or not?"

Winnie haughtied her right back. "Don't you think we're a little old for this?"

No, they didn't.

Winnie finally gave up arguing, partly because it wasn't doing any good, and partly because Sugar Beth was finally showing some of her old spirit. Besides, Winnie really wanted to be a Seawillow.

They bundled her off to the living room. Where she waited.

And waited.

The minutes ticked by. Finally, she got fed up and stormed back to the sunroom. "Do you mind telling me what's taking so darned long?"

Merylinn pointed toward Amy, who was sprawled on the floor. "Oh, we voted a long time ago, but Amy wanted to show us her new sit-ups, and we forgot to call you."

That got Winnie upset all over again. "I won't be forgotten, do y'all hear me? Just because Miss High and Mighty's back in everybody's good graces doesn't mean I'm going to let any of you start walkin' all over me."

Sugar Beth sniffed. "Touchy."

"Always was," Merylinn agreed.

Leeann regarded Winnie smugly. "You'd better watch how you talk to us. You haven't gone through the initiation ceremony yet, so we can withdraw your invitation any time we want."

Winnie crossed her arms over her breasts and tapped her foot. "Initiation ceremony?"

That was all it took to set off a big debate, because nobody could remember exactly how the initiation ceremony went, except they all agreed on one thing. They needed a photograph of George Michael.

"For what?" Winnie asked with exaggerated patience.

Leeann tugged on her bra strap. "You have to swear to love him forever."

"That is so not going to happen."

"You have to," Merylinn said. "It's a Seawillow ritual."

"Except we don't have a photo," Heidi pointed out.

Amy reached inside her purse and pulled out her Bible. "I've got an idea."

"We are *not* using a picture of Jesus!" Merylinn exclaimed.

Amy looked disappointed but gracefully gave in to group

pressure. The discussion continued, but went nowhere. Finally, Leeann took it upon herself to investigate Colin's CD collection. "Look! Here's the new U2 album. Winnie can swear allegiance to Bono instead."

Heidi studied the album. "It just doesn't seem the same."

Sugar Beth passed the album over to Winnie with a grin that nearly made it to her eyes. "Kiss Bono's picture and swear to love him forever."

Winnie regarded her loftily. "Only because of his dedication to good causes."

Unfortunately, that wasn't the end of it. Apparently they had a secret handshake, but nobody could remember what it was. They also used to sit in a circle and pass around some kind of necklace, but it had been lost years before.

"I remember one thing for sure," Merylinn said. "You have to tell what boy you like."

"Gosh, I'll have to think about it," Winnie said sarcastically.

"She's not displaying proper Seawillow spirit," Heidi pointed out.

"She also has to tell a sex secret," Leeann said.

"Sex secret?" Winnie rolled her eyes. "You guys were eleven. How many sex secrets could you have had?"

"Quite a few. Merylinn found her mom's copy of *Joy of Sex*."

Winnie threw up her hands. "All right. A couple of nights ago I had an erotic dream about Edward Norton."

"Like who hasn't?" Heidi said, unimpressed. "We need a better secret than that."

Winnie's biggest sex secret—the lack of desire she'd once felt for her own husband—was something she didn't intend to share with anybody. She pretended to think it over. "Okay, how about this? Merylinn, do you remember the time you kept Gigi so Ryan and I could go to that conference in Miami?"

"Uh-huh."

"There wasn't a conference in Miami. We took a hotel room in Memphis and spent the weekend playing sex slaves."

It was a lie, but their reactions more than satisfied her.

"You slut!"

"Sex slaves?"

"Did you use handcuffs and everything?"

"*Everything*," Winnie said.

Sugar Beth wasn't buying it, but she stayed loyal and kept her mouth shut, which made Winnie think about how nice it was to finally have a sister.

"She's getting tears in her eyes," Merylinn exclaimed. "That must have been one hell of a weekend."

Winnie smiled at Sugar Beth. "Unforgettable."

Sugar Beth returned the smile. "Even I can't top an entire weekend playing sex slaves."

Winnie shifted her position on the couch before another wave of sentiment caught up with her. "Isn't it time to light the initiation candle?"

"Not quite." Sugar Beth lifted an eyebrow in calculation. "There's one more thing . . ."

Amy shot up from her chair. "No. We are *not* doing that."

"We have to," Sugar Beth said, "or Winnie'll never be an official Seawillow."

"Oh, God . . ." Merylinn threw her head back and started to laugh.

Leeann groaned. "I shouldn't have eaten so much."

"If we do, we can't tell anybody," Heidi said. "You know how my mother-in-law hates me. If she finds out, I'll never hear the end of it."

"Do what?" Winnie asked, not entirely sure she wanted to know.

A few moments of silence fell over the group. They looked at one another. Finally, Amy spoke in a hushed voice. "We have to strip down naked and run around Frenchman's Bride three times."

Winnie regarded them incredulously. "You're making this up."

Leeann snorted. "I wish."

Amy shook her head. "It's true. Whenever anybody new came into the Seawillows—"

"Which thankfully wasn't too often," Merylinn interjected.

"—we'd wait for a night when Sugar Beth could talk Diddie into letting us have a sleepover."

"Preferably during the summer so we could sleep outside on the veranda," Heidi added.

"Once Diddie and Griffin fell asleep," Amy went on, "we'd strip down, and all of us would run naked around the house."

"I never heard a word about this," Winnie said.

"It was our best secret."

"Our only secret," Leeann said dryly.

"Even the guys don't know."

"It's barely dark," Winnie said. "And it's not even sixty degrees outside."

Sugar Beth grinned at her. "Then we'd better run fast."

A debate over terms and conditions followed, but in the end, they only made one concession to maturity. They agreed they could keep their shoes on.

"I knew I should have thrown out these ratty panties," Leeann said a few minutes later as they stood in the sunroom peeling off their clothes.

"Somebody make sure *all* the lights are off."

"I'm savin' up for liposuction. I really am."

"I liked it better when we hated Sugar Beth. Look at her legs."

"Ohmygod, Winnie has a *humongous* hickey!"

Naked and giggling, they clustered at the back door. "Y'all ready?" Merylinn asked.

"Ready!" they declared.

Sugar Beth grabbed the knob and threw it open. "Seawillows forever!" she cried.

And then they flew.

* * *

Ryan and Gigi's impulsive late-night walk took them to the end of Mockingbird Lane. As they reached the drive that led to Frenchman's Bride, they came to a dead stop at the exact same moment.

Gigi found her voice first. "Do you think they went crazy or something?"

"Sure does look like it."

They didn't say anything for a few moments, but Gigi finally grew so horrified she couldn't stay quiet. "You shouldn't watch."

"Honey, I wouldn't miss this for anything."

High-pitched giggles drifted toward them, a curse, a shush. The women disappeared around the side of the house.

Gigi scowled. "If the kids at school find out about this, I'm not going back. I mean it."

"We'll leave town together."

"Nothing like this ever happened before Sugar Beth came back."

"If she stays, it'll only get worse."

"Still, I don't want her to leave."

He squeezed her shoulder. "Neither do I."

Gigi sucked in her breath as the women reappeared from the other side of the house, this time with her own mother in the lead. "This is *so* embarrassing."

"The sad thing is, I doubt they've had a drop of liquor."

"I used to think Mom was perfect."

"She can't help it, honey. Southern women are born with the insanity gene."

"Not me."

He sighed. "Sooner or later, you'll go the way of the rest."

With a hissing noise, the automatic lawn sprinklers came on, and all of them began to shriek.

"I can't look anymore."

Ryan buried his daughter's face in his chest and smiled. "In the morning, we'll pretend it was all a bad dream."

* * *

Sugar Beth shut off her alarm. It was Tuesday, the day she'd planned to leave Parrish. She turned her head into Colin's pillow, and as she drew in his familiar scent, she prayed he'd come home before she had to change the sheets. Misery washed over her. She fought it off by remembering last night and the Seawillows. She smiled. Winnie had given her a priceless gift.

She managed to pull herself out of bed—not an easy task these days—and get dressed before she headed for the bookstore.

"I thought you'd be packing now," Jewel said as Sugar Beth handed over the blueberry danish she'd intended to eat but couldn't quite stomach.

"A temporary change of plans. I'm hanging around a little longer."

Jewel's tiny face brightened. "For real?"

She nodded and filled her in on what had happened with Colin.

"He left? Just like that?"

"Just like that," Sugar Beth replied, warmed by Jewel's expression of outrage.

"What are you going to do now?"

"Keep trying to get hold of him."

Jewel regarded her sympathetically. "From what you've said, that could take a while. He doesn't seem to want to be found."

"I'm calling his editor. Somebody has to know where he is."

"You'd better come up with a more believable story than that Oprah thing you told me about."

"I will."

Colin's editor answered on the second ring. "Neil Kirkpatrick."

"Lady Francis Posh-Wicket here calling from London."

"Who?"

"I'm the director of Her Majesty's Royal Office of the Garter. Her Majesty has some rather exciting news for one of your authors. Sir Colin Byrne. Ah, but what a stupid cow I am. He's not Sir Colin yet. Which is why I need to ring him up. But he doesn't seem to be answering his bloody phone."

"I'm afraid I don't know where he is."

"Bollocks, sir. Am I to believe you've lost one of your most important authors?"

"Excuse me?"

"Perhaps *you* would like to be the one to tell Her Majesty that Sir Colin has disappeared because I'm sure I don't want to."

"Who is this?"

"I must insist you locate Sir Colin im-*me*-jetly."

"I don't know who you are, but I have work to do here."

"Not until you tell me where the hell he is, you *wanker*!"

There was a long pause. "Sugar Beth, is that you?"

This time she was the one who hung up.

"They're all mad, every one of 'em," said Rupert with conviction.

GEORGETTE HEYER, *Devil's Cub*

Chapter 23

*B*lazes of azalea and dogwood announced the arrival of April. Northern Mississippi had never been more beautiful, but Sugar Beth was miserable. She lived her days in limbo, taking comfort only in the fact that no moving company had appeared to pack up Colin's things. Sometimes she managed to convince herself that Colin was simply trying to manipulate her and that he'd be back soon. But as one week gave way to another, she began to believe he'd meant exactly what he'd said.

Two weeks after Colin had driven away, Ryan appeared at her door with the news that he'd finally called. "He's rented a house—he didn't mention where. He says he's working round-the-clock to finish his book."

"What about me? What did he say about me?"

Ryan made a business of examining his car keys. "I'm sorry, Sugar Beth. He said he didn't want to talk to you yet—maybe when his book is done. And he said to stop harassing his publisher. Oh . . . he asked about Gordon."

Bloody wanker.

He *was* manipulating her! A flood of righteous indignation drove away the tears that were so close to the surface these days. She pushed past Ryan, headed for the Lakehouse, and spent the evening dancing with Cubby Bowmar.

Her anger carried her through the next two weeks. And then *Reflections* hit the stores . . .

"I've never seen anything like it," Jewel crowed. "The book hasn't been out a full week, and I've already sold three hundred copies."

"*Hoo*-ray," Sugar Beth said glumly.

Sue Covner regarded Sugar Beth smugly from behind Jewel's shoulder. "Look on the bright side, Valentine, honey. Not everybody gets to be immortalized in great literature."

Marge Dailey poked her head out from the inspirationals. "I think you're holdin' up pretty well. If it was me, I swear I'd move to Mexico. Although I suppose that's not really far enough away, still bein' in North America and all."

The whole town was laughing its collective ass off.

The book immediately shot to the top of the *New York Times* bestseller list, and a reporter from *USA Today* showed up. Although stories about Colin's mysterious disappearance had begun to appear in the press, the reporter was more interested in searching out the real-life characters from *Reflections*. The diabolical Valentine was at the top of his Most Wanted list.

"Why, that's Sugar Beth Carey you're looking for," Amanda Higgins said about five seconds after the reporter arrived in town. "Sugar Beth Carey Tharp Zagurski Hooper."

"You might remember reading about her a few years back," her husband volunteered. "She was that waitress who married the oil tycoon. Emmett Hooper was his name."

The story hit the papers twenty-four hours later, and even Tibet wasn't far enough away to hide.

Early in May, a month after Colin had left, the painting went up for auction, and the J. Paul Getty Museum bought it for a little over three million dollars. Even though Jewel and the Seawillows did their best to celebrate with Sugar Beth, she wanted Colin. More than any one of them, he'd understood what this meant to her. But the fact that he didn't bother to call with his congratulations added another log to the smoldering pyre of her resentment.

She completed the paperwork for the trust that would ensure Delilah's care, then flew to Houston to spend a few days with her and take care of other business. *Reflections* stared back at her from the window of every bookstore she passed. She treated herself to an appointment at the city's best salon, followed by a shopping spree, but not even fresh blond highlights and a pair of Jimmy Choo stilettos could lift her spirits.

She returned to Parrish late on a Tuesday night, six weeks after Colin's desertion, tired, lonely, and teary-eyed. Just as she began to turn off her bedside light, the phone rang, and when she answered, she heard a familiar imperious voice. "Where the bloody hell have you been for the last three days?"

Her legs collapsed. "Colin?"

"What other man would be calling you at midnight, pray tell?"

Everything she'd planned to say flew out of her head. "You *bastard*!"

"Reached you at a bad time, did I?"

"You manipulating *bastard*!" Everything spilled out, all her anger and frustration. She yelled and cursed until she was hoarse, but when she finally wound down, he only said, "Now, now, my love," which wound her up all over again.

"I'm not your love! I'm not your anything! You deserted me, you limey prick, and I'll never forgive you. But I'm glad you left because now I don't ever have to look at your ugly face again. And guess what? When I told you I loved you, it was a big joke, do you hear me? All this time I've been laughing at you behind your back. I don't love you! The whole thing was a big fat joke!"

"I'm sorry to hear that," he replied, not missing a beat. "But since I love you enough for both of us, I'm not too concerned. It's embarrassing, really, how much I miss you."

That calmed her down a little.

She abandoned the side of the bed to sit cross-legged on the rug so Gordon, who'd slithered under the bed during her tirade, could emerge and put his head in her lap. Her eyes had started to leak, but she took deep breaths so Colin didn't know his desertion had turned her into a regular little watering pot. "How could you have left?"

"An animal in pain. That sort of rubbish." He sounded haughty, vaguely bored, but she knew him too well, and she wasn't fooled. She'd hurt him, all right, maybe more than he'd hurt her. She leaned down and blotted her eyes on one of Gordon's ears. "I didn't mean to hurt you. You know I didn't."

He replied with the same jaded tones. "The fact that you couldn't help yourself only made it more painful."

"You were right," she said in a miserably small voice. "I never gave us a chance. I realized it as soon as you drove off."

"Of course I was right."

"Could you come back now?"

"Under what terms?"

"This isn't a business negotiation."

"Just so we're clear."

"I love you," she said. "I can't be much clearer than that. But we need to have this discussion in person. Where are you?"

"As to that . . . I'm not quite ready to say."

She sat a little straighter. "Then why are you calling? What do you want?"

"I want your heart, my darling."

"You have it. Don't you know that?"

"And I want your courage."

She bit her lip. "The courage thing is starting to come together for me. It's not happening overnight, but I'm getting there. And I don't want to lose you. I haven't really thought this through all the way, but it seems to me that Parrish can survive the scandal of two people who love each other living together for a while, don't you?"

There was a short pause. "That's what you want, then? For me to come back so we can live together?"

"I know it's a big step, but I'm tired of being scared—you have no idea—and I'm ready to take that step if you are."

"I see."

"You mentioned an engagement. I'm . . . I'm honored, Colin. I know this is just as hard for you as it is for me. This could be our first step." He didn't say anything, and she wondered if she'd shot too far ahead. "But if you're not ready to live together, I understand, and forget about the engagement— it's way too soon. I'll move back to the carriage house so you have some room. I won't push, and I won't crowd you. I know how that feels. Take all the time you need. Just come back."

She waited.

"Colin?"

"You still don't understand, my darling."

She was perspiring from nerves. "Understand what?"

"I'm returning on our wedding day. Not a moment before."

"Our wedding day!" She jumped to her feet. Gordon slithered back under the bed.

"I'm sure Winnie and the Seawillows will be more than happy to help with the arrangements, and Ryan can expedite the paperwork."

"You can't be serious."

"Oh, but I am."

"An engagement, yes." She shot across the room. "After we've lived together for a while. But we're not jumping into marriage. We aren't prepared."

"I'm afraid I have to go, Sugar Beth. I need to get back to work. Congratulations on the sale of your painting. I only wish I could have been there to celebrate with you."

"Don't you dare hang up! Are you telling me that you're not coming back unless I agree to marry you?"

"Of course not. That would give you far too much wiggle room. What I'm telling you is that I won't come back until you're standing inside the church, at the altar, with all our friends there as witnesses."

"That's ridiculous!" She kicked a magazine out of her way. "This isn't one of your books, Colin. This is real life. People don't do things like this."

"But then we're not ordinary people, are we?"

She'd started to hyperventilate and sank down on the chair. "Use your head. Neither of us can afford another mistake. We have to be sure we're completely comfortable with each other."

"I was sure a long time ago. I'm very much in love with you."

She gripped the phone tighter. "Come home, Colin. Now."

"And put myself at your mercy again? I'm hardly that foolish."

"Then how are we going to settle this?"

"Inside a church in front of a minister. Take it or leave it."

She jumped back up. "I'm leaving it!"

She heard a bored sigh. "Fortunately for you, I'm prepared to be patient for another day or so, which, more than anything else, bears testimony to the depth of my feelings for you."

"Stop talking like a fop!"

"I'll check in with Ryan periodically. But—and listen very carefully, my darling—I will *not* be calling you again. If you were a sane woman, I would, of course, behave in a more rational fashion. Since you are a lunatic, however, this is the only way."

"You planned this from the beginning, didn't you?"

"Let's simply say that you're not the sort of woman who can be permitted to run amok."

She clenched her fist. "Colin, please. We have the chance for a future together. Don't screw it up by making unreasonable demands."

"How could I screw it up when you're doing that so very well all by yourself?"

"I'm pregnant! You have to come back right now to take care of me."

"No, my love, you are not pregnant, and I won't be manipulated. Now, this conversation has grown tedious beyond belief. I love you with all my heart, and I— Are you crying, my sweet?"

"Yes." She sniffed. "That's practically all I've done since you left."

"Truly?"

"I'm afraid so."

"How splendid."

And that was that.

Sugar Beth stomped through the house for a few hours, cried some more, and ate her way through two bowls of oatmeal. The next morning she woke up even angrier, grabbed the phone, and hired Bruce Kleinman, Amy's first boyfriend and the best contractor in town, to start work on the depot. She no longer owed Colin a thing. Right after, she reached Jewel. "Remember when I told you I had this fantasy about opening a children's bookstore in the depot?"

"I'm hardly likely to forget it. I told you I thought you should do it. You were the one with cold feet, remember? You said you couldn't do anything permanent because of Colin."

"That's not a problem anymore, since I officially hate him. And I hope you meant it about us being partners."

Sugar Beth pulled the receiver away from her ear to keep Jewel's celebratory hoots from rupturing her eardrum.

She showered, slipped into a new pair of orange capris along with a sleeveless white shirt and sandals, and called Winnie to bring her up-to-date. Afterward, she set off to meet Bruce at the depot. When they were done, she went to see

Jewel so they could discuss their partnership agreement, and following that, she snatched Charlie from his baby-sitter and took him to the park to play. She ended the day with a quick drop-in at Yesterday's Treasures.

"Jewel's worried about you," Winnie said as she entered the store. "I just talked to her on the phone, and she said you refused a Goo Goo Cluster. She thinks I should call an emergency session of the Seawillows to do some triage."

"Jewel should stay out of the Seawillows' business," Sugar Beth retorted. "She laughed in my face when I told her how much we wanted her to join."

"You probably shouldn't take it personally."

"How can I not take it personally? Next to you, she's my best friend, not to mention my future business partner. And she's not half as funny as she thinks she is. She said joining the Seawillows was the first step toward putting on a hoop skirt and standing on the front lawn of Frenchman's Bride waving a parasol and going fiddle-dee-dee."

Winnie sighed. "This isn't about Jewel. It's about you."

Sugar Beth sank down in an oak farm chair, the emotions of the past two days catching up with her. "Just because a person understands something about herself doesn't necessarily mean she can fix it."

"I'm guessing we're talking about you now."

"Think about it. A woman who's always been overweight, for example. She knows exactly what she needs to do to keep off the pounds, but that doesn't mean she can do it, right?"

"You've got a point."

Sugar Beth pressed her stomach. "Call me crazy, but taking a fourth trip down the aisle doesn't seem like the best way to fix whatever's broken inside me."

"Unless whatever was broken is already fixed."

"Just thinking about all this is making me queasy. I've gotta go." She grabbed her purse, gave Winnie a peck on the cheek, and made her way out of the store.

The heat had begun to settle in, and as she hit the sidewalk, she slipped on her new sunglasses, a trendy pair of aviators. A man she didn't know tripped over his feet rubbernecking at her. She was too tired to appreciate the attention.

Gordon greeted her at the door. He'd gotten clingy since Colin left, and she sank down on the tile to give him love, but he was the product of a broken home, and he was too depressed to do more than roll over on his back. Afterward, she made her way to the kitchen, grabbed a carton of strawberry yogurt, and began to pace. Finally, she lay down on the sunroom couch, only to jolt awake a few hours later and begin pacing all over again.

Night settled in, and her agitation grew. By eleven o'clock, she'd worked herself into such a state she couldn't stand it any longer, so she marched down the street and banged on Winnie's door.

Her half sister answered in a pair of pajama tops, hair tousled, beard-burn reddening her cheek. Sugar Beth stormed inside. "Can't the two of you spend just one evening talking like normal people?"

"Don't take out your sexual frustration on me. What's wrong?"

"I need to talk to Ryan."

"He's asleep."

"Not for long." Sugar Beth pushed past her and stalked upstairs. Winnie followed, bitching all the way.

Ryan lay on his stomach, probably naked, although a thin blue blanket covered him from the hips down, so she couldn't be sure. She punched his shoulder. "Wake up!"

He rolled over, the sheet twisting around him, blinked, and looked past Sugar Beth to his wife, who crossed her arms over her chest and glowered. "She's your old girlfriend. I barely know her."

Sugar Beth had started to shake, but she kept her voice low so she didn't wake Gigi. "Listen to me, Ryan Galantine. When that bastard calls back, you tell him he's won this round. I'll marry him. But I don't take well to being blackmailed, and tell him I intend to spend the rest of my life making him miserable, got that?"

Ryan pushed himself up into the pillows. He looked sleepy but amused.

Sugar Beth bore in. "I mean it. If he wants this marriage so bad, he can have it, but he'd better be prepared to suffer serious consequences." She spun around, marched past Winnie, stormed down the steps and out the door.

Ryan gazed at his wife. "They deserve each other."

Sugar Beth refused to have anything to do with the arrangements other than to say she wanted a private ceremony, just Gigi, Ryan, and Winnie as her matron of honor. No one else, not even Jewel or the Seawillows.

Which wouldn't do as far as Winnie was concerned. She called the Seawillows together, minus Sugar Beth, and even coerced Jewel into attending. Since Leeann didn't have a baby-sitter, they met around her kitchen table, where Winnie took out a yellow pad and got down to business. "We'll have to plan the whole thing ourselves. Luckily, Colin's given us an unlimited budget. He told Ryan he wants the ceremony by next Saturday at the latest, which gives us ten days. He's afraid she'll bolt if we wait longer."

"I'll make sure the video store hides *The Runaway Bride*," Merylinn said. "No sense in giving her ideas."

"If Colin wants to keep her from running off, why doesn't he get back here and see to it himself?" Heidi asked.

Winnie gazed down at her yellow pad so she didn't have to meet their eyes. "He said he had to finish his book first."

That didn't set well with any of them. "You'd think she'd be a little more important than finishing a book." Merylinn sniffed.

"I've never understood that man."

"I hope Sugar Beth doesn't figure out how far down she is on his priority list."

"You know how sarcastic he can be," Jewel said, doing her best to defend him. "Maybe Ryan misinterpreted."

But a sense of uneasiness undercut the rest of their planning.

Ignoring Sugar Beth's wishes, Winnie decided on a Saturday evening ceremony at the Presbyterian Church followed by a tent reception on the front lawn of Frenchman's Bride. With no time to issue formal invitations, Jewel and the Seawillows called everybody they could think of, and by the time they were done, three hundred people had accepted. Sugar Beth went ballistic when she heard. Winnie told her to shut up and find a dress.

Ryan managed the license, and Leeann dragged Sugar Beth to the lab for her blood test. Sugar Beth had no idea how Colin was handling his end of the process, and she was too busy nursing her grievances to care.

On Friday morning, the day before the wedding, a crew arrived at Frenchman's Bride to erect the tent for the reception, and not long after, a rental van appeared with tables and chairs. Sugar Beth strapped a headset over her ears to shut it all out and spent the day petting Gordon and making plans for her bookstore while an old Pearl Jam CD blared in her ears.

There'd been no time to put together a shower or a bachelorette party, which wasn't a problem, since Sugar Beth wouldn't have attended either. The night before the wedding Winnie tried to talk her into staying in the Galantine guest room, but she refused to leave Frenchman's Bride. This forced Winnie to put her alternate plan in place, and at six o'clock on Friday evening Gigi showed up at the door with three large pizzas, Gwen Lu, Gillian Granger, Sachi Patel, and Jenny Berry.

"Mom said we could have a sleepover here. Everybody wants to hear your power speech. Plus Jenny really needs help with her eye makeup."

Sugar Beth marched to the phone and called Winnie. "Is

this what my life has come to? I'm being guarded by thirteen-year-olds?"

"You're a little nervous," Winnie replied. "I decided you needed a distraction."

"A *little* nervous! I've pegged the Richter scale on nerves! This is all a setup. The final piece in his plan to get revenge. I'll march down the aisle, and he won't be there. He's going to leave me stranded at the altar. I'm telling you right now, he's not showing up tomorrow."

"Standing you up at the altar would be overkill," Winnie pointed out. "He already finished you off when he wrote *Reflections*."

Sugar Beth hung up on her.

Winnie proved to be right about one thing. It was impossible to brood with a houseful of thirteen-year-olds demanding her attention. Gigi's new friends were geeky and awkward, but sweet and funny, too. Someday the Seawillows might need to form a junior auxiliary.

She slept badly that night and rose long before the girls. She came downstairs in an old pair of shorts and one of Colin's work shirts, with her hair hanging in a ratty tangle and a crease across her cheek. Her wedding day. Again.

After she'd let Gordon out, she disposed of the pizza boxes, then sat at the counter, brooding. Her legs needed shaving, her fingernails were ragged, she'd made no plans to have her hair done, and the only thing she really wanted to do was go back to bed and pull the covers over her head. She let Gordon in and did just that.

Winnie woke everybody up a few hours later. She bustled around the house, full of phony cheer and annoying platitudes. Sugar Beth lunged for the jar of peanut butter, then put it back because her stomach was in no state for food.

Ryan was taking the girls to Denny's for a late breakfast, then delivering them to their homes to dress for the ceremony. Gigi hugged Sugar Beth before she left. "Don't worry. You can still claim your power even after you get married.

Look at Mom." And then she startled Winnie by hugging her, too.

After that, Winnie went into hyper drive. "You do have your gown, right? You promised you'd take care of that, and I know you had to buy it off the rack, but you look disgustingly gorgeous in anything."

"I have it," Sugar Beth said, "and it's locked up where you won't find it."

"Why can't I see it?"

"Because it's a big freakin' surprise, that's why! Is Colin here yet?"

Winnie didn't meet her eyes. "Not as far as I know. But Ryan talked to him. He'll be here."

"Yeah, right." Sugar Beth slapped the counter. "I told you what's going to happen. He won't show up. It's why I didn't want the entire town invited. But would you listen to me?"

"Of course he'll show up. He loves you. Now go take a shower. Janice Menken is coming to do your hair at four. You need to be at the church by five-thirty."

For a moment all of Sugar Beth's defenses fell away. She gazed at Winnie. "Tell me I'm doing the right thing."

"I'm sure you are," Winnie replied, in a way that told Sugar Beth she wasn't sure at all.

Sugar Beth slammed the barricades back in place. She showered and shaved her legs. Afterward, she permitted Janice Menken to construct an elaborate hairstyle that looked like a wedding cake had landed on her head. She took it apart as soon as Janice left and reconstructed it more simply closer to the back of her head. She refused to wear a veil, and she kept her makeup subtle, with the emphasis on her eyes and only a tawny gloss at her lips. The familiar rituals did nothing to calm her, and she grew even more agitated as various Seawillows kept sweeping in and out to check on her.

None of them had seen Colin, but they were all very certain he was around somewhere.

She decided the less time she spent at the church the better, so she fetched her gown from the attic where she'd hidden it and got dressed in Colin's closet. Just as she slipped into her shoes, Jewel and Leeann appeared to drive her to the ceremony. They frowned when they saw her gown.

"You're not really wearing that, are you?" Leeann said.

"It's my fourth marriage," Sugar Beth retorted. "What did you expect?"

Jewel shot Leeann a meaningful look. "Winnie said she was in a bad mood."

"You still look beautiful," Leeann conceded. "More than beautiful. But Colin's going to have a fit."

"Have either of you seen him?"

"He's probably with Ryan," Jewel said uneasily.

"Or on his way to South America." Sugar Beth kissed Gordon good-bye and stomped out to Jewel's car, her beaded stiletto sandals making lethal clicks on the pavement.

The nostalgic smells of old hymnals, Pine-Sol, and long-forgotten potlucks enveloped her as she entered the back door of the redbrick Presbyterian church. Winnie, stylish in gold silk, waited just inside. Her eyes narrowed with displeasure as she took in Sugar Beth's dress, but she wisely held her tongue.

"Tell me you've seen Colin," Sugar Beth said as Winnie steered her toward a small anteroom just off the narthex.

"Ryan's in charge of Colin."

"So you haven't seen him."

"I haven't had time to look. There was a misunderstanding about the music, and the altar flowers weren't right, then Gigi glittered her eyelids. Did you teach her to do that? Never mind." Winnie's face set in a chipper smile. "We didn't do anything about something old and something borrowed. You have a new dress and blue eyes, but we need the rest."

"When it's your fourth marriage, you tend to lose faith in superstitions."

"This is your last marriage, and tradition is important." She reached into her small beaded bag, drew out Diddie's pearls, and clasped them around Sugar Beth's neck. "Don't get attached. I'm taking them back as soon as the reception's over."

Sugar Beth touched them with her fingers, and her eyes filled up with tears. "Oh, Winnie . . ." She turned and hugged her sister. "I love you."

"I love you, too," Winnie replied, and promptly burst into tears herself.

The organist began to play the prelude, and they hopped up and down and waved their hands in front of their faces to stop themselves before they ruined their eye makeup. Winnie blew her nose. "Colin's definitely here. Mrs. Patterson never starts to play until everybody in the wedding party has shown up."

"She's hated me ever since my ninth-grade recital when I got to dance the Sugar Plum Fairy instead of her precious Kimmie."

"Everybody in Parrish isn't involved in a conspiracy against you."

"We'll see."

The prelude came to an end. Winnie thrust a cascading bouquet of white Casablanca lilies into Sugar Beth's hands and picked up a smaller bouquet for herself, then drew her out into the narthex. Sugar Beth could only see the last two rows of pews, but even they were filled. "What possessed you to invite so many people?"

"You and Colin are going to be a big part of this community," Winnie retorted. "Everybody deserves to see you married."

"If he's here."

"Of course he's here."

The organ launched into the processional, and Sugar Beth's teeth began to chatter. "I'm not walking down that aisle until you peek around the corner and make sure he's there."

"He has to be. If he weren't, Ryan would—"

"I don't want to hear another word about Ryan!" she hissed. "Your husband has reason to hate me, too. He's probably in on the whole thing."

"True." Winnie lifted her bouquet. "And then there's me." With those ominous words, she stepped around the corner and disappeared down the aisle.

The music swelled. Sugar Beth straightened her shoulders and fought her fear. As she made her way around the corner, the congregation rose, temporarily blocking her view of the altar. She clutched the bouquet more tightly, her palms sweaty. Four husbands! What kind of fool got married for the fourth time?

A sea of faces turned toward her, three hundred of them, but not the one she most needed to see. Until she took her place at the end of the aisle . . . There he was, with Ryan at his side, both men dressed in black tuxedos. Colin wore his as comfortably as other men wore jeans. The tucked white shirt gleamed against his tan face, which was thinner and more angular than when she'd last seen him. Apparently she wasn't the only one who'd had trouble eating. The knowledge gave her just enough indignant satisfaction to propel her down the aisle.

Colin's heart swelled as he watched Sugar Beth approach him. She was dressed entirely in black. He chuckled, and for the first time in nearly two months, he began to relax.

Her gown was beautiful despite its color. Long, slim, and strapless, it had diagonal panels of tiny black beads that grew wider as they reached the hem. She floated toward him, exquisite in form, countenance, and movement, her blond hair and smooth white shoulders rising from the gown like foam from a stormy sea. The brittleness she'd worn like a second skin when she'd first come to Parrish had broken away. She was softer, more exquisite, more precious to him than he'd ever imagined, but the perilous flash of silver in those pale blue eyes reminded him of what a dangerous game he'd been playing. And it wasn't over yet.

She stopped at his side and passed over the bouquet to Winnie. He took her hands. They were cold as ice, but his weren't much warmer.

The ceremony began. He'd have preferred writing his own vows, ones that spoke more personally to the depth of his feelings for this magnificent woman, but then she would have had to write hers, too, and he hadn't trusted her not to curse. Browbeating her was the only way he'd known to slay the dragon that had held this princess as a prisoner for far too long. They belonged together, and he'd been determined to put her out of her misery as quickly as possible.

The minister's voice broke into his thoughts. Pastor Daniels was a traditionalist, and it hadn't occurred to him that he should modify the ceremony.

"Who gives this woman to be wedded to this man?"

There was a long pause. The congregation began to stir uneasily. Colin frowned. Ryan smiled and stepped forward. "I do."

The pastor came to his senses after that and quickly deleted the *speak now or forever hold your peace* part, which would surely have sent people hopping to their feet all over the place.

The vows followed. Sugar Beth spoke hers flatly, almost angrily. He understood. She'd lost faith in vows, and this particular ceremony held a lot of unhappy memories for her. Still, it had to be done.

The rest of the ceremony passed in a blur, something to be endured rather than cherished. She had a ring for him, which was a surprise, a simple white gold wedding band. He slipped a perfect two-and-a-half-carat diamond on her finger. She wasn't a woman for subtlety.

More vows and the pronouncement. "You may kiss the bride."

He gazed down at her and, as he drew close, whispered against her lips, "Don't bite."

She didn't. But she didn't really kiss him back either.

Ryan and Winnie whisked them to Frenchman's Bride for the reception. The white tent had billows of net at the entrance and a swagged ceiling. Crisp linens draped with sheer gold overskirts covered the tables, each of which displayed a trailing centerpiece of lilies, hyacinths, and ivy. Long serving tables held platters of lobster tails, crab claws, and shrimp, along with an assortment of hot and cold dishes. He couldn't imagine how Winnie and the Seawillows had managed to do all this so quickly or how he would ever thank them properly. There was no band, no dancing. Winnie knew he and Sugar Beth needed to get through this reception as quickly as possible so they could be alone. He watched Sugar Beth bypass a tower of chocolate-dipped cream puffs for the relish tray. He frowned.

The guests seemed to have entered into a conspiracy to protect him because no one suggested he and Sugar Beth stand still for wedding photographs, and not a single person tapped a knife on a water goblet to encourage them to kiss. When it came time for the wedding cake to be cut, Winnie jumped up with a panic-stricken expression and said she and Ryan would do the honors. Only Cubby Bowmar seemed disappointed that he wouldn't get to see Colin's face decorated with vanilla fondant.

Sugar Beth spent most of the reception with either the Seawillows or Gigi and her teenage friends. Finally, Winnie drew her away to throw her bouquet, and Sugar Beth aimed right for Jewel, which he thought was a nice touch. No one mentioned a garter ceremony.

As it came time to leave, Winnie retrieved the pearls Sugar Beth had been wearing. "You can't take them back!" his outraged wife exclaimed. "That's what I want for my wedding present."

"Forget it. I have more important plans for these." Winnie kissed her cheek and slipped the pearls into her bag. "Your present will be waiting when you get back from your honeymoon."

"What honeymoon?"

Winnie pushed her toward Colin.

Eventually, he was able to get her to his car, which had been decorated with white streamers and a sign on the passenger door that read *4th Timz the Charm.* Rice flew. Merylinn stuffed Sugar Beth into the front seat. Heidi threw her overnight case in the back. Someone triggered an air horn. And then they were off.

The interior of the car grew tomblike. Sugar Beth stared straight ahead. Colin tried to think of something to say, but he hadn't slept well in weeks. Most nights he'd stayed at his computer till dawn, caught a few hours of rest, then gotten up and begun to write again. Except for a weekly trip to a convenience store, he'd seen no one. He'd forgotten to shave, forgotten to eat. Occasionally he'd subjected himself to brutal daylong hikes in the desert, hoping the exertion would wear him out enough so he could sleep for more than two hours at a stretch, but it seldom worked. He'd had no taste for food, no taste for much of anything except writing and torturing himself with thoughts of Sugar Beth.

They passed the Quik Stop, and she finally broke the silence. "What honeymoon?"

"I considered the Virgin Islands, but for now I think it's better if we just head to the lake. Amy and Clint have given us their cottage for the night. Why were you eating cauliflower?"

Her gown gave an angry rustle. "Tell me where you've been for two months."

"A little adobe house I rented outside Taos. Three rooms near an aspen grove. Simple but serviceable."

"You look tired. And you've lost weight."

He heard concern in her voice—a chink in the armor of her resentment—and his fatigue instantly vanished. "I'm exhausted. Tired to the bone." He gave a weary sigh and studied her reaction through the corner of his eye. "It's been an extraordinarily difficult two months. I haven't been well at all."

"Probably suffering from overacting disease."

He smiled and turned his head to drink in that perfect face. "Do you hate it so very much? Being married to me?"

Her eyes flashed. "We didn't even sign a prenup! And I'm a wealthy woman."

"Are you worried, then?"

"Of course I'm worried! I just got married for the *fourth* time! But I've never had a lick of common sense, so why should I be surprised."

"You have a great deal of common sense, not to mention an exquisite body . . . which I intend to enjoy to the fullest as soon as possible."

"Good, because sex is the only reason I'm going along with this."

"I understand."

They remained silent for the rest of the trip to the lake. She seemed resigned, if not overjoyed, and the atmosphere no longer felt quite so oppressive, but he knew he wasn't out of the woods yet. He carried her case inside the cottage—his was already there—and wasted no time drawing her toward the bedroom. She came to a dead stop just inside the door. "Oh, my."

Mountains of fresh flowers and masses of white pillar candles occupied every corner of the gray and white bedroom. Music played softly in the background, and in a particularly nice touch, the covers on the bed had been turned down to display white rose petals scattered across the pale gray sheets. Even the draperies over the wall of windows that faced the lake had been drawn. Amy's mother had followed his directions to the letter.

"Dreadfully excessive," he sniffed. "These Southerners."

"It's beautiful," she whispered.

"Well, if you think so . . ." The candlelight caught the black beads of her gown, and her skin looked iridescent, as if it had been dusted with crushed opals. "I have a wedding present for you," he said.

"I have a present for you, too."

"If it ticks, I'm calling the police."

She smiled. His muscles relaxed enough for him to cross the room and retrieve a thick sheaf of papers tied with a red bow from his overnight case. As he handed it to her, he wished he'd had more to drink at the reception. "I . . . didn't finish until yesterday, so there wasn't time for a fancy gift wrap."

Sugar Beth gazed at him and realized he was nervous. The knowledge gratified her more than anything else that had happened that day, and the final layers of her resentment began to peel away at the corners. She sank into the room's only chair and gazed down at what he'd handed her. "You finished your book."

"Very late last night."

He'd dedicated it to her. That must be his surprise. She smiled to herself and pulled at the lopsided red bow he'd wrapped around the manuscript. He shifted his weight, cleared his throat. His agitation warmed her even more. And then she gazed down at the title page. Her breath caught in a tiny gasp.

A Love Story for Valentine
by
Colin Byrne

"Oh, my . . ." A thousand questions sprang to her mind. Her voice, when she finally rediscovered it, sounded thin and faint. "But . . . what happened to your other book?"

"This needed to be written first."

She ran her fingers over the title page, and the hard knot of fear she'd been carrying inside her for longer than she could remember dissolved. In its place she felt a deep-rooted sense of peace. A man who would do this for the woman he loved was a man for the ages. Her smile wobbled at the corners. "When male authors write love stories, the heroine tends to end up dead."

"Not this time, I assure you." His voice was no steadier than hers. "I'll never be able to hold up my head in literary circles again."

"Oh, Colin . . ." She drew the manuscript to her breasts, and her eyes filled with tears. The remnants of her fear fell away as she gazed into the eyes of her fourth and last husband. "I do love you, my darling."

"That's what I've been counting on."

He set aside the manuscript and pulled her to her feet where he began taking the pins from her hair one by one. As it tumbled down, he kissed her neck, her shoulders, whispering sonnets of love that grew earthier and more explicit as their clothes fell away.

"You're exquisite," he whispered as he laid her in the rose petals. She ran her hands over his body, reacquainting herself with its hard slopes and muscled ridges. He found other petals, soft and moist, plump with need, fragrant with desire, and she grew wild with need. Wilder still when he finally entered her and she saw the emotion burning in his eyes.

"I love you," he whispered. "I love you so, my darling."

She whispered her own love words in return, and the sweet storm swept them up.

The next morning Sugar Beth propped herself on her elbow and gazed at her sleeping husband. He'd worked hard last night, making love with her until they were both exhausted. Resisting the urge to wake him, she slipped out of bed and pulled on a pair of panties along with his tuxedo shirt. In the kitchen she found Gordon, a pitcher of freshly squeezed orange juice, and a basket of warm muffins. No woman had better friends than she did, and as soon as she got the chance, she intended to throw them a bridal shower in reverse.

She drank a glass of juice and gave Gordon some love, but left him behind as she made her way through the rear sliders and down to the lake. The early-morning sun sparkled on the extravagant diamond her husband had given her. He didn't want her to forget she was married, as if she could. She smiled, and a sense of peace flowed through her in a deep, quiet stream. Forever was a long time for love to last, but when it came to Colin Byrne, forever felt exactly right.

"Bored with me already?"

She turned to watch her husband coming toward her, his bare feet leaving tracks in the dew-soaked grass, Gordon trotting at his side. Colin wore jeans and a white T-shirt, all gorgeous and sloppy—unshaven, rumpled, munching on a muffin, and as he kissed her, she tasted banana-nut crumbs, toothpaste, and sex.

"Not bored at all." She smiled and brushed his cheek. "I've been thinking about my wedding present."

"I put my heart on every page," he said so sweetly she would have teared up all over again if she hadn't needed to do something else first.

"Not that present," she managed. "My present to you. I hope you like it because I can't take it back."

"It's impossible to imagine returning anything you've given to me."

"Hold on to that thought."

And then she told him.

He looked stunned.

She wasn't surprised. She'd needed time to adjust, too.

Eventually, he recovered enough to ask a few questions. Then he started kissing her again, but just when their breathing got heavy, he broke away. "I'm sorry, my darling. I know it's our honeymoon, but . . ." He removed his hand from her bottom with the greatest reluctance. "Would it be possible for you to entertain yourself for an hour? Two hours at the most?"

"You're deserting me *now*?"

"Ordinarily I wouldn't think of it, you understand, but in light of your amazing news . . ." He gazed down at her, his heart shining in his eyes. "I'm feeling a pressing need to write an epilogue."

Epilogue

$\mathcal{E}$veryone called her Honeybell, except her father, who referred to her as Eugenia . . . or Eugenia Frances the morning he found his new Helmut Lang necktie swimming in Gordon's water bowl. Next to her mother, she was the joy of his life, an imp with his dark hair, Sugar Beth's dazzling eyes, and her own feisty spirit. Every morning when he carried her downstairs, she squealed in his arms as she spotted the life-size portrait of Diddie and Sugar Beth that once again hung in its former place in the foyer. All his threats to torch the bloody thing fell on deaf ears. Sugar Beth declared that Winnie couldn't have given her a more perfect wedding gift. Except for Diddie's pearls.

"Don't even think about wearing them," Gigi whispered to the baby on Eugenia's christening day, when Winnie formally presented the contents of the blue velvet box to her new niece. "You'll look like a dork."

On Sunday afternoons, they all gathered at Winnie's for potluck—the Seawillows and their husbands, Leeann and her "significant other." The fact that Jewel and Leeann were now a permanent couple had thrown the town into a tailspin, but Leeann said she couldn't live a lie any longer, and she was truly happy for the first time in her life, even though Jewel steadfastly refused to join the Seawillows, although she never missed their potlucks.

Colin watched Heidi coming toward him with a carving knife. "You're the only man here who can cut up a ham without mangling it," she said. "Give Honeybell to me."

"I'm not eatin' anything but my Lean Cuisine," Merylinn declared, heading for the microwave. "Slap me if you see me even look at anything else."

Sugar Beth caught his gaze across the women's heads and gave him one of those smiles he cherished, a hint of bewilderment still clinging to its edges, as if she couldn't quite believe all this was hers. Sometimes he had a hard time believing it himself.

A Love Story for Valentine had lived up to Sugar Beth's prediction and had become his most popular book, although he could have done without the resultant publicity, not to mention his editor's pleas that he someday write another romance novel. Colin shuddered. Sugar Beth, of course, thrived on the publicity and gave interviews at the drop of a hat. Valentine's Books, the name she'd settled on for her store, was an immediate success, and Jewel had expanded Gemima's. The Depot Coffeehouse that Heidi managed for Sugar Beth had turned into the gathering place for everyone in town, and a bigger hotbed of gossip he never hoped to witness.

Life was good but not perfect. He and Sugar Beth still argued whenever the mood struck them. The Seawillows were involved in a cockamamie scheme to find a sex partner for Merylinn's widowed mother. Gigi had a boyfriend, which was driving Ryan wild. And sometimes when the moon was full, Cubby Bowmar and his cronies still showed up on the front lawn of Frenchman's Bride to bay for Sugar Beth. Colin mainly put up with it because he knew she enjoyed the attention.

"Dinner's ready." Winnie took the platter of ham from him and shooed everybody toward the dining room.

"One of these days I'm bringing sushi," Heidi said. "They're sellin' it at Big Star now."

"I'm not eatin' sushi," Deke retorted. "I doubt it's even legal in Mississippi."

"Time for grace," Amy announced. "Everybody hold hands."

"Come here, Honeybell."

Sugar Beth took the toddler from Heidi and wove through Ryan and Deke to get to Colin's side, where she clasped his hand and they both gave thanks for more blessings than either of them could ever have imagined.

Acknowledgments

$\mathcal{B}$ ouquets of magnolia blossoms to everyone who helped me with my Mississippi research, especially Susan Jordan and Sherry Colhoun at the Holly Springs, Mississippi, Chamber of Commerce; Bridgette Correale for the photos; and Adele San Miguel for making certain I received them. Thanks to Elizabeth Baucom, Donna Barnes, Melanie Noto, Lynn Pittman, and Carol Jackson for observations and yearbooks.

Thank you, Peter Janson-Smith and Sir Richard Rougier, for permission to quote from the works of the incomparable Georgette Heyer.

I've received information, advice, and support from so many friends and associates. Thank you, Steven Axelrod, Jill Barnett, Jennifer Crusie, Lisa Gallagher, Kristin Hannah, Alison Hart, Cissy Hartley, Cathie Linz, Lindsay Longford, Meryl Sawyer, Suzette Vann, Matthew Verscheure, Margaret Watson, everybody on the SEP Bulletin Board, and the entire Phillips gang, including Dana, our newest member, and Nickie Shek, who set me straight on thirteen-year-old girls.

At William Morrow and Avon Books, I am forever grateful to Carrie Feron, my fearless and peerless editor. Also Nancy Anderson, Richard Aquan, Leesa Belt, George Bick, Ralph D'Arienzo, Karen Davy, Darlene Delillo, Gail Dubov, Tom Egner, Seth Fleishman, Josh Frank, Jane Friedman, Heather

Gould, Brian Grogan, Cathy Hemming, Angela Leigh, Kim Lewis, Selina McLemore, Brian McSharry, Judy Madonia, Michael Morrison, Jan Parrish, Shelly Perron, Chadd Reese, Rhonda Rose, Pete Soper, Michael Spradlin, Debbie Stier, Andrea Sventora, Bruce Unck, and Donna Waitkus.

Bless all your hearts,
SUSAN ELIZABETH PHILLIPS

You met Kevin Tucker and Molly Somerville in *This Heart of Mine*. Now get ready to meet Kevin's shark of an agent, Heath Champion, and Annabelle Granger, the girl least likely to succeed.

MATCH ME IF YOU CAN
by Susan Elizabeth Phillips

On sale August 2005
A William Morrow Hardcover

$\mathcal{I}$f Annabelle hadn't found a body lying under Sherman, she wouldn't have been late for her appointment with the Python. But there were those dirty bare feet sticking out from beneath her Nana's ancient Crown Victoria . . . One extremely cautious glance under the car revealed they were attached to the body of a homeless man known only as Mouse, who was famous in her Wicker Park neighborhood for his lack of personal hygiene and fondness for alcohol. An empty bottle of three-buck Chuck lay near his chest, which rose and fell with the sounds of his wet snorts. It testified to how important her appointment with the Python was that she momentarily considered trying to maneuver Sherman around the body. But her alley parking space was too tight.

She'd allowed plenty of time to get dressed and make the trip into the city for her eleven A.M. appointment. Unfortunately, Mr. Perkins had caught her at the front door and refused to leave until he'd had his say. Still, this wasn't an emergency yet. All she had to do was get Mouse out from under Sherman.

She gingerly prodded his ankle with her foot, noting as she did that the emergency mixture of Hershey's chocolate syrup and Elmer's glue she'd applied to a scuff mark on the heel of her favorite pair of strappy sandals hadn't entirely camouflaged the damage. "Mouse?"

He didn't stir.

She prodded him again, this time more vigorously. "Mouse, wake up. You have to come out of there."

Nothing, which made it time to revert to more drastic measures. With a grimace, she bent over, grabbed one filthy ankle, and gave it a shake. "Come on, Mouse. Wake up!"

Nada. If it weren't for his slurpy snorts, he might have been dead.

She shook him more vigorously. "This happens to be the most important day of my professional life, and I could use a little cooperation here."

Mouse wasn't interested in cooperation.

She needed more leverage. Gritting her teeth, she gingerly slid up the skirt of the buttercup yellow raw silk suit she'd bought yesterday for 60 percent off at a Field's Day Sale and crouched down by the bumper. "If you don't get out from under there, I'm calling the police."

Mouse snorted.

She dug her heels into the ground and yanked on both filthy ankles. The morning sun beat down on her head. Mouse rolled over just far enough to wedge his shoulder under the chassis. She yanked again. Beneath her jacket, the white sleeveless shell she'd chosen to complement Nana's antique pearl teardrop earrings had begun to stick to her skin. She tried not to think about what was happening to her hair. This hadn't been the best time to run out of styling gel, and she prayed the ancient can of industrial strength Aqua Net she'd found under the bathroom sink would tame the bedlam of her red curls, always the curse of her existence, but especially so during a humid Chicago summer.

If she didn't get Mouse out in the next five minutes, she was in serious trouble. She made her way around to the driver's side door. Her knees cracked as she crouched down again and peered into his slack-jawed face. "Mouse, you have to wake up! You can't stay here."

One grimy eyelid flicked open, then slid shut again.

"No!" She poked his chest. "Look at me. If you come out from under there, I'll give you five dollars."

His mouth moved and a guttural rumble oozed out, along with a string of saliva. "G'way."

The smell made her eyes water. "Why did you have to pick today to pass out under my car? And why my car? Why not Mr. Perkins's car?" Mr. Perkins lived across the alley and spent his days coming up with new ways to make Annabelle crazy.

The minutes were ticking by, and she was starting to panic. "Do you want to have sex? Because if you come out, we could maybe talk about it."

More drool and another putrid snort. This was hopeless. She jumped up and dashed toward the house.

Ten minutes later, she finally managed to lure him out with an open can of beer. Not her proudest moment.

By the time she'd maneuvered Sherman from the alley to the street, she had only twenty-one minutes left to navigate the traffic into the city and find a place to park. Dirt streaked her legs, her shirt was crumpled, and she'd broken a fingernail when she'd opened the beer can. The extra five pounds that had accumulated on her small-boned frame since Nana had died no longer seemed like such a big problem.

10:39.

She detoured down Halstead to avoid road repair on the Kennedy. As she maneuvered Sherman's tank-like bulk through the traffic, she scrubbed at her dirty legs with the damp paper towel she'd snatched up in the kitchen. A cab cut her off. She laid on the horn, and a trickle of perspiration slid between her breasts. She glanced at her watch. 10:50. The light at Halstead and Chicago turned red. Her hair was sticking to the back of her neck, and more curls were springing up. She tried to do her yoga breathing, but she'd only been to one class, and it wasn't effective. If only Mouse had picked a day when Annabelle's economic future wasn't at stake to pass out under her car.

She crawled into the Loop. 10:59. She didn't have time to follow her customary practice of cruising the streets until she found a metered parking space large enough to accommodate Sherman's bulk. Instead, she wheeled into the first exorbitantly expensive parking garage she could find, threw Sherman's keys at the attendant, and took off at a trot.

11:05. No need to panic. She'd simply explain about Mouse. Surely the Python would understand.

Or not.

A blast of air-conditioning hit her as she entered the lobby of the art deco office building. 11:08. The elevator was blessedly empty, and she punched the button for the fourteenth floor.

Don't let him intimidate you, Molly had told her over the phone. *The Python feeds on fear.*

Easy for Molly to say. Molly was sitting at home with a hottie football player husband, a great career of her own, and two adorable children.

The doors crept shut. Annabelle caught sight of herself in the mirrored wall and gave a hiss of dismay. The raw silk suit had turned into a limp mass of buttercup wrinkles and dirt smudged the side of the skirt. Worst of all, her hair was uncoiling from the Aqua Net curl by curl, with the hair spray weighing it down just enough so that the escaping locks hung lank around her face like bedsprings that had been tossed from a tenement window and left in an alley to rust.

Usually when she got upset about her appearance—which

even her own mother described only as "nice"—she reminded herself to be grateful for her good features: a pair of very nice honey-colored eyes, thick lashes, and—give or take a few dozen freckles—a creamy complexion. But no amount of positive thinking could make the image that stared back at her from the elevator mirror anything but horrifying. She scrambled to tuck a few curls behind her ears and smooth her skirt, but the elevator doors opened before she could repair much of the damage.

11:09.

In front of her, she saw a glass wall imprinted with gold letters: **CHAMPION SPORTS MANAGEMENT**. She hurried across the carpeted hallway and entered through a door with a curved metal handle. The receptionist had short, steel-gray hair and a thin-lipped mouth. She took in Annabelle's disheveled appearance through a pair of half glasses with blue metal frames. "May I help you?"

"Annabelle Granger. I have an appointment with the Py— with Mr. Champion."

"I'm afraid you're too late, Miss Granger."

"Only ten minutes."

"Ten minutes was all the time Mr. Champion had available in his schedule to see you."

That confirmed what Annabelle had suspected from the beginning. He'd only agreed to see her because Molly had insisted. She glanced in desperation at the wall clock. "I'm really only nine minutes late. I have one minute left."

"Sorry." The receptionist turned back to her computer and began tapping away.

"One minute," Annabelle pleaded. "That's all I ask."

"There's nothing I can do."

Annabelle needed this meeting and she needed it now. Pivoting on her heels, she rushed toward the paneled door at the far end of the reception area.

"Miss Granger!"

Annabelle dashed into an open hallway with a pair of offices on each side, one of them occupied by two buff young men in dress shirts and neck ties. Ignoring them, she headed for an imposing paneled door set into the center of the back wall and turned the knob.

The Python's office was the color of money: lacquered jade walls, thick moss carpet, and furniture upholstered in varying shades of green accented with bloodred pillows. The Python himself sat behind a sleek, U-shaped desk, his high-backed chair turned toward the window, where Lake Michigan was visible in the distance. She took in a state-of-the-art desktop computer, a small laptop, a PDA, and a sophisticated black telephone console with enough buttons to land a jumbo jet. An executive headset lay abandoned next to it as the Python spoke directly into the receiver in a voice that was deeply resonant, crisp, Midwestern.

"The third-year money is good, but not if they cut you early. I know it's a gamble, but if you sign for one year, we can play the free agent market." She glimpsed a strong tanned wrist, a rugged watch, and long tapered fingers curled around the receiver. "Ultimately, it's your decision, Jamal. All I can do is advise you."

The door burst open behind her, and the receptionist flew in like an offended parakeet. "I'm sorry, Heath. She got past me."

The Python turned slowly in his chair, and Annabelle felt as if she'd been punched in the stomach.

He was square-jawed and tough—a roughneck who'd flunked charm school the first couple of times around, but finally gotten it right on the third pass. Everything about him proclaimed a brash, self-made man. His hair was thick and crisp, its rich color a cross between a leather stock portfolio and a bottle of Bud. He had a straight, confident nose and bold dark eyebrows, one of which was bisected near the end with a thin pale scar. The firm set of his well-molded mouth proclaimed a low tolerance for fools, a passion for hard work that bordered on obsession, and possibly—although this might be her imagination—a determination to own a small chalet near St. Tropez before he was fifty. If it weren't for a vague irregularity to his features, he would have been unbearably gorgeous. Instead, he was merely drop-dead good-looking. What did a man like this need with a matchmaker?

As he spoke into the phone, he turned his eyes on her. They were the exact green of a hundred-dollar bill singed at the edges with displeasure. "This is what you pay me for, Jamal." He shot the receptionist a hard look. "I'll talk to Ray this afternoon. And tell Audette I'm sending her another case of the Krug Grande Cuvee she liked."

"Your eleven o'clock appointment," the receptionist said as he hung up. "I told her she was too late to see you."

He shoved aside a copy of *Pro Football Weekly*. His hands were broad, his fingernails clean and neatly clipped. Still, it wasn't hard to imagine them ringed with motor oil. She took in the perfect fit of his pale blue dress shirt, custom made to accommodate the width of his shoulders before tapering toward his waist. Unless she missed her guess, his navy print necktie cost more than her entire outfit.

"Apparently, she doesn't listen well." His shirt molded to a broad chest as he shifted in his chair, making Annabelle uncomfortably aware of a junior high science lesson she vaguely remembered about pythons.

They swallowed their prey whole. Head first.

"Do you want me to call security?" the receptionist asked.

He turned his predator's eyes on her, leaving Annabelle on the receiving end of another of those knockout punches. "I think I can handle her."

A jolt of sexual awareness shot through her—so inappropriate, so unwelcome, so totally out of place that it threw her off balance and she bumped into one of the side chairs. She was never at her best around excessively confident men, and the absolute necessity of impressing this particular specimen made her silently curse her clumsiness right along with her rumpled suit and medusa hair.

Molly had told her to be aggressive. *He's fought his way to the top, one client at a time. Brutal aggression is the only emotion Heath Champion understands.* But Annabelle wasn't a naturally aggressive person. Everyone from bank clerks to taxi drivers took advantage of her. Even her own family—*especially* her own family—walked all over her.

And she was sick of it. Sick of being condescended to, sick of too many people getting the best of her, sick of feeling like a failure. If she backed down now, where would it end? She met those money-green eyes and knew the time had come to tap deep into her Granger gene pool and play hard-ball.

"There was a dead body under my car." It was almost true since Mouse had definitely been dead weight.

Unfortunately, the Python didn't look impressed, but then he'd probably been responsible for so many dead bodies that he'd grown bored with the whole concept of corpses. She took a deep breath. "All that red tape. It made me late. Otherwise, I would have been punctual. More than punctual. I'm very responsible. And professional." Just like that, she ran out of air. "Do you mind if I sit down?"

"Yes."

"Thank you." She sank into the nearest chair.

"You don't listen well, do you?"

"What?"

He gazed at her for a long moment before dismissing his receptionist. "Hold my calls for five minutes, Sylvia, unless it's Phoebe Calebow." The woman left, and he gave a re-signed sigh. "I assume you're Molly's friend." Even his teeth were intimidating: strong, square, and very white.

"College buddies."

He tapped his fingers on the desk. "I don't mean to be rude, but you'll have to make this fast."

Who did he think he was kidding? He thrived on being rude. She imagined him in college dangling some poor computer geek out a dorm window or laughing in the face of a weeping, possibly pregnant, girlfriend. She sat straighter in the chair, trying to project confidence. "I'm Annabelle Granger from Perfect for You."

"The matchmaker." His fingers tapped away.

"I think of myself as a marriage facilitator."

"Do you now?" He drilled her again with those money-hard eyes. "Molly told me your company was called Myrna the Matchmaker."

Too late, she remembered that she'd overlooked that particular point in her conversations with Molly. "Myrna the Matchmaker was started by my grandmother in the seventies. She died three months ago. I've been modernizing since then, and I've also given the company a new name to reflect our philosophy of personalized service for the discriminating executive." *Forgive me, Nana, but it had to be done.*

He leaned back in his chair. "I'm going to cut to the chase and save us both time. I'm already under contract with Portia Powers."

Annabelle was prepared for this. Portia Powers, of Power Matches, ran the most exclusive matchmaking firm in Chicago. "I know you signed that contract a few weeks ago, but that doesn't preclude you from also using Perfect for You."

He glanced toward the flashing buttons on his phone. A long, vertical slash of irritation bisected his forehead. "Why would I bother?"

"Because I'll work harder for you than you can imagine. And because I'll introduce you to a group of women with brains and accomplishments, women who won't bore you after the newness wears off."

He lifted an eyebrow. "You know me that well, do you?"

"Mr. Champion . . ." *Surely that wasn't his real name?* ". . . you're obviously accustomed to being around beautiful women, and I'm certain you've had more opportunities than you can count to marry one of them. But you haven't. That tells me that you want something more multifaceted than simply a beautiful wife."

"I barely have time to deal with Power Matches let alone adding anybody else to the mix." He uncoiled from his chair. He was tall, so it took awhile.

She'd already noted the wide shoulders. Now she took in the rest of him. He had an athlete's body, but not a thick physique. Instead, he was lean and muscular. If you liked your men swimming in testosterone and your sex life dangerous, he'd be number one on your automatic dial. Not that Annabelle was thinking about her sex life. Or at least she hadn't been until he stood up.

He stepped around the corner of his desk and extended his hand. "Good effort, Annabelle. Thanks for your time."

He wasn't going to give her a chance. He'd never intended to do more than go through the motions so he could pacify Molly. Annabelle thought of her hopes for this meeting, her dreams of making Perfect for You unique and successful. Years of frustration boiled inside her, fueled by crappy judgment, bad luck, and missed opportunities.

She ignored his hand and rose to her feet. He was at least a head taller, and she had to tilt her neck to meet his eyes. "Do you still remember what it was like to be the underdog, Mr. Champion? Do you remember when you were so hungry to close a deal that you'd do anything to make it happen? You'd drive across the country without sleep just to meet a Heisman candidate for breakfast? You'd spend hours hanging around the parking lot outside the Bears practice field trying to catch the attention of one of the veterans? Or what about the time you hauled yourself out of bed with a raging fever so you could bail another agent's client out of jail?"

"You've done your homework." He cast an impatient eye at the blinking phone buttons. He was clearly unimpressed, but he hadn't thrown her out, so she kept going.

"When you started in business, players like Kevin Tucker

wouldn't give you the time of day. Do you remember what that was like? Do you remember when reporters weren't calling you for quotes? When you weren't on first-name terms with everybody in the NFL?"

"If I say I remember, will you leave?" He returned to his chair and reached for the executive headset that lay next to the telephone console.

She curled her hands into fists, hoping she sounded passionate instead of loony. "All I want is a chance. The same chance you got when Kevin fired his old agent and put his faith in a fast-talking, sports-savvy guy who made his way from an armpit town in southern Illinois to Harvard Law."

One dark eyebrow angled upward.

"A blue-collar kid who played college football for the scholarship, but counted on his brains to get ahead. A guy with nothing more than big dreams and a strong work ethic to recommend him. A guy who—"

"You're makin' me cry," he said dryly.

"Just give me a chance. Let me set up one introduction. Just one. If you don't like the woman I choose, I'll never bother you again. Please. I'll do anything."

That caught his attention. He pushed aside the headset, tilted back in his chair, and rubbed the corner of his mouth with his thumb. "Anything?"

She didn't flinch from his assessing gaze. "Whatever it takes."

His eyes made a calculated journey from her rumpled russet hair to her mouth, down along her throat, and lingered at her breasts. "Well . . . I haven't gotten laid for a while."

Her constricted throat muscles relaxed. The Python was toying with her. "Then why don't we do something about that on a permanent basis?" She dug into her new fake-leather tote for the folder she'd finished preparing at five o'clock that morning. "This will tell you a little more about Perfect for You. I've included a timetable, a fee structure, our mission statement."

Now that he'd had his fun, he was all business. "I'm interested in results, not mission statements."

"And results are what I'll give you."

"We'll see."

She drew an unsteady breath. "Does that mean . . ."

He picked up the telephone headset and hooked it around his neck leaving the cord dangling down his shirtfront in a serpentine tail. "You've got one chance. Tomorrow night. Hit me with your best candidate."

"Really?" Her knees went weak. "Yes . . . Fantastic! But . . . I need to clarify exactly what you're looking for."

"Let's see how good you are." He flipped up the headset. "Nine o'clock at Sienna's on Clark Street. Make the introduction, but don't plan on leaving. Stay at the table and keep the conversation going so I don't have to. I work hard at what I do. I don't intend to work hard at this, too."

"You want me to stay?"   •

"Twenty minutes exactly. Then take her away."

"Twenty minutes? Don't you think she'll find that a little . . . demeaning?"

"Not if she's the right woman." He gave her his country boy's smile. "And do you know why, Miss Granger? Because the right woman will be too damned *sweet* to take offense. Now get the hell out of here while you're ahead."

She did.

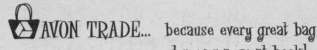

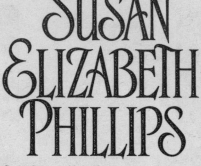